BLIGHT

ALEXANDRA DUNCAN

BLIGHT

GREENWILLOW BOOKS, *An Imprint of* HarperCollins*Publishers*

Blight. Copyright © 2017 by Alexandra Duncan

The text of this book is set in Melior Medium. Book design by Sylvie Le Floc'h

On page 71, the song quoted in English and Spanish is "His Eye Is on the Sparrow," written by Civilla Durfee Martin (1869–1948) and included in Methodist hymnals as early as 1881.

The song quoted on page 230 is "The Unquiet Grave," a very old folk song included in the Child Ballad collection. The version used here can be found at: http://www.contemplator.com/child/unquiet.html

Library of Congress Cataloging-in-Publication Data

Names: Duncan, Alexandra, author.
Title: Blight / Alexandra Duncan.
Description: First edition. | New York, NY : Greenwillow Books, an Imprint of HarperCollinsPublishers, 2017. | Summary: When an agribusiness facility producing genetically engineered food releases a deadly toxin into the environment, seventeen-year-old Tempest Torres becomes entangled in a war she never knew existed.
Identifiers: LCCN 2016049147 | ISBN 9780062396990 (hardback)
Subjects: | CYAC: Virus diseases—Fiction. | Survival—Fiction. | Genetically modified foods—Fiction. | Hispanic Americans—Fiction. | Science fiction.
Classification: LCC PZ7.D8946 Bl 2017 | DDC [Fic]—dc23 LC record available at https://lccn.loc.gov/2016049147

17 18 19 20 21 PC/LSCH 10 9 8 7 6 5 4 3 2 1
First Edition

 Greenwillow Books

TO IZZY,
WHO WILL SAVE THE WORLD
WITH SCIENCE

There is...

"There can be no civilization without wildness . . .
no sweetness absent its astringent opposite."
—Michael Pollan, *The Botany of Desire*

.1.

CORN
ZEA MAYS

I brace the rifle against my shoulder and press my eye to the sight. The night pulses with cricket chirps and the deep, throaty calls of frogs somewhere in the neighboring forest. The moon has long gone down.

"Two scavengers outside the south perimeter," I mutter into my coms. "Engage?"

"Hold." Crake's voice crackles back to me. "Scanning."

The wind stirs, lifting my hair and carrying the scent of new corn over the company fields, up to the guard nest where I stand. I pull back my rifle's bolt and chamber a round in preparation, then follow the scavengers with my scope. There are two of them this time, thin things in drab clothes, about thirty yards out. One male, one female. They run forward at a crouch.

"Approaching the fence," I tell Crake.

Metal glints in the moonlight. I refocus my scope. One of them—the man—clutches a pair of wire cutters. The other one will have the sacks, then. She scuttles through the brush, two hanks of long, matted blond hair escaping her hood.

"Permission to engage." Crake's voice flares in my headset. "Looks like we have some repeat offenders out tonight. Fire when ready."

I steady the rifle and find the man's forehead in my sights. He kneels beside the fence, already making fast work of the chain links beneath the first run of razor wire.

"Gotcha." I move my finger to the trigger.

Just then, he whips his head up to say something to his accomplice, and the moonlight catches his face. He's young. My age, maybe a little older. His dark hair sticks up as though it's been cut with a blunt knife. The girl grips his hand and strokes the back of his palm with her thumb. My throat closes.

"Tempest." Crake's voice cuts in. "What are you waiting for? Take them out."

I swallow and refit my eye to the scope. The boy has cut two of the links already. Any second, they'll have a hole big enough to wriggle through.

Old enough to know better. I try to talk myself up to it. *Old enough to have made his choice.*

He's stealing the company's lifeblood, stealing the food straight from my mouth. He's a shirk, a parasite, living off hardworking people. But for some reason, I can't shoot.

"Tempest!" Crake shouts. "You deaf, girl? Fire."

His voice jolts me into action. On instinct, I drop my sight from the boy's head to his hand and fire. The cutters fly from his fingers exactly as the rifle's recoil jostles my shoulder, ruining my view. A smothered yelp echoes through the night.

"Did you get them?" Crake is in my ear again. "Are they down?"

I swing my scope over the dense brush, trying to find them. There, the fence. A four-link section partially pried up from the dust. I scan the no-man's-land between the fence and the woods. A flash of white flits through the weeds. The girl's hair in the moonlight. They're doubling back to the forest.

A burst of static crosses my coms. "Tempest—"

"Negative." I trail the rifle's sight across the field, closer to the tree line. "They've gone rabbit." A stir of movement. Found them.

"You *missed*?"

"Shit," I mutter. Now all I can do is make this look good enough to keep a reprimand off my file. "I'm on it, Crake. Just let me do my job."

I snap off my coms and focus on the pair running full tilt for the trees. The boy cradles his right hand against his chest as the girl pulls him along through the dark. I aim low and fire into the dust at their feet. Clods of dirt kick up as the rifle cracks again and again. The scavengers burst forward, hands locked.

I fire a final shot, high this time. It sinks into one of the trees, spraying bark as they finally cross beneath the arms of the oaks bordering the wood. And like that, they're gone.

I shoulder my rifle. The gunshots fade, and the night holds its breath. I close my eyes, inhaling the mix of fresh burned powder and sweet corn.

"Tempest?" Crake's voice spills out of the guard nest's loudspeakers, ruining the quiet. "You care to tell me what in the great bleeding hell that was?"

I flip on my coms again. "I'm here, Crake. You don't have to yell."

"The hell I don't," he says over the loudspeaker. Then back in my ear again. "They got away."

"Sorry."

"Sorry, my ass." Crake's tone softens to a grumble. "I'm sending Seth to relieve you. You're shift's almost up anyway. Get down here and write your incident report before you clock out, you hear me?"

"Loud and clear." I switch off my coms and drop my head against my knees. What was I thinking, getting all sappy over a pair of shirks? I've shot my efficiency stats to hell and made myself look disastrously incompetent in the process. But what's done is done. I can't stay curled up in the guard nest all night.

I check my rifle to be sure the chamber's empty before swinging it onto my back. I stand looking at the forest, a dense pool of black at my feet, blacker even than the sky. Somewhere in the darkness, a lone cricket trills, and as if it's called all clear, the whole night resumes its song. I climb down from the guard nest and make my way to the bunker.

A gust of stuffy heat hits me as soon as I key myself past the blast doors with my data band. Our condensers have been down all week, but the maintenance teams have been slammed, probably upgrading equipment at the research and development lab at the center of the compound or one of the other facilities that take precedence over our satellite bunker. I pass Seth on the way in, decked out in a spotless gray company sweater and regulation black knit cap that would match my own if I weren't so rumpled and sweaty from standing watch since 2300.

"Way to go, Eagle Eye." He sights me along his fingers and pretends to shoot.

Seth's parents are only sharecroppers, but his family has been with the company since this compound was founded. They're legacy. Early on in our training, he figured out I was a charity case, the daughter of a shirk who died right outside the compound gates, and made it his mission to remind me of his staggering superiority every chance he gets. He's one of those people who fit in effortlessly wherever they go. He never stands awkwardly on the edge of a briefing room or digs his nails into his palms while he's waiting for monthly deterrence and accuracy stats to post. He doesn't need to worry about proving his loyalty to AgraStar, because no one would ever think to question it, least of all him.

I roll my eyes, pull off my cap, and keep walking. Track

lights run the length of the bunker's broad, windowless corridor, angling subtly down into the earth. For some reason, the sight of those lights makes me more tired than being out in the dark. I check my data band . . . 0428. I should have enough time to finish my report and hit the mess hall before the morning rush. I might even get in an hour of sleep before daybreak.

I shoulder open the door to the Eye, our security monitoring center. I scan my rifle in and stow it back in the specialty weapons rack beside the other company firearms. One of the cheery AgraStar Conglomerate posters that line our halls and dormitories looks back at me from behind the guns—a determined-looking young man caught in midjog, with a golden field of ripe corn and a bluebonnet sky stretching behind him. FOOD IS FUEL read the bold white letters overlapping his feet.

"Tempest?" Crake calls from the feed room, his head silhouetted against the sickly green-blue glow of the monitor bank.

"Here." I tug off my sweater over my head, accidentally pulling my hair free of its high pony tail. The night's humidity has turned my curls into an unruly mass of frizz, and the bunker's heat is already getting to me. My undershirt is soaked through.

Crake leans back in his chair so he can see me through the doorway. His red hair sticks up in wisps above his frog-belly-white face. "What the hell happened out there? You think I don't have enough to worry about with the moles and anarchists trying to hack us all the time?"

I concentrate on folding my sweater. What am I supposed to say? That I can still see their hands intertwined? That no one has ever touched me with such tenderness?

"He moved at the last second," I say. "I would've got him otherwise."

Crake grunts. "You know what I tell you. The majority of system failures—"

"Are the result of human error," I finish for him. I give up trying to fold the sweater and chuck it into the rolling laundry bin parked in the corner. "I had a bad night, okay? And maybe I could shoot better if I didn't have someone buzzing in my ear every second."

"Hmmph." Crake looks at the bank of displays. Over the feeds, the grainy figures of guards change places. The view flips between the guard nests and known weak spots in the compound's acres-long fence, the grain elevators, and the sharecroppers' homesteads in an endless loop. What was I thinking? I owe my whole life to AgraStar. Without it, I'd be one of those sorry wretches skulking the perimeter, stealing food out of other people's mouths. They took me in when I was a kid, begging at the gates. They gave me food and shelter, all free, until I was old enough to start learning a trade, giving back. And this is how I've repaid them.

"I nicked him, at least. Scared them both off." I say in a quieter voice, as much to myself as to Crake. "It's not like they got anything,"

"Yeah, and now we've got a hole in the fence big enough

for any scavenger to waltz through." Crake still sounds mad, but I can tell he's winding down. "Who's going to fix that, huh?"

"I will." I sigh. "Okay? If it'll get you off my back, I'll go as soon as it's light." So much for getting any sleep before dawn.

"Fine." He turns back to his feeds. "Don't forget your report."

I knock out the incident report—0506 now—and head down to the mess for my morning rations. On the way, I pass the women's quarters, still dark except for small rectangles of predawn blue creeping in through the high windows. I stare past the sleeping shapes to my own bunk by the far wall, directly beneath the fire escape, and for a moment, I let myself imagine falling face-first on my mattress, pulling the blackout curtains closed, and passing out until lights-on at 0600.

But no, I have a fence to fix.

Hardly anyone is up as I fill my tray with a bowl of plain cornmeal grits and a shrink-wrapped green apple from our sister farm facility, several hundred miles northeast in the Appalachian Mountains. That's one of the benefits of being a company employee, getting in on the shipments of food from other facilities. The bulk of our crop is destined for ethanol production, but we eat the excess. Everyone gets sick of corn after a while, but at least with AgraStar's model, you get some variety. I don't know how those monoculturalists up at Bloom—one of our competitors—cope with growing only soybeans. Eat a lot of tofu, I guess. Poor bastards.

I drop my tray at a table, peel off the apple's wrapper—
*AgraStar Conglomerate: Leading the Way to a Healthy
Planet*—and bite into it. It's dry and underripe, but at least it's
not corn. Might be the Appalachian facility is having trouble
with white rot again; maybe that's why they're harvesting their
crop so early this year. Last year, we lost nearly half our apple
harvest to blight. We would have lost all of it if our scientists
didn't have a fail-safe built into the company model. We
always distribute two variants per harvest, each genetically
engineered to resist all known pests and diseases. If one fails
or turns out not to be as rot resistant as we thought, we have
the other variant to fall back on. Production might drop, and
we might go a little hungry some years, but we never starve.

I gnaw the apple down to its core and am about to start on
the pool of congealed grits when a pack of boys from security
forces strolls in, led by Ellison Long.

I freeze, spoon halfway into my bowl. Ellison is the best
shot on the whole security force. At nineteen, he's already
good enough to lead his own hand-selected team on special
enforcement missions, and he's in charge of sniper training
for new sharpshooters. He's the one who taught me to load
and fire a rifle, to spot movement in the dark and determine if
it's an animal or a scavenger.

And he was a charity case, like me. A patrol found him
next to his dead mother when he was only a few months old,
and now he's shooting up through the security ranks. Leticia
from dispatch told me she heard corporate is interested in

him for a position at AgraStar's facility in Charlotte, or maybe even at their headquarters in Atlanta. I don't usually get caught up in things like this, but no one would deny Ellison is nice to look at, too, with his close-cropped hair, his big, black-lashed eyes, and his dark brown skin. I would have a crush on him if it weren't impossible to think he might remember I exist, much less like me back.

Please, please, please, I say silently. *Don't let him have heard about this morning.*

But no such luck.

Ellison breaks from his group and meanders over to my table. "Hey, Torres." He's always called me by my last name, as if we're both still in training. "Heard you had a bad morning."

"Yeah." I turn my spoon over in the glop that's become my breakfast and sincerely wish I'd thought to shower before coming to the mess. One minute under Ellison's gaze and I'm thirteen again, his hand on mine, guiding me as I pull back the bolt on my rifle. I blush. "Guy moved at the last second."

Ellison shakes his head. "Happens to the best of us." He pulls out the chair next to me and sits down. "This one time I took a shot at this scavenger. I thought I had the back of his head, but instead I ended up hitting the bag he had slung over his shoulder."

I manage a weak smile. "Yeah?" *He's sitting with me. Ellison Long is sitting with me.*

"I'm talking corn everywhere." Ellison spreads his arms

out over his head, miming an explosion. "Crake was pissed, but I told him, hey, at least the shirks didn't get it."

I laugh, but it comes out high-pitched and childish. What's wrong with me? Ellison says something to me and all of a sudden I turn into one of those idiot girls who can only giggle when a boy's nearby? I clear my throat. "Thanks, that—"

"Hey, El," one of his friends shouts across the mess hall. "You eating with us, or what?"

"Hold up a sec," Ellison yells back. And then, to me, "What you've gotta do is get back on the horse, you know what I'm saying?"

I nod. "The horse. Right."

"You on duty this afternoon?" Ellison asks.

"Duty?" My mind goes suddenly, horribly blank. It's been too long since I've slept, and Ellison Long is talking to me. Apparently, his presence has the same effect on me as a frontal lobotomy. I force my mind back on target. "No. I'm on night shift all this week."

"Good." He smiles. "I'm going up to mile marker two-twenty-six this afternoon, and I need another pair of boots. You game?"

For a moment, I can't wrap my mind around what he's asking, and then it hits me like a thunderclap. "You want me for your team?" Everyone wants to be chosen for Ellison's enforcement missions. It's not just me. No matter who you are, there's something about him that makes you want to please him, to make him proud, to make him notice you.

"Yeah," Ellison says. "You're serious about your job, Torres. I like that. I need that in my ranks."

My chest goes as hot as my face. Is he giving me a pity mission because of what happened this morning? Or showing me some preference because I grew up like him? But no, Ellison never treated me any different than the other trainees when I was learning to shoot. That's one of the things I've always respected about him. He judges people on their abilities, not where they came from.

"What do you say?" Ellison asks.

I don't deserve it, I want to blurt out. *I let that scavenger go.* But I don't. I say the only thing there is to say. "Of course."

"Great." Ellison smiles again and pushes his chair back from the table. "Meet me at the motor-pool yard at sixteen hundred, and make sure you bring your M4."

"My M4?" I'd expect to bring a handgun, maybe, but an M4? That's an assault rifle. Mile marker 226 is square in the middle of sharecropper territory. What kind of trouble is Ellison expecting on our own land?

Ellison must see the look on my face. "I don't think you'll need it, but you never know what you'll run into. Can't hurt to be prepared."

"Right." I make myself smile.

Ellison backs away. "Don't forget, sixteen hundred."

"Sixteen hundred," I echo as he rejoins his friends.

I stare down at my bowl. Ellison Long wants to try me out

for his team. If I do well on a mission with him, everyone will forget my sloppy shooting this morning. Maybe he'll even ask me to join him on a regular basis. That would shut Seth up. No more midnight guard duties, only special assignments and intensive training and sitting with Ellison's team at meals. Sitting with *Ellison*.

Whoa. I bring myself back down to earth. *First things first, Torres. Do your job. No more screwing up. No more soft-headed mercy for scavengers. Ellison wants only the best.*

I shovel down my breakfast and swing by the women's showers to splash cold water on my face. As I stand hunched over the sink, the door creaks open behind me, and a parade of bleary-eyed girls from the children's quarters stumble in to brush their teeth.

Their minder, a bear of a woman with pale skin and heavy brown bangs, shrugs apologetically. "Sorry. Water's out in kid land again."

"No problem." I smile at the girls in what I hope is a kind way. These are kids like I was, charity cases and the children of AgraStar employees who've died in the line of duty—mostly transport drivers and security forces on duty rotations outside the compound. The oldest one is probably eight, the youngest five. They stare at me with big, nervous eyes.

"It's all right, girls," their minder says. "Security forces are our friends. They keep us safe, right?"

The girls all nod solemnly.

The minder sighs and gives me an apologetic eye roll over the tops of their heads. *Kids, you know?*

I keep the smile plastered on my face, but something heavy settles in my gut. I back out the door and take the stairs to Requisitions for the spare parts I'll need to fix the fence. Metal corrugate, welding mask and torch, gloves.

The sun has broken the horizon by the time I make it outside, and the world is heating up. Soon the bunker with its vents hissing lukewarm air will be the coolest place for miles. I tramp past the grain elevators and down a red-dirt service road cut through the acres of corn. *La milpa*, my brain tries to say, but I swat the word away. English only. That's the official language of AgraStar. I learned that lesson my first year on the compound. I sigh, annoyed with myself. If I want to be the perfect AgraStar recruit—good enough for Ellison's team—I have to get rid of these last vestiges of the things my father tried to program into me before he died.

The crickets keep up their calls from the shade—they don't know it's day yet—and the thin *whist* of the sharecroppers spraying pesticide somewhere in the tall green rows floats over their voices. Harvest is almost here, and then the rumble of combines will overtake this quiet morning song. Near the perimeter, I come upon a sharecropper refilling his backpack tank from a drum parked along the side of the road.

He's old enough to be my father, but he tips his hat at me. "Ma'am." The sun has baked his skin the deep red of the dirt.

I smile and return his salute. Not all sharecroppers are

so polite. Some of them, the young ones mostly, resent those of us on security forces, call us pigs and cogs. But they could have chosen to go out for the forces, the same as I could have chosen to start sharecropping.

When I turned twelve, the recruitment officers took me aside, just like everyone else. I had been living, eating, learning to read and write, all at AgraStar's expense, since the company found me outside the gates of our compound, SCP-52, when I was five. I could start working in the fields immediately, they said, paying back my debt, and either be free to leave the compound or begin working toward a homestead of my own by the time I was nineteen. One year of work for every year I'd been under the company's wing. Or I could continue my training and education. I could study and become a scientist for them, or a teacher, or a member of the security force. My years of debt service would be longer, but I'd have more variety in my work. I'd learn special skills. The company would value me. I could grow up to be somebody.

I finished my training and earned my first security post the year I turned fifteen. Eight more years, and my debt will be paid back. I can start contracting with the company on my own by the time I'm twenty-five. Not bad for someone who could have ended up a shirk.

I reach the perimeter. The sun is out in full force now, no clouds, no wind, only a white-hot sky cut by a twenty-foot tall chain-link fence festooned in stripes of razor wire. Our compound covers a few hundred square miles, most of that land devoted to growing corn. Four security substations are positioned north, south, east, and west, with an R&D facility and ethanol production plant at the heart of the territory. The security fence encircles it all, keeping out the shirks and road gangs and anarchists. A breach puts nearly six thousand loyal AgraStar contractors and sharecroppers at risk.

I drop the corrugate against the links, fit the welding mask over my head, and tug on my gloves. The sooner I get this done, the sooner I can go back and grab some sleep.

I kneel in the dirt and let the torch's blue flame kiss metal. Embers spark and fall around me, cooling from white to red by the time they hit the ground. Slowly I fuse the arm-long square of corrugate to the links, then stand back and inspect my work as it cools. It's a simple job, but a good weld. I pull off my mask. Sweat rolls down my back and my hair is soaked through. I shade my eyes and look down the line of fence to where it disappears into the curve of cornstalks. Reinforced squares like mine dot the length of it as far as I can see. Someday the entire lower third of this fence is going to be nothing but overlapping metal patchwork.

Something glints in the scrub grass beside the fence some ten paces down the line. I walk over and squat in the dirt. *What . . . ?*

I lie down and work my hand through the bottommost link. *There.* The metal is hot from lying in the sun, but I pull it through anyway. I sit up and examine my find. The cutters, the ones the scavenger boy was using last night. A scoop of metal is missing from the outer edge of the business end, where my bullet must have hit it after clipping the boy's hand.

The still air pulses with heat. I stare out at the forest, insects trilling in my ears. What happened to that boy? Is he lying in the heat somewhere, sweating out a fever from the wound? Is that girl with him, laying her cool palm over his forehead? Are they waiting for darkness to fall so they can try again? The image of their hands laced together surges in my mind again, but this time, all I feel is hate. No one has ever held my hand that way. No one has ever led me through the dark. I do fine on my own, thanks. I'm no shirk who needs to live off other people. I should have done everyone a favor and put them both out of their misery.

I stand and brush the dust from my shirt. No use beating myself up. I know what to do next time. I stuff the cutters in my pocket, gather my welding torch and mask, and start walking back through the shimmering heat to the bunker. If I don't stop thinking about it, I'm never going to get to sleep. I need to be rested for my first mission with Ellison.

.2.

HONEYSUCKLE
LONICERA JAPONICA

I stand outside the motor pool with my rifle over my shoulder. I've traded my sniping gear for a short-sleeved day uniform with the company's signature starburst emblazoned over my heart. My hair is pulled back in a braid, still damp from the shower. I caught a few hours' sleep in the women's dormitory, but I could have used more. The day has that unreal feeling it takes on when you wake up in midafternoon, like you're out of step with the rest of the world.

I shift from one foot to the other. It's 1559. No sign of Ellison yet. My chest tightens. Should I have come earlier? Are they already gone? Or was this some cruel joke all along? Ellison's never seemed like the type to play pranks, but maybe I've had him wrong. After all, who am I to think I deserve a shot like this? Tempest with the dead shirk dad, capable enough not to be singled out for hatred, but not vibrant or legacy or *enough* of anything to be welcomed in, either. I should stick to spending my time shadowing Crake in the Eye or, better yet, at the firing range, convincing everyone I really did miss and I'm trying to make up for it.

The readout on my data band flips over to 1600. On cue, an open-topped truck swings into the motor yard, spitting a cloud of dust in its wake and filling the air with the smell of burning corn oil. Two boys and a girl, all sporting bare, tanned arms and mirrored sunglasses, fill the backseat. I know them by sight. The girl is Danica Hwang, and the boys are Will Betts and Marco Etowah. Ellison's handpicked team. The tightness in my chest releases.

"Torres!" Ellison waves to me from the driver's seat.

I jog after them and stow my rifle alongside the others in the gun rack bolted to the back of the truck. Ellison's teammates watch me like foxes. They're all a few years older than I am, close to Ellison's age. I swallow and try to smile, but I think I might come off more nervous and crazed than friendly and competent. *Don't screw this up, Tempest.*

Ellison pats the seat beside him in the front. "C'mon, Torres. Saddle up."

I boost myself into the cab and clip the seat belt across my chest. The wire cutters press against my lower back. I don't know why I've kept them. As a reminder, maybe, to do my job, not to be soft when duty calls.

Ellison twists around in his seat. He's left his uniform unbuttoned in the heat, so the white of his undershirt shows. "Torres, this is Hwang, Betts, and Etowah. Y'all, this is Torres. She's filling in for Max today. She's a solid shot."

"Usually," I add, and am relieved to see Danica crack a smile. So they've heard.

Ellison shifts the truck into drive and swings us around. As we pull out of the motor-pool yard, we pass Seth trudging back to the bunker. His eyes catch mine, and for one brief second I have the satisfaction of seeing them go wide. Then we're gone, past our outpost's thick concrete walls and onto one of the long streaks of dirt road that radiate out from the heart of the compound.

A thrill runs through my stomach as the truck jounces over the uneven road. I'm on a mission with Ellison Long. Soon my poor marksmanship will be nothing more than a funny story I tell new recruits to cheer them up.

Fields and fields of head-high corn go by, broken only by secondary roads and the occasional glimpse of sharecroppers bent among the bright green rows.

Marco leans forward. "Where we off to, boss?" I can barely hear him over the engine and the wind whipping past my ears.

"Mile marker two-two-six." Ellison squints at the road and fishes up the pair of sunglasses hooked to his shirt.

"The Kingfisher share again?" Danica asks.

Ellison nods. "One of the pest eradication patrols up in the northeast sector found some nonstandard seed varieties floating around. They want us to look in, see what we can see. It could simply be an invasive species drifting in on the wind—"

"Or it could be Harry Kingfisher." Marco finishes for him.

I crane my neck to look back at Marco. "You think he's growing an invasive species on purpose?"

"Not just growing," Marco says. "Distributing."

Even Will, who's been staring out the window through his black mirrored sunglasses this whole time, nods.

"But. . ." I frown. I can't think of a good reason why anyone would jeopardize our harvest by planting invasive, nonstandard seeds. Our R&D teams pour so much work into calibrating and tweaking AgraStar seeds to produce the most disease-resistant, high-yield crops possible. "Why? Who'd want them?"

Ellison shakes his head. "Not everyone's an upstanding citizen like you, Torres. If you ride with us, you're going to see the ugly side of things." He spares a glance at me. "You up for that?"

"Of course." I wish I could see his eyes, but all I can see is the reflection of myself, sitting ramrod straight in the passenger seat, tendrils of dark brown hair escaping my braid in the wind. I tuck the wayward strands behind my ears. "Whatever you've got, I'm up for it."

"That's my girl." Ellison holds out one hand and locks our wrists together in a quick, tight grip.

We bump over the unpaved roads at top speed. Mile 224. 225. 226. Abruptly, the corn drops away to reveal a standard sharecropper homestead—red tin roof, cinder-block walls, a simple vinyl awning stretched over a porch along the front of the house. A small boy dressed only in a pair of old canvas pants sits under the awning, scratching a greasy-looking beagle behind the ears. His head snaps up at the sound of our engine. He takes one look at us, overturns his chair, and lights out across the small patch of unplanted dirt in front of the house. He crashes into the corn and disappears before Ellison can even kill the engine.

"See," Marco says. "What'd I tell you?"

"Bad sign," Ellison agrees.

We step out of the truck. The dog rises to its feet and lets loose an uneasy half bark, half growl.

"Rifles," Ellison reminds us. "Safety on."

I wait my turn and unload my gun from the rack. This is what everyone loves about Ellison. He's tough-minded, but fair. He looks out for people like Harry Kingfisher, even when those people flout the company rules and put us all at risk with their own stupidity. He was that same way with us trainees when I was younger—he'd call us out for being careless with our weapons or talking shit about the company, but he wouldn't report us if we shaped up. And wanting him to like us was enough reason to shape up. I shoulder my rifle and approach the house alongside Will, Ellison, and Danica. Marco stays posted, standing in the back of the truck.

The Kingfishers don't grow pleasant runs of company-issued chrysanthemums and black-eyed Susans in front of their house, like most sharecroppers. Instead, they've filled the ground around their porch with untamed bushes of flowering chamomile and great, shaggy tomato plants bearing purple-red fruit. A run of white honeysuckle engulfs one end of the porch and spills up onto the roof, a blatant violation. I can see why Ellison and his crew suspect Harry Kingfisher. As invasive species go, honeysuckle comes in second only to the kudzu that creeps up from the forest surrounding the compound.

A tall, stocky man with a full head of gray hair pulled back in a ponytail appears in the shadow behind the screen door. His face is brown and lined.

"Harry Kingfisher?" Ellison calls.

The dog sounds a warning bark and takes a step forward.

"Easy, girl." The man pushes open the door. "What d' you want this time?" The dog backs behind his legs with a snarl.

"You want to tell me what this is about?" Ellison waves at the honeysuckle.

"I told you before, the stuff just grows." Kingfisher crosses his arms. "Nothing for it."

Danica tosses a look over her shoulder and rolls her eyes at me.

"What about the tomatoes?" Ellison nods at the plants. "You got a permit for them?" Since the company considers sharecroppers independent contractors leasing company land, rather than company employees like us, they don't get a share of produce from other facilities, except when their land becomes part of the Fallows once every six years. Instead, they're allowed to grow a certain number of subsistence crops—tomatoes or green beans, maybe—to supplement their diet. So long as they meet their corn quota, anyway.

"Course I got a permit." Kingfisher steps out into the yard and lets the screen door slam behind him. "What, do I look stupid? Growing contraband in my own front yard?"

"Let's see it, then," Ellison says.

The man's eyes tighten. "I showed it to you last month when you were out here."

"If you'll just oblige us, sir."

Kingfisher curses and reaches into his back pocket. "One day a bunch of self-important kids are going to show up on your doorstep and harass *you* about some meaningless bullshit, you know." He pulls out a well-creased paper and shakes it at Ellison. "Here."

"Thank you," Ellison says.

"You know, people like us used to stick together." Kingfisher shakes his head. "Life's hard enough without some suits picking apart everything we do."

Ellison raises an eyebrow. "People like us?"

"You know what I mean." Kingfisher nods at Ellison's bare forearms, and I realize he's talking about his skin. Kingfisher looks at me. "You too, miss. You ought to be looking out for us, not grinding us down."

A bone-deep discomfort rears up in me. I scowl and adjust my grip on my rifle. That's the old way of thinking, from before the company came in and made everything fair and equal. No wonder Harry Kingfisher's always getting himself in trouble.

"You know it's not like that anymore," Ellison says without looking up, and from the tired way he says it, I can tell they've had this conversation before. "If somebody hears you talking that way, corporate's going to hit you with a libel citation."

"You keep telling yourself that," Kingfisher says. "Someday you're going to learn who's really looking out for you and who's using you. I just hope it's not too late."

Will backs up next to me and stares at the homestead's roof, careful not to look my way. "Boss man and I can keep him dancing. Walk the perimeter. See if you spot anything."

I nod and start around the house in a wide circle as Ellison unfolds the permit and inspects it. A peeling black oil tank hunches along the building's side, surrounded by weeds. The dirt under my feet is hard packed as concrete.

"Hey," Kingfisher calls out behind me. "Where's she going?"

"Mr. Kingfisher—"

"Hey, girl! There's nothing you need over there."

"Mr. Kingfisher." Ellison's voice rings out, loud and commanding. "You don't need to concern yourself with her. You only need to worry about our conversation, right here."

I refocus, keep walking. Nothing unusual at the back of the house. Faded bedsheets and a woman's blue denim dress flap on the laundry lines strung between two T-shaped poles. A rusty generator against the house. A plywood chicken coop. In fact, nothing is strange about the Kingfisher homestead at all, except how quiet it is. No sounds carry over the corn, not voices, not even the gentle hiss of pesticide raining down on crops. All the other homesteads I've visited have been lousy with kids scampering across the lawn or busy at some chore or another, their parents shouting for them to hurry up with this or fetch that. It's far too quiet.

I make for the wall of corn. Kingfisher's voice comes back into range behind me, angry and unintelligible, followed by the murmur of Ellison trying to keep him calm. The cornstalks crackle as I push them aside. The leaves are tough as ribbed canvas beneath my hands. I unsling my rifle and use its muzzle to push my way through. The quiet grows thicker the deeper I go. No wind, no insects, only sun and corn.

"Ow." A muffled yelp. I freeze.

"Watch it," a kid whispers.

"No, *you* watch it," another kid rasps back.

"Boys." A woman. "Hush."

I advance slowly, careful not to step on the dry husks that have fallen to the dirt and give myself away. Maybe I'm going crazy—the sharecroppers all tell stories about sound traveling funny in the corn—but I swear the voices are coming from ahead of me and under my feet.

"He started it," one of the boys whines.

"I don't care who started it." The woman again. "We ain't got time for this. You want your daddy to get taken away by those security cogs?"

I push forward through another row, and the corn drops away. A small, empty square of land, about the size of the monitoring room in the Eye, lies in the center of the corn.

Sets of tall wooden tripods fashioned out of stakes and twine dot the space, all heavy with full-grown runner beans. I count quickly. Fourteen, maybe fifteen plants in total, all definitely contraband. I whistle low to myself. Ellison should see this.

"Listen," one of the boys says, closer than ever. "Did you hear that?"

I drop into a crouch and scan the ground. There's more here than a contraband bean plot. Then I spot it. A clear space in the corner, covered only by dirt and husks. I approach softly, heel-toe, heel-toe. There, a mud-caked metal handle. I kneel and gently scrape away the soil around it. *Not so much as a loud breath.* A trapdoor comes into view, cut from a piece of roofing tin.

I smile. *Got you.* I grab the handle and heave up. The trapdoor flies open, scattering dust and debris through the air. I flip my rifle's selector from safety to single shot and aim down into the gap that's suddenly appeared in the earth. A woman screams, and someone else shrieks behind her.

"Everybody drop what you're doing." I squint into the darkness. "Don't move."

I descend the stairs slowly, rifle at the ready, giving my eyes time to adjust to the shadows. A middle-aged woman with tanned skin and long salt-and-pepper hair stands beside a weathered wooden sideboard, a jar of golden corn seeds uncapped in her hand. Two small boys peek out from behind her, and a girl of maybe twelve sits on a low stool on the other side of the narrow room, cutting out squares of plastic with a paring knife. Makeshift plywood and cinder-block shelves line the earthen walls behind them, each cluttered with grimy jars holding seeds. A clutch of radio equipment—transmitter, headphones, receiver—has been shoved in beside them.

My eyes widen. There's too much here for simple contraband, too much for a farmer who might want to organize a little behind-the-barn trade in exchange for extra fructose rations or a favor down the line. And the radio equipment . . . Marco's right. The Kingfishers must be distributors. The woman—Kingfisher's wife?—places the seed jar carefully on the sideboard.

I set my jaw. I've got to take charge while they're still stunned enough not to run. "Okay, everybody up and out." I gesture at the daylight with my rifle.

The woman lets her fingers linger on the jar's lid, as if she's caressing something precious. "Come on, little ones." She speaks quietly, even though there's no reason to hide now. "Do what the lady says."

The girl and boys file up the steps. Pity strikes me. Unless Harry Kingfisher does some fast talking, these kids aren't going to be seeing their parents again. They're probably going to be stuck in a dormitory on sharecropping detail, at least until they're old enough to strike their own deal with the company. And with a history of illegal seed hoarding and distribution on their files, it'll be hard for them to ever score a good assignment like security forces or research and development.

The woman moves to follow her children. My pity turns to anger.

"You." I turn my rifle on her. What kind of mother makes her kids into criminals, saddles them with that label for the rest of their lives? "Hand me that container."

The woman places a trembling hand over the jar of corn seeds. "What, this?"

"Yes." I let acid drip into my words. "That. Hand it over, now."

Her gaze flicks to the rifle, and then back to me. She holds it out.

I snatch it from her. "Now up the stairs. We're going to take a little walk and see what your husband has to say about this operation you've got going here."

"He doesn't know anything." Her voice warbles. "This was all my idea. He doesn't know a thing."

"Uh-huh." I follow her up the steps, my rifle trained on her back the whole way.

The girl and one of the boys are waiting next to the trapdoor. The youngest kid is gone.

"Dammit." I scan the corn, careful to keep my rifle on Mrs. Kingfisher. "Where'd he go?"

The girl and her brother stare at me.

I turn to them. "Which way did he go?"

The boy whimpers and moves closer to his sister. She clutches him, eyes on my rifle.

Good, let them be afraid. Not that I would shoot a bunch of kids—that would be unprofessional—but they don't need to know that.

"I'm going to ask one more time." I narrow my eyes at the girl. "Where did he go?"

"I . . . I don't know." She doesn't blink. "He got scared and ran. I . . . I think he was headed for the house."

I heave a sigh. What else am I going to do? The kid won't get far once we've called in our findings, anyway. He'll probably turn himself in once he figures out his family is gone.

"C'mon," I grunt, and march them back in the direction of the house.

"Please." Mrs. Kingfisher turns to me. Tears streak her face. "Just let our kids go. They ain't to blame for this."

"You should have thought of that before." I poke her in the chest with my rifle's muzzle. "Move."

By the time we break through the corn, the woman is stumbling through hiccupping sobs, and the boy has caught her hysteria. Only the older girl stays silent, eyes straight ahead, as we step into the homestead's side yard. Mr. Kingfisher and my teammates are more or less arrayed as before, Ellison at Kingfisher's side, Marco atop the vehicle, Will and Danica spread out on guard.

"Hey, guys." I hold the jar of corn seeds aloft with my free hand and shake it. "Look what I found."

Kingfisher catches sight of us. I see him counting and coming up one shy. "What—" His voice rises. "Marie? Where's Micah?"

"Harry!" Mrs. Kingfisher goes hoarse. "The kids, Harry—"

Kingfisher locks eyes with me. "What did you do to them? What did you do with Micah?" He steps onto the grass.

"Mr. Kingfisher." Ellison plants a warning hand on his chest.

"No." Kingfisher shoves Ellison aside and strides full bore at me. His eyes have gone black and dilated. "Where's my son? What the hell did you do with him?" He's charging now, all two hundred pounds of him barreling down on me with a fury that makes me take a step back.

"Harry, no!" Mrs. Kingfisher screams. "Stop!"

A surge of adrenaline hits me. My training clicks in. I drop to one knee, brace my rifle, and aim for Kingfisher's shin. A wounding shot. I don't want these kids to see me kill their old man, even if he is a criminal. "Mr. Kingfisher, stop."

He keeps coming. The world slows and sharpens. I tighten my finger on the trigger. Last warning. "Mr. Kingfisher—"

A sickening thud smacks the air, the sound of meat on meat. It happens too fast for me to see, but somehow Kingfisher is down in a flail of arms and legs, wrestling with someone in the dirt. I blink and lower my rifle. Will's head surfaces in the fray.

"Stay down, you sonovabi—"

Kingfisher gets in a solid hit across Will's jaw. I hear the bones crunch from where I'm standing. Danica flies in from the right, brandishing her rifle like a bat. She swings the butt in a downward arc and cracks Kingfisher across the face. He screams and then there's blood, and Danica and Will won't stop hitting him and, no, his kids shouldn't be seeing this, no matter what their father did, and all of a sudden I'm remembering what I don't want to remember—my own father on his back in the leaves, a single snowflake falling to rest on his still, unseeing eye—

A gunshot rings out. "That's enough." Ellison steps forward.

For a moment, all I can hear is my own quick breath and a high ringing. Danica and Will let Kingfisher drop. His head thumps against the ground. An animal moan rises from him.

"I think he's sufficiently subdued." Ellison's face has gone a sick shade of gray, but he doesn't drop the command in his voice. He looks at me. "What's this about? Who's Micah?"

I lower my rifle and swallow. "The littlest kid, I'm guessing." I climb to my feet. "The one we saw make a run for it earlier. I was subduing the mother, and he went rabbit. Slipped me."

Ellison grunts and nods. "He'll turn up." He tilts his chin at the jar of corn. "Is that all you found?"

I shake my head. "There's a whole underground room out in the field, about sixty paces in. I left the door open. Shouldn't be hard to spot."

Ellison casts a disgusted look at Kingfisher and his wife. "Torres and Etowah, load 'em up in the truck. We'll let the administrators figure out what to do with them. Betts, call in the eradication team and report the kid's data band number to admin for an APB. Hwang, with me."

"Sir." The rest of them salute, so I copy and follow up with my own belated "Sir."

Ellison and Danica disappear into the corn, while Will

climbs into the truck's cab to call in what we've found. Marco hops down and helps me lift Kingfisher so we can fasten his hands behind his back with a zip tie and haul him to the truck. His wife and kids follow sullenly.

Harry Kingfisher slumps in the bed of the truck. His breathing sounds wet and strained. Mrs. Kingfisher sits with her head in her hands, trying to hide the fact that she's still crying. The boy whimpers, but the girl is strangely silent.

"Right," Will says into the truck's coms. "See you in a few."

I shake out my hands to cover their trembling and make a close circuit around the vehicle.

You've still got to do your job, Tempest, I tell myself. *You knew this might happen. What would Ellison do?*

Gather intelligence, I think. *Take advantage of your opponent's disorientation.* Right. I take a deep breath. Only the girl looks up as I approach, but no matter. She's the one I want to talk to anyway.

I sit down next to her on the truck's bumper. "What's your name?"

"Juna." She looks at me warily.

"It's all right." I try to smile kindly. "How old are you, Juna?"

"Eleven and a half," she whispers.

"Almost old enough to make your own contract." I flood my voice with cheer. "Have you thought about what you'd like to do when you're older?"

She shrugs. "I guess I'll help my dad run the share."

Pity wells up in me again. No way are the Kingfishers keeping their share after what's gone down today. Contraband, distribution, and resisting arrest? Maybe even proselytizing, depending on what they have to say for themselves.

I clear the rifle's breach and click the safety back on. "You know this isn't how most people live, right?" I turn to look at her. "Selling contraband? There are other ways to live. Honest ways."

Juna narrows her eyes. "Like what?"

"Well." I clear my throat. "You could become a scientist, come up with new disease-resistant strains of plants. Or you could be an instructor or work in laundry services or transport or pest eradication."

Juna stares at the dirt.

"Or you could be like me," I say.

Juna looks up sharply. "Like you?"

I nod. "I'm not so different from you. I would have ended up a scavenger if it weren't for AgraStar taking me in when I was your littlest brother's age." I smile. "You wouldn't know that to look at me now, would you?"

Juna shakes her head. "I guess not."

"Juna," I say gently. "You know where your brother's gone, don't you?"

Her eyes dart to mine.

"It's okay to tell me. I only want to keep him safe, is all."

She opens her mouth, but hesitates.

"I could put in a good word for you," I say. "If you help

us, I can make sure you get the assignment you want when you make your contract."

"I . . ." She shoots a glance at her parents, caked in dust and bound with zip ties, then up at me.

Right then, an engine backfires on the road behind us. A high-sided pickup rumbles into the yard. Two figures in white jumpsuits and filtration masks climb out of the truck and begin unloading tanks of chemicals.

I look back to Juna, but her eyes have gone hard again.

Ellison and Danica reappear at the edge of the field.

"Oh, good." Ellison waves to the eradication team. "It's this way. Danica'll show you."

The white jumpsuited team lugs their chemicals across the yard and follow Danica back into the corn.

"Load up," Ellison calls to us. "We've got to clear out of here so Eradication can do their work."

My head snaps up. "What about the kid?"

"Admin says he's not registering in this quadrant." Will cranes his head around to look at me. "Wherever he is, he's well clear."

"Oh." Of course he is. Eradication would never go ahead with their work if the kid was anywhere close. *Way to show you're green, Torres.*

I help the Kingfisher kids into the front seat and make sure their parents are securely bound in the cargo area. I slam the tailgate closed and come face-to-face with Ellison.

He leans a hand against the spare tire bolted to the

truck. "You did good out there, Torres. I don't think I've ever seen anyone perform that well on their first day of a new assignment. You're a real professional." There's something in his eyes. Respect? Admiration? But no, it's something more than that. He's not looking at me like a student anymore. I'm his equal in the field.

"Th—thanks."

Ellison touches my upper arm, and my breath catches in my throat. "Tempest. Can I call you that?"

My mouth gapes open like a fish. I manage to nod.

"Maybe you can ride with me again soon." He squeezes lightly and grins. "We make a good team, huh?"

My face goes hot. "Yeah." I duck my head and look down at the truck's tire treads. "We do."

Danica jogs back across the yard. "They're ready. We can move out."

We pile into the jeep, Danica, Will, and Marco in the backseat, and Juna and her brother crammed between me and Ellison in the front. Ellison guns the engine, and we pull away from the Kingfisher homestead. As the house shrinks from view, a dull thud shakes the earth, followed by a louder, crackling boom. Everyone but Ellison looks back. A thick black cloud billows up from the Kingfishers' field.

"I'll never be like you," Juna whispers, so soft I almost can't hear. "Not ever."

.3.

SNAKEBERRY
SOLANUM DULCAMARA

Afternoon thunderclouds mass overhead as Ellison speeds toward the nearest security substation. A cool breeze moves through the fields, sweeping back the sluggish summer air. The sky is pink and electric. Ellison clicks on the headlights.

"E.T.A., ten minutes," he says into the radio. "Y'all got someone from admin ready to take the Kingfishers into custody?"

"Roger that," the radio crackles back. "You better gas it if you want to beat that storm front, though. You know how the roads get."

Ellison frowns, concentrating on driving. In the backseat, Danica, Will, and Marco have begun retelling the story of the afternoon, complete with sound effects. I can already tell the version that makes it back to the bunker is going to be slightly more badass than the reality.

"I . . ." I clear my throat and steal a glance at Ellison. "I liked how you handled everything. Back there, I mean."

Ellison flashes a grin at me. "You didn't do so bad yourself." He smiles and spares a look away from the road for me. "Do you mind me asking—what made you decide to join up with security forces?"

"I . . ." I blush. "It's kind of stupid."

Ellison rolls his eyes. "It can't be that bad."

"Okay, so . . ." I take a deep breath. "There was this woman, Rosalie MacLeod, on security forces when I was a kid—"

"Oh, Rosalie. I remember her." Ellison waves his hand in apology. "Sorry, go on."

"There's not much to it." I look out at the corn rushing by, its greens deepening under the darkening clouds. "She was nice to me. I wanted to be like her."

Ellison nods. "I get that." He glances over at me again. "It's not stupid."

In the distance, thunder rumbles, and the whole world sighs, expecting rain.

"She was the one who found me," I blurt out. I breathe in sharply, as if I could suck the words back. I never talk about that, not with anyone.

Ellison looks at me more intently now, so long I'm sure he's going to run us off the road. Then he turns forward again. "I liked her, too. She was good at what she did."

"Yeah," I agree.

"What ever happened to her?"

"She got hurt on a transport security mission." I twist my fingers in my lap. "After that, she transferred to communications down at the R and D facility. I don't see her anymore."

We lapse into silence. I stare out at the fields and glimpse their reflection rushing along in the side mirror. A flash clips the corner of my vision. I turn and look back. Lightning? No, there's a steady light behind us. Two lights, in fact. The high beams of another truck.

"Will?"

He stops teasing Danica midsentence and looks up, a goofy grin plastered on his face.

"Did admin send out backup for us?"

"No." He catches the troubled look on my face. "Why?"

"Nothing," I say. I'm only being green again, probably. "I just wondered if that truck—"

"Truck?" He snaps his head around, but the road bends and the cornfields swallow the headlights. He turns back to me. "I don't see anything."

"It's there," I say. "Watch."

Raindrops hiss on the hood. We both stare back at the road reeling out behind us. It straightens again, and a few heartbeats later, the headlights strike our rearview mirror. They're closer this time, close enough for me to count three figures riding in the cab.

Ellison glances up and squints into the mirror. "Who's that?"

"Backup?" I try to make out what kind of vehicle it is, try to see the riders, but the rain is coming down harder now, and I can't see anything in the gloom.

"The substation didn't say they were sending anyone." Ellison spares another glance in the rearview. "Besides, if they're backup, why haven't they radioed us?"

Will casts a look at our rifles, clipped securely into the gun rack at the back of the truck, and then at Danica and Marco. Should we go for them? Or maybe the other vehicle's radio is simply broken, and they're trying to catch up to escort us or share some news? After all, what else could it be in the heart of company territory?

Ellison looks at me, and then up to the mirror again. "Another five minutes and we'll be at the substation."

He tightens his grip on the wheel and guns the gas. The engine revs. We edge faster, but the truck behind us isn't nearly as weighed down. It's closing the distance. Fifty feet. Forty. Twenty-five. Fifteen.

"What's happening?" Juna's brother tries to twist around in his seat.

"Shh," she whispers. Her eyes catch mine. "Stay down."

I look back again. Lightning crackles across the sky, illuminating our pursuers. An open-top Humvee, mottled with rust. The engine cranks and grinds as they move closer. Something is wrong. Very wrong. Any company vehicle making that kind of sound would have been retired, scrapped for parts.

"Ellison . . ." My voice wavers.

One of our pursuers rises in the front seat. Two hanks of white-blond hair hang down her shoulders, almost silver in the storm's light. The girl steadies a rifle on her shoulder and takes aim at our back left tire.

"Ellison!" I scream.

He jams his foot all the way down to the floorboard and swerves, but it's too late. A bang rocks our back end, and our truck careens across the wet road. Everyone screams. Juna's brother latches on to my arm as we fishtail off the road and crash into a wall of wet green corn.

Stalks snap against the truck's grill and thump the windshield. Ellison jerks the wheel, trying to pull us back under control, but the ground is slick and uneven, and the back left side drags along on its rims. We hit a rut. I throw my arms around Juna and her brother as the truck tips up on two wheels. Everything slows. The ground comes up to meet us on Ellison's side, a mash of mud and pulped corn.

Impact. The front window splinters. The sudden change of momentum throws me and the kids against Ellison, and then, for a brief moment, my stomach drops and I'm weightless. I don't seem to be in the cab anymore, but before my brain can process what this means, wet leaves brush my shoulders and I hit the ground with a thump that knocks the breath from my lungs.

↓ ↓ ↓

My head pounds. I stagger to my feet, but the world spins around me. Green earth, wet sky, fire. I close my eyes and stand still, waiting for the spinning to stop. The world has gone quiet without the grind of diesel engines and tires rumbling over the road. Rain patters on the leaves and spits in the crackling fire. All quiet, except for the voices.

Voices yelling over the corn. The metallic thunk of a car door slamming. I open my eyes. Several dozen yards in front of me, our truck lies on its side in the mud, a small, acrid-smelling fire licking from its undercarriage. I drop into a crouch and run along the deep furrows our tires left in the wet clay, toward the wreck. I register dully that I'm not feeling much pain, but I'm pretty sure that's going to change once the endorphins flooding my bloodstream wear off.

Three of the rifles are missing from the jeep's gun rack. I pull mine out and check its magazine, though the world is going to have to stop swirling before I can do much good with it.

"Torres?" A hoarse whisper from the far side of the truck.

"Who's there?" I whirl, rifle up at the sound.

Danica pokes her head over the vehicle's upturned side. "Back here."

Danica, Will, and Ellison huddle in the jeep's shadow, rifles at the ready. Juna crouches beside them with her hand clamped over her brother's mouth to muffle his whimpers. Mrs. Kingfisher's zip ties have been cut away, and she sits with her husband's head in her lap. His left leg bends back at the wrong angle and blood soaks his pant leg. His eyes are closed, but he's breathing.

I kneel beside Ellison. "You're okay." I brush tears away. It's only a physiological response to the wreck, that's all. It's not like I'm really crying. "Where's Marco?"

Ellison focuses his gaze over my shoulder and nods.

I look up. Marco's body hangs slack in the seat restraints. He looks fine from the ground—unconscious, maybe—but then I stand to get a better view. Blood cakes Marco's hair and the right side of his face, and there's an unmistakable stillness to his chest. I take in a sharp breath. I haven't seen a dead body since my father's, at least not up close. The disposal teams usually take care of the shirks we pick off, if their fellow scavengers don't drag the bodies away first. I reach out and touch Marco's shoulder, half expecting him to startle and blink awake, but he doesn't. His body jostles softly and his head lolls back.

Footsteps squelch through the mud. A man's voice drifts over the corn.

". . . told you to be careful. You'd better hope Harry and his brood aren't dead."

"How was I supposed to know he'd go off the road like that?" a girl's says. "It's not like I took out the driver or anything."

I drop down behind the truck.

Mrs. Kingfisher's head snaps up at the sound of the girl's voice. Our eyes meet. She looks away quickly.

"You know her?" I whisper.

Mrs. Kingfisher shakes her head, but her eyes are open too wide. I start to press her, but Ellison signals for us to be silent.

"Might as well have shot him." Footsteps splash closer.

The girl huffs. "How else was I going to stop them?"

"Quiet, both of you." A new voice joins in, a younger man's. "There it is."

Ellison quietly thumbs his gun's selector over to semi-auto and gestures for the rest of us to do the same. I try not to breathe. The world swims at the edges.

Ellison holds up a hand and counts with his fingers. One. Two. Three.

"Go," he mouths.

As one, we rise and level our rifles at the girl and her companions. Her eyes go wide, and they swing their firearms up at us.

"Drop your weapons." Ellison's tone has gone hard and dangerous. "Now."

"You first." The girl adjusts her grip on her gun. She wears the same ditch-water brown tunic she had on the night before, only with the hood thrown back, and a faded red handkerchief loose around her neck. She and the middle-aged man both carry automatic rifles, older versions of our own, but the younger man has only a heavy black revolver and a bandaged hand. I stare at it. The last three fingers on his right hand are splinted and bound with rags.

"You," I breathe.

He stares blankly at me from beneath his ragged black hair. How could he know who shot the wire cutters from his hand last night? To him, it would have been a crack of pain in the dark, and then a mad dash through the weeds. My chest fills up with anger again. I never should have let him run, him or the girl. I should have aimed true, and then Marco would still be here.

"Hand over the Kingfishers, and we'll let you go," the girls calls.

Ellison laughs. "How about you lay down your weapons and I let you live long enough to face the disciplinary board?"

She snorts. "Seems to me you're not in much of a position to be making demands."

"You think so?" Ellison says. "Any minute now, a team from the substation's going to be rolling along, wondering why we haven't showed yet."

"And if you don't hand over Kingfisher and his kids, all they're going to find are your bodies," the girl says.

"Jesus, Eden," the scavenger boy mutters.

"We've got a job to do, Alder." She takes her eyes off Ellison for a split second to glance at the boy. "Or have you forgotten what AgraStar does to seed savers?"

I take my chance. Now, when she isn't looking. I won't make the same mistake twice. I shift my aim to her chest, hold my breath so the world will stop spinning, and fire.

The shot goes wrong, but lucky wrong. Her chin jerks

up, as if some invisible force has pulled her by the hair. She falls, squeezing the trigger convulsively and spraying an arc of bullets into the air. To the left of me, someone screams—Will?—and the field erupts in gunfire. The Kingfisher kids clap their hands over their ears and crouch in the mud. The older scavenger backs to the wall of corn, firing steadily. The younger one sends off a few wild shots, and then drops to his knees and crawls through the mud to the girl's body.

Bullets ping off the truck's undercarriage. My mind and body snap together. This is what I've been trained to do. *Calm breathing. Use your adrenaline.* I focus on the older man. I'm no good for precision shots with my vision still skewed, so I fire in a sweep across his position. One of my shots rips through his neck—a flesh wound—but most of them patter harmlessly into the corn like hard rain.

A bullet bites Danica's shoulder. She grunts in surprise as it throws her back into the dirt, but that gives Ellison enough time to bring his rifle to bear and execute a neat shot to the center of the man's chest. He drops.

I let myself breathe. "Nice."

Ellison grins at me. "Thanks. I try."

A single shot cracks the air, a paltry sound after the air-ripping exchange. Ellison's face goes slack.

"Tempest," he says in surprise, and falls.

I whirl around, rifle up. The scavenger boy stands over the girl's body, pistol raised and pointed at the spot where Ellison stood mere seconds ago. At his feet, the girl's skin has gone pale as her hair. A dark ruby spot spreads steadily across her neck, blood mixed with rain and red clay.

Ellison lies head back in the mud. One heaving, wet gasp wheezes out of him, and then he freezes midbreath. I keep waiting for him to draw another, but he doesn't. The seconds keep going by, and he doesn't. I stare at him. Ellison—good, even-handed, handsome Ellison, who gave me a chance to join his team when everyone else was snickering behind their hands at me—is dead. And it's all my fault. My fault for not taking care of the shirks when I first had the chance.

No. I look up at the boy. *Scratch that. It's* his *fault.*

I pull my trigger, but the rifle only clicks. Empty. I drop down behind the truck as he returns fire.

A magazine, I need a fresh magazine. I grope at my waist as the bullets ricochet overhead. I normally carry several reloads and a spool of zip ties on my utility belt, but now the whole belt is gone. I glance at the Kingfishers, huddled together, trying to shield one another, and then at my teammates splayed out across the field. Danica lies in the mud five feet away, moaning. The others are dead. Ellison's dead. I'm on my own.

My eyes tear up again, and I swipe at them furiously. I have to focus, live through this, hold out a few more minutes until the team from the substation arrives. I can't think about Ellison, about the pride and warmth in his smile the second before he fell, about what could have been. I glance at him. His utility belt is still in place, with its regulation spare mags.

I don't breathe. I don't think about how he won't feel me tug the magazine from him. I just make my fingers move closer and closer. Pop open the snap case. Pull out the extra mag. Ignore how his body rolls as I tug it free. *Don't look at his face.* Mud and blood slick my fingers as I release the old mag and jam the new one in its place. I let out a breath.

Silence drops over the field. The scavenger boy must have run out of ammo, too. The air rings with sudden quiet. Thunder still rumbles, but the downpour lightens, signaling the storm's retreat. Juna lifts her head and stares at the bodies and churned mud around her, then over to me.

"Hey, Cog!"

It takes me a second to realize it's me the scavenger is shouting for.

"Cog Girl, you still there?" He's close, on the other side of the jeep.

I clear my throat. "What?" My voice comes out hoarse and shakier than I mean it to be. "You ready to surrender?"

He laughs, but there's something hollow to the sound. "No. You?"

I look at Juna again, then over at Danica. She's going to bleed out if I don't do something soon.

I close my eyes. "Listen, if you want the Kingfishers, take them. Just let me get my teammate to the substation. I won't get in your way; you won't get in my way. Deal?"

He laughs again, then stops abruptly. "So now you want to deal?" A click and snap—he's loading fresh rounds. "Eden . . ."

He stops and starts again. "My people are dead."

Anger surges back through me. So is Will. So is Marco. So is Ellison. All because I thought I saw something human in a pair of shirks last night.

I rise to a crouch, careful not to make a sound or lose my footing in the slimy clay. My heartbeat thumps in my ears. *Slow, controlled. Like a viper in the grass.* I pause and listen. A soft squelch in the mud. A metallic click and the unmistakable catching sound of the revolver's cylinder snapping into place. He's exactly on the other side of the truck from me. I dig in my feet. All I have to do is stand and fire down. Behind me, Juna draws a shaky breath.

I rise and swing my rifle in an arc over the side of the wreckage. The boy looks at me, and in the second before I'm going to pull the trigger, I see his eyes. They're dark, like mine, and full of the same mess of fear and anger and shell-shocked distance I know mine must show. But I'm going to do it anyway. I'm going to put an end to this, once and for all. I'm going to—

A whine rises around us. I glance up. A blinding flash, and then, seconds later, a boom rattles the air, and a thick column of awful light shoots from the earth to the lingering thunderclouds. A shock wave slaps past me. I stumble back onto the ground in time for the second explosion. The corn bows down suddenly, as if struck by an invisible hand, and far off, the emergency claxon winds into a blaring wail.

I push myself to my feet. Several dozen miles away, across

acres of prostrate corn, a column of midnight-black smoke tumbles into the sky. It fans out as the higher air currents catch it, sinking its fingers into the clouds and staining the sky a sickly yellow-green. I glance at my data band. Due southeast. What the hell is due southeast of mile marker 226 that could make a cloud like that?

The research and development labs. The ethanol processing plant. The heart of the compound.

Something begins falling from the sky. At first I think it's rain, but then I see it's ash and cinders. Ash and cinders drifting and sparking in the fields, like an awful mimicry of the fireflies that come out in the early summer dusk. The ashes land on the bright, spear-like leaves of the corn, and immediately, the leaves shrivel and wither. The early corn blackens in its husks and drops to the wet ground. Miles of corn, a whole season's worth of work, falls to rot in a matter of seconds.

And that's when the scavenger's pistol strikes the side of my head.

.4.

TREE OF HEAVEN

AILANTHUS ALTISSIMA

I come to on my knees. The ground rocks beneath me, and a diesel engine drowns out every other sound. A painful thud fills my head with each heartbeat, and my throat is raw, as though I've been inhaling paint thinner. It takes me a moment to recognize the smell flooding my nose. Vinegar. A deep cough wracks my chest. I open my eyes.

I'm kneeling on the floor in the back of a Humvee, facing the bench that runs along the sides of its cargo area. A zip tie binds my blistered wrists to the safety bar above the seat. Juna sits beside me, a damp bandanna pulled up over her nose and mouth.

"She's awake," she yells over the engine's steady grind.

Boots clomp behind me, and the scavenger boy—Alder?

Is that what the blond girl called him?—drops onto the bench on the other side of me. Rust-colored splotches stain his pants and shirt; mud or blood, I'm not sure. He wears a bandanna over the lower half of his face. Above it, his eyes sag with fatigue. He still holds the gun in his uninjured hand, and I remember. Will and Marco dead. Danica dying. Ellison falling, and the blood and stillness that followed. He won't ever grin at me again. He won't ever guide my hand along the bolt action of a rifle.

I muster what strength I have and glare at the scavenger boy. "Where are you taking me?"

"The forest." He shifts his gaze behind me. "You can thank Mrs. Kingfisher you aren't dead yet. She spoke up for you."

I twist around, but it's Harry Kingfisher lying on the bench opposite me, his broken leg propped up in his son's lap, both of them with their mouths covered. Mrs. Kingfisher hunches over the Humvee's steering wheel as we fly over the road. My team's rifles stand barrel-up in the passenger seat beside her. All around us, the light looks wrong. I stare at the road receding into the spoiled rows of corn. A red line of fire burns on the horizon. Toxic yellow mist hangs over what's left of the fields, muting the sun to a blurry white disk.

Something heavy and soft knocks against the sole of my boot. Two bodies lie on the floorboards, jackets thrown over their faces. A lock of white-blond hair escapes the smaller bundle. Her shoes have been stripped off, and her naked feet rock limply with every rut we hit.

Juna leans down next to my ear. "Not me," she whispers. She's wearing the dead girl's boots, and her makeshift mask is sharp with vinegar. "I told him I wanted you dead."

I ignore her and bring my eyes back to Alder's. "What happened? Our crops—"

He shakes his head. "I don't know."

"Was it you?" I tug against the zip ties, even though I feel like I'm going to vomit. The air smells wrong, too. "You did this, didn't you?" But even as I say it, I realize it doesn't make sense. Why would the scavengers try to wipe out our crops? Steal them? Yes. But destroy them?

"More like you." He shoots me a disgusted look.

"We would never—"

"There's no limit to what AgraStar will do," he says.

But no. He's wrong. The company would never do this. Why would it wipe out its own product, its employees and contractors' livelihoods?

Alder holds something up. "Where'd you get these?"

I drag my eyes back up to him. The wire cutters. I forgot about them.

"Was it you?" Alder tries to trap my gaze.

I look away. "I don't know what you mean."

"Where did you get them?"

"Nowhere," I say. "I found them."

"Where?"

"In a field."

He slumps into silence. The perimeter fence comes into

sight. A convoy of white company trucks passes us, speeding the other way, toward the R&D facility.

"Hey!" I scream and try to stand. The zip tie allows me to rise, but only to a stoop. "Help!" The wind whips my voice away. I jerk at the tie, even though I know it won't break. It cuts deeper into my flesh.

"Sit down." Alder pushes me back to my knees.

Juna gives him an appreciative smile. "You'd better cut that tracker off her, too." She turns her own wrist to show the naked patch where her data band should be. "Otherwise they'll find us later."

I press my lips together and glare at her. I can't believe I felt sorry for this kid. She's as much a hardened criminal as her parents.

Alder shoots a weary look at my wrist, and then at Juna. "You do it. I'll mess it up."

Juna shrugs. "You got a knife?"

Alder pulls a folding knife with rusted hinges and a fat, serrated blade from his belt. "That do?"

Juna nods. She leans in close and cuts her eyes at mine. "Hold still." She smirks and fits the blade between the soft flesh of my inner wrist and the data band's polymer backing. "Wouldn't want me to slip, would you?"

A faded gold AgraStar emblem inlaid in the knife handle catches the light as she pries upward with the blade. I grit my teeth. The shirks must have taken this knife from another company soldier, and now here they are, using it on me. An electric burn sparks my nerve endings, and the band pops free. It clatters to the floor. Two pinpricks of blood well in the center of the pale strip of exposed skin, like a snakebite, where the power prongs used to feed in. A tremor passes through me and my body turns rubbery, as if I've just finished a five-mile run.

I wrestle my face into a blank mask, refusing to show how much it hurts. I slump on the floor and stare at my wrist. I've had my data band since I was a kid. A flash of memory— my feet dangling off a table covered in crinkly paper. "Just a pinch," the medic says, pressing the installation gun against my wrist. My eyes water, but I don't cry, and Rosalie claps me on the shoulder and says I'm brave. That band has always been there, monitoring my heart rate, keeping time, tracking my duty roster, helping me tell north from south and poison sumac from harmless ferns. How am I going to get back to my station if they take me out past the perimeter fence?

A cloud of sharp-winged chimney swifts funnels overhead, overtaking us as they streak to the trees.

I look up at Alder. "They're going to stop you at the gate." I fight to keep my voice even, so he won't hear the pain and panic growing in it. If I can get him to cut the zip ties, maybe I can wrestle the gun out of his hands, take control of the vehicle. Or at least jump out and disappear into the fields. I lift my bound hands. "This isn't going to win you any favors with the border guards."

Another truck streaks by, barreling toward the chaos we've left behind.

Alder nods at it. "You seriously think anyone's watching the perimeter now?"

"Maybe." I grimace. "Maybe not. But if they are, don't you think having me trussed up like this is going to tip them off?"

He and Juna share a look over my head.

"She's right," Alder says.

Juna makes a face.

Alder pushes the revolver into her hands. "Keep that on her." He clicks open the same rusted knife and takes hold of my hands. His touch is positively gentle compared to Juna's. "Don't move, okay?" He looks briefly into my eyes, and then goes to work sawing at the zip tie.

I glance at Juna. She scowls and adjusts her grip on the gun. She looks like she wouldn't hesitate to use that thing on me, but if I'm fast enough, I can be over the side of the truck before she has time to aim. Juna's a little thing. Even the kick from a standard pistol will throw her off.

My hands spring free. I see Juna clench the trigger, but I knock the gun from her hands and bolt.

I clear the Humvee's tailgate, hit the ground rolling, and jump up again as the truck screeches to a halt. I make for the wilted corn and crash through the dry, rustling stalks. But my adrenaline is spent. Every inch of my body aches. *Keep moving.* Boots crunch behind me in the corn. I dart left, into another row, and hunch down as I run. My chest burns, but I force my breaths low and quiet.

A blur streaks by. Alder throws himself into a side tackle.

I stop short and try to lurch out of the way, but he catches me around the shoulders, and we both hit the ground. For a moment, my lungs stop working. They won't draw air. I remember the time Seth accidentally-on-purpose kicked me in the throat in combat maneuvers training when we were thirteen, and how our instructor used our accident as an opportunity to demonstrate more disabling strikes. *The fingers present an excellently sensitive yet nonlethal option. . . .*

I grab Alder's splinted fingers, pull back. He yelps and throws a punch, knocking me into the dirt. My head spins.

In the few seconds it takes my vision to clear, Alder has my wrists cinched together in front of me with a new zip tie. He hauls me to my feet. We trudge along in silence for a few minutes, back to the road.

"What do you want me for, anyway?" I say. "It's not like I'm going to stop you from getting back to your precious forest."

Alder pushes me along wordlessly.

"I could be helping with the fire." My eyes sting and blur, and a bubble of helpless panic rises in my chest. "They need me. They need all the security personnel they can get."

Alder shakes his head. "You killed Eden."

He speaks so quietly, I don't think I've heard him right. "What?"

"You killed Eden," he repeats, louder this time. He looks up at me through red-rimmed eyes. Is it the smoke, or is he close to tears?

"And you killed Ellison," I shoot back. "And Marco, and Will, and Danica. What about them?"

He clenches his jaw. "That's different. Eden wasn't doing anything to you. She—"

"—was pointing a gun at us," I finish for him. "She was interfering with an authorized prisoner transport. You all were."

"You didn't have to shoot her." He drops his head. "She was only bluffing. She would never have hurt anyone."

I remember Ellison's smile the moment before he fell. I make my face hard, and shrug. "That's the chance you take when you pull a rifle on an armed security detail."

Alder rounds on me. "Is that the chance she took when she tried to feed us last night, too?"

I've lost people, too, I want to spit. *Who knows what might have happened with me and Ellison if you hadn't killed him? I could have had friends. People I trusted. Even love.*

But I'm not going to waste my breath. I'm not going to let some shirk in on my sappy half fantasies. I'm not going to let him know the least little thing about me. I stare evenly back at him. "I don't know what you mean."

"Eden was right," he says after a few seconds. "Cogs really don't have souls."

I stumble to the Humvee with Alder's pistol at my back. Juna meets us at the side of the road, a rifle over her shoulder. Her face falls when she sees me. Clearly she was hoping Alder would finish me off and leave me to rot alongside the crops.

The two of them boost me up into the Humvee. I sink down on the empty bench and lean forward, elbows on my knees. My head pounds. Juna and Alder position themselves on either side of me, weapons at the ready.

"Loaded up?" Mrs. Kingfisher calls.

Alder nods. "Did you raise the Deacon's team?"

She shakes her head. "Nothing but static. Might be the mag-pulse rounds they were using took out their radios."

"Keep trying," Alder says. "We have to get through to them."

The engine turns over. We crawl forward, past the unmanned security fence and along the road to the forest.

We skirt the woods, coast down a hill blanketed with head-high grass, and pick up one of the old hardtop roads. The company's ethanol tanker trucks still use the short section of hardtop leading to the interstate highway, so we keep it pretty free of new growth, fill in the cracks and potholes. But farther out, it disintegrates into a patchwork of crumbling asphalt, spidery goose grass, and horse nettle.

Alder hoists himself up on the Humvee's roll-over bar to keep watch. "Everyone quiet," he says. "Eyes sharp." Young ferns and undergrowth crackle beneath the tires.

I swallow and scan the road for any movement. Out here, we're as likely to run into hijackers as an AgraStar patrol. If I have a choice, I'd rather stick with the shirks than take my chances on a bunch of jackers.

We roll through the shadow of an overpass and pull off onto a slight grassy incline leading up to the northern edge of the forest. Alder pulls the bandanna down around his neck and heaves in a deep breath. The air is wet and clean here. Whatever hangs over the compound hasn't drifted this far yet.

Vast shrouds of kudzu have overtaken this end of the wood. It looms above us as we approach, changing the familiar shapes of oak and pine trees to the corpses of half-hidden monsters slumbering beneath the green.

Something about the kudzu forest has always frightened me. Maybe it's the silence that hangs over it, as if the vines have wrapped around the forest's throat while they suck the life from the trees. Or maybe it's the childish fear that if I part the veil of leaves, I'll fall out of my own world and into whatever uncanny land exists on the other side.

Whenever I'm on duty guarding an eradication team outside the compound gates, I spare a few minutes to hack at the vines with my machete, drive the mass back at least a few feet. But the kudzu is always creeping closer to the compound, swallowing old power lines and the husks of abandoned, gasoline-fueled cars along the sides of the highway. Eradication spends half their time holding it off with flamethrowers and chemical sprays along the southern perimeter, but it always grows back. I glare at Alder and then up at the wall of kudzu before us. Maybe we should have taken some napalm to the whole thing, killed two birds with one stone.

Mrs. Kingfisher slows to an idle. Alder hops over the Humvee's side, tucks his gun in his belt, and wades through the scrub to the curtain of green.

"What's he doing?" I ask.

No one answers. Alder reaches into the vines—*no, it can't be*—and pulls back a tangled mat of leaves. A shadowy opening tunnels into the kudzu, large enough for the Humvee to pass through.

The hairs on the back of my neck rise, and my peripheral vision darkens. The scavengers' camp is through there, in the kudzu forest.

Alder holds the vines aside as we drive into an archway of green. As soon as we pass through, he drops it again, plunging us into thick near-darkness. His boots thump on the Humvee's tailgate, and the vehicle dips slightly as it takes his weight. Mrs. Kingfisher clicks on the headlights. Alder is across from me again, the glare of the high beams emphasizing the circles beneath his eyes. We roll forward, passing skeletons of dead trees muffled in kudzu. I make myself keep breathing. *Stay calm. Stay limber. Stay ready.*

The tunnel's ceiling lifts and parts, letting a smattering of daylight through the canopy high above. I smell smoke again, but not the acrid, chemical-laced stuff that choked our fields and left my lungs raw. This is the ancient, alien scent of wood smoke.

Memory knocks the breath from me. A man's hands—my father's?—stripping the skin from a squirrel. Smoke drifting sweetly up to the golden sky. The spit of fat on embers. My father. His laugh, always fast and nervous, as though he wasn't sure it was allowed—

No. I don't want to remember. My father was nothing but a shirk, and he made me one, too. I didn't understand until later what our constant wandering meant—that he had most likely broken his contract somewhere. He was worse than those born outside the company's embrace, who were raised to be stubborn or maybe didn't know better. He knew what he was doing, what it would mean for me, and he did it anyway.

We come to the bottom of a steep rise and park alongside an old steel-framed motorcycle with a sidecar and a pickup truck with a canvas awning suspended over its bed. Mrs. Kingfisher throws the Humvee into park while Juna and her brother help their father down.

"Easy, now. No running." Mrs. Kingfisher's hands close in a bony grip around my elbow as she leads me to the embankment.

I glance back as I stagger up the hill. Alder lingers behind. He stands at the rear of the Humvee, leaning heavily on it. As I watch, he reaches down and brushes something from Eden's cold ankle. His fingers trace the arch of her foot and the jut of bone at her joint, as if he could tender her back to life. Then his jaw tightens, and he looks at me. I snap my head away. I won't be sorry. Ellison and my teammates are just as dead. I have to focus on not slipping as Mrs. Kingfisher half guides, half pulls me to the crest of the hill. The tailgate slams, and Alder tramps after us.

A pale, balding man with a rangy build and a single-action shotgun balanced across his shoulder awaits us at the top. He squints as we approach, counting our number, clearly coming up short, counting again. Alder jogs ahead to meet him.

The older man lets the muzzle of his shotgun drop to the dirt. "Eden?" Everything—hope and fear and the unwanted weight of knowledge—comes loaded in that one word.

Alder shakes his head. "I'm sorry. She and Malcolm—"

The other man doesn't wait for him to finish. He brushes past Alder, picking up speed as he descends the hill on a slither of decomposing leaves.

"Grebe," Alder calls after him. "Wait! Don't go down there."

But Grebe isn't listening. He slows when he gets to the side of the Humvee and looks down at what's inside. Alder turns away and continues up the incline.

A moan starts behind us. "No. No, no, no." And then louder, breaking. "Eden!"

"Keep walking." Mrs. Kingfisher tugs at my elbow, and I realize I'm frozen in place.

A glade opens at the top of the rise. Small groups of scavengers, maybe twenty people in all, cluster outside structures patched together from ragged plastic tarp, car hoods, rusted metal corrugate stripped from the perimeter fence, and woven branches. Inside one, I glimpse a jumble of radio equipment on a table. A low, smoky fire burns in a pit at the center of the makeshift village. The ground is mud and moss. No crops grow here beneath the overhanging trees.

A skinny, shirtless boy zips to us and crashes into Mrs. Kingfisher's legs. "Mama!"

Micah, I realize. The one who ran.

At his shout, the other scavengers look up. They're mostly kids, with a smattering of teenagers and adults.

"Micah." Mrs. Kingfisher bends to kiss his head. "Thank you, baby," she whispers into his hair and holds him tight to her. "You saved us."

The older scavengers burst into murmurs and a flurry of sideways glances at me. I realize with a growing sense of dread that they aren't all speaking English. I think some of them might be using the language my father spoke—I recognize the cadence of it, even if the meaning of it falls through me like a sieve—but others speak something I've never heard before. I can't understand them at all. The children stare openly. On the far side of the glade, a middle-aged woman with one foot bound in rags and a burst of tight gray curls drops a bundle of newly shucked corn.

"Malcolm?" She limps a few steps toward us and stops dead.

Alder shakes his head again.

The lines on her dark brown face deepen. She purses her lips.

"I'm sorry, Laurel," Alder says. "Have the other groups come back yet?"

"Groups?" Laurel repeats. She blinks herself back to the present. "No, you're the first."

"We need the Deacon." Alder's voice dips low and urgent. He turns his back to me and says something more to her, but I can't make out his words.

The muttering in the camp grows louder.

". . . that cog . . . without Eden . . . bodies in the truck . . ."

". . . con una prisionera pero sin su novia?"

". . . sǐ wáng . . . fāshēngle shénme shì?"

"Alder?" Mrs. Kingfisher clears her throat. "Son, I think we'd better get the girl inside." She glances meaningfully at the circle of scavengers tightening around us.

Alder sees them, too. "Right."

Mrs. Kingfisher pats Micah's back. "Go and help your sister with your daddy now."

Micah scampers off, and Alder marches me toward one of the larger hovels. I keep my head low and my eyes sharp, trying to remember everything I can. Six structures in a circle around the fire. About sixty steps across the circumference. Only two guards that I can spot, aside from the balding man down by the Humvee, who I'm guessing must be Eden's father.

"Hey!" one of the women shouts. She coughs. "She's the one, isn't she? She's the one that killed Malcolm and Eden."

Mrs. Kingfisher and Alder don't answer.

A clump of muck and rotten leaves strikes the nape of my neck. The crowd's muttering intensifies.

"Murderer!"

"Rén zhā!"

Someone lobs a shriveled corncob and catches me in the lower back. Someone else hurls a chunk of peat.

"¡Vete a la mierda!"

"Butcher! Child killer!"

Mrs. Kingfisher pulls me along. *Child killer?* That girl was no younger than I was. We both chose to fight. But somehow I don't think these people will see it that way. Crake used to tell us stories about what a pack of shirks would do if they found you alone in the woods. I never used to give those tales much thought, beyond retelling them to scare the younger trainees, but now all I can think is that this mob might really flay me alive and use my skin as paper or hack off my limbs and roast them in front of me.

Something foul splatters at my feet—dog or human filth.

"Hey!" Alder lets go of my arm and rounds on the other scavengers. "We have laws. This isn't what the Deacon would—" A poorly aimed hunk of moss and clay hits him in the gut.

"Company whore!" a woman screams, and flings a handful of compost. Her face flushes red and her mouth twists in an ugly way. This frightens me most of all. I can see the twisted logic in calling me a killer. I've taken lives in the service of AgraStar, to keep our compound and our people safe. But *whore?* The most I've ever done is stare at Ellison across the mess hall, and now that will never happen again.

A rock packed in mud grazes my temple. *Enough.* I'm not going to die here at the mercy of a bunch of shirks and children. I twist my arm from Mrs. Kingfisher's grip and run.

"Stop!" Alder shouts.

I break into the brush, bound hands stretched in front of me in an effort to keep my balance. Ferns and low-reaching branches smack my face. I leap a fallen log and come down in a stretch of wet clay. It sucks at my boots, but I won't stop, won't slow down. Alder's breath rasps harsh and close behind me, and the curses and shouts of the scavengers follow at his heels. I'm completely out of adrenaline now, feeling every sprain, every bruise, the rawness in my throat from breathing in that smoke. I splash across a shallow creek and grab on to the exposed roots of an oak to pull myself onto the opposing bank.

A gunshot echoes through the wood. I drop into a roll— leaves, sky, leaves, sky—and come to rest in a shallow ditch. The sun streaks through the trees and catches in the pollen like fairy lights. I lie faceup, staring at the towering pines, trunks gilded by the late light. *Am I hit?* I scan myself for any pain, any numbness. No. The shot must have gone wide.

"Up, then." I hear Crake in my ear. *"Up and run."*

Too late. Alder crashes through the underbrush and stops short above me, breathing hard. He cocks his revolver and points it, shaking, at my face.

"You ran." Betrayal shoots through his voice. "Why did you run?"

I freeze. My tongue sticks to the roof of my mouth. Shaking hands don't mean a person won't fire. They only mean he's more likely to pull the trigger by accident.

"They were going to kill me." I struggle onto my elbows. "What did you expect me to do?"

"Nothing." He steps back, closing his eyes, and uncocks the gun. "Exactly what you did."

Voices approach and boots splash through the creek.

"She's here." Alder's voice cracks. "I've got her."

The scavengers appear between the pines. The guards come first, with their shotguns, then the rest of them with sticks and rocks clutched in their hands. They stare down at me with the same blunt, dilated gaze cats get when they've cornered their prey.

One of the guards levels her shotgun at me. "Step back, Alder."

Alder steps in front of me. "No."

"What do you mean, *no*?" Laurel pushes her way to the front of the crowd. "She killed Malcolm and Eden. *Your* Eden."

Alder drops his eyes to me. "I know." His gaze rests on me for a moment before he looks away. "But she's just a cog. The Deacon says they don't know any better. The company trains them up to kill, and they don't learn anything else."

The other guard spits in the dirt. "All the more reason to put her down now."

"No." Alder tucks the revolver back in his belt. "That won't bring Eden or Malcolm back. It won't change anything."

The female guard, a towering woman with light brown skin and freckles, narrows her eyes. "Except we'll all sleep better with one less cog in the world."

"No." Mrs. Kingfisher steps forward, raising her voice. "Listen, we got bigger problems than her. Something went wrong out there."

Laurel turns to her. "How wrong?"

"Bad wrong," says Mrs. Kingfisher. "Something got out of that R and D complex—"

The crowd breaks into murmurs.

One of the men snorts. "More of AgraStar's dirty tactics."

"It wasn't us," I burst out. "You're the ones who've killed off our crops, you lazy-ass mother—"

"Enough." Mrs. Kingfisher cuts me off with a look that tells me I'm not doing myself any favors. "Something blew at the complex, maybe the ethanol processing plant or one of the labs close by, and something in the fallout killed the corn."

A shocked silence strikes the crowd.

"The corn?" The woman guard repeats. "*All* the corn?"

Mrs. Kingfisher nods. "I never seen a blight like that. It was spreading as we drove."

"What do we do?" Laurel's voice edges over into hysteria. "Oh, God. What do we do?"

Alder clears his throat and looks down at me as he speaks. The setting sun turns his hair to a halo of fire. "We wait for the Deacon."

.5.

SPEAR THISTLE

CIRSIUM VULGARE

I lie on the dirt floor of the largest shelter, breathing deep and even so Mrs. Kingfisher will think I'm asleep. She and Alder agreed she was the only one who could be trusted not to slit my throat in the middle of the night, though I'm not completely sure she could stop someone else from doing it. She sits in an old lawn chair by a smoky oil lamp, mending clothes, while Mr. Kingfisher and the kids sleep on wooden pallets beside her.

Every sound snaps at me: the crinkle of blue tarp walls as the wind moves them, the low pop of the logs in the fire pit, the rustle of the guards' footfalls. A girl brought a plate of hot corn tortillas to the Kingfishers earlier, and the aroma still lingers in the air, making my stomach grumble. Flashes of sense memory come when I close my eyes—my father's weathered hands patting a small tortilla into shape with practiced turns, the sizzle of lard in a cast-iron pan nestled in the coals of a campfire.

"*These taste funny, Papi. I like the ones Mami makes better. The ones from the bag.*"

"*Well, we're camping, cielo. This is special camping food.*"

I remember a pair of boots stepping over a log. Riding high on someone's shoulders, my father singing to me in words I couldn't understand or can't remember. I squeeze my eyes shut and try to smother the memories. I need to concentrate. I need a clear head so I can escape.

Somewhere outside, maybe in that praying tent, there are people singing, too, all together in one voice.

"I sing because I'm happy,
I sing because I'm free.
For His eye is on the sparrow,
And I know He watches me."

Then again, the same tune, but in another language.

"¡Feliz, cantando alegre,
yo vivo siempre aquí;
Si Él cuida de las aves,
cuidará también de mí!"

My mind scrabbles at the words. There's something faintly familiar about them, their cadence, but I can't quite latch on to their meaning. It's as if I'm trying to climb a rock wall, but I keep slipping on slick stones. *Dammit.* I want to kick something, hit something, but I remember in time that I'm supposed to be asleep. I squeeze my eyes shut. This was the language my father spoke to me. I know it in my bones. And that means it's dangerous. I shouldn't want to remember it. So why am I still trying?

Footsteps approach, and then pause on the other side of the tarp beside me, scattering my thoughts.

"Grebe." A familiar voice. Alder.

"It's done," the older man says. "She and Malcolm are both in the burial tent."

"Thank you. I'm sorry I couldn't . . ." Alder's voice falters, and he clears his throat. "I'll come help wash her when you're ready."

"Thank you," Grebe says. "She would have wanted you there."

"Did she tell you where she wanted to be buried? She always said—"

"Beside the sitting oak, yes."

They both fall silent.

"Listen." Grebe coughs. "I know you two were . . . I know what Eden meant to you." He drops his voice when he says her name, as if it were burning his throat.

"Don't—"

"No, let me," Grebe says. "I only want to say, I've thought of you as a son for a long time. And you're still a son to me, even with her gone."

"I shouldn't have let her go." Alder's voice is muffled. "I should have told her to stay behind."

Grebe laughs. "You think she would have listened? Not my Eden."

"No," Alder says. "No, she would have tried to get me to stay here instead, with my hand and all."

A knot rises in my throat, and suddenly my heart is pumping rage instead of blood. *It's not my fault. It's not my fault. It's not my fault.*

"What do you think the Deacon will do with her?" Alder asks.

"The cog girl?" Grebe's voice goes hard. "Put her down, most like. I don't think the camp would stand for anything else, even if there was another option."

Silence. "I guess not," Alder says.

Grebe laughs. "Don't tell me you want her alive."

"No. Of course not," Alder says. "It's only . . . I killed some of them, too."

"They fired first," Grebe says. "They had the Kingfishers. You had no choice."

"I know. I just . . . I didn't think it would be like that. It was awful. And it doesn't change anything. Eden's still gone."

"It's hard." Grebe's voice softens. "Especially the first time. All the things you make yourself do to protect your own. You've got more restraint than me, son. If it had been me out in the field today, I would've left that cog girl with a bullet in her belly."

Danica's face floods my memory, her body lying still in the corn. I pull against my restraints.

"Eden wouldn't want you beating yourself up. She would have been proud of you."

Alder is silent for a moment. "You're right."

Grebe clears his throat. "Did you get through to Charlotte?"

"Yeah," Alder says. "The sat phone's almost dry, but I passed along the basics. They'll get it up on the Latebra Congress site, but I don't know if some of the more remote camps will be able to get a signal."

Charlotte? Does he mean a person, or the city to the north of us? AgraStar has a strong hold there, so strong they host trade talks with our competitors in the shiny office towers and never worry about jackers inside the freeway loop. The idea that there could be shirk sympathizers there is crazy. And what the hell is a Latebra Congress?

Mrs. Kingfisher's chair squeaks, and I realize I've forgotten to breathe. I let out my breath quietly and feign sleep again.

A distant rumble builds in the woods, overwhelming the soft sounds of night. Diesel engines. I sit up. The rest of the Kingfishers blink awake. The shirks surely haven't got that many vehicles between them. My heart surges. AgraStar? Harry Kingfisher stares blearily at me from two blackened eyes, but Juna bolts for the flap of tarp that serves as a door.

"Juna!" Mrs. Kingfisher casts a quick look at me and hurries after her. "Get back here, girl."

Outside, the camp quickens with shouts, footsteps running, lamps flaring, flashlights scattering their beams across the walls.

Alder pulls up the tent flap. "Get up."

I draw back. "Why?"

"Because otherwise I'm going to drag you out."

I struggle to my feet as best I can with my hands tied in front of me. "What's going on?"

Alder checks my bonds. "We're walking."

He's too calm. If AgraStar were here, he wouldn't be this calm. Something's wrong.

"Come on." Alder marches me out of the tent into the firelit clearing.

"Where are you taking me?"

"To see the Deacon."

The black wall of forest looms beyond the edges of the firelight. The engines rattle the night, and the thick smell of corn diesel drifts up from the other side of the rise. Below, two ancient pickup trucks, a jeep, and a van with the roof sheared off sit idling, headlights flooding the base of the incline. A man standing in the bed of one of the pickups shakes a rifle over his head and whoops something, but the grumble of the engines muddies his words.

"Deacon Ward!" Alder pushes to the front of the crowd with me in tow. "Deacon!"

The drivers kill their engines, and one by one, the lights die out.

"Deacon Ward!" Alder shouts again.

"I hear you, boy." A woman's voice, low and roughened, surfaces in the shadows below. "We're coming."

Car doors slam. My eyes adjust to the darkness. A line of figures trudges up the rise and slowly resolves in the fire pit's glow. They all haul hundred-pound cornmeal sacks, stamped with the AgraStar emblem, over their shoulders. A tall, muscular woman leads the group. Her skin is browned with dirt and sun, her hair pale silver. Beneath a faded company flak jacket, sweat and blood stain her shirt and the damp bandanna tied around her throat. A pair of pistols is strapped to her sides. Her skirt kicks out with every stride, revealing thick leather boots and canvas trousers underneath.

She stops before Alder and pulls the bandanna from her neck. "You got the Kingfishers out, then?" Her voice is raspy.

Suddenly it comes slamming home to me who Deacon Ward must be. The moon-pale hair, the command in her voice, the confidence in her step. In every way, she's a match for the girl I killed today, if that girl had lived another twenty years.

Shit. Instinctively, I try to back away, but Alder yanks me closer.

Deacon Ward turns, taking in my uniform and bound hands, before dismissing me and looking back to Alder for her answer.

"Yes, ma'am." Alder hesitates. "It cost us, though."

Deacon Ward nods and scans the crowd. "Where's Eden?"

A heavy silence falls. Alder opens his mouth, but nothing comes out. He tightens his fingers around my arm and stares down at the dirt.

The Deacon looks behind Alder. "Grebe?" Worry breaks her voice. "Where's Eden? Didn't she come back with the rest?"

The crowd shifts around me. I feel their anger buzzing in the air again, their eyes boring into me. I take a deep breath.

"She's dead." My voice ricochets through the silence. "I shot her."

Deacon Ward's face goes blank with shock. She blinks at me, then at Alder and Grebe. "What?"

"We got bogged down trying to get the Kingfishers back," Alder says quietly. "Eden went in and . . ."

The Deacon closes her eyes. For one terrible moment, I think she's going to break down like Grebe did, shout the girl's name and fall to pieces. But no.

"Take me to her," she says.

Alder starts to hand me off to Mrs. Kingfisher, who's surfaced again, Juna in tow, but the Deacon stops him.

"No, bring her." She turns to me, and her expression stops me cold. "I want a word with her."

"Everyone else . . ." Deacon Ward raises her voice and points down the hill to the vehicles. "We have food stores to be unloaded and wounded to tend. Lend a hand where you can." She winces and rubs her throat.

"You were there," I mutter at Alder. "You know I only—"

"Shut up." Alder stops me. "Just shut up."

"Que Dios te mate," one of the women spits at me as she brushes by.

Grebe leads the way into the camp, the Deacon a step behind. When they think no one is looking, she doubles her step and they grab tightly on to each other's hands. Alder walks me after them in a parody of their embrace. *He would have held Eden's hand like that.* I stare at their clasped fingers. *Ellison might have held my hand that way, too.*

Stop, I tell myself. Thinking like this doesn't do anyone any good, least of all me. *She had a gun on you. You did what you had to do. You did your duty to the company.*

Grebe leads us to a tent on the edge of the camp. It's woven from strips of plastic bags and old packing material; they come together like a quilt. A lamp burns inside. The tent's fabric catches the glow and bleeds it out into the night, so it looks as though the plastic itself is radiating light. It's almost beautiful.

Alder hurries us forward. "Deacon." He speaks low and casts a look behind us to make sure no one is following. "I know now isn't the time, but we need to talk—"

She stops. "The crops," she finishes for him.

"They turned to ash before our eyes," Alder says.

"I know," she says.

"I mean, thank God you got the food, but next year . . ."

"Alder." Her voice is weary. "I promise we'll talk it over.

I know what it means. But give me a moment now, okay?"

"Of course." He backs off. "Of course. I didn't mean to . . .
Sorry."

"It's all right." She squeezes his shoulder awkwardly. "Let
me be with her a little, and then you can bring the cog girl in."

"Yes, ma'am," he says. "Sorry."

As she lifts the tent flap and ducks inside, I catch a brief
glimpse of Eden. She lies on a sawhorse table in the center of
the space, her mud-streaked hair gathered over her shoulder,
her arms stiff at her sides.

The flap falls and I turn away. Is that what Ellison looks
like now? And Danica and Will and Marco? Are they still
lying in that field beside our overturned truck, watering
the ground with their blood? Or has someone come along
and carried them off, zipped them safe in the black cocoon
of a body bag? My throat burns. A strangled sobbing sound
escapes me before I even know it's coming.

Alder narrows his eyes. "You're crying?"

I swallow and wipe at my cheeks furiously. I don't answer.

Alder's eyes snap wide and his Adam's apple bobs in his
throat. "You are." Then he gathers himself and tightens his
grip on my arm again. "Good."

I let out a bark, something between a laugh and a sob.
"You think I'm crying for her?"

"Who are you crying for, then?"

I dig my fingernails into my palms. "No one," I say.
Everyone.

Deacon Ward ducks out of the tent and turns to Alder. "Go gather everyone. Tell them to meet around the fire once they've finished unloading the trucks."

Alder looks at me. "What about her?"

"She'll stay with me."

"Are you sure?" Alder shifts his feet. "She's already run—"

"Alder." The Deacon stops him. "You trust me, yes?"

Alder hesitates. "Of . . . of course."

"Then leave her with me. Besides . . ." Deacon Ward fastens her gaze on me. "There's nowhere for her to go."

Something tells me this isn't like the other times I've been left more or less unguarded. There will be no more chances. I step into the tent. Malcolm lies barefoot on another table. He's been washed and dressed in patched, clean clothes. For a moment, I think he's only sleeping, except that his chest is so still. Someone—her father, probably—has closed Eden's eyes, but otherwise her body still bears all the marks of the battlefield. The mud in her hair, the freckling of blood across her lips and pale cheeks, the ragged hole in her neck.

Silently, Deacon Ward circles her daughter. She picks a wet cloth from the plastic water jug balanced by Eden's side, wrings it out, and gently wipes the smudges of blood and dirt from her face.

"I didn't want to kill her," I hear myself say, even though my brain is screaming, *Shut up, shut up. You're only making it worse.*

Deacon Ward looks up and raises her eyebrows.

I swallow. "They attacked us. I didn't have a choice."

The Deacon stares at me until I drop my eyes. *Stupid.* Even I hear how weak my protests sound. This is her daughter. She doesn't care who fired first.

"I'm sorry." My voice wobbles, and I hate myself for it.

"That's war." Her voice is rough. She finishes wiping Eden's face clean and begins on her arms. Outside, the scavengers' shouts echo up the hill as they carry their pillage into the camp.

"Are you going to kill me?" I ask.

Deacon Ward doesn't answer. She holds her daughter's hand tenderly as she scrubs her fingers.

"They wanted to earlier, but Alder said you should be the one to decide."

The Deacon sighs and drops the wet cloth back into its jug. She leans against the table for a moment, eyes shut tight, and then she opens them again and draws herself up. "You know where our camp is." She speaks softly as she combs her fingers through Eden's hair. "And what you did . . ."

"I told you, I didn't want—"

"I know," she says. "Like I said, that's war."

I can't look at her, so I keep my eyes on Eden instead.

The red bandanna is gone from her neck, and in its place hangs a chain with a carved wooden symbol on its end. I've noticed some of the other people in the camp wearing it, too. It's that cross shape I've seen beside the road out on eradication duty, the one people sometimes put to mark where somebody died. Those things aren't official, just something you do if you lose someone, and AgraStar management mostly looks the other way. An uneasy feeling comes over me. I've seen Rosalie plant one of those. She would never have done that if she knew it was a scavenger symbol.

"What did you mean, there's nowhere for me to go?" I ask.

"You saw what happened out there. We were trying to blow a door. We didn't—" She clears her throat and swallows painfully. "Things didn't go as we planned."

"*You* set off the explosion?" Cold shock races through me. Here is this woman blaming me for taking one life, when she's good as killed us all, even her own people. I step forward, my voice rising with my anger. "You . . . Do you have any idea how many people spent their lives building that compound? And now you destroy everything, *everything*, all because you're too lazy to work a day in your life."

"Don't you dare." The Deacon grabs me by my collar and pulls me so close I can smell the stench of sweat and gunpowder lingering in her clothes and hair. "Don't you dare, after what you've done, you little cog bitch."

Tears prick my eyes. I don't care anymore that she could order me dead, that she could shoot me herself with the brace of pistols at her hips.

"What have I done?" My body, my eyes, my throat are all on fire. I'm a column of fury. "What have I done that you haven't done a thousand times over? This is your fault. Yours." I spit the final word in her face.

"I know," she thunders back at me, eyes sparking. Then pain twists her face. Her voice drops to a rasp, and she lets my shirt go. "We didn't mean it to happen that way. Those bombs, they were only supposed to be a diversion, so we could raid the distribution warehouse. But we placed them too close to the R and D labs. . . ." She closes her eyes.

I stand frozen. The air between us hums.

When the Deacon speaks again, it's in a whisper, as if she's talking only to herself. "There must have been something volatile in there. Something that aerosolized. We should have waited instead of rushing in when we heard about the Kingfishers." She opens her eyes. "You were out in the field when it happened?"

I nod.

"Then you saw what it did to the plants."

It isn't a question, but I nod again anyway.

"Whatever it was, it works the same way on people, but more slowly." She rubs her throat again, fingers her damp bandanna. "If we hadn't brought protection for tear gas . . ."

"But the substations . . ." My own voice croaks.

Deacon Ward shakes her head. "It's spreading. By the time we hit the gates, all we saw were bodies."

"Spreading," I echo. "Is it coming this way? Will it reach us here?"

"I don't know." The Deacon smooths the hair from her daughter's forehead. "Twenty years I've lived here. I'll bury my Eden here. But I think . . . maybe we should go. The land is dead. This place is dead."

"You don't know that." My eyes tear up again. "AgraStar could fix it. The company can fix anything." Even if I'm about to die, I feel a sudden, urgent need to know that life will go on as usual, that the world I know will be there without me. I look at her, almost pleading.

Deacon Ward stares back. I have the disconcerting feeling she's looking straight through me, though, as if I'm nothing more than a thin sheet of plastic.

She's decided something. "Come with me."

She grabs my arm and hauls me roughly from the tent, out into the open air. Dawn has come creeping up while we were inside, a breath of dusky rose hanging in the air. The scavengers sit sullen and tired around the fire, where one of the younger boys is tending a pan of cornmeal griddle cakes.

They look up when they see us. I spot Juna in the crowd, hefting a plastic water bucket. A satisfied smirk lights her face when she sees me. Alder is there, too, silent and watching on the other side of the fire.

The Deacon marches me forward without a word.

The strength anger lent me has gone. My vision blurs. She's going to kill me. She's taking me out to the woods to kill me and leave my body to rot like Will and Danica and Marco and Ellison. I shake my head to clear my eyes. My wrists are slippery with my own sweat and blood, and I try one last time to twist them free of the zip ties. No luck. It's all I can do not to trip over the brambles and brome as Deacon Ward leads me into the trees.

The first eddy of sunrise streams into the forest, lighting the mist before us in gold. The high call of a morning bird echoes in the treetops. A few times I almost think I hear someone following us, but when I glance over my shoulder, I see only trees. No one is coming to save me. The world is dew bright and fresh, and I am going to die.

The terrain edges up again, and up and up, until we emerge on the lip of an escarpment. Deacon Ward stops before a jut of land anchored by a live oak. Its trunk bends low to the ground to form a natural bench, and then branches out over the drop, into the open air. *The sitting oak.* This must have been Eden's place. Below, separated from us by a few acres of forest, the AgraStar compound spreads out its neat circle. But where the bright green fields of corn should be, a sickly grayish-brown stain has taken over. It bleeds out beyond the perimeter fence and touches the forest edge with uneven fingers, like a spreading rash.

Deacon Ward stands still, regarding the spoiled land below us. Then she turns to me and rolls up her jacket sleeve. "Let me show you something."

I tense. This is it. I should run. But there's nowhere to go.

"Look." Deacon Ward holds out her right arm, clenched fist facing up.

"I don't see—" I start to say, but then I do.

Two pale, twin scars mark the inside of her wrist, like a viper bite. I touch my own raw wrist where my data band was. "You were with the company."

Deacon Ward nods. The morning sun shines on her face, bringing out its thousand spidery wrinkles and care lines. "I was a biochemist."

All the air has gone out of me. "You left?" I always thought scavengers were too lazy to strike a contract with a company, or else people who grew up outside the gates and didn't know any better. Who in their right mind would leave the comfort and security of the company for this? Who would betray their friends, their contract, leech off their own people?

"You never heard about anyone doing that?" she asks.

"No." I've heard of people transferring to other facilities, even rewriting their contracts so they can go from transport duty to sharecropping. But leaving? Terminating a contract? "Never." I stare at her. Is she lying, trying to trick me, playing some last game with me? She must be, except I don't see why she would.

"It happens." Deacon Ward eases one of her revolvers, an old-fashioned .22, from her belt. She flips open its cylinder and begins slipping tiny rounds into its chambers.

This is it. I've thought about how I'd want to die. Everyone in security forces has. We all tell each other we'd be calm and noble, professionals to the end. Now, standing dirty and bloodied, hands tied, in the clean wash of morning, I can't stop shaking. I look down and try to focus on the dirt, try to come up with a plan to get me out of this, but I'm like an engine that won't turn over. None of this feels real. Not the gentle breeze in my hair, not the fresh, wet scent of dew, not the delicate click of Deacon Ward loading her weapon.

She snaps the cylinder closed and levels a look at me. "Put your back against the tree."

"What?"

She raises the gun and cocks the hammer. "Put your back against the tree."

I do as she says. Pine needles cushion my feet and the sun brightens. I grit my teeth and squeeze my eyes closed. The world is fire behind my lids.

Something tugs at my wrists. I look down. Rope. Deacon Ward is wrapping rope around my already-bound hands.

"What are you . . ."

She's circling my body, circling the tree, finishing each rotation with a slipknot that will only tighten if I struggle. She's tying me to the tree. Why would she bother doing that if she's just going to shoot me?

My training kicks in. *Flex your muscles. Make yourself bigger so there will be slack left later, when she's gone.* I arch my back ever so slightly. Bow out my elbows a fraction, enough to give me room, but not enough for her to notice.

In the valley below, the last of the mist burns away. All that remains of our crops is an uneven band of green near the perimeter fence. Everything is still. It's another thick, humid, summer day, like any other, though it seems impossible that the sun can still be climbing. It should have stopped when everything else did. As I watch, the edges of the blight creep outward, spreading like a slow-moving stain.

Deacon Ward ties off the end of the rope and steps back.

"What are you going to do with me?"

"Nothing." Deacon Ward looks out on the fields. "How long can a body survive without water, do you think? Three days? Four?"

I don't respond. She and I both know the answer. Not long.

"Will it be that or the blight, I wonder?" she says. "What will happen if you're still here when it reaches this tree?"

I forget myself and struggle against the ropes. The knots tighten.

Deacon Ward watches me. "I'm sorry I can't let you go. Maybe you would have seen AgraStar for what it is, with a little more time. But Eden . . ." She looks into my face. Her eyes are dull and dead. "I'm not above revenge. Especially when it's what my people need."

She turns, her footfalls muffled by the carpet of fallen leaves and pine needles.

Don't do this. I almost shout after her. But if I beg for mercy, she might give in and shoot me. If I stay silent, at least I have a slim chance of getting away. I stand with my back to the tree, my arms rigid in front of me, watching her disappear. Below me, the blight advances on the edge of the forest.

.6.

BRACKEN

PTERIDIUM AQUILINUM

The moment the Deacon is out of sight, I relax my arms and shrug one shoulder up, then the other. The first of the knots is near my clavicle. I work my fingers up, against the rope's rough fibers. My tactics have bought me a few millimeters of space—maybe enough, maybe not. Sweat breaks out under my arms, my breasts, along my neck. The sun hits the tree's exposed roots.

A twig snaps in the woods. I stop, holding my breath, listening. Nothing. I inch my fingers up again. The rope scrapes my skin. My hands are wet, and mosquitoes cluster around me. I can't think about them or the tips of my fingers going numb or how the wetness on my hands is probably blood. I'm going to get out of this. I'm going to survive.

The sun is above the tree line when I reach the first knot.

My stomach rumbles and my tongue sticks to the roof of my mouth. *One at a time*, I tell myself. *Stay focused.* I pick at the loops, but they're tight, tight. I close my eyes and bang the back of my head against the tree in frustration. The image of Ellison's body wells up in my mind—him lying on his back in the rich dirt, the blue sky above, no breath passing his lips. I don't want him there, out in the open. I don't want the ants and the weevils crawling over him. He needs to be safe beneath the ground. All of them do—Ellison and Danica and Will and Marco.

I start again. I am a machine. It doesn't matter if I rub my fingers raw. It doesn't matter if my nails split or the ropes cut my skin. All that matters is this one knot. I am going to get free. I'm going to live, and I'm going to bury them.

One of the loops gives. I pull, and it comes easier, and then it's loose. The ropes slacken. Instead of millimeters, I have inches. I work over to the next knot. My wrists may still be bound with the zip tie, but I have more latitude to move them, and the second knot comes easier. The sun glares down at a steep angle. I squint at it. Late morning, maybe 1030 hours. Already the earth is baking. Sweat soaks my clothes. I count back. It's been at least fifteen hours since I last had water. The blight has sunk its fingers into the forest. Once it reaches me, how long do I have?

I start on the next knot, and the next. My shoulders are free, and then my elbows and waist. Only my bound wrists are slowing me now.

The sun is nearly at its zenith and my hands are a bloody

mess by the time I untie the last knot. I stumble away from the tree. My head spins. I'm not going to die. I'm not going to spend my last hours watching the fields and forest below me curl with rot and liquefy. A laugh almost escapes me.

Keep it together, Tempest. First things first. *Water.* I'm going on seventeen hours now, and the base of my skull has begun to ache. I could make my way back to the compound. There's a footbridge and a stream somewhere along the way, I think. But that would take an hour, maybe two. I know I can live a few days without water, but how long can I keep moving without it, especially in this heat? I shade my eyes and look out in the direction of the compound. Brown-and-gray patches of dead leaves mottle the forest canopy. The blight is still spreading. Will it infect the stream, too?

The shirk camp is closer. It's risky, but I could keep to the woods, circle it, and see if they're gone. They might have left some water behind. Maybe a knife, too, so I can cut my hands free.

I move through the trees. Ahead, something small rustles in the undergrowth, but nothing comes at me. No footsteps, no voices, no engines. How long did it take the Deacon to walk me out to the sitting oak? I'm fairly sure I'm going in the right direction, but the world was mostly dark when we started off, and I wasn't the most calm I've ever been.

And then I'm at the camp. I jump back behind a tree, heart thumping. *Very smooth, Torres, blundering right into it.* I peer around the side of the trunk. Nothing stirs. The campfires are ash and damp coals. Debris litters the ground—a shirt trampled in the mud, an empty coffee tin, a ripped sack, and a scattering of corn kernels, little flecks of gold in the dirt. I creep out, all my senses alert. A small breeze sways the treetops, but where normally the sound would soothe me, today it reminds me of masked footsteps and poisoned air.

Everything made of tarp has been torn down, but a few of the more permanent structures still stand—the funeral tent where Eden lay, some kind of shack made of particleboard and stripped tree branches, a small aluminum trailer raised up on struts. I find crushed glass, empty jugs, and a single shoe without a sole, but no water. No sign of Eden or Malcolm's bodies, either. The Deacon must have decided there wasn't enough time to dig a grave and taken them along.

I tear through the bottles and coffee tins strewn across the clearing, but none of them has so much as a drop left. I sink down next to the muddy ash of the fire pit. Tears spike my eyes. Going on eighteen hours. I've stopped sweating. Not a good sign. I look down at my raw wrists and the zip tie crusted in my blood. I need water. I need medicine, bandages, food. And that means one thing. Blight or no, I have to make my way back to the AgraStar compound.

The forest ends at the bottom of the hill. I blink against the dazzling sheet of sunlight and step out into a field of pale, feathered silvergrass that reaches past my waist. There, beyond the lip of the field, the red dirt road cuts its way east to the compound.

The entire world stays silent. The only sound is the gentle scrape of my boots on the hard-packed clay. After the rain yesterday, the road would have been a muddy wash, but the sun has already baked it solid again. I feel as if I'm breathing in pure heat.

Maybe Deacon Ward was wrong about everyone being dead. Maybe there will be a med team waiting for me on the other side of the fence. She must have been wrong. She must have been lying. She and her team were out in the field for hours with only vinegar-soaked bandannas to protect them, and my own throat feels less raw than yesterday. There's no way AgraStar would let R&D keep something on the premises that could kill us all. Would they?

Ahead, a weather-grayed bridge made of old railroad ties spans a ditch. I remember the jolt and drum of our vehicles passing over it on past missions, and then another memory follows close on its heels. My patrol got caught out in a rainstorm one time, and on our way back to the compound, the ditch had turned to a rush of brown water. This is it—the stream. The grass around it is still full and green. The blight hasn't spread this far yet.

I push myself into a shuffling run. *Please let there be some left, please let there be some left.* There must be, after the storm yesterday.

I spot a muddy glimmer below a delicate fringe of grass. I ease myself down to the bank and scoop up a handful of water. It tastes of dirt and algae, but I don't care. It's water, and that's all that matters. I drink until my throat stops aching and my head doesn't throb in time with each heartbeat.

The sun beats down, full and bright. I look over at the bridge, at the square of deep shade beneath it. I could lie down and sleep. But there's no time. I have to get back to AgraStar and get some supplies. I have to make sure the Deacon was lying. I have to bury my friends.

The road wavers before me, but I continue down it until the stark line of the perimeter fence shimmers into view half a mile ahead. The only thing between me and home is an open scrub field, most of it reduced to rot. I scan the length of the fence and the guard nests perched above it, looking for signs of life. Nothing. Behind me, a crow takes flight, croaking a warning to its mate. Ahead, there is only silence. If Deacon Ward was lying, if someone is still alive, then they'll surely be manning the guard nests. My eyes snap to the nearest post. Was that the glint of a rifle sighted on me, or simply a ripple in the air?

I raise my hands above my head as best I can. "Hello?" I step forward. "Hello!"

The air muffles my words. Behind me, dead leaves rattle and scrape. I advance across the field, hands still high. "This is Tempest Torres, security substation west. Is anyone there?"

No answer. The dead scrub drops away and the fence rises high above me, the guard nest a dark perch in the sky. I slow as I come up next to it. The fields of shriveled corn stretch for miles. A heavy column of green-black smoke rises in the north. The R&D facility. I drop my hands. It will take days for the fires to die down.

I swallow and glance down the length of the fence. Nothing moves. I look up at the guard nest again. I'll have to break in. I almost laugh at the thought, but the laugh turns into a sob as it rises in my throat.

I pick out a patched spot on the fence, a weak one with an old, rusted weld, and kick. The sound splits the air like thunder. I start back in surprise and look up at the guard nest, half expecting Seth to swing a rifle over the side. But no. A hot breeze washes my shoulders and rustles across the field, a slow, quiet sound, like the creep of a snake's belly over dry grass.

I clench my teeth and kick again, almost falling over. This time, one side of the patch breaks free. I regain my balance and kick again and again, until the rest of the weld gives and the metal plate rattles to the ground.

I stand back. I'm in. A gust of elation catches me up, but then drops me just as quickly. Without guards posted along the fence, anyone could get in as easily as I did. Scavengers, jackers, anybody. I curse and duck through the ragged hole. I need my hands free. I can't defend myself like this.

A quarter mile into AgraStar territory, I find a motorbike overturned in the middle of the dirt road. The driver lies facedown in the dead corn, a dark-skinned woman with short-cropped hair who I think might be Vonia from the east substation security team. But I don't dare turn her over to find out. The thick, queasy stench of rot reaches me even before I hear the flies.

I double over and dry heave into the dirt. I don't want to know if it's Vonia, with her tiny gold earrings that bucked dress regulations. Who once showed me and a gaggle of other trainees the puckered scar from a bullet wound in her upper arm, and grinned like crazy when we made fake gagging noises and told her it was disgusting.

I cover my mouth with the crook of one arm and try not to think about any of that as I pull the utility knife from her belt. I saw a dead fox once when I was training. Insects had eaten away its eyes and its ribs had caved inward. It was collapsing in on itself. I felt an inexplicable sadness. I hadn't known this animal, had never seen it alive, yet I wanted to reverse time, put it back together. But I couldn't. It was something beautiful that was gone and couldn't be restored. It was unfixable.

All of this is unfixable.

I head back up the road, brace the knife between my feet, and saw at the bands around my wrists. The sun beats down on my head as I slowly shred the zip tie. I slip a few times and nick my raw skin, but by now I don't care. I would gnaw through the plastic if I could.

Finally the tie pops free. My uniform is soaked with sweat, but my hands are mine again. I flex my fingers and assess the damage. I should be safe from infection if I can see to my wounds soon enough, but they're definitely going to scar.

I tuck the knife into my belt and walk back down the road to the overturned motorcycle. I hold my breath as I pass the body that might be Vonia. *Don't look, don't look, don't look.* I right the bike. *I'll come back*, I think. *I'll get a shovel and I'll bury her, too.* I kick the starter. The engine roars to life, and I push myself away from the scene. *Don't look back, don't look back, don't look back.*

I take the road north, toward the nearest substation. More abandoned vehicles and bodies litter the sides, and several miles in, I come across an overturned Humvee. I don't look inside as I slow the bike and weave my way around it.

A bitter, caustic taste builds on my tongue as I ride, and my nose and throat begin to burn again. I pause at the next crossroad. The bike idles under me. I shade my eyes and stare out over the fields. Without the corn rising in its green walls, I can see for miles. Nothing moves. No wind, nothing except the tower of smoke on the horizon.

Something warm and wet trickles from my nose and spills into my mouth. I taste copper and salt. I reach up to wipe my lip, and my hand comes away smeared with bright red blood. I stare at it, heart quickening. I can taste it in the back of my throat now, too.

Filtration masks. Crake kept filtration masks in the Eye. That might buy me some time to do what I need to do. I gun the engine and turn west, toward my own substation. There will be coms there. I can send out an SOS to the nearest AgraStar compound. Doctor my wrists. Find some clean water. Bury Ellison and the rest while I wait for rescue.

I don't hear the alarms until I hit the access road leading into Substation West. The wail builds as the flat roofs of the bunkers come into view, until I'm swimming in the sound. My pulse pounds with it. I can feel it in my teeth.

I cut the bike's engine and lean it on its kickstand. I make myself walk through the sound, down to the bunker entrance. The blast doors have jammed halfway open, their standard override position when the fire alarms trip, and the smell of burned plastic gums the air. Emergency lights flicker along the sloped corridor inside. Underneath the burned smell hangs the sickly sweet odor of rotten meat.

I hesitate. I need those filtration masks. And medicine, water, food.

But I also know that smell. I know what it means.

I force myself forward through the heat and stink and blaring alarms. My training isn't doing me any good. My brain won't switch into its calm, professional mode and let me see only what I need to see. It jumps from the ill-lit recruitment posters—a long-haired, smiling woman with blue-patterned gardening gloves and a basket of corn balanced against her hip; AGRASTAR CONGLOMERATE, COME GROW WITH US—to the dark shapes sprawled across the floor or slumped in shadows. My breath comes fast and shallow. It's too easy to imagine those shapes rising silently, following me, blocking the exit.

I stop, close my eyes, and breathe.

"You're panicking," I say aloud. "That's not helping."

I open my eyes. The body of a young woman lies in front of me, the low glow of the emergency lights gleaming dully on her sightless eyes. It's only then that I register the array of smaller shapes collapsed behind her. The minder, the one I saw in the women's showers yesterday, and all her students.

It's all right, girls. Security forces are our friends.

I turn away and gag, but there's nothing in my stomach.

I reach the door to the Eye. It's sealed and the retinal scan system is down, but the battery-powered keypad is still up, and I know Crake's door override code by heart. The doors disengage with a sudden jerk and a hiss of air. I step in cautiously and push the door closed behind me. Crake's chair is empty, and all his screens are dark. The only illumination comes from the weapons locker. The door stands ajar, the automatic light buzzing steadily inside. I push the door open the rest of the way. Someone has emptied it hurriedly and left a mess. The few remaining rifles lean against one another haphazardly, like a child's game of pickup sticks. Loose rounds litter the floor and spill out into the Eye, a handful of filtration masks among them.

"Tempest."

I spin around, clamping my jaw closed so I won't scream.

Crake lies on the floor beside the uniform laundry bin. The florescent light gives his already-pale face a gray-blue cast. A smartfabric filtration mask covers his nose and mouth, but a dark stain has already spread across it.

"Crake." I drop to my knees beside him. He was never my friend, exactly, but he let me lurk around the Eye when I didn't have anything else to do. My throat goes tight and my eyes prickle.

"Tempest." He can barely lift his head from the floor. "What are you doing here, girl?"

"The shirks grabbed me, but I got away." I reach out to

support his head, but then I wonder if that's what he'd want me to do, and I pull back. I don't know how to help him. "What happened to you?"

Crake shakes his head. "You've got to get out of here." He coughs. "Far as you can."

"But where am I supposed to go?"

"Anywhere." Crake wheezes. "Not here. No good here." His eyes roll back and close.

"Atlanta?" I pull at his shirtfront. AgraStar's headquarters is in Atlanta. "Should I go there? I can warn them."

Crake opens his eyes. "Already did." He looks at his computers. "They're sending a containment team."

He fumbles with his mask and pulls it down. I try to push it back in place, but he bats my hands away.

"It doesn't matter." He unhooks the mask from around his ear and lets it fall. Dried blood streaks his chin and throat. "It's no good."

"I can get you out of here." I hear myself say it, high and girlish, even while my mind is calculating. He's right, it's too late. He's been breathing in the fallout too long.

Crake shakes his head. "It's no good." His eyes swim and then fix on me, suddenly lucid. "You've got to leave before the containment team comes."

"But they can help," I say. "They're coming to help. Right?"

He shakes his head harder. "Not help. Contain."

"Contain." I repeat. What's wrong with that? Who knows how far the blight will spread if no one stops it?

Crake nods faintly and closes his eyes. "Quarantine. They can't let anyone know."

"Know what?" I say.

Crake takes a shuddering breath.

I shake his shoulder. "Know what?"

His eyes flutter open again. "What?"

"You said they can't let anyone know," I say. "Know what?"

"R and D's controlled blight initiative," Crake says. "It's not just a regular herbicide. It was supposed to target Bloom's soybean crops, only we didn't have it right yet. The strain was too strong."

I rock back on my heels. "Bloom?" Why would AgraStar do that? Why would we need to? Corn is a better source of both fuel and grain than anything our competitors grow.

"Not just Bloom," Crake says. "Progress Multinational and Apex Group and Fuel Solutions United. All of them."

I feel as if someone has kicked me square in the stomach and knocked out all the air.

"Why? Why would we do that?"

Crake laughs, but then the laugh turns into a shuddering cough that wracks his whole frame. "Someone had to do it first." Wetness bubbles in his throat. "If we hadn't, it would have been one of them. This way—" His words deteriorate into a thick cough, each spasm bringing up a fresh clot of blood.

I look around. Water might ease his pain, but I don't see any, and I don't dare leave him long enough to make my way down to the mess hall. I wait until his coughing subsides.

"We would have gotten it right." He sighs. "A little more time, and they would have had it." He exhales, and his shoulders relax against the floor.

"Crake?" I jostle him.

His body moves limply under my touch. His half-lidded eyes stare up at the ceiling. He's gone.

I tilt my head back to keep the tears from falling. I hate crying. I hate when anyone does it, but I hate it most when I can't keep from doing it. It's stupid, useless. What good has it ever done anyone?

AGRASTAR CONGLOMERATE—REFUELING THE FUTURE. A woman in protective goggles and a white lab coat holds up a beaker of ethanol and smiles down at me from one of the posters tacked on the wall.

Rage surges through me. It fills my stomach and my mouth and ears and eyes, until I think I'm going to choke on it. I bolt up, eyes brimming—*stupid, stupid*—and stride over to the poster. Then I'm tearing at it, ripping it from the wall, tears streaming down my face—*stupid, useless*—throwing the woman's smiling face to the floor and stomping, shredding, destroying it with my boots. And all the while I'm screaming and screaming like I could never spill enough anger from me, like I'll never be emptied of it. Everything is gone, ruined. There are too many people to bury. There's no fixing it. There is no going back.

.7.

TAPROOT

RADIX

My inner soldier finally takes over, and I go blessedly numb. I grab a filtration mask from the weapons locker—it bought Crake some time; it might do the same for me—and select one of the remaining guns. The only rifles left are bolt-actions for sniping, so I pick a nine-millimeter handgun. I find a backpack, cram it full of food and water from the kitchens, then pick my way over to the infirmary to doctor my hands. The alarms blare on, but I'm immune to them now.

I hiss and bite my lip to keep from screaming when I splash rubbing alcohol over my raw flesh, but even the pain doesn't bring me out of the fog.

It's better this way, I think, as I wrap my wrists and fingers in gauze. *It's better not to feel too much right now.*

I shove extra medical supplies in my bag—bandages, alcohol, antibiotics, water filtration pellets. I don't know how long it will take the quarantine crew to get here. Hours? Days? But I do know I can't stay much longer, not without my lungs liquefying. Better to stick to the woods where the blight hasn't reached and watch for the crew, turn myself over when they arrive. I'm not afraid of being quarantined, no matter what Crake thinks. I've always been a model employee. They'll look up my records and see they can trust me. At the very least, it means a real medic can check my hands.

There's only one thing left to do. I find a shovel and retrace my steps through the bunker until I'm back at the entrance. I loop the handle through the straps on my backpack and climb onto the motorcycle. I sit for a minute, watching the scattering of white clouds drift across the crystal-blue sky. Then I kick the engine into gear.

I ride out to the spot where Ellison and the rest of my team fell. No one has moved them. Marco still hangs in the truck's restraints. Will and Danica lie sprawled in the trampled corn. The air is thick with fat black flies. Whatever R&D engineered, it isn't lethal to them. My filtration mask blocks most of the smell, but it hovers around the bodies, reminding me how little time I have.

Despite the sun, the mat of rotten cornstalks and shriveling root systems have kept the clay moist. It parts easily for my shovel. My throat burns less with the filtration mask on, but the faint taste of blood still lingers in the back of it. I clear out a four by six area, about three feet deep, breaking every twenty minutes or so for water. I know I should bury them properly, but I don't have the energy for anything more than a shallow grave.

When I'm done, I drag them over, one by one. I lay Danica and Will down first, shoulder to shoulder, then free Marco and arrange him by their side. Death has made their bodies heavy and unwieldy, and I barely have the strength I need. Last is Ellison. He stares wide-eyed at the blue, blue sky, mouth parted, as if he's surprised to find himself this way. The scavengers have taken his rifle. I lift his hand and hold it in my lap. It's cold, the same temperature as the clay.

Not now. I grit my teeth. *Hold it together.*

I drag him to the grave and nestle him among his team. I brush the dirt from his clothes, even though I know it won't make any difference soon enough.

I reach for the shovel again, but I feel a flutter of unease. This isn't right. Something is missing. I drop the shovel and kneel next to the grave. Marco is the only one who looks truly peaceful, I guess because he died so quickly, without really knowing what was going on. I wish I could wash them and dress them in clean clothes, the way the scavengers did for their dead, or fill their hands with flowers. It seems wrong to cover them with dirt without some word or gesture to mark their passing.

But I have no flowers, much less words. My friends' bodies blur and my throat tightens. I see my father again—his blank stare, the falling snowflakes, and then the crack of dry winter branches behind me. . . .

No, no, no.

. . . the branches cracking and my heart's sudden jump. I turned, and there was a woman, leveling an assault rifle at me. . . .

Rosalie.

. . . leveling a rifle at me and speaking into her coms. *He's got a whelp with him. Advise.*

My breath came hard in my scrawny bird chest, looking into the mouth of that gun. . . .

But Rosalie would never shoot you. She saved you, remember? She brought you in from the wilderness.

. . . terrified, and its mouth was still staring me down, and the woman was still waiting with it leveled at me. And then she touched her ear.

Roger that. She shouldered her rifle, and suddenly all the menace lifted. She held out her hand. *Here, kid. Come away now. Come with me. You're safe.*

And then walking away from my father's body and the sniper's mark, the hole in his forehead.

For a long time, all I can do is breathe and hold myself and rock back and forth over the grave. Rosalie killed my father. Did we ever bury him? Or did we leave him to rot outside the perimeter fence or be dragged away in the night, like we do with most scavengers? I don't remember.

Something scuffs the dirt behind me. I lunge for the

shovel and whirl around, raising it in the air like a bat.

Alder stands ten paces away. He holds an old bolt-action hunting rifle, angled down at the dirt. He frowns at me as if I'm some type of animal he's never seen before.

I step back. "What do you want?"

Alder's eyes are fixed on the bodies behind me. "I . . ." He glances at my face. "The Deacon told us she tied you to the sitting oak."

"Yeah." I swipe at my eyes and adjust my grip on the shovel. "She did."

"I thought . . ." He clears his throat. "I thought she was making a mistake, leaving you there like that. I thought you might . . ."

"Live?" I finish for him. I'm raw. Raw, and too angry to get killed now, after so much.

Alder steps forward. I feint with the shovel and shoot him a look of pure menace. He holds up a hand—*wait*—and lowers his rifle the rest of the way. He walks to the edge of the pit and looks down at my teammates laid out in the dirt.

"You're burying them." He looks back at me. "Deacon Ward always told us you burned your dead."

"We do. So we can use the land for farming. But that doesn't matter now." I wave my hand at the destruction around us.

He looks down at the grave again and swallows. "We did this. Eden and me."

"Yes."

We both stand, awkward and tense, as if we're waiting for some signal to tell us what to do.

Finally Alder lays down the gun and holds out his hand. "Give me your shovel."

"Why?"

"You want them buried, don't you?"

"Not by you," I spit.

"Look, just . . ." He sighs and runs a hand through his hair. "Just give me the shovel, okay?"

"Fine." I toss it at his feet. He doesn't have a filtration mask, and if he ends up killing himself filling in Ellison's grave, that would only be sweet justice.

He picks up the shovel and digs into the pile of loose dirt beside the pit. The only sound is the heavy patter of dirt on cloth and flesh. I watch him for a few minutes, and then circle the grave and crouch. I sink my fingers into the soil and scoop wet clumps into the hole. I try to do it gently, pretend I'm covering my friends in a warm blanket, rather than burying them forever.

We work in silence until the grave is nearly full.

"Where will you go after this?" he asks.

"I don't know."

"Won't your company take care of you? Send you to another compound?"

I shake my head. *My company.* How could my company have done the things it's done?

He falls silent again, looks off at the afternoon sun sinking lower in the sky, everything gold light and lengthening shadows. "Deacon Ward will have missed me by now. She'll be wondering where I am."

"And I care . . . why?" I snap.

His eyes flash, and I hope he'll come at me, hope he'll hit me. I want to pound his face into the dirt. I want something brutal and simple. But then he glances down at the mound of earth between us. "You're right. You don't."

"Did you bury her?" I ask. "Eden?"

His head snaps up at her name. Our eyes catch, and then his shoulders drop. "No. The Deacon said there wasn't time."

"Is that why you haven't left?"

"No." He looks at me. "I was going to kill you first."

Surprise flushes through me, and then something else. . . . Respect? If our roles were reversed, I might have done the same.

I try to keep from smiling, but I can't. "You probably should have waited to fill in the hole, then."

A ghost of a smile flits across his face.

"I thought it was cruel, leaving you to die slow. It wasn't justice. The Deacon would have regretted it." He nods to his gun. "So I came back to make it quick."

"But I was gone."

"But you were gone," Alder agrees. "So I tracked you. And now here we are."

"Here," I dig into my backpack, pull out an extra filtration mask, and toss it to him.

Alder catches it. He hesitates, looks at it, then me. "Thanks."

"You should leave," I say. "Crake—before he died, he said they were coming to quarantine the area. You've got to clear out before they come."

Alder freezes. "Quarantine?"

"Yeah, Crake said . . ." I look up, and the words die in my mouth.

Alder stands stock-still, all the color drained from his face. "Quarantine?" he says again.

"Yeah." I frown at him. "What, you never heard the word?"

"We have to get out of here." Alder drops the shovel and tries to grab my arm.

"Hey!" I shout, dancing out of the way.

"You don't get it." He checks the horizon. "That's not what you think it means."

"What is it, then?"

"It's code." Alder snatches up the rifle and snaps it open to check his cartridges. "Whatever's left, they're going to burn it to the ground. Make it like this place never existed."

I bark out a laugh. "They wouldn't." After all, what's left to burn? But then I remember Crake, blood flecked over his chin. *They can't let anyone know.*

A sick feeling creeps into my stomach. "How . . . how do you know?"

"The Deacon." Alder slings his rifle back over his shoulder. "She used to be one of you."

The earth turns under me, slow, slow, like the minute hand of an old clock. "She told me," I hear myself say.

"We've got to move." Alder grabs for my arm again.

"Don't touch me."

"Fine." He holds up his hands in surrender and backs away. "Don't believe me. You want to stay and get yourself killed, that's nothing to me. But I'm going."

"Good," I shout after him, picking up the shovel. "I'll finish this myself."

Alder turns to say something else, but then his eyes go wide. "Listen." He scans the sky. "Do you hear that?"

I hold my breath. At first I don't, but then I hear it, far off in the distance. The drone of a plane. No, more than one. They pop into view on the horizon, two specks tearing toward us at top speed.

"Run!" Alder yells.

I'm already off, scooping my bag from the dirt and throwing myself onto the motorcycle. "Come on!" I shout, kicking the starter.

Alder hesitates. For a split second, hate and suspicion cross his face, but then he's clambering onto the back of the bike. He grabs my waist and holds tight. I gun us forward, onto the road leading to the nearest substation.

"No, left!" Alder shouts in my ear.

"Left?" I yell back. "Kingfisher's?"

He says something, but a sudden roar overhead mutes his words, and the horizon to the west ripples with fire. Orange flames blossom, and then the aftershock hits us, a ripping series of booms that echo through my chest.

"Holy hell." I push down the throttle and lean forward over the handlebars. "C'mon, faster!"

Another line of fire blooms to the west, closer this time. I catch sight of one of the planes, a sharp black shape circling out of the smoke. It strafes the land as it comes in for another pass, and more fire leaps up in its wake.

"They're trying to kill us!" I scream.

"No, really?" Alder shouts back. "What did you think they were going to do?"

Smoke billows up and blankets the sun. The whole world turns a sickly yellow, the same jaundiced hue that creeps in before a hurricane. The Kingfisher homestead comes into view a mile out. I can see farther without the corn, but that also means the pilots overhead won't have so much trouble spotting the bike, unless the smoke is thick enough to hide us.

"Where?" I yell over my shoulder.

"The house!"

Another line of fire ignites behind us, closer than before. Glowing cinders rain down on the road and the dead corn, as if all the stars have burst and fallen from the sky. Points of heat sear my shoulders and arms. I smell my hair burning.

The Kingfishers' tin roof sharpens into detail. Scorch marks score the side of the house, where the honeysuckle grew, and laundry still droops on the line. I brake and swing the bike into a sudden stop. Alder races to the porch and I follow, close on his heels.

As I pass the front stoop, something red flashes in my periphery. I look back. Tomatoes, ripe and full. Something alive in the midst of all this rot. Time stops. My heart stops. How is this possible? The blight has killed everything, but it hasn't touched them.

"Alder."

He turns. I read terror all over his face, but then he sees.

"Hurry." He holds out his hands. "Give me your bag."

I shrug it off and pull open the drawstring top. Alder grabs a handful of ice packs and painkillers and extra gauze and chucks it all on the porch. He rips the tomatoes from the vines with both hands and stuffs them into the bag.

Overhead, the planes fill the air with a heavy buzz.

"Alder," I say.

"Done." He cinches the bag closed and pushes it into my hands as he brushes past me into the house.

Antique junk clutters the space, in the way of homesteads that have been in a family for years, and the air smells of must. I catch only fleeting glimpses of the front room as I hurry after Alder: a sunken couch, a camp stove, pictures of trees done in coffee grounds and red clay hanging on the wall. I nearly trip over an old wooden footstool.

Alder flips back a rag rug and reveals a trapdoor. "The Kingfishers' cellar. We'll be safe here."

"I'm not going down there."

Alder grabs the pull ring and yanks the door open with a squeal. "I don't think you've got much choice."

"What good's that going to do if they bomb the house?" I shoot back. "Then we're trapped beneath a burning building instead of inside it. Either way, we're dead."

Outside, a sonic boom claps the air. The walls shake and a lamp falls to the floor and shatters.

Alder hops down onto the stair leading to the cellar. "Trust me," he says. "If I were going to kill you, I'd have done it already."

"That's reassuring," I mutter, but I follow him into the dark anyway.

.8.

CHEROKEE PURPLE
SOLANUM LYCOPERSICUM

Alder strikes a match and feeds it into a lamp at the bottom of the stair. An oily circle of light fills the room. Another impact shudders the ground, and a dusting of silt rains down between the floorboards.

"Great," I say. "You'd rather be buried alive than burn to death. Is that it?"

Alder glares at me. "You want to go back up there?"

"No." I roll my eyes.

"Then will you shut your cog mouth for a second? I know what I'm doing."

I briefly entertain the idea of ramming Alder's head into the dirt wall and digging an escape route that way.

"Fine," I say through gritted teeth.

Alder stalks to the far end of the room, where black metal shelves stocked with AgraStar brand pesticide tanks and fertilizer line the wall. He grabs a full bag and throws it on the floor.

"Come on," he says. "Help me."

I drop my backpack and join him, shoving pesticide tanks, boxes of spare tractor parts, and bags of fertilizer out of the way. Alder grabs one side of the shelving and drags it away from the corner. I lift the other side, and slowly, we walk it away from the wall, revealing a stack of tin roofing corrugate.

I glance at the ceiling. "This is supposed to help . . . how?"

"You'll see." Alder slides the tin out of the way. A hole, three feet wide, maybe four feet tall, is cut into the cellar wall. He crouches down and holds the oil lamp out into the darkness. It's a tunnel, a passage boring into the earth as far as I can see. Roots vein the walls and roof. We'll have to duck, but there's enough room to pass through single file.

A bone-shaking boom throws us to the ground. The spaces between the floorboards overhead flash white. I lie stunned, my brain scrambling to make sense of the sound and light above me. Then the heat hits me, and the smell. Fire. The Kingfishers' house is on fire.

"Move." Alder is beside me, tugging me to my feet, pushing me into the tunnel.

"My pack!" I stagger back for the bag of supplies.

The blaze moves fast, eating the floorboards overhead with a crackling fury. Heat pulses down from the ceiling and orange flames curl around the wooden beams. Behind me, a damaged beam gives way and plummets to the ground in a cloud of sparks.

"Hurry!" Alder shouts.

I run for the tunnel, duck, and barrel forward at a stoop. Alder follows. As he clears the threshold, a thunderous crack sounds and the floor collapses into the cellar in an avalanche of flaming beams and dirt.

"Go!" Alder shouts. "Run, run!"

But I'm already running, shoulders hunched, head low, hoping the many feet of earth above won't cave in. The air is thin and hot, and Alder's lamp dances crazily, illuminating flashes of terrain ahead me.

The tunnel turns left, and the noise and heat fade. I stop and pull my filtration mask down around my neck. The sharp smell of smoke hits my nose. "Give me a minute," I pant. "Not enough air."

The lamp lights Alder's face. "It's not much farther. Keep moving."

I stumble forward, catching my hair in the roots and tripping on the uneven ground. I'm about to give up when the tunnel widens and the ceiling rises and I can walk almost completely upright.

"Here." Alder jogs forward, and I step aside to let him squeeze by. Better. He can light the way, and I can see what he's up to.

The ceiling rises another foot. Alder's lamp illuminates a rough-cut archway, and beyond it, a wide room. Three of the walls are lined with shelves, but the fourth is an enormous vein of muddy yellow quartz that curves up and forms part of the ceiling. The lantern light glimmers on its surface. Half of the shelves are empty, but labeled jars of seeds fill the others— runner beans and okra, tomatoes and yellow squash. Bins of tubers and garlic cloves sit at the foot of the shelves. Contraband.

I let my pack drop and walk to the center of the space. "The Kingfishers weren't the only ones, were they?" I shoot a look at Alder. There's no way they stored all of this themselves, in addition to their other stash beneath the green-bean plot.

"Of course not." He turns his back to me and scans the shelves. I spot what he's looking for at the same moment he does. An old sat phone. He grabs it from the top shelf and holds down the ON button to test the power.

I take a step back. "Who are you calling? The Deacon?"

"No one." He frowns at the screen. "Can't get any connection down here."

"What about the . . ." I struggle to remember what he and Grebe said last night. "Charlotte? The Latebra Congress?"

Alder freezes. "Where did you hear about that?"

"You said it. Back at your camp, when you were talking to Grebe."

He's silent now, staring at me, and my anger and frustration rush back. It's his fault this happened, him and the Deacon, and now he wants to play games?

"Must be important." I plant my feet. "If you don't want me knowing about it."

Alder advances on me. I step back, ready to throw up an arm and block the blow I'm sure is coming, but he leans into my face instead.

"Never repeat those words, Cog Girl." He spits. "Forget you ever heard them."

I work up a sweet smile. If anything was going to sear those words into my memory, it's being told to forget them.

"Goddammit." He snatches up my bag and arranges himself on the floor next to a bin of sweet potato roots. He starts rifling through the bag's main compartment, pulling stuff out, sorting it on the dirt next to him. Aside from the tomatoes, we have three bottled waters, five filter masks, a tube of antiseptic gel, a roll of gauze, a bottle of painkillers, a flashlight, and two boxes of protein bars.

I look around the room. Empty trays and rolls of mesh sit next to pieces of equipment I don't recognize. There's something that looks like a radar gun, but smaller, and with bars across its mouth. I pick it up. Where did they get equipment like this? Did they steal parts from R&D? They must have, unless someone there slipped it to them. Maybe that's not so far-fetched. How many others were doing this? How many more secret rooms beneath homesteads? How many people mistrusting AgraStar enough to throw their lot in with the Deacon and the scavengers?

But then, maybe I shouldn't blame them. If Crake is right and AgraStar created the blight as a weapon . . . no. It was an accident. A regular experiment gone wrong. We're constantly trying to stay ahead of the weeds and pests developing resistance, come up with newer, more powerful herbicides that will kill the invasives and spare the crops. AgraStar would never have created something this devastating on purpose. If I can bring the tomatoes to our scientists, they can fix it. The fruit resisted the blight, which means it might hold the key to protecting the rest of our crops somewhere in its genes.

"What is all . . ." I look down. Alder is pulling apart one of the Kingfishers' tomatoes. Juice runs over his fingers and into the dirt.

"What are you doing?" I lunge for the fruit.

Alder holds it out of my reach. "I'm saving the seeds. They'll rot if we leave them in."

"Oh." Of course. Contraband crops have live seeds that can be planted and grown, unlike the varieties AgraStar distributes each year. Ours are robust, high yield, and supposedly disease-resistant, but if you tried to save the seeds and replant them the next year, you'd get nothing. They're a genetic dead end.

Alder finds a tray with a fine mesh base and spreads the jam-like insides of both tomatoes over it. I step beside him to watch.

He uncaps one of the water bottles and raises an eyebrow at me. "You've never done this?"

I shake my head. He shrugs and goes back to work, washing the seeds, collecting the water below, and running it back through the sieve until they're clean.

"Hand me that sun gun?" He raises his eyes to the device I was examining earlier.

I hand it to him. He flips it on, and a glow like perfect afternoon sun pours out of the barred end. He moves it gently back and forth over the thin layer of seeds scattered across the mesh. They're so small. Vulnerable. Drop them and they're lost.

"Here." Alder hands me one of the de-seeded tomatoes, all skin and meat. He picks up the other one and chews it while he makes another pass with the sun gun. "This isn't the best way to save seeds, but it'll have to do."

I stare down at the gutted fruit. The last thing I want to do is eat, but I need something if I'm going to keep going. I take a tentative bite and freeze. The tomatoes I'm used to are bland and mealy. But this one has a taste to it. Tart, on the edge of sweet, and juicy.

"This is smart," I say grudgingly, nodding at Alder's work. "We can get them to Atlanta easy this way."

"Atlanta?" Alder frowns, eyes still on the seed tray.

"Yeah," I say. "They can analyze them, figure out what made them resistant. Blend that into the genetic mix."

He looks up at me and switches off the sun gun. A muscle in his jaw ticks. "What?"

"AgraStar's headquarters," I say. Is he dense? "We have the top R and D facilities in all the company-states. They'll fix this. They—"

"AgraStar!" Alder explodes. "They just set your whole compound on fire. They tried to kill us!"

"I didn't have my tracker on. If you hadn't taken it from me—"

"What the hell is wrong with you?" Alder stares at me. "Are you that brainwashed? Don't you think they swept for signs of life? That's the whole point. You're expendable. They're covering their tracks. They're making sure no one ever finds out what happened."

I turn away, face hot. He's wrong. Someone would notice, ask questions. Wouldn't they? A whole compound wiped out, a break in production, altered shipping routes? True, there are hundreds of other farm compounds, other facilities exactly like ours spread throughout the southeastern corner of the continent, but . . .

My head aches. I haven't slept in over a day and there's not enough air down here. Would I notice the difference between one shrink-wrapped apple over another? Would I think anything of a delivery delay? I press my fingers against my temples. No. I would assume trouble with jackers or a road washed out—some everyday inconvenience, not a catastrophe like this.

"You don't know that," I say. "Maybe fire's the only way to stop the blight spreading." A strategic sacrifice. Like cutting off an arm to stop gangrene.

"Believe what you want." Alder shakes his head and turns the sun gun back on. "Like hell am I letting AgraStar get its hands on these seeds. These are heirlooms, not company property. They belong to us."

"What are you going to do with them?" I plant my hands on my hips. "Keep them for your little shirk camp and let everyone else suffer? Do you know how many people AgraStar feeds?"

Alder keeps his eyes on the tray. "They might feed a million people now, but look at the cost. They own everyone. They control what you plant, who gets to eat, who gets to live. And what do you do? You thank them for it." He shakes his head.

I roll my eyes. "What do you want? To go back to the old days of nation states? Elect a bunch of idiots who argue all the time and never get anything done?"

"Does that scare you?" Alder smirks. "Losing your little trigger-happy, power fantasy? Being no different than the rest of us?"

"I'm nothing like you," I say. "I work for a living."

"You work for a system that has everyone so scared to lose what little they have, they'll let AgraStar do anything it wants." He's shouting now, red-faced. "Any tiny thing we can do to bring them down is worth it."

Blood pulses hot in my face. "Oh, so blowing up our R and D facility and killing everyone in the compound is a 'tiny thing' now?"

Alder closes his eyes and rubs a hand over his brow.

"That's not . . . it wasn't supposed to go that way. You know that. It was supposed to be a simple raid." He opens his eyes again. They're red rimmed and circled by shadows.

"Shake you up. Steal some food. Distract you while we got the Kingfishers out."

"Fine." I look away. I don't want to see his sad, tired eyes. "Whatever."

Alder sets the sun gun aside. "It's true," he says quietly. When I don't reply, he takes a small cloth bag from the shelf and begins brushing the dried tomato seeds into it.

I clench my jaw. I mean to keep an icy silence, but I can't. "Why couldn't you just leave us be and grow your own food if you hate us so much?"

Alder pauses. He blinks up at me, and then suddenly bursts into laughter.

I narrow my eyes at him. "What?"

He stops. "You're serious." His eyes go wide and his mouth drops into a grim line. "AgraStar doesn't tolerate competition, even from small growers. You're either with them or against them. And you see what happens if you're against them." He looks up at the dirt above our heads.

"That's not the same. That would never have happened if it wasn't for—"

"Isn't it?" Alder's gaze drops back to me, and it's pure fire. "Your eradication teams, the ones that took out the Kingfishers' stockpile? You don't think they really spend all their time fighting off kudzu and honeysuckle, do you?"

"Yes." I try to sound certain, but my voice wavers. "And taking down bootleggers."

Alder laughs once. "Is that what you call them?"

I fold my arms across my chest. "That's what they are."

"Or maybe they're independent farmers." Sarcasm edges his voice "Maybe AgraStar shows up and claims they've been growing AgraStar seed strains without authorization, violating the company's intellectual property rights. And then maybe they give them a choice: hand over control of their land and contract out with AgraStar, or have their crops burned."

I scowl. I've been on missions out to farms bootlegging our seed strains, and I've never had any reason to think the raids were more than the higher-ups said they were. The bootleggers who didn't want to contract would try to stop us, of course. Like that one old man who met us on the road with a shotgun. I had to knock him out with a stun charge, and when he came to and saw his crops in flames, he spit on me and cried. Another time, we found a little girl— maybe seven or eight—crawling around under the combine Eradication brought in, trying to sabotage it. Seth thought she was hilarious, at least until she bit him. But isn't that exactly how criminals act? Wouldn't an innocent person let AgraStar finish their inspection without fighting?

"How do you know they weren't skimming seeds?" I say uncertainly.

"They could have been," says Alder. "Or it could be their farms were next to an AgraStar compound, and the wind and bees cross-pollinated their crops with AgraStar's without them knowing or even wanting it to happen. Could be if AgraStar says you're guilty, there's no one who can prove otherwise."

I drop my eyes and kick at the floor. It all sounds like ignorant shirk propaganda, except I can't forget what Crake said about the blight. *"Someone had to do it first."* And the new, raw memory of Rosalie with her rifle. *"He's got a whelp with him. Advise."* Maybe AgraStar isn't all good—no one is all good—but the company can't be as dirty as Alder says. It can't be *evil*.

"We didn't always burn them," I say quietly, still looking at the floor.

Alder doesn't answer. He cinches the seed bag closed and tucks it into his pocket. He throws me the backpack. "Load up."

"You think the fire's out?" I glance down the tunnel, back the way we came. We're too far away to see or hear anything, and it's hard to tell time underground, with no wrist coms. But the air is getting thin. It's definitely been an hour, maybe two.

I repack our supplies while Alder selects a few extra seed jars to add to them. When he isn't looking, I snatch one labeled TOMATO, CHEROKEE PURPLE HEIRLOOM and wedge it into my pocket. I don't know if it's the same kind that survived the blight, but it can't hurt. Our scientists will want to analyze it either way.

We make our way back through the tunnel. The heat increases as we go, tendrils of steam escaping the soil around us. I feel like we're walking through my substation's crowded showers on an August night.

I almost don't see the entrance until we're upon it. Roof beams and ragged pieces of tin have fallen across the opening, letting in triangles of smoky light. Alder shoves one of the beams, but it doesn't budge.

"Dammit." He drags an arm across his forehead and kicks the wreckage. It shudders, but stays firmly in place.

"Are we trapped?" My throat is dry. We have only two bottles of water, thanks to Alder's seed saving, and our masks won't keep out whatever killed Crake and the rest of the compound forever.

"I don't know." Alder kneels down and looks through a small opening between the beams. "Maybe . . ."

He lies on his back and tries to fit into the gap. A red flush creeps up his face, and sweat streaks his skin and hair. He lets out a grunt. "No."

I crouch down. A maze of wood and debris blocks the way, but I can still see sunlight.

"Move," I tell Alder. "Let me try." I'm smaller.

I shrug off my pack and maneuver my head and torso through the gap. If I angle right and then left, that will get me most of the way. Nails and plaster shards litter the floor, and some of the wood still smokes.

"Shit." I hiss as I put my hand down in hot ash, and my eyes water. My fingers are already raw, and now this.

"You okay?" Alder calls.

I realize only then that I've cried out.

"Fine." I choke. I crawl forward on my elbows, clenching

my teeth. Nails and splinters rip at my shirt and scratch my arms, but I barely feel them. I shove a sheet of roofing with my shoulder. It falls away, and I roll out into the rubble. The sky stretches above me, solid gray like winter. Falling ash lands softly on my face.

I stagger to my feet.

"Are you out?" Alder's voice is muffled. "Did you make it?"

I don't answer. The stairs are still there, the cinder block scorched and blackened, but standing. The wind kicks up a puff of ashes. I look at the pile of rubble blocking the tunnel entrance, then up at the stairs, then back again. A thought snakes through my mind. I could leave him trapped in there. He would die, and that would be some small revenge for Ellison and everyone else the shirks killed. I could set off on my own for Atlanta or one of the other AgraStar compounds.

But he could have shot me in the head while I was burying my team, and he didn't. He could have let me burn up during the quarantine, and he didn't. Besides, he has my pack. And he has the seeds. I need a new mask, and I can't turn up at AgraStar's headquarters empty-handed, with nothing to back up my story.

"I'm out," I say. "I made it."

"Can you move some of that debris out of the way? I think I can push this beam aside if there isn't so much blocking it."

Not for the first time, I wish I'd found some gloves back at the station. My bandages are charred and smudged with soot and stiff with dried white blood cells yellowing in the air. I'm not even bleeding red anymore.

"Give me a minute." I push over one of the roofing sheets. Everything is still hot to the touch, some of it smoking. I squeeze myself behind one of the heavier beams and push back against it with all my weight. It falls to the ground in a flurry of sparks.

"Keep going," Alder calls. "Almost there."

I shoulder another beam to the side and grunt. "Shut up." I'm not taking encouragement from a shirk like we're some kind of team.

Something comes loose in my lungs. I bend over, hacking wetly. I can't breathe.

"You okay?" I barely register Alder shouting. "Hey, Cog Girl, you okay?"

I touch my mask. Blood. *Shit.*

"I can't—" I swallow. "See if you can push from your end now."

The beam blocking the tunnel shudders and slowly bows out. "I think . . . ," Alder grunts, and all at once, the wood tumbles sideways. It collapses with a thud and another explosion of sparks.

"Alder?" I start toward him.

Alder coughs and stumbles out into the open, waving his hand to clear the smoke and blinking at the gray-bright sky.

My legs waver under me, and I sit down heavily on a chunk of concrete.

"Jesus, Cog Girl," Alder says. "You look terrible."

"It's Tempest," I say. "Not Cog Girl. Now give me my pack."

♦♦♦

All that's left of the motorcycle is a twisted hunk of metal, so we hurry across the blackened fields on foot. Ash falls like snow, gathering in the furrows and turning the red dirt gray. We stop only to change our masks and re-dress my hands. The closest exit to the compound is due west, so we head that way, even though it will mean doubling back south later.

Alder pulls out the sat phone and tries to power it on as we walk. It lights up, but he scowls at the screen.

"Battery's low." He scrubs a hand over his face. "And none of our satellites are in range."

"Scavengers have their own satellites?" I snort. "What, did you make them out of twigs and shit? Maybe that's why they don't work."

Alder gives me a withering look. "No. We hack them."

"Who, you?" I scoff.

Alder turns back to the phone. "Not everybody who wants to see AgraStar taken down lives in the woods."

Interesting. If I can keep him talking, maybe I'll have more than a handful of seeds and a sad story to bring to headquarters.

"Who are you calling?"

"The Deacon," Alder says.

"So you can tell her about me?"

Alder gives me a tired look. "It's not all about you. I know they're headed south, but I don't know where they're stopping. The Deacon herself probably won't know until they find the right spot."

He trudges ahead, staring down at the sat phone's screen. I jog to catch up with him. "You won't tell her about me, then? That I'm alive?"

"I haven't decided yet." Alder looks up at the sky as though a satellite might pop into view, then down at the rotting earth. "Right now, I'm more worried about making it out of the blight zone. I don't think these masks are doing much good."

I swallow. Even with a new mask, my throat feels seared. I taste a salty mixture of blood and mucus pooling at the back of my mouth. Alder's right. If we don't get clear of the blight, these masks are only delaying the inevitable.

Alder checks the phone again and grunts. "Still no signal."

"Can't they track us with that?"

"Who?"

"AgraStar. Your Latebra Whatever." I shrug. "Anyone."

Alder shakes his head. "That's why we only hack a few satellites, not your whole network. So we don't draw attention to ourselves. Besides, it keeps us from getting too dependent on technology. That's what the Deacon's all about. Getting us back to the essentials of life. Depending on the God-made, not the man-made." He says it as if he's repeating a slogan.

I frown. "Is that what you're all about, too?"

"I'm about staying free," Alder says. "And alive."

The sat phone beeps.

"Ha!" Alder's face brightens. He punches in a number. Digital static burbles on the other end, loud enough for me to hear, and then a two-tone chime. Alder lets it ring, and ring, and ring.

"They're not picking up." His face clouds over.

"They're probably still on the run." If I were them, I'd want to put as much distance as possible between me and ground zero. I take the phone from Alder and turn it off. "You can try again later. Now we have to move."

We walk in silence for a time, our breath muffled by the masks.

"You still going to turn yourself over to AgraStar?" Alder asks.

I shrug. What else am I going to do? Like hell am I becoming a shirk again.

"You really don't think they'll make you . . ." Alder points two fingers at his head and makes a shooting motion. "Disappear?"

I glare at him. "What do you care?" They won't. They can't. If I bring them good intel and promise not to talk, surely they'll trust me. I've always been a reliable asset.

Alder raises his hands in surrender. "Whatever."

The perimeter fence approaches, and the kudzu forest beyond. Fire has burned away all the creeping vine and reduced the trees to blackened skeletons for as far as we can see. Once we're past that, we'll be in a no-man's-land of jackers, shirks, and delusional separatist farmers who think they can outlast everyone.

"Do you think they got it all?" I ask. "The blight?"

"Hope so." Alder's eyes flicker over the smoldering forest.

"Looks like they burned, what, a mile, mile and a half out past your perimeter?"

"What are you going to do?" I watch him. He keeps his head up like I do—alert. Always scanning the horizon for trouble.

"Head south," he says. "Find the Deacon."

I swallow the blood in my mouth. "AgraStar's headquarters is south, too."

"Meaning?"

I look away. "The road's less dangerous with someone to watch your back. We could sleep in shifts, keep watch. . . ."

Alder smirks. "You trust me to watch your back?"

"About as much as you trust me." I look him over. We've both had plenty of opportunities to kill each other by now. "I'd take you over a band of jackers, anyway."

He snorts but doesn't say anything. We walk in silence past a collapsed section of the border fence and through the charred field separating the compound from the forest. Evening is finally coming on, the sun low and muted, looking out at us from behind the haze like a red eye.

Alder stops at the burned-out tree line. "Okay."

"Okay?"

"Yeah," he says. "We stick together part of the way. Till our paths split. No farther."

.9.

MARIGOLD

CALENDULA OFFICINALIS

We camp in a copse of trees about four miles beyond the perimeter gates. The sky has gone dark, and the smell of smoke still lingers in the air, even this far away. At least we seem to be outside the blight zone, though, and I've stopped coughing up blood.

I drop my pack next to an elm. "You're sure no one will find us here?"

"If they do, it'll be my people," Alder says. "We've used this spot as a hideout before."

"Hmph." I inspect my almost-empty water bottle. I'm too tired to argue, much less keep walking. My legs are shaking with fatigue, and the forest is starting to jump and blur.

"I'll take first watch," Alder says.

"Fine." I collapse by the tree and grab a protein bar.

"Give me one?" Alder says.

I narrow my eyes and toss one to him. "Didn't you bring anything with you?"

"Just that." He nods at the rifle. "I didn't think I'd be more than a few hours behind everyone. I thought I'd, you know . . . catch up."

"You hunt?" I tear into the bar, ignoring the unspoken words between us. *I thought I'd kill you quickly.*

He rolls a shoulder, a kind of shrug. "Yeah, but unless we see a deer, that's not going to do us much good. Blow a rabbit or a squirrel apart."

"Traps would be better," I say, my mouth full. "In case we need that for other things."

Alder looks away. He has to know as well as I do what's out here on the roads. The kind of men who aren't afraid to attack a company tanker won't bat an eye at a single rifle.

"Yeah," he agrees. "Quieter."

I ball up the protein bar wrapper in my hand. It's gone too quickly, and now I'm thirsty. I finish off my water, shaking the last few drops onto my tongue.

"There's a creek another half a mile in," Alder says. "We can head that way in the morning. Follow it down to the Catawba River, even."

"The Catawba bends southeast," I say, stifling a yawn. Atlanta is southwest. "I'd rather stick to the road."

"Suit yourself." Alder leans against a tree and pulls out

the sat phone. "You want some sleep, now's your chance. I'm waking you up in four hours."

"Like you can even tell time in the dark," I say. But if Alder has a comeback for me, I don't hear it. I'm fast asleep.

I come awake with something clamped over my mouth. Alder's hand. I buck and kick, but he holds me still.

"Shh," he hisses in my ear. "Down by the road. Look."

I stop fighting, but my heart pumps hard against my chest. Several sets of headlights burn white through the underbrush, and the steady sound of engines idling fills the night. Alder removes his hand.

"Yours?" I whisper.

He shakes his head, barely visible in the glow of the headlights.

Someone's moving through the weeds by the road. Then the sound of a man pissing in the grass.

"Hurry it up!" A shout from the truck—a woman. "We've got to get the sweep started by oh-six hundred."

"I'm comin'. I'm comin'," the man mutters.

I squint through the brush. *0600? Sweep?* She sounds organized, professional.

The man in the grass is a silhouette against the headlights, but then he turns, and I glimpse the logo on the back of his flak jacket. A four-pointed starburst, the bottom half growing out of two stylized leaves like an ear of corn. I have that same symbol carved into the rubber treads of my boots. It's engraved on our rifles and printed on our produce stickers. AgraStar.

Alder grips my arm.

"Don't," he whispers. He's seen it, too.

I know I should run to them, wave my arms, identify myself. Some instinct is keeping me down on the forest floor, though. I should be flooded with relief, but all I feel is dread. *Quarantine.* I scan the convoy waiting on the road. No medic wagons or personnel carriers that I can see. Everything out there is an armored vehicle. That means every person carries an automatic rifle on his or her back that makes Alder's bolt-action look like a child's pellet gun. Whatever they're doing, they aren't on a rescue mission. *Expendable.* Alder's words echo in my mind.

"Let's go," Alder whispers in my ear.

"No, stay still," I hiss back. "They'll move on any minute."

"Did you hear that?" The man by the road sweeps his flashlight over the underbrush. Alder and I hit the dirt.

"Leave it," the woman calls. "It's probably a groundhog or something."

His machete glints in the moonlight as he pulls it from his belt.

"Hey, pig pig pig!" he calls, wading into the brush.

Shit. I glance at Alder. He jerks his head at the deeper woods behind us, and I nod. We start crawling backward, slowly, quietly.

"Hucks, come on." Boots hit the asphalt, and the woman's voice gets louder.

A stick snaps beneath my knee.

I freeze and look at Alder. His eyes are big, like a deer's. Flashlight beams sweep over us.

"Run," Alder says.

We jump up and bolt through the undergrowth.

"There!" someone shouts. "In the woods."

The forest explodes. Splinters fly from the trees as bullets hit them. I duck and run forward at a crouch, close behind Alder. The gunfire follows us like a terrible rainstorm. The forest is darkness and hook-thorned vines, branches thrashing out and whipping my face, snatching at my clothes. Alder threads us through it as fast as he can. My blood is pure adrenaline. I match his pace, heedless of the thousand scratches and cuts from the undergrowth.

"This way." His breath is harsh. We run and run, jumping deadfall, dodging saplings, half blind. The gunfire fades behind us.

Alder slows as we enter a less-dense tract of trees. We don't speak, our breath the only sound between us. The forest opens onto a moonlit clearing. A shape rises out of it, huge and looming, draped in kudzu vines, a denser dark than the sky. A house. Or what used to be a house.

Alder pulls the vines away, uncovering an open doorway and complete darkness beyond. "Careful," he says. "The floor's caved in near the back."

I duck under his arm and walk slowly, feeling ahead with the toe of my boot. The floorboards are slightly soft and spongy with rot.

"What is this place?" I ask, rummaging in my bag for a flashlight.

"Safe house," Alder says. He lets the vines fall behind us. "Sort of."

I click on the flashlight. We stand in a large, open front room. The entire back half of it has collapsed, the floor giving way to a shallow pit. A portion of the ceiling has fallen through, leaving a clear view up into the second floor and the kudzu-wrapped rafters above. Floorboards and broken beams curve over from the upper level, as if the house is a waterfall frozen midstream. Particleboard covers the windows, but kudzu runners have crept in between the gaps and climbed the walls all the way to the ceiling.

"Turn it off," Alder says. "They could still be out there."

I press the flashlight's head against my hand, so all it gives off is a dim, red glow. "How did you find out about this pl—" I turn to Alder.

Blood covers the left side of his face from temple to neck. It soaks his collar and shoulder, dark in the red light.

"They hit you."

Alder touches the wound gingerly. He winces, looks at the blood on his fingers. "I think it's only a nick."

"Here." I shove the flashlight at him and reach into my bag for the antibiotic gel. It would be better to clean it with water, but I've drunk everything in my bottle and Alder can't have much left in his, either. Gel will have to do.

"Hold still." I squeeze out a glop and smear it over the cut.

His skin is hot. I fish out the roll of self-adhesive gauze and begin wrapping it tightly around his head, over the wound, around again, until the blood stops seeping through. "There." That'll have to do.

My eyes go to his, and I suck in a breath. His pupils are huge and black, like an animal about to pounce, or else be slaughtered. I don't know how to read the intensity in them. I step back.

He looks away. "Thank you."

I shrug and sling my bag down on the floor. Alder stands still, watching me. The hairs on the back of my arms and neck rise, but I try to ignore him and concentrate on finding my empty water bottle.

"You could have gone to them," he says.

I shrug again. "Not without getting shot. I don't have my tracker, remember? Stepping out of the forest right then would have spooked them."

He says nothing but keeps staring at me. I have the feeling that if I look up and catch his eye again, he's going to wrap his hands around my neck and crush my windpipe or maybe do something entirely different and far more confusing. Eventually he turns away and balances the flashlight facedown on the floor. A small ring of light escapes around the edges, giving me enough illumination to find a dry spot to sit.

Alder settles himself a few feet away and leans his rifle against the wall. He closes his eyes and rolls over on his side, his back to me. "Your watch."

I sigh and tilt my head back. A colony of mud dauber wasps have built their papery, fluted nest in the corner of the room, above my head. I get up and switch off the flashlight. Better to let my eyes adjust to the darkness. I stand there, listening to the house's stillness. I may have had only a few hours of sleep, but I'm wide awake, alert to every creak and sigh. Alder shifts, and then his breathing slows.

I wander up the staircase to the second story, careful where I step. Moonlight creeps in around the leafy vines. All the rooms on the first floor are empty, but upstairs I find an abandoned iron bed frame with hearts and curlicues molded into the headboard, a pile of rotting clothes, and another room scattered with plastic bottles and broken glass. The walls are thick with graffiti. FUK COGBITCHES and BLACKTOPS R PUSSYS and BURN in big, sloppy letters. Alder and his people aren't the only ones to use this place, then. I have the feeling their messages would be more spiritual, if they were the type to mark up a place at all.

My body tenses before I know exactly why. From far away, the thrum-hum of a surveillance drone reaches my ears. I drop into a crouch. I used to wake in the night sometimes to the buzzing of them—a benign sound, almost comforting. But now I break out in an icy sweat and my head is full of fire. I can almost feel the plane's cold electronic eye sweeping back and forth over the forest. Will the patchy roof and layers of kudzu be enough to mask our heat signatures? I press myself into the corner and hug my knees. I am small. I am nothing but a bobcat or a fawn. I am nothing to investigate further. For the first time, I'm glad my data band is gone. Without it, I am nothing but another animal, untethered and untraceable.

I press my knuckles against my forehead. *What's wrong with you? Don't you want them to find you? Don't you want to go back? How can you expect them to trust you if you don't trust them?*

Of course I do, I snap at myself. But on my own terms. In daylight, with intel to share. I don't want them finding me in a half-rotten shack with a scavenger boy in the middle of the night.

The sound recedes. I stand, every muscle stiff and aching. Is it really gone? I wait another fifteen minutes, listening in the dark, but the drone doesn't return and no rumble of ground vehicles disrupts the chirp of frogs and crickets. I make my way back downstairs. Alder is fast asleep, his breath deep and even. I stare at his back. I could leave him here. No harm done. Disappear into the night and veer southwest, toward Atlanta. I'm better off approaching an AgraStar outpost without him. Besides, the longer I stay here, the greater the chance the patrol we evaded or a jacker gang will happen by. But Alder has the seeds, the resistant ones, and if I'm going to talk my way back into AgraStar's good graces, I need something to bargain with. I need to prove I'm loyal.

I kneel over him, barely breathing. The bag of seeds is in his jeans pocket. I reach for it, but Alder's breath hitches. He moans, something animal, something that sends a brief shiver of pity through my chest. He rolls on his back, eyes closed tight, a frown pinching his forehead. I know he needs those seeds. His people need them to survive. But I need them, too. I finger the edge of the bag and slowly pull it from his pocket.

It comes free with a whisper. I clutch it to my chest and freeze, certain Alder is going to open his eyes and see me. But he doesn't.

I stand and back away. Better if he doesn't know, isn't it? He'll come after me if he knows. I crouch in a sliver of moonlight, open the pouch, and shake all the newly dried seeds into a plastic bag from my pack. Then I refill the pouch with seeds from the jar of Cherokee Purple I took back at the Kingfishers'. They look more or less the same to me. Alder might be able to spot the difference, but hopefully he won't have a reason to examine them. Who knows, maybe the Cherokee Purples will end up being resistant, too.

I stuff the bag inside my bra and cinch Alder's pouch closed again. The moon has slipped away, taking my spot of light with it. Night is ending. I start to tuck the pouch back into Alder's pocket. He's skinny—all bones and muscle—and his pants are too large, held up by an ancient belt patched with strips of duct tape. My fingers barely graze him, but suddenly he twitches in his sleep and cries out.

"Eden!" He grabs my hand, and I freeze.

Shit. His eyes are still closed. His face is dotted with sweat and crumpled in a frown. I start to pull away, but he says it again, soft and pleading this time.

"Eden."

Something about the way he says her name sends pain through my whole body, as if his words have brushed up against a raw nerve. His fingers are strong, the skin smooth except for a patch of roughness around the heel of his hand. If I close my eyes, I can pretend it's Ellison's hand, which I'll never hold. Ellison's hand, which will never brush the hair from the back of my neck on a hot day, like I've imagined so many times. If I close my eyes, I can pretend I have everything I'll never have.

I sit there, pretending, as the light coming in through the kudzu softens to gray. Alder relaxes again. His fingers go slack and his brow unfurrows. I let his hand drop, and stand. Soon he'll be awake, and I'll be gone.

I step out from beneath the vines overhanging the front door and adjust the straps on my backpack. Thick gray fog covers the clearing behind the house. I walk out into it. There must be a body of water nearby, with all the moisture in the air. And I heard frogs earlier. The ground grows soggy, sucking at my boots, and the pine trees are muted shadows. I come to a lake and stop. Small waves lap at the shore. The mist makes everything feel close and soft, and even though I know the fog and the soft slosh of water are the perfect cover for someone to sneak up behind me, I still feel safe—cocooned, hidden. Maybe I'm just tired. Maybe if I squeeze my eyes shut, no one will see me.

I kneel to refill my water bottle. Somewhere in the mist, a mourning dove calls out, its cry echoing over the water. A chill sweeps over me. *"Eden."* And a wave of rage and loneliness hits. I sit down in the mud and damp grass. I could tear up my little plastic bag of seeds, ball it up and throw it out into the middle of the lake where no one would find it, and then we would all die. We would all be dead, and there would be no more scores to settle.

My limbs feel so heavy. I should keep moving before Alder wakes and finds me gone, but my body won't let me. I pull out the plastic bag. The seeds are tiny, a pale yellow-brown, and thin. Like babies' teeth, only smaller. It seems impossible that anything could depend on these—a red, round fruit, a future harvest, maybe even the lives of everyone the blight touches. If the other plant varieties the Kingfishers kept aren't resistant, if this strain is the only one and the blight keeps spreading, Alder's people really might die without it. Not at first, of course. First they would scavenge wider and wider, and then they would raid someone else's stores, and *then* they would die, either from hunger or violence. I look out at the lake again. Two days ago, I wouldn't have cared either way, but today I don't want to be the cause of any more death. We can split the seeds—some for AgraStar to study, some to keep the scavengers alive.

I get up and trudge back to the house. As I reach a slight rise, the sun comes out, burning away the fog shrouding the forest. I stop dead. Where yesterday the trees were in the full, thick green of summer, today they are bare. Shriveled and blackened leaves hang from their branches like tattered cloth. The blight has touched the edges of the meadow, turning the grasses gray.

"Alder!" I stand in front of the house, my eyes locked on the dead trees. The firebombs didn't stop the blight. It's closed the miles between us and the compound in one night. "Alder!"

"What?" He appears in the door, eyes puffy and hair sticking up. He looks from me to the forest, and his eyes snap wide. "Oh, God."

"We've got to go," I tell him.

"Oh, God," he whispers again. He doesn't move.

"Alder, come on. We have to get out of here."

"What did we do?" he says, but he isn't talking to me, not really.

"Here." I hand him a water bottle. He needs a task, something to help him focus. "Get your gun. Follow me."

To my relief, he obeys. I lead him down to the lake and away from the spreading destruction as fast as our feet can carry us.

.10.

DOGWOOD
CORNUS FLORIDA

We've been walking along the wooded banks of a stream for an hour when Alder stops.

"Where are we?" he asks.

"I dunno exactly." I look up. The sun shimmers through the treetops. "We went south from the lake, and then came across this creek, so I started following it, like you said."

He blinks as if he's just come awake. "Upstream or down?" he asks.

"Huh?"

"How do you know you're going the right way? Did you turn upstream or down when you got to the creek?"

"Downstream," I say. "Southeast. To the Catawba, like you wanted."

He stares at me. "Oh."

I roll my eyes and keep walking. "I'm not a complete idiot, you know. They gave us some wilderness training before they sent us out on road-clearing patrols. In case we got lost. Or captured."

"We don't go out trying to capture you," Alder says. "That was a fluke."

"I meant the jackers."

We both fall silent. He has to know as well as I do that learning how to start a campfire or telling your cardinal directions by the sun won't do you much good if it's jackers that have you. That's why road-clearing duty would get you ration increases or earn you double time on your contract. That's why guards got pulled for it, why we always had a lookout. The teams that ran across jackers mostly got away. Except when they didn't.

"You ever run into them?" Alder asks.

I shake my head. "We heard stuff, though."

"Like what?"

I roll my shoulders uneasily. It feels like bad luck to talk about it. "About two years ago, they hit one of our eradication teams. We lost two—a guard and a clearer."

"You knew them?" Alder says.

I shake my head. Neither was from my substation. I look around the bright woods, suddenly on edge despite the lush trees and lazy stream.

"They said the clearer made it back in the middle of the night. She was naked and caked in blood from head to toe." I swallow. "They evacuated her straight to Atlanta. The higher-ups thought no one would volunteer for clearing duty again if they saw her."

"But you did," Alder says. "You volunteered?"

"It was only a rumor," I lie, and shrug. "Besides, every other guard my age was almost ready to contract out on their own. I needed the double time. I didn't want to be twenty-five and still paying back my keep."

The expression on Alder's face is something between confusion and pity.

I look away, at the stream. "Anyway, you can't keep the supply trucks moving if the road isn't clear."

"Why do you care so much about some company?" Alder asks. "They're not your family. You don't belong to them. You don't owe them anything."

"I owe them my life. They took me in when . . . when my father died. They raised me." Only my father didn't simply die. They killed him. *Rosalie* killed him.

I try again. "They could have shot me. They could have let me starve."

"What saints." Alder shakes his head. "They didn't murder you when you were a little kid."

"It's not like that." I start walking again. Is it so wrong to want to belong to something, to be a part of something? I belonged with Ellison and his team, however briefly. It was probably the closest I'll ever come to knowing what family feels like, and now it's gone.

"What about you?" I bend back a branch in my way. "Do you belong to the Deacon and them?"

"No," Alder says abruptly. I think that might be the only answer I get out of him, but then he takes a deep breath.

"There's a difference between belonging with and belonging to." He keeps his eyes on the path. "I belonged with Eden."

I don't say anything. A mosquito buzzes past my ear.

"Sometimes . . ." He clears his throat. "Sometimes I used to think about the two of us—me and Eden—making a homestead in the mountains near where I grew up. Little cornfield. Chickens, maybe. Someplace none of the companies would care enough about to bother with."

He doesn't sound angry. Just sad. Defeated.

"That sounds nice," I say quietly.

"It wouldn't have worked, anyway," Alder says. "Eden wanted to fight, same as her mother. She would have been our next Deacon if she hadn't . . ."

If I hadn't killed her. The guilt is nearly enough to stop me in my tracks, but I keep walking. I had no choice. Did I? What would have happened if I hadn't shot Eden? If we'd simply handed over the Kingfishers? Would everyone still be alive, or would Eden have lined us up and shot us by the side of the road anyway?

I imagine Ellison alive, rallying the blight's survivors. He would know exactly what to do, how to get us safely back to AgraStar. We wouldn't be following a twisting creek through a mosquito-infested forest, trying to find our bearings.

"You should try to reach the Deacon again," I say. I'm guessing Alder doesn't want to think about this any more than I do.

"Yeah." He stops to pull out the sat phone and powers it up. The low battery tone chimes immediately.

"Dammit." He punches in the number.

I squat beside him and finger a three-leaf clover. In my mind's eye, a spot of gray appears on it and withers it to a gray husk. We've walked away from the blight, but I know it's back there, hard on our heels. By nightfall, this clover and the trees overhanging the creek might be dead. Will it catch up to us again when we stop to sleep?

"It's ringing." Alder's eyes go wide. "Hello? Hello? This is Alder . . . Rose? Is that you? Can you hear me?"

A piercing screech leaps from the sat phone. Alder grimaces and tries again.

"Rose? Yes . . . no. No, they didn't. I went back and . . . Listen, I don't have much time. Can you tell me where you're headed? I thought I could find . . ." He pauses. "Hello?"

Alder lowers the phone and looks at it.

"Hello?" he says again, his voice rising, frantic. "Rose? Hello?"

"What's wrong?" I say, even though I know. The sat phone is dead. His chances of finding the Deacon are shrinking by the minute.

"Goddammit!" He hurls the phone against a tree. It shatters, showering plastic shards over the forest floor.

"Alder, what the hell—"

"Goddammit." He races forward, pulling at his hair, and doubles back. "So stupid."

"Shhh." I move toward him, shaken. I've seen him focused, angry, sad, but never out of control. "Shut up. Anyone within a mile could've heard you."

"Let them." Alder glares at me, his eyes wet. "I'm an idiot. I lost all of them, and I don't even have anything to show for it. I deserve to get caught."

"Well, I don't." I stoop to pick up the broken phone. I'd be hopeless at trying to put it back together, but I don't want to leave a trace behind. AgraStar may claim this territory, but it belongs to them in name only. There are worse things in the wild than quarantine procedures.

"Come on." I stuff the pieces of the sat phone in my pack and start walking. We need to put as much distance between ourselves and this spot as possible.

After a while, I hear Alder behind me.

"I'm sorry." He comes up even with me. "I didn't mean to lose it back there. It won't happen again."

"Better not." I look sideways at him. "I felt like doing the same thing, back at the cabin."

"Yeah?" He meets my gaze.

"Yeah." I look away. "Don't worry. You'll find them. You must have contacts, people who can help you reach them, right? Other scavengers? Besides, you tracked me all the way across the compound. And they *want* you to find them."

Alder nods. "You're right. I'll find them. I have to." He pats his pocket, the bag of seeds. "If AgraStar can't stop the blight, this is our best hope."

I want to admit what I've done, but my mouth is dry. There's nothing to do but keep moving.

At midday, we rest at a bend in the creek where a pool has formed, surrounded by dogwood trees.

"Food's running low," Alder says, leaning on his rifle as I roll up my pant legs and wade in to refill our bottles.

"I know." I don't look up. My nine-millimeter is heavy on my hip, but any gunshot will echo for miles. Hunting is out of the question.

"If we had some wire, I could make a snare," says Alder. He glances at my boots, partially unlaced on the bank.

"Don't even think about it," I say. "I need those."

"You're in the water," he says.

"But I'm not staying here," I say. "Use your own shoelaces."

He raises an eyebrow. I look down. Alder's shoes are held together by twine and duct tape. My laces are new poly-nylon, perfect for slipknotting.

"Fine," I say. "I'll just sit here in the water until you come back."

"Couldn't hurt," Alder says.

"What's that supposed to mean?"

Alder raises his other eyebrow.

"Are you telling me I stink?" Of course I do. Who wouldn't

after surviving an ambush, a fire, and two days on the run? No need to rub it in.

He smiles and crouches down to unlace my boots.

"Like you smell any better," I mutter.

Alder snorts and pulls the laces free, then walks off into the woods.

I sit on a rock next to the water and unwind the bandages around my hands. They're crusty with blood and dried gel, and they stick to my skin in spots. I hiss as I pull them free and lean down to submerge my fingers in the current. I close my eyes. The water is cold and perfect. I could nearly cry with relief. I sit bent double, listening to the rush of the stream, my mind calm for the first time in days.

A mosquito lands on my forearm, then another, and another, drawn by the shade and the promise of warm blood.

Screw it. I unclip my holster and lay my nine-millimeter on the rock, within easy reach, then pull out the bag of seeds and lay it alongside my weapon. I slip into the pool, clothes and all, and sit on the riverbed with only my head above the water. My clothes need it as much as I do. I allow myself a tiny smile. There's a reservoir, banked by gravel and dotted with irrigation pumps, in my compound's north quadrant. Our wilderness survival instructor taught us to swim there, and we're allowed to go on Founders' Day and Contractor Recognition Day. After training drills, we sometimes had a little free time before we were bussed back to our substations. I would swim out a few dozen yards, past where the other trainees were splashing and climbing on one another's shoulders and float, alone in the middle of the lake. I liked to rest my palms on the surface, test the water's tension, and enjoy the way it muffled the rest of the world.

I close my eyes. The sun is warm and the woods are quiet. I barely hurt at all.

The image of a washroom pops into my mind, smaller and brighter than anything at my substation. A single tub with high sides, and a woman kneeling, a washcloth in her hands. *Here, m'ija, put this over your eyes so I don't get soap in them. . . .*

My eyes spring open. I surge up out of the water, staggering under the weight of my wet clothes. *What was that?* I can hear my own breathing, harsh and fast, like I've been running the track by the perimeter fence. Did I fall asleep? Was that a dream?

But it didn't feel like a dream. It felt like a memory.

"Tempest?"

Alder stands on the riverbank, a rabbit in one hand and his shirt gathered up like a sack in the other. I didn't even hear him. He could have been anyone.

He stares at me, wide-eyed and wary. "What's the matter? Did you hear something?"

"It's okay." I swallow. I'm wide awake, shot through with adrenaline. "I'm okay. It's nothing."

"You sure?" He unloops my shoelace from the dead rabbit's neck. "You look like you saw a ghost."

I shake my head. "It's nothing." I palm the seed bag, then

grab my holster and fumble to fasten it around my hips.

Alder's expression says he doesn't quite believe me, but he shrugs and looks away. "You know how to dress a rabbit, or you want to gather wood?"

"Now?" I need a second, a minute, an hour to settle myself in my skin again.

"A fire'd be less likely to give us away in the daytime," he says. He unrolls his shirt to reveal a handful of brown button mushrooms. "Unless you're not hungry."

"I'll find the wood." A walk will calm me down, give me time to hide the bag clenched in my hand. I nod at the mushrooms. "You sure those are safe?" I remember just enough of my survival training to know some mushrooms are poisonous, but not how to recognize them.

Alder pops one in his mouth. I roll my eyes and stuff my feet in my boots.

"Dead wood only," Alder calls as I squelch into the trees. "Green wood'll make smoke."

"I know, I know," I mutter.

We eat and go on our way. Later that evening, we reach the Catawba, the last rays of the setting sun making its muddy waters shine like polished bronze. We bed down in an abandoned boathouse. Or more of a boat shack. It has two empty docking wells, each the right size for a rowboat, with a small pier between them, and a little more floor space on the shore side. There are no boats, but when I look down into the water, I can make out a pile of rotten boards and a rusted gas can on the riverbed beneath us.

Alder volunteers to take first watch, which is fine by me. I stake out a spot, stuff my backpack under my head, and close my eyes, listening to the water lapping underneath the boathouse floor. The image of the washroom creeps back again, but I shove it away. I don't have time to think about what it means right now. It's only going to distract me and get me killed.

"What you said this morning. . . ," Alder says suddenly. "About earning your keep?"

I roll over. He's sitting on the stubby pier, his face turned away. "Yeah?"

"They don't own you, you know." His voice is firm. "You don't owe them anything."

I don't reply. I pretend to be asleep, but it's a long time before my mind quiets enough to allow me some rest.

"Tempest." Alder shakes my shoulder. "Your watch."

I blink. The moon has risen, flooding the boathouse with silvery light. For a few seconds I stare at it. The world looks unreal in black and white. *Am I still dreaming?* Then I remember.

"You awake?" Alder asks. He's settling down on the pier, as far from me as the small space will allow. He rests his rifle at his side.

"Of course I am." I stand and run my hands through my hair. My stomach complains, and I turn my wrist to check the time on my tracker, only to remember it's gone. It was afternoon when we ate the rabbit, and now the moon is up. We're going to have to do something about our food situation tomorrow. Alder isn't always going to find wild game, and we have only four protein bars left.

"Do you know of any . . ." I turn to Alder. He's dead asleep.

I can still feel the plastic bag in my bra, the seeds almost weightless inside it. I'm going to do what I should have done yesterday before Alder woke up. Or undo what I did. Give some of the seeds back to Alder. Let the scavengers have a chance, however small. Of course I'll keep some. If anyone has a shot at defeating the blight, it's AgraStar, but why not hedge our bets? *"The more eyes on a problem, the better,"* Crake always said.

I watch Alder sleep. It's going to be harder this time. There's less room to move around in the small boathouse, and he's lying on his back, not his side. I wait until his breath slows and deepens.

I crawl forward and crouch on the narrow span of floor between the docking wells. His left pocket. That's where he keeps it. I sit close, not touching him, but near enough to feel the heat radiating off his body. I reach over, careful not to jostle him, and feel for the lip of his pocket. I pinch the pouch and pull it up, slow, careful. . . . Suddenly I become aware of my own breath, harsh and loud in the small space.

I swallow and get a better grip on the bag. Then I slide it out the rest of the way—slow, gentle, quiet.

I sit back, clutching the seeds to my chest. Alder never

has to know. AgraStar never has to know. All I have to do is—

"What are you doing?"

I snap to attention.

He sits up. "What is that?"

"Nothing." I rock back on my heels and stand in one quick motion.

He's wide awake now. "You were going to do something to me. What were you . . ." His eyes go first to the gun, then he slaps his pockets. He jumps up. "Give it back."

"I don't know what you're—"

Alder rushes me. I turn to run, but he grabs my hair. "Give it back! I know you have it."

I spin, trying to wrench myself free, and come face-to-face with him. His eyes narrow. I scowl back. "It's not what you think. I wasn't trying to—"

"Enough." Alder snatches the bag of seeds and shoves me back. I sprawl on the floor, shocked and winded. *I was trying to do the right thing.*

"I can't believe I trusted you." He stuffs the bag in his pocket. "Stupid. You're just another unthinking cog bitch, like all the rest of them."

"Don't say that." I stand. I hate that word. "I'm not—"

"Shut up. I don't care. You killed Eden."

"I—"

"You killed Eden!" he screams.

"And you killed Ellison!" I scream back. "You killed everyone I know. I had my whole life planned out, and you took that from me. You took everything from me!" I grab the front of his shirt and twist it in my fists.

"Go on," Alder says through his teeth. His face is wet. His chest heaves beneath my hand. "Do it. Kill me."

The words bring me back into my body. I'm not going to lose control. He can't make me. I let go of his shirt and back away.

"What, are you afraid?" Alder holds out his hands in mock surrender. "Don't want to take me on without your fences and your guns?"

I shake my head. My body is hot with anger. There's nothing I'd like better than to pound Alder's face in, and I'd probably win. I'm better trained, better fed, and just as angry. But it's what he wants, and I'm not going to give it to him.

"You're nothing." Alder spits. "Without that cog compound, you're nothing at all."

"What are you, then?" I pick up my backpack, trying to keep my voice calm. "Leeching off us? Nothing but bottom-feeders and parasites."

"We're free," Alder says. "More than you'll ever be. Even after all this, they've still got your mind. You'll never be anything but a cog."

"Better that than a shirk," I say, and shove out into the night. I've spent too long with Alder, been too soft. I've let him push me off track. I need to head southwest, to AgraStar, back to what I know. The moonlight hits me, and I run.

.11.

SILVER DOLLAR PLANT
LUNARIA

The forest gives way to a field, and I stop. I've been going west for an hour or so. The moon is full and bright above the tree line. I stare at the scrub and overgrown grass in front of me. Open space means no cover, nowhere to hide. I check left and right. The field is more than a field, now that I look closely. It's a long, wide break in the trees, as if someone clear-cut the whole tract of land at some point. A dull glint catches my eye. Railroad ties. Of course. AgraStar doesn't use the old rail lines, but our transport routes cross them, and I've seen their steel bones out on eradication missions a few times.

I adjust my pack and check my ammo. Something about the tracks raises the hairs on the back of my neck. It's been decades since anyone used freight trains. Shouldn't this whole area be overgrown with saplings and brambles? Unless someone has been clearing it . . . I step back and chew on my lip, looking for movement in the grass and shadows. Nothing. I don't like the idea of exposing myself and running across the tracks, but I don't have much choice. There's no other way to reach the safety of the thicket on the other side. Better to go now, when I have a little more cover than I would in daylight.

I dart out at a crouch, trying to keep my head below the grass and weeds. *Swift and silent.*

I'm nearing the other side. Only five yards, then two . . .

"Tempest!"

I hit the ground. What the hell?

"Tempest!" Alder hisses again. "Wait!"

I crawl the last few yards to the trees and hide behind a cluster of lunaria. Its round, paper-white leaves shine in the moonlight. I catch sight of Alder racing across the field, jumping the rails. *Idiot.* What's he doing?

A pair of headlights flash on. Alder freezes, caught in the high beams. An engine revs—a diesel roar breaking the night—and the lights lurch forward. Alder bolts, first toward me, then back in the direction he came from. Whoops and shouts rise above the engine. The vehicle jolts and jumps over the uneven terrain, careening after Alder. *Jackers.* They cut him off, circle him, drive him back into the open. I can't make out any faces, but it's men's voices taunting him as they let him run, then drive him back again. Shaved heads above the open-top jeep. M4 carbine rifles on their shoulders. They're playing with him.

I press my back against a tree and check my rounds again. What am I going to do? Me and a clumsy pistol versus a truck full of men with M4s that have probably been modded to be fully automatic? The math isn't good. If I had my rifle, my scope, a better vantage point, maybe. . . . The best I can do with a pistol is cause a distraction before they spot my muzzle flash and come after me. The image of that captured clearer, naked and covered in blood, flickers through my mind. I see her walking, the flames of the R&D facility rising behind her, the corn shriveling beneath her feet. *It's not real. It's only a story. You're mixing it all up.* My breath comes short and fast.

A burst of machine-gun fire echoes across the field. Alder is frozen in the headlights, but he hasn't fallen. He holds his hands above his head. One of the men climbs down from the jeep, his movements slow. I saw a swamp cat once on wilderness training—a mountain lion, Rosalie called it, even though there are no mountains for at least a hundred miles west of the compound. This man moves like that. Slow and sure. Dangerous, as if he's conserving his energy to strike.

He looms over Alder. I hear a muffled exchange, some kind of question, and Alder shakes his head. The man steps closer. Alder shakes his head again. The man raises the butt of his M4 and clocks Alder across the temple. Alder falls, a dark shape beneath the high beams. I clap a hand over my mouth.

The man who hit Alder points to the others and then to the woods. They pair off, two on one side of the jeep, two on the other, raise their rifles, and point them at the trees. *Shit.* At me.

They're pointing them at me. The clearing explodes with sound. Bullets rain against the trees and zip past my head. I scramble back on my hands and knees. A wide trunk. An oak. I throw myself behind it and hunch down, arms over my head, squeeze my eyes closed. *Hold still. Stay silent. Make yourself small.*

The gunfire stops. *Don't come into the woods. Please don't come into the woods.* I try to listen past the ringing in my ears. Shouting. Rustling. Laughter. Then car doors slamming. The engine guns to life.

I raise my head and draw my nine-millimeter. I peek out from behind the tree. The jeep's brake lights wash everything in red. I catch sight of something on the tailgate as it lurches over the railroad tracks and pulls away—a crudely drawn hand. I've seen that symbol before, but where?

Alder is nowhere to be seen.

My blood is ice. This is worse than AgraStar catching him. I could maybe have made things easier for him if it were one of our patrols, stopped them from killing him outright, the way he stopped his people from murdering me before Deacon Ward had her say. The scavengers and us, we both believe in some kind of order, some kind of justice. But these men . . . jackers. What are they going to do with him?

I step out of the trees and holster my weapon. I study the trail of flattened grass the jeep left behind. To the south, I make out two receding spots of red light. I can't let them have him. He's going to make it home, back to his people, the same as me. I break into a jog and follow the jeep's tracks.

The brick wall is ridiculously low. It must have been made for decoration, not defense, back during a time when that sort of thing made sense. CA TON WOOD, the rusted letters read. Smeared handprints surround the words. Past the sign, down an arrow-straight boulevard broken by weeds and potholes, stand rows of nearly identical two-story houses. The clapboard siding has fallen off in places, and the windows are dark. Kudzu and creeper vines have grown over some of them. Downed fir trees have crushed the roofs of others.

I crouch in the ditch across the street from the houses, trying to figure out my next move. If I were these men, I'd post guards, give them coms and rifles and have them watch the road. Which means I should approach from the side or the back, unless I want to be target practice.

I slink into the woods and circle around to a hill overlooking the houses from the northwest. *The hand.* Crake kept a file of the road jackers' signs and symbols. He used to make those of us training for eradication duty flash through them. A *V* with its wings bent like a bird for the Carrion Brothers. A wheel for the Blacktops. An eye with lashes like daggers for Las Zorras, one of the few all-female gangs. A smeared handprint, bloodred and dripping.

The Red Hand.

Las Zorras and the Carrions and most of the others, they're ruthless, but not cruel. You can bargain with them, give them something in exchange for your life. But AgraStar and the other company-states won't even negotiate with the Red Hand. If they're the ones who get you, you're counted dead. I sift through what little I remember from Crake's dossiers and cafeteria gossip. Pockets of them throughout the southeast. Homogenous—everyone is white, with shaved heads, tattooed with the same symbols, crooked crosses, numbers, lightning bolts. If there are Red Hand women, they don't go out on raids. Religious, but not like Alder's people. I feel sick.

I crest the hill above the development. From up here, I can see their whole compound. A cluster of houses built around a cul-de-sac are lit up. Floodlights and generators, men sitting on the hoods of cars, razor wire accordioned around the perimeter. I catch sight of the jeep, but not Alder. I'm guessing they've taken him inside. The surrounding streets are shadowed and deserted, dark buildings lined up like identical ghosts.

This is the stupidest thing I've ever done. I should go, run, and be glad it isn't me down in that compound. But the image of Alder caught in the high beams still burns against the back of my eyes. He was looking for me. Never mind that he was being an idiot. They never would have found him if he hadn't been looking for me. He would never have been looking for me if we hadn't fought. And we never would have fought if I hadn't stolen the seeds.

I check my pocket to make sure I still have them. Seth and all the other perimeter guards would laugh at me, trying to save a scavenger. But Seth and all the rest of them are dead.

I half crawl, half slide down the hill and approach the houses from the back. Dark windows watch me. The chains on a swing set creak in the breeze. The lights from the Red Hand base, several streets over, bleed up into the sky. I stick close to the walls and overgrown bushes, darting from house to house as I make my way closer to the lighted cul-de-sac. Every window could hide a lookout, a sniper. Every corner, a guard patrol. I keep my body low, my feet soft.

I spot the gutted frame of a car in the middle of the street, duck behind it for cover, and then dash to the next row of houses. I need an exit plan, a way out. Maybe I can steal the jeep? But they have other cars, and they outgun us. Better to sneak out, never let them see us in the first place.

I peer into the darkness. Someone has built an enormous chain-link cage in the dead grass, top open to the sky. The fencing is twelve feet high, and each side is twice as long. A tennis court? We have one of those—*had* one of those—near the living quarters at the R&D facility. Someone has strapped floodlights to the corners, but they're dark. A single cloud drifts over the moon, deepening the shadows around me. Something thick and uneven covers the court's floor. I creep closer. The gate is padlocked.

Gravel crunches under my foot. One of the shapes on the court sits up.

I suck in a breath. It lifts its head and lets out a low growl that raises the hair on the back of my neck. Eyes flash phosphorescent green. Other shapes shift around it, and then more eyes wink on in the dark, more throaty rumbles join the first. *Dogs.* They erupt in barks and snarls. One of them lunges at the fence, eyes rolling, white foam frothing around its mouth. I stumble back. The others throw themselves after the first, their eyes wild. There are dozens of them.

Rabid. They're rabid.

I run. Houses flash past, blurs of white in the moonlight. Behind me, the floodlights stagger on, and shouts echo across the empty streets. I throw myself behind a garden shed, panting. What the hell? Why is the Red Hand keeping rabid dogs? I close my eyes and pull my knees close to my chest. Crake had me put down a raccoon with rabies one time. It had that same vacant, glassy look in its eyes. *"You're doing it a kindness,"* Crake said.

I peek out. Several men with shaved heads are down by the court, one of them inspecting the chain link, the others fanning out with flashlights. I pull my head back and press myself flat against the shed.

"Anything?" someone yells.

A beam of light sweeps the house beside me. "Nah." The light moves the other way. "Probably just a possum or something. They're all worked up 'cause they're hungry."

"You hungry, huh?" The fence rattles. "Are you some hungry dogs?"

The snarling and barking start up again, savage and deafening.

"Stop riling 'em!" another man shouts over the racket.

"They've got a job to do. You'll wear 'em out."

"You hear that?" The first man says to the dogs. "You're getting fed soon. But first we're gonna have some fun."

Something about the way he says it sends a chill through me. *Alder.* What are they planning to do?

I crawl away from the shed and work my way back toward the cul-de-sac. *Slow. Quiet. Invisible.* I strain to hear past the rushing in my ears.

A makeshift barricade of razor wire, old cars, and fencing surrounds the houses on the cul-de-sac. Floodlights face out, forming a perimeter, as bright and dangerous as day. There are six houses on the circle, a hodgepodge of trucks and armored cars parked on the curb. Music blares from one of the cars, all thumping bass and shrieking guitars. A hoarse, gravelly voice shouts along. Several men sit on the hood of a low-slung sedan with reinforced sides, drinking and pitching empty bottles over the razor wire. One of them has his shirt off. An enormous cross in a circle covers his pale back, with numbers flanking it—an 88 on his left shoulder blade, a 14 on his right. A chill runs down my spine. Crake might have known the exact meaning of those marks, but even I can tell it isn't anything good.

Thump. Something hits the window of the darkened house above me. I freeze. Isn't this place empty? It's outside their perimeter. Slowly I lift my head. *It's nothing. Nothing. Only an animal. Only the wind* . . . I look up. There's a man's face pressed against the glass several feet above me. I stumble back, biting off a cry. He moans—a low, animal noise—and slaps his palm against the window. He's looking at me, but I don't think he sees me. His eyes are vacant and drool seeps down his chin. *Like the dogs. Exactly like the dogs.*

I circle around to the front of the house and peer in through the big bay window beside the door. Bodies cover the floor, some of them moving, some of them not. A faint odor of rot and feces seeps through the walls. Two people stand silhouetted against the glare of the floodlights bleeding in through the back windows. One of them sways in place, like a pine tree rocking in the wind. The other stands stock-still, a statue listing to one side. I cover my mouth. *The dogs . . . all these people . . .*

Rabies. Don't they have the vaccine? With all those dogs around, they must know the risk. Fever, hallucination, dying of thirst but afraid to drink. Then death. Unless . . . I steady myself against the house. The dogs. *"But first we're gonna have some fun."*

Sadistic fucks. They wouldn't let their own people suffer like this. These must be prisoners, captives. They're exposing them on purpose. Is this what they do to people who don't cooperate? Or who don't have anything left to offer?

The moaning starts again. A woman this time, though the noise she makes is barely human. Another voice joins her, then another, and another. *Thump. Thump. Thump.* Hands on walls. Hands on glass.

I run.

.12.

YELLOW NUTSEDGE

CYPERUS ESCULENTUS

More clouds roll in, snuffing out the moon. I work my way along the empty streets and crouch in the shadows when a Red Hand patrol rolls by. I'm not afraid anymore. I'm angry, and they are going to pay.

I stalk up to the dog pen. A low growl rises from the pack. No hesitating. Time for a distraction. I raise my gun, aim it at the padlock looped through the gate, and fire.

The night explodes in howls and snarls as the dogs burst through the opening. I sprint around the closest house just as its lights snap on and two men tumble out the front door.

"Hey!" I hear behind me. Then, "Shi—" The word dissolves into a wet scream, a wild snarl, and a burst of gunfire.

I glance back. One of the men is down already, the body of a dog slumped over him. The other is turning, bringing his M4 to bear on the oncoming rush of teeth and fur. Then one of the dogs leaps for his throat, and the pack overwhelms him. Engines rev to life and shouts fill the night. I put on a burst of speed. Three lots down, there is an empty house with an unlocked door. I made sure of it. Now I have to reach it.

A growl, the clicking of toenails on the street. *Shit.* I push myself faster. Ten feet to the door, seven, five, two . . . I crash into it, fumbling for the knob, fall into the open foyer, and twist around as the dog leaps over the front step, teeth bared. I kick the door and it swings shut right as the dog's body collides with it. The door rattles. I can hear the animal throwing itself against it, scrabbling with its nails.

I'm up again, running down the dark hallway, through the kitchen, out the back door into the glare of the floodlights. I switch my pistol's safety on, tuck it into my holster, and run at a crouch along the barricade at the heart of the Red Hand compound. Shouts, barks, and gunshots echo over from the next street.

One guard stands at a break in the barricade, his back to me. *Quiet.* I swallow.

I'm on him in a second, my arm around his throat, choking off any sound he might make before he can fully turn and see me. He's bigger than me, but I let my weight go dead. He stumbles back and falls on me, but I hold tight, even when he lands on my leg, driving his elbow into my thigh. His eyes bulge, his face reddens, the cords in his neck strain. He smells like beer and burned plastic, sweat sticking his skin to mine. I tighten my grip and look away. He flails against me silently, arches his back, and then, at last, he falls slack.

I drop him and run to the house on my right, the one with the open-top jeep parked on the patch of dirt out front. Alder's rifle is still upright behind the backseat. I think about grabbing it, but my nine-millimeter will be better in close quarters, if it comes to that. I dash up the steps and push open the front door. The smell of diesel hits me, thick and sweet. Voices drift down from upstairs, but the main floor seems empty. Flags I don't recognize hang over the windows, muting the floodlights. Someone has punched a hole in the drywall. Boxes of liquor and ammunition are stacked against the wall, alongside fuel cans.

I grab a liquor bottle like a club and go up the stairs. Better not to shoot if I don't have to. Gunfire is going to bring every man in the camp running. A hallway branches in two directions—three doors to the left, two to the right. Muffled shouts rise and fall behind one, on the left. I creep toward it, bottle raised. It swings open silently, and I freeze.

Two boys—scrawny, maybe ten or eleven, with smears of dirt on their clothes—stand in the far corner of the room, shoving and screaming at each other.

"Fuck you, shithead!"

"No, fuck you, you fucking shithead!"

A toddler dressed in a man's filthy undershirt sits on the

floor between the boys and me, playing with a mechanic's wrench. He—she?—twists around to look at me with big brown eyes and then turns back to the wrench. The boys don't notice me at all. I back away, pulling the door closed behind me.

The next room holds a pair of bare mattresses and several sleeping bags crumpled in the corners. The one after that is a bathroom, with a double-doored metal cabinet shoved into the alcove where the shower used to be. I make myself breathe. *Dammit.* What if he's not in here? What if he's in a different house, or they took him someplace when the dogs broke out?

I try the first door on the right. There's a woman on a mattress in the middle of the floor, under a heap of blankets, a cluster of empty bottles near her head.

"Erik, I told you all that bullshit is hurting my skull." She starts to get up, and a current of fear bolts through me.

But she falls back on the mattress. "Keep the goddamn door shut, I said!" she shouts.

I move to pull it closed, but in that moment, the last door to my right flies open, and a man bursts out. Shaved head, puffy, bluish circles under his eyes.

"I swear to God, Karlee, if you don't stop complaining—"

He stops dead when he sees me. All the air goes out of my lungs. I swing the bottle. He ducks, but I'm faster. It catches him across the side of the head and explodes in a shower of shards and blood. He sags, and I bring my knee up and catch him in the throat. Alcohol stings my nose and the sores on my hands.

He crumples against the wall, leaving a smear of blood across the plaster.

"Erik, what the hell—"

I whirl around, pulling the gun and flipping the safety off in one movement. The woman stands in the doorway, staring at the man's body, her skin pale and her brown hair wild. Heavy smudges of eyeliner ring her eyes. She sways a little on her feet.

"Get back in the room," I say, quiet and calm. If the younger boys hear me, if they come running . . . I swallow. I don't want to have to do that.

She lifts her eyes to me and narrows them. "You little bitch," she spits. "You're going to pay when my boys find you. They're going to turn you over to the dogs."

"First they have to find me." I move my finger down to the trigger. "So get back in the room."

She takes an unsteady step backward.

"Now sit on the mattress." I gesture with the gun. "Put your hands behind you."

She complies. I switch the safety on again and scan the room. There's an old belt in the corner, next to an empty coffee tin that smells like urine. I snatch up the belt and kneel behind her.

"Don't test me," I say, looping it around her wrists. "I don't want to hurt—"

The woman slams her head back, into my nose. I hear the crunch of cartilage and taste blood, and then she's on me, raking at my face with her fingernails.

I roll away and aim a kick at her side. It connects. She stumbles, but then she's up again, fast as a cottonmouth. She lunges. I bring up my elbow and catch her across the face. We topple over in a pile of arms and legs. My back hits the wall, and suddenly I'm fighting blind, gouging with my thumbnails and pulling hair. Then I'm on her back, pinning her to the floor. I twist one arm behind her, grab her hair, and yank her head back. She screams.

"Quiet!" I press up on her arm. "I swear I'll break it."

She stops struggling. I let go of her hair and grab the belt again, then cinch it tight around her wrists. I prop her against the wall.

She spits at me. One of her eyes is swelling closed. "You'll be sorry," she pants. "They'll make you one of the dead men."

I grab a sock from the floor, stuff it into her mouth, and rip a strip of fabric from one of the shirts piled by the door to make a gag.

I pick up my gun. "Not if I make them dead men first."

One more room to check. I leave her there and push open the last door.

A pop-up hurricane lantern stands in the center of a soiled carpet. On the far wall, someone has painted an eagle, its outspread wings feathering into fingers, as if a thousand hands dipped in blood have given it form.

A moan. I spin around. Alder hangs by his hands in the closet, a length of rubber hose looped over the metal clothing rod and tied around his wrists.

"Alder!" I run to him, try to lift him up, but he's dead-weight, barely conscious. A bruise the size and color of a plum has pushed one of his eyes shut.

A fresh wave of anger surges through me, and with it, a shock of adrenaline. I storm back out to the hall, kick the Red Hand guard over onto his back, and kneel down to search his body. He wears a double-barreled, sawed-off shotgun in a holster and a stupidly flashy knife with a blade formed to look like a lick of silver flame. Whatever. If it's sharp, it will do.

I run back to Alder, slide the blade between the hose and the rod, and start sawing. Either the guard in the hall was an idiot, or he kept his blade dull on purpose.

"Tempest?" Alder blinks at me through his bruises and matted hair. "What are you doing here?"

"Saving your ass." I go back to sawing. "Obviously."

He shakes his head. "You've got to get out of here. They'll come back. I can't—"

"Alder." My voice is harsh. We're short on time. "Can you stand?"

"I think so," he says.

"Good." I pull the knife up one last time.

He nearly falls, but catches himself against the wall. I grab one of his arms, drape it over my shoulder, and drag him out of the closet.

"Tempest." His voice breaks. Outside, diesel engines rumble like thunder.

I stop and look at him. Patches of blisters and raw pink burns cover his arms and throat. The urge to bash in someone's face—whoever did this to him—floods my body.

"The seeds," he croaks. "They took them."

Guilt washes over me. There's no time to explain. Brakes shriek. They're coming.

"Let's get out of here." I guide him to the door. "Quiet and quick as you can, okay?"

We step over the guard, descend the stairs, and make our way to the kitchen with its sliding glass doors.

The doorknob rattles and the front door swings open just as I push back the sliding door.

I shove the knife into Alder's hands and palm my own pistol. "You with me?"

Alder blinks again, a little more clear-eyed, and nods.

"Can you run?"

He nods again.

"Okay," I say. "Run."

I bolt for the closest break in the fence, a wedge-shaped opening at the base. The links scrape my back as I wriggle through. I turn to help Alder.

"Hey!" A man dashes out into the yard. "Got 'em running! They're running!"

I tug Alder up, and we sprint for the dark houses. Two more streets, and then we'll hit woods. We can lose them there.

More shouts behind us, and the sound of gunfire. I race around a house and dart across the street, boots pounding against the asphalt. I hear Alder behind me, breathing hard, stumbling, but still moving.

Something flashes across the corner of my vision. A low, wet growl and the solid slap of bodies colliding, and then an ugly, animal scream. I turn back.

"Tempest! Get it off me!" Alder shouts. A dog crouches over him. It has Alder's arm clamped between its teeth, shaking the limb as if it could rip it from his body.

No. I feel the word through my body. *Rabies. Hydrophobia. Madness. Death.* Time slows and the night snaps into focus. I raise my gun and square the dog's torso in my sights. One heartbeat. *Breathe.* And I fire.

The shot rings out through the compound, sharp and clear. The dog slumps over Alder. The engines rev again, and shouts fill the night. We're out of time. I've pinpointed our position.

I shove the dog off Alder and help him up. Blood runs down his forearm, welling from the deep puncture wounds. He sucks a breath through his teeth and clutches his arm to his chest. He needs a tourniquet, but there's no time. We run for the trees, Alder struggling to keep pace with me. The memory of those people in the abandoned house, dead eyed and howling, smeared with their own waste—will that be him? Is it always a sure thing?

I turn back, lock his arm around my shoulder, and hurry

into the woods. Lights sweep the tree trunks behind us.

"Keep moving," I whisper.

His breath comes short and uneven as we hobble deeper into the trees. "Tempest . . . ," he gasps.

I angle us north, where a scrubby patch of land slopes up to the overlook. "Only a little farther. To the top of the rise." We'll be able to see them coming from there.

Alder stumbles, but I haul him back to his feet. He's getting heavier, leaning more on me as we struggle uphill. I slip, too, and then right myself. The burst of adrenaline is wearing off, leaving me weak and shaky. We aren't going to make it to the top, not like this.

I stop and scan the hillside. There. A dip in the terrain, shielded by an overgrown mat of sedge. I pull Alder behind its cover. He collapses, breathing hard, sweat glistening over his face and neck.

"Stay here." I raise his wounded arm above his head. "Keep this elevated. I'll be back."

"Tempest." He catches the edge of my shirt. His eyes are wide and black in the dim. "They got the seeds. They found them—"

"Alder . . ."

"They took them. I was so stupid. I came running after you, and they—"

"Alder!"

I hang my head and sigh, then reach into my pocket and pull out the bag of blight-resistant seeds.

He stares at them. "But I . . . I don't understand."

"I wasn't trying to steal them from you. I took them on my first watch, back when we were camping in that ruined house."

He presses his lips together. His skin is ghostly pale, and he looks like he's going to be sick.

"That's what I was trying to say earlier." I look at him through the hair falling across my face. "I was trying to give them back."

Alder frowns, and he opens his mouth to say something.

"Don't," I say. "Just stay here, okay? Keep quiet. I'll be back."

I run the rest of the way up the hill at a crouch, my ears pricked for engines, or the click of a round being chambered. I grab my backpack from where I stashed it, sling it over my shoulder, and stare down at the compound. Beams of flashlights and headlights flare and weave through the woods below.

I half run, half slide back down the hill to Alder. He lies still, eyes closed.

"Alder." I shake him.

His eyes fly open and he sits up, chest heaving, cradling his arm.

"It's okay. It's me." I pull a roll of gauze and the tube of antiseptic from my pack. In a better world, we'd wash his arm in clean running water. But we're here, so I squeeze the last of the ointment onto his wounds and start wrapping the gauze fast and tight around his forearm.

He watches me. "That was one of their dogs. The ones they keep penned up."

I nod.

"You let them out, didn't you?"

I hesitate, then close my eyes. "I had to create a distraction. To get you out."

He swallows and nods. "They have—"

"Rabies." I look up at him. "I know."

His other hand begins to shake, and he balls it into a fist. "I'm going to die."

"No," I say. "There's a vaccine. If we get it in time—"

"How much time?"

I grimace. "Seventy-two hours, I think. Three days."

He laughs and rolls his eyes skyward. "And who has it? Them?" He waves at the compound below.

"I can go back in," I say. "I can find it. I—"

"No. You're not going back in there. You saw what they did . . . what they do to people. That's worse than suicide."

"They aren't the only ones with vaccine," I say. "Any settlement, any company farm is going to have it on hand. We just have to talk someone into giving it to us." It's only a little thing. One dose and done, not like in the old days when it took weeks of shots to cure.

He snorts. "With what?"

"I don't know. We'll figure it out. We'll—"

"Wait!" Alder grabs my arm. "Do you hear that?"

I turn my head and listen. A diesel engine is approaching,

growing louder and louder as it climbs the hill.

"Down!" I push both of us flat behind the sedge.

The jeep rocks its way into view, headlights illuminating the weeds. I press my face to the dirt and count. *One Mississippi. Two Mississippi. Three Mississippi.* It passes us, crawling higher, to the overlook.

The overlook. *Shit.* They'll be able to see everything from there. Including us.

I nudge Alder. "Come on."

"What?" Even in the dark, I can tell he's looking at me like I'm crazy.

"They'll see us," I whisper. "We've got to move."

I scramble up the hill on my hands and knees without waiting to see if he follows. A plan is forming in my head. A truly terrible, ill-conceived plan.

The jeep reaches the top of the hill. I stop and flatten myself against the dirt, and watch as two men climb out, rifles slung over their shoulders. They begin a sweep of the ridge, walking past the spot where my bag was stowed a few minutes ago.

Alder crawls up behind me, panting. "What are you doing?"

"We're never going to make it on foot." I track the men's movement against the tree line. They're farther from the vehicle than I am. Now's my chance.

I look over my shoulder at Alder. "Stay here. Be ready."

"Tempest, don't—"

I jump up and race for the jeep. My feet thump the ground and my breath sounds impossibly loud in the night air. Far off to my right, a faint blue glow is bleeding from the horizon. Morning.

The driver's side door is missing, so I boost myself onto the runner board and slide into the driver's seat. I start to reach beneath the steering column to pull out the wires, and stop. They've left the key in the ignition.

"Thank you," I whisper, and turn the key. The engine revs.

"Hey!" I barely make out the shout over the engine. A bullet pings off the roll bar, less than a foot above my head.

I wrench the wheel, stomp on the gas, and take off down the hill. Bullets patter against the back of the vehicle. I glance behind me. One of the men is kneeling, taking aim, and the other is running wildly after me.

I jam on the brakes when I catch sight of Alder. "Get in!"

He pulls open the passenger door and jumps in. Then we're off again, careening down the hill, weaving, me crouched over the steering wheel and Alder slouched low in his seat. I head west, in what I hope is the direction of a road, leaving the Red Hand and its dead men in our dust.

.13.

CRABGRASS
DIGITARIA SANGUINALIS

We drive west through abandoned fields. I keep an eye on the cracked rearview mirror. Still no headlights behind us. We have maybe a five-minute head start, if the guards on the hill ran straight back to their base—maybe more if the dogs were still causing chaos. But the grass is high enough to slap the jeep's front grill, and we're leaving a flattened trail behind us. We might as well be carrying a strobing LED sign saying WE WENT THIS WAY!

I spot a weed-cracked blacktop road and take it. It doesn't matter where it goes, so long as it leads away from Red Hand territory. We'll figure out where we are later.

Alder slumps, silent and pale, in the passenger seat.

"You okay?" I glance at him and then up at the mirror again.

"Fantastic," he says. "Never better."

"We should get off the road." I scan the fields. The first touches of dawn are lightening the sky behind us. "Hide out. See if they're following us."

"We should ditch the jeep," Alder says.

"Not yet." The blacktop is broken and rocky. I grip the steering wheel tighter. "We'll never outrun them without it." *Or find help.*

"What about there?" Alder points to a barren stretch of land to our right. Bare, hard-packed dirt spreads out for acres, ending against a wall of kudzu. We could cross without leaving tracks and hide the jeep in the vines.

I pull off the road and drive across the empty field. The first rays of sun hit the hood as we near the kudzu forest.

I lean forward and squint. "What is that?"

Several long, low shapes project from the woods, perfectly parallel and shrouded in vines.

"Buildings?" Alder says.

I slow. Beside the kudzu-draped structures are two huge square troughs cut into the ground, like shallow dirt swimming pools.

I let the jeep roll to a stop. "What the hell is this place?"

"Does it matter?" Alder looks tired. "It's deserted and off the road, like you wanted."

We circle around the back of one of the buildings. Alder wanders toward it as I pull down vines and arrange them over the jeep.

"Tempest, look." He pushes back a bunch of kudzu,

revealing faded letters on the side of the building. FAIRFIELD HOG FARM.

I peer through the filmy windows. Empty concrete stalls line the room, with a long gutter running down the center aisle.

"Factory farm?" I look at Alder. "I wonder why it closed down?"

"Maybe it couldn't compete with AgraStar."

I cut my eyes at him. "AgraStar doesn't trade in livestock."

"Apex does," he says.

"What, like they have some kind of trade deal?" I say. "We'll make sure there are no pig farms in our territory if you make sure there's no one growing corn in yours?"

Alder just looks at me.

"You can't be serious." I stare back at him. Why would Apex care about a few pig farms in AgraStar territory? It would be nothing next to what we import from them.

"Believe what you want." He turns away. "I'm going to see if there's a way inside."

I follow Alder to the front building, where we have a clear view east across the fields to the road. Chains and padlocks hang on the doors, but one of the windows is boarded up with rotten plywood that falls away with one sharp tug. I climb through and help Alder in after me.

Morning sunlight filters in between gaps in the kudzu—little glimmers of gold. Alder coughs in the dust stirred by our footsteps.

I hold out my water bottle to him. "Here."

He shakes his head.

"You're not thirsty?" I frown. Rabies victims stop drinking, but he can't be having symptoms yet.

"I just want to lie down," he says.

"Suit yourself." I stare out at the road through the vines. I didn't notice earlier, but a few patches of crabgrass have broken through the dirt. When I look back at Alder, he's lying in the middle of the floor, eyes closed, injured arm held to his chest. He's bled through his bandages.

I turn back to the window and prod my nose gingerly. I'm not sure if it's broken, but it's definitely swollen. A truck appears on the road, then another, and another, all crawling along slow enough to scan the countryside. The Red Hand. I duck below the window, even though there's no way they can see me.

Breathe, Tempest, breathe.

If they turn this way, we need to be ready to run. I peek out again. The last vehicle in the caravan rolls slowly out of sight. I let out a breath and rest my forehead against the sill. There's no telling how far they'll go or when they'll be back.

"You awake?" I ask Alder.

He nods.

"They passed us by," I say. "I'm going to see if I can find more water."

Alder doesn't answer.

"You think there's a creek nearby?"

Alder doesn't open his eyes. "How should I know?"

I bite back a retort. I'd be in a shitty mood, too, if I'd been tortured and then attacked by a rabid dog.

"Stay here, okay?" I say. "Get some rest. I'll be back soon."

I head south toward a dip in the landscape, hugging the tree line as I go. The sun is up, but the light is still soft and the mosquitoes haven't come out yet. The trees creak under the kudzu. Alder needs help. Painkillers. Vaccine. We both need food and water. But I don't even know exactly where we are. Somewhere west of the Catawba and east of the highway that runs south past my compound to Atlanta. The nearest AgraStar holdings are north, in Charlotte, and GAP-12, somewhere west of the highway, in the foothills. Charlotte is out—that's back the way we came, back toward the blight. But if we can reach the highway and I can remember which exit to take . . .

I stop. A smell travels on the breeze. Charcoal and meat cooking. My stomach clenches and my mouth waters. A haze of blue smoke drifts from the woods ahead.

People.

I hesitate. It could be scavengers, maybe even the Deacon and her caravan. But it could just as easily be another Red Hand encampment. I touch my nine-millimeter. Whoever they are, they could have medicine, vaccine, a sat phone. Alder isn't going to make it without help. I have to risk it.

I push aside a train of kudzu and step into the forest. It's cooler in here, dim and thick with insects. I try to walk quietly, but it's next to impossible. Half the trees around me are dead, leaning against one another or downed and reclaimed by vines. I follow the smell of smoke to a narrow creek, small enough to jump over. I pause and refill my water bottle, then push on, into a wide meadow.

A house stands on the far end, encircled by a razor-wire fence, with solar panels arrayed across its tin roof. Smoke pours from a close-topped grill in the yard. The wind shifts, and suddenly the cooking smells are gone, replaced by a stench of rotten meat and manure. I turn away and gag.

What the hell is this place? A farm of some kind? I spit bile into the undergrowth and wipe my eyes. The farms we saw on eradication duty kind of looked like this, but they had more land, and they weren't hidden in the middle of a forest. I creep closer. There are pigs rooting around behind the wire—no, hogs, huge and hairy. A pinkish moat surrounds the property. The closer I get, the stronger the rotten smell. That water—it's coming from that pink water.

I fight the nausea building in my throat. The nervous hope I had curdles into a brick of pure anxiety.

Keep it together. Just because their land smells like warm death doesn't mean they're as vicious as the Red Hand. I step away from the cover of trees and into the clearing. A morning mist hangs above the moat. There's an enormous metal box of some sort built into the fence, like a drawbridge. And there's something inside it, something moving, something I can't quite make out. Warning flares go off in my brain.

"Hello?" I call. "Is anyone there?"

A sallow-faced man steps out from behind the house, wearing a blood-stained apron and rubber gloves. He stops when he sees me and unslings a rifle from his back.

"What d' you want?"

I hold out my hands to show I'm not going for my weapon.

"My . . . my friend," I say. "He got attacked by a dog. Please, I know it's a long shot, but do you have any rabies vaccine? Or a sat phone?"

"Maybe." He lowers his rifle. "What'll you give me for it?"

I scramble to inventory what we have. The jeep, my gun, the seeds. We can't afford to give up any of those. And I doubt our last few protein bars are worth anything.

"Information," I say. "You know the AgraStar compound north of here? SCP-52?"

He steps closer to the fence. "What about it?"

"There was an attack," I say. "An accident. Something killed all the crops, and it's spreading. Coming this way. You have to leave, go south, before it reaches here."

His face hardens and he laughs. "Interesting story you've got there." He saunters toward the drawbridge. The thing inside bangs against the metal. "Pretty convenient."

I take a step back. "What do you mean?"

"Well, you're one of them." He gestures at my clothes. "AgraStar. You think I don't know they hate people like me signing no contracts, living free? You think this is the first time they've tried to scare me off my land?"

"It's not about that—"

"Everything's about that, darlin'." He pulls a linchpin from some sort of wheeled contraption by the drawbridge. The metal box shudders.

"Now, I'm going to have to ask you to leave." He raises a whistle hanging from a chain around his neck.

"Wait," I plead. "I'm telling the truth. My friend needs help. He's not AgraStar. He's just a scavenger, like you."

The man goes still. "Scavenger, huh? Is that what I am?"

"I mean . . . no." *Dammit, Tempest.* "He's not signed to anyone. He's free, like you said."

"All right," the man says. "I'm going to count to ten, and then I want you gone."

"Please," I say. "Look, what about my gun? I can trade you that. Just to use a sat phone. Isn't that worth it?"

"Ten," he says. "Nine, eight, seven . . ."

I step back, hands still held up. "We have a truck. A jeep."

"Six." He starts to turn the wheel. "Five, four, three . . ."

The thing in the box lets out a low, guttural growl.

"I'm leaving." I stumble over my own feet as I back away, and catch myself. "Please . . ."

". . . two, one." The man turns the wheel.

The front end of the box opens with a metallic squeal, slowly lowering to form a bridge over the moat. Two eyes flash in the shadows.

I stand frozen in the middle of the clearing, staring into the depths of the box. The man puts the whistle to his lips and blows a two-note tone. An animal lunges from the darkness, huge and muscled, its ribs visible through its striped hide. *Holy shit . . .*

Instinct kicks in, and I turn and run. I can hear it behind me, gaining, paws slapping the ground. A tiger. How does this guy have a fucking tiger? I crash through the tree line and fight my way through the undergrowth. The creek opens up beneath me. I glance back and catch a flash of white muzzle and claws, and trip.

I splash down into the creek. The tiger leaps through the space where I was mere seconds before and lands on the opposite bank. I stagger up and pull my gun. The animal rounds on me, ears flattened, lips pulled to show its teeth.

I fire. It screams and startles back. I chamber another round and brace myself, panting. Anyone could have heard that shot for miles around. If the Red Hand is in range, I've just sent up a beacon. The tiger stares at me, eyes dilated and a single bloody paw raised.

"Get out of here!" I shout. My wilderness training is coming back to me. What to do if you come across a mountain lion. Make yourself big. Hold the animal's gaze. Be as loud as you can. Hopefully the same thing works on tigers. "Go on!"

It snarls and slinks back a step.

I raise my arms above my head and look the tiger in the eye. "Get away! Leave me alone!"

Far off, the two-note whistle sounds again. The tiger turns

its head toward the noise and, with a snarl, limps off along the creek. I stand with my back against the bank, watching it go and willing my heart to stop straining against my chest.

When I'm sure it's gone, I race back through the woods and out into the sunshine. Did anyone hear? Is the Red Hand turning around to find us this very moment? Is the tiger behind me somewhere, waiting to pounce? I've heard stories about people who used to keep exotic animals for pets or run private zoos, in the old days, before AgraStar put an end to that kind of insanity, but I always thought those were stories about how broken everything was before. Not warnings about what might still be out there.

I meet Alder outside the building. He staggers toward me, still cradling his arm against his chest.

"What happened?" His eyes are wide, with dark circles beneath them. "I heard a gunshot."

"No time." I hurry to the jeep. "We've got to move."

"But the Red Hand—"

"We have to risk it," I say, yanking the vines away from the jeep. "We can't stay here."

Alder slides into the passenger seat without another word. I jump behind the wheel and pull out onto the dirt field, trailing lengths of kudzu behind us.

.14.

CLOVER
TRIFOLIUM REPENS

The road rolls bright and cracked beneath us as we ride south through the midday heat. It's obvious no clearers have stopped on this stretch of highway in months. Weeds and trees have grown in, thick and dangerous, right up to the lip of the road. Excellent cover for an ambush. One of the jeep's tires is blown, making a rhythmic whapping sound against the asphalt, but we don't have a spare. It doesn't matter if I warp the rims, anyway. We're going to have to ditch the jeep when we run out of gas. I'm just hoping I recognize the turnoff for GAP-12 before that happens.

We haven't seen the Red Hand caravan all morning, but then, we haven't seen any AgraStar convoys, either. And even if we do, it's not like they'll hand over corn diesel out of the kindness of their hearts. Best-case scenario, they'd take us captive and I could talk them into using some of their vaccine reserves on Alder. More likely, they'd shoot us on sight, especially with a Red Hand symbol emblazoned on the side of our vehicle. That's what I was trained to do. Not that I'm complaining. If nothing else, the jeep has helped put some miles between us and the front edge of the blight.

I glance at the fuel gauge, and then over at Alder. He's slumped against the passenger-side door, eyes closed. Sweat slicks his forehead, and his skin is greenish pale. We found a bottle of some sort of yellow rotgut in the glove compartment, and I talked him into drinking some of it, then splashing the rest over his wounds. He threw up after that, and now the cab smells like alcohol and vomit, but at least he knocked himself out.

I squint against the glare. My eyes feel like they're full of sand, and all the bruises I've collected have flared from a background ache to insistent pain. I should have told Alder to save some of the rotgut for me. I spot a break in the trees and pull off the road, into a sort of natural alley carpeted with clover and overhung by oaks and pines. The moment we pass into the shade, the knots in my spine begin to unravel. I'm too tired to be afraid. I sit with the engine running for a moment, numb with relief, before I kill the motor and let the silence wash over me.

Alder stirs. "Where are we?"

"Eighty miles northeast of Atlanta," I say. We passed one

of the old, faded highway signs a few miles back. "Give or take."

I reach behind the seats and pull out our one remaining water bottle, half full and warm. I hold it out to Alder. "Here."

He shakes his head.

"Come on." I jiggle it at him so the water sloshes against the sides. "You've got to want to wash out your mouth, at least." I look pointedly at the empty liquor bottle lying at his feet.

"No." He looks at me, dead serious, deep gray circles under his eyes. "You shouldn't waste that on me."

My throat catches. So that's what this is about. "You don't know—"

"Yes, I do. There's no point pretending we don't know what's going to happen." He doesn't sound angry, only tired. Somehow, that makes it worse.

"There's still time, if we can find a vaccine," I say. Three days. Seventy-two hours. Or more like sixty-five now, but still. Almost three days.

Alder snorts. "And who's going to give it to us? The Red Hand?" He nods back the way we came.

"AgraStar could," I say quietly.

Alder gives me sharp look.

"I'm only listing our options," I say quickly. "What about your people? Do you have any settlements outside Atlanta? Allies?"

Alder shakes his head. "There're some caravaners to the

south we know, but they move around. No one wants to dig in too close to the heart of a company."

"What about your Latebra Congress? If we found another satellite phone or a different way to contact them, could they get help to us?"

"Yes." Alder presses his fingers against his mouth, and then shakes his head. "Maybe. But we don't have a sat phone."

I huff, frustrated. "What about the Deacon? Don't you at least have a guess where they might have gone?"

Alder looks away, out at the deep green shadows of the forest around us. "She would have picked someplace remote, but we didn't have enough diesel to get us out of AgraStar territory entirely. Sea islands off the east coast, maybe. Or west, someplace deep in the Smokies. Maybe even down as far as the Everglades." He shakes his head. "Nowhere we can reach on what we have left in that tank."

Deep in the green, a cricket pulses.

"We have to do something," I say. "We have to try."

"It's not worth it."

Pressure builds behind my eyes and in my throat. I shove myself out of the cab and stomp away, crushing the clover beneath my boots. How can he just give up? And how could I let this happen? It's my fault. I should have come up with a better distraction. Something that didn't involve the dogs. And if I weren't so stupid, so caught up in making sure AgraStar was the one to figure out what to do with the seeds, I wouldn't have taken them from him in the first place.

I kick a fallen log, knocking away the rotten bark. If I were back at home, back on the compound, I would run or go out to the firing range until I had myself under control again. But I'm not. I'm here. And Alder's going to die, and it will be my fault.

I rub angrily at my eyes. *No.* He won't. Not if I can help it. Maybe he's given up, but I haven't.

I storm back to the jeep. He's lying on the ground beside it, his good hand splayed out in the grass, his wounded arm tucked beside his chest. His eyes are closed.

I grab the water bottle and stand over him. "Drink this."

He opens his eyes. "Tempest . . ."

"No." I stamp my foot. "Get up. You're going to drink this."

He sits up awkwardly. "You're the one who's going to need it."

"Alder." I grit my teeth. "If you don't drink the damn water, I'm going to have to go back to my original plan of murdering you."

He cracks a ghost of a smile.

I flop down next to him, exhausted, my back against the jeep. The clover is cool, alive.

"Okay." He unscrews the cap. "I'll make you a deal. You drink half, I drink half."

I roll my eyes and snag the bottle from his hands. "Fine." I tilt it back and down half the water in a few gulps. It's warm as tea, but that doesn't matter to my cracked lips and aching throat.

I wipe my mouth and hand the bottle back. "Your turn."

Alder laughs once, low, and sips. I lean back against the wheel well. We sit in silence while he finishes the water.

"Did you ever make chains out of these?" Alder runs his hand over the tops of the white flowers dotting the clover. "When you were a kid?"

I frown at him. "No."

"Really?" He plucks a flower and looks at me like I'm the crazy one.

"Really," I say, pulling my own flower. But as I do, something hazy flashes in the back of my mind. A clover flower with a long stem wrapped around my finger like a ring. *"Look, Papi!"* I blink.

Alder pierces a hole in the stem with his thumbnail, plucks another flower, and threads its stem through the hole. "Eden and I used to make them," he says, not raising his eyes from his work. "I would make necklaces for her, and she would make me a crown."

That pressure builds in my throat again.

"I think . . . I think maybe I did make them. For my father." I look up at him. "I think I used to bring him bunches of wildflowers. He would pull out the yellow dandelions and we would chew on them." I taste it in my mouth as I say the words.

Alder frowns. "Deacon Ward said most company farms raise the kids in barracks, away from their parents."

I nod. "I didn't always live on the compound. My father,

he was like one of you. I think we wandered a long way, tried to stay away from the company farms." I shut my eyes, a tumble of images coming at me. Memories. "Then it was winter one year, and we were out of food. An animal got into our packs—a bear, I think—and ate it all. So he thought . . . my father, he decided to make for a compound after all. And then . . ." An image of my father fills my mind—eyes wide, on his back, a clean red hole in his forehead and snow drifting down gently all around.

Something squeezes my arm. My eyes spring open on green and more green, the clover and earth and trees. And Alder, crouching beside me. When did he move so close? I shiver.

"You should sleep a little," he says.

I shake my head. "We have to keep moving. I'll sleep after we've found help."

"You'll crash the jeep."

I press my fists against my eyes.

"We'd sweat out all the water we drank, going back on the road now, anyway," Alder says. "Just an hour's rest. I'll keep watch."

I feel myself slipping, my vision going bleary. "One hour."

"Good," Alder says, and play punches the spot where he held my arm moments before. "Right answer."

I curl up on the clover. I can smell the earth and the plants, the greenness of them. *It wouldn't be so bad to die here,* I think. To sink down and let the cool earth wrap around me, to let crickets sing me to sleep forever. But how long will this place still be here? Will it be gone in a matter of days, like my compound and the trees around the lake?

I open my eyes. Alder is staring at me with an expression that makes his face look like it's about to fracture.

"I'm sorry." I swallow against the hardness in my throat. About everything, I mean. About Eden. About Ellison. About what he suffered with the Red Hand and the virus that's probably coursing through his blood. About the loss of everything we've known.

"It's not your fault," he says.

I squeeze my eyes shut against the hot tears welling in them and turn my face to the earth.

"Tempest," Alder says, in a way that makes me look up again. "It isn't. It's not your fault."

I blink the blur from my eyes.

"No crying, huh?" He makes an attempt at a smile and raises an eyebrow. "Don't go wasting all that water I so generously gave you."

I laugh.

"Sleep," Alder says. "I'll wake you in a little while."

And at last, I do.

I wake sometime later to the sound of thunder. Wind blows through the trees, flipping the leaves pale side up. I sit and hug myself. A small circlet of flowers lies next to me on the grass. I lift it gently and turn it over in my hands. A bracelet. Not a crown or a ring. Something else. A truce. Maybe forgiveness.

Soon Alder comes back, carrying a bundle in the front of his shirt. I quickly tuck the flowers into my backpack.

"There's a meadow back there." He displays a handful of small green apples. "I found these."

I grab one, bite into it, and immediately spit it out. "Ugh. Sour." I roll my tongue. "What are they?"

"Crab apples." He takes a bite, screws up his face, and keeps chewing. "Taste terrible, but they're better than nothing."

I try another bite and grimace. I shuffle through my backpack and pull out the last of the protein bars. That's it. The end of our food.

"I put the water bottle in the meadow," Alder says. "With any luck, we'll catch some rain."

I nod. "We'll drive again, as soon as the storm passes."

Another gust of wind rolls over us, and rain patters down on the canopy above.

"We should change your bandage," I say.

"I guess so." He extends his arm and starts unrolling the gauze gingerly. He sucks in a low hiss when it sticks to his skin.

I lean over the wound. "You need stitches."

"And a whole roast turkey. And a gold-plated helicopter."

I roll my eyes and look closer. "Doesn't seem infected, at least."

He shrugs. We both know it's not first on our list of worries.

"Maybe go wash it off in the rain," I say. "Then we'll re-dress it."

He does. When he comes back, I start wrapping his arm again, more carefully this time.

"Your father was a scavenger," Alder says, watching me work. "What about your mom?"

I shake my head. "I don't remember her."

"Not at all?"

"She must have died when I was really little." I tuck the end of the bandage back in around itself. "What about you? Your parents must be with the Deacon."

"No." He flexes his arm, testing the bandage, and winces. "We lived in a settlement northwest of here, in the mountains. Near the French Broad River. AgraStar raided our camp when I was four or five, flushed us out. Some people went west, farther into the hills. The rest of us struck out east, met up with the Deacon."

"And your parents?" I'm holding my breath.

"They didn't make it." He looks away. "Jackers. They would have gotten me too, but one of the men traveling with us boosted me up into a tree and told me to keep quiet."

"So who raised you?" I ask.

"Everyone. No one." He shrugs and plucks another flower from the clover. "Same as you, really."

I look up. The rain has eased, and the sun is creeping back. The whole world is hazy gold and steam. "We should go," I say. "While there's still daylight."

Alder nods. He heads off to fetch the water bottle and returns with it half full. We pile into the jeep and drive south.

Thirty miles down the road, the engine starts to sputter, and the power steering goes out.

"Dammit." I struggle to hold the wheel steady as I pump the brake. We coast to a stop in the middle of the road.

"What's wrong?" Alder sits up straight.

"Don't know." I tap the fuel gauge on the console. It doesn't move—still on a quarter tank. I tap it again, and it hits me. It's been stuck there for miles.

I curse and slam my hands against the steering wheel. I look over at Alder. "We're out of gas."

He nods and studies the road in front of us. Then he reaches over, shifts the jeep into neutral, and slides out of the passenger side. "Come on."

I follow him around to the back of the vehicle. "What are we doing?"

He leans against the tailgate. "We've got to get this thing off the road. We don't want to leave any clues for the Red Hand."

"Wait." I grab my pack and the water bottle, then lock the steering wheel to the right.

Together, we push. The jeep rolls off the road, slow at first, then it catches momentum and disappears into the thick mass of vines and ferns growing along the roadside. The forest swallows it up.

I watch it go, feeling sick. Finding someone to help when we had the jeep to speed us along was going to be difficult. Finding GAP-12, or anyone else, on foot is going to be next to impossible. I count down the hours. Half a day since Alder was bitten, maybe more. How long until he starts hallucinating? Until he can't swallow? A day and a half? Two? Once he's reached that stage, there's no turning it back.

"Tempest!"

I turn. Alder is several yards down the road already.

"Coming?" he calls.

I hurry to catch up to him. "What do we do now?"

Alder shrugs. "We walk."

.15.

MEADOW FOXTAIL

ALOPECURUS CAROLINIANUS

The fever hits Alder after sundown. The world has purpled into dusk, and the crickets and frogs have started up their pulsing song. I turn around and find him lagging several yards behind me on the road. His face is pale and slick. Heat still radiates from the blacktop, but he's shivering.

"We should stop," I say reluctantly. We need to keep moving if we're going to find help, but Alder looks like he'll collapse if he takes another step.

He doesn't argue. He doesn't say anything.

"I can try to make a fire," I say.

Alder shakes his head. He points to the skeleton of an old billboard a quarter mile down the road, its silhouette barely visible against the darkening sky. "There."

I nod. The sides of the road here have been cleared recently, all the green things between the highway and the tree line shriveled up and chemical-dry underfoot. Less chance of an ambush, but no cover, either. Someone—a guard or a clearer—has planted a whitewashed cross in the dirt to mark the spot where a team member fell. I touch the flimsy wood and remember the same symbol around Eden's neck. I don't want to have to make one of these for Alder.

We climb the billboard's access ladder. Alder stops every few rungs to rest, but at last we reach the narrow platform below the board. A light wind ruffles the sweaty curls at the nape of my neck. I breathe in. The highway stretches behind us, running through the thick shadows of the trees. The blight is out there, hidden in the dark. Has it reached the pool where I soaked my burned fingers? The boathouse? The Red Hand compound? Ahead of us, the lights of Atlanta twinkle in the distance, skyline haloed in a pink glow, as if the sun has set there instead of along the western horizon.

I didn't know I'd be able to see it from so far away. AgraStar is there. That means medicine. Civilization. Safety for me, a return to normal. Death or imprisonment for Alder. If he makes it.

"You want to go there, don't you?"

I shake my head. "I'm just thinking they'd have medicine."

He sits slowly, as if it pains him, and lets his legs dangle off the side of the platform. "They wouldn't give it to me. Besides, I'd rather die out here."

"No, you wouldn't." I drop down next to him and let my legs hang beside his in the open air.

"Rather than have them heal me, only to execute me later? Or make me into one of their cogs?" He leans back so he's looking at the sky. "I think I would."

My stomach twists. I look away.

"Tempest."

I turn back to Alder.

His face is drawn, serious. "If we don't find the vaccine—"

"Stop it." I know what he's going to say.

"No, listen. If it gets bad, if I'm too far gone, I want you to promise me something."

I fold my arms tight across my chest and glare at him.

"Promise me you'll end it." He nods at my gun. "Don't let me suffer like those people the Red Hand kept. Okay?"

I turn away. I can't keep insisting we're going to find help, because we're not. I'm only lying to myself and Alder, and Alder isn't fooled.

"You'd be doing me a mercy." His hand touches mine, sudden and warm. "I'd be with Eden."

I snatch my hand back. Her name is like a cold knife. A reminder of what he did, what I did, what happened to everyone around us. Ellison in the open dirt. Eden laid out and washed in the glowing tent. The creeping death following us. The woman clothed in blood.

"You're tired," I say. "You should sleep."

"I'm not—"

"You need to rest." I stand and walk to the other end of the platform. The remnants of a faded image rise on the billboard above me—half a smile, red lips, white teeth. "I'll take first watch."

"Tempest . . ."

"Just go to sleep, Alder." I lean against the safety rail. I can't look at him. "If you still want me to kill you in the morning, we can talk about it then."

Dusk drifts into night, and the chorus of insects rises, invisible, from the sea of treetops around us. I pull my hair out of its ponytail and comb through it with my fingers. Why does it feel like my lungs are caving in when I think about Alder dying? Less than a week ago, we were trying to kill each other, but now . . . I drop my head into my hands. He's my ally. I think I trust him. And he must trust me. Mercy killing, that isn't something I'd leave to just anyone. If it were me, I'd want only the right person to do it. Someone who would make it quick and clean. No hesitating, no botching it.

I lean back and look at the giant mouth. Alder may trust me to do the right thing, but I don't know if I trust myself. I don't even know what the right thing is anymore.

I reach for the seeds and turn them over in my hands. I should braid my hair, clean myself up as much as I can. That will make me feel better. More like a soldier. More in control. But my arms are so heavy. Every muscle in my body quakes with fatigue. I want to lie down and let the kudzu and weeds grow over me. I trace the tiny teardrop shapes of the seeds through the plastic. AgraStar shouldn't have them. The company might be able to clone the seeds, extrapolate which genes gave them their resistance, and transfer that resistance to other crops, but they'll also hoard that information, profit from it, maybe even use it to build a more devastating biological weapon. Maybe I don't know what the right thing is, but I do know one thing I can't allow.

Engines startle me awake. I sit up straight. A line of headlights moves through the night—it looks like two trucks, a car, and a small V of motorcycles bringing up the rear. Someone stands in the bed of the lead truck, sweeping a handheld floodlight across the trees bordering the road. I flatten myself against the platform and peek over the edge. Not an AgraStar caravan. The Red Hand? Are they still hunting us? Another dozen miles closer to AgraStar territory and they might not risk it, but here we're still in no-man's-land.

The flood lamp sweeps up over the billboard, and I freeze, praying the angle is enough to hide us. Alder moans in his sleep.

"Shh." I reach out and squeeze his ankle, the only part of him I can reach. *Please be quiet. Please stay still.*

The beam drops and plays over the trees to our right. I let out a breath but stay flattened against the platform, every muscle rigid. I lie there as the caravan passes, and as it doubles back an hour later, still strafing the trees with light and filling the night with rumbling.

✦ ✦ ✦

I don't sleep again, even though shadows are starting to jump before my eyes and I can feel my heart beating too quickly. I'm dehydrated. But Alder is worse. His fever is high, flushing his cheeks and bringing a glassy sheen to his eyes. His hair is soaked with sweat. He watches me through barely open lids as I change his bandages.

"You didn't wake me for my turn on lookout," he says as I peel back the last layer.

"You—" I catch sight of his wound and choke down a gasp.

"What?" He sits up.

In silence, we both stare at his arm. His flesh is swollen, and red streaks radiate out from the punctures. Infection. I curse.

"It's okay," I say quickly, stupidly. The fever. I should have known. I should have brought more antiseptic with me. I start rewrapping his arm. "It's going to be okay."

"Tempest—"

I ignore him. "Can you climb down?"

He pushes himself up on shaky arms. "I'll have to."

"Don't go plummeting to your death, okay?" I try to give him a smirk. It doesn't hold.

"I can do it." He looks me in the eye as he says it, but that doesn't change the fact that he's swaying on his feet.

"I'll go first," I say. "I can try and catch you if you slip."

We make it down. Alder sits in the billboard's shadow

for what feels like a quarter hour, while I scan the horizon for movement, toes squirming anxiously in my boots.

"Okay," he finally says.

I hold out a hand, and he lets me help him up.

We tramp through the waist-high ragweed and foxtail along the side of the road, ready to drop down if we see anyone coming. Every few feet, I stop and look back, both to check on Alder and to scan the horizon for vehicles. We're moving slow, covering barely two miles an hour. The sun is hot and my head pounds. We might get another afternoon thunderstorm—they come like clockwork every summer—but that's still hours away.

The sun climbs high above us, and the road ripples with mirages, quicksilver pools that shimmer into view and then disappear. At some point, I stop sweating, which I know is bad, but I keep walking, checking behind me, walking again.

A roar rips across the sky. I look up, expecting to see thunderheads rolling in, but the sky is a perfect blue. The sound grows louder, closer.

"Get down!" I grab Alder and throw us both on our bellies in the weeds.

A trio of jets scream overhead, angling northeast, in the direction of the Red Hand base and my compound.

"What are they doing?" Alder asks as the sound fades.

I stand and dust seeds and burrs from my legs. "I don't know."

The words are barely out of my mouth when we hear a distant *boom-boom-boom*. A wall of smoke appears on the horizon. It must be at least thirty miles north of us, maybe more, rising above the treetops.

"The blight?" Alder says.

I have a vision of it spreading, seeping out in evil wisps like the red streaks on Alder's arm. Touching all the creeks and rivers veined across the landscape, carrying the infection in the current.

"Must be. They're trying a firebreak, I think."

"Fire didn't stop it before," Alder says grimly.

"Maybe they didn't get all of it the first time." My mouth is dry. I'm not sure even I believe me.

Alder doesn't answer. We wait in the grass as the jets circle back around and disappear to the south, in the direction of the city. Then we wait a few minutes more before we stand again and keep walking.

The retaining wall appears several quiet miles down the road, a concrete barrier that starts at knee height and steps up until it towers six feet above our heads. It runs beside the highway as far as I can see.

"Can we go around?" Alder looks weary. "Through the woods?"

I lean over a waist-high section of wall. The ground slopes up sharply behind it, covered in a dense undergrowth of briars and weeds.

I grimace. "We can try."

We try to pick our way through the thicket, but it's no use. Thorns snag our clothes and slice red lines across our skin. Alder's ankle turns in the soft, uneven mud, and I barely catch him before he rolls down the slope and crashes into the back of the retaining wall. After half an hour, we turn back. I can still see the highway behind us. We've made it only a handful of yards.

"How long do you think it goes?" I say as we stand, scratched and sweaty, back where we started.

"I don't know." Alder stares at the wall. "Couple miles? I've never been this close to the city before."

I gnaw on the inside of my lip. Even if it's only a couple of miles, that's a long time with no way to run off the road and take cover. If we keep following the highway, we're exposed, trapped. But if we veer off into the woods now, we risk getting lost.

"Can you run?" I ask him.

"I can try," he says, but the sickly sheen on his face makes me think it won't be very far or very fast.

"We'll walk," I say. "Quick as we can."

Alder opens his mouth, but I cut him off. "I'm not leaving you behind, okay? Stop telling me to."

We start out at a brisk pace, but before a mile is out, Alder is lagging again, and the wall shows no sign of ending. Somewhere behind it, a bird calls, an off-kilter sound, a warning. I don't like this. I look back. Nothing emerges on the horizon, but I'm on alert, my heart pounding as if I'm on patrol. I can almost hear the soft crackle of Crake's open com line in my ear.

Another mile passes, the only sound our shoes on the pavement and Alder's labored breathing. Mosquitoes buzz around us. I look up. A quarter mile away, the wall is lower and the land drops back into a gentle slope topped by pines.

"Almost there!" I call back to Alder.

He raises his head, relief written on his face for a brief moment, and then it's gone.

"Do you hear that?" He turns and squints back at the rolling road.

"Hear what?" I say. But then I do. *Engines.* A glint of metal appears on one of the rises in the highway behind us.

"Run!" I grab Alder's hand and pull him forward. I can see the end of the wall. We can make it if we're fast enough. Twelve hundred feet, a thousand, eight hundred . . .

Alder stumbles and smacks the ground. The sound of engines grows at our backs. There's more than one. A dozen, at least.

"Go!" Alder yells. "I'm slowing you down."

I yank him to his feet. Blood seeps through his pants at the knees and covers his hands and chin. I point to the end of the wall. "There's still time. We can make it."

"Tempest . . ."

"Move!" I shout.

We run. Five hundred feet, four hundred, three hundred. I look back. Two lines of tanker trucks crest the last hill between us and begin their descent, led by guards on motorcycle. We have a minute—maybe—before they're on us.

One hundred feet, seventy-five, fifty . . .

"Almost there," I pant. *Please don't let them see us. Let them think we're a mirage.*

Thirty, twenty, ten . . .

The diesel engines reach a roar. The wall drops to knee height. I link my arm through Alder's and pull us over it. We hit the dirt a half second before an entire caravan of tanker trucks blares by. I lift my head as much as I dare and squint against the dust stirred up in their wake. Fourteen tankers, all with the AgraStar logo printed in green on their sides, surrounded by armed guards riding jeeps and motorcycles. They fly past, in close formation, and then they're gone, their deafening blare fading with them.

I lie with my head pressed to the dirt, heart pounding.

"You okay?" Alder asks.

I nod and make myself sit up. "You?"

"A little banged up."

"Can you walk?" I offer him a hand.

He takes it gingerly. "I think so."

We trudge along the road. My knees are jelly and my head aches. I keep my eyes on the pavement in front of me. We have to stop soon. Even if we're nowhere near water, I need to rest.

"You see that?" Alder says.

I lift my head. Alder is pointing to something ahead of us—a rise and an overpass, an old highway exit, with the flat roof of a service station barely visible above the hill.

"You think anyone's up there?"

Alder shakes his head. "Hope not."

I lick my cracked lips. "There might be water."

We look at each other, passing a silent calculation between us. No doubt scavengers and jackers have picked off whatever was left behind in the decades since stations like this one were closed down. Then again, someone could be using it to stash supplies. Or trap unsuspecting travelers.

"We'll be careful," I say.

Alder nods.

"If anything's off, we run for the woods." I try to swallow. I don't know what's worse—making a bad call by accident, or doing something incredibly stupid because you have no other choice.

The air is quiet at the top of the ramp. The covered filling area stretches out cool and empty against the glare of the sun. Our footsteps echo. Some of the pumps have been ripped out, and warped pine boards cover the windows of the building.

I squint up and down the long strip of road beside the station. Other buildings and a series of transformer towers dot the gentle folds of the landscape, all half eaten by vegetation.

Alder tugs at the boards. "They're on tight."

I lean in to peer through a gap near the front door, and draw back in surprise. Sunlight floods the interior of the building. A section of roof has fallen through to the floor, and a circle of sourwood trees in full, feathery bloom has grown up on top of the pile of shingles, dirt, and leaves. Dust motes float in the column of light surrounding them.

"What's wrong?" Alder tenses beside me.

"Nothing." I move away so he can look, and scan the horizon again. I could shoot out the lock, but anyone within a mile radius would hear it, and the last thing we want is the wrong kind of attention. There has to be another way in.

"Like a fairy circle," Alder says quietly.

I glance up. "Let's go around."

We find a utility ladder at the back of the building, its rungs sunk directly into the cinder-block wall.

"Stay here, yeah?" I say, climbing until I can peek over the lip of the roof.

"What do you see?" Alder calls.

"Not much." The top of the building is mainly dirt and concrete, except for the hole. A stack of empty mason jars with rusted caps sits jumbled in one corner of the roof. Someone might have been using this place as a stash once, but not anymore.

I edge closer to the hole and peer down. It's too dark to see anything past the sourwood branches. I lie flat on my stomach and lower my head and shoulders, ponytail dangling straight down. Slowly my eyes adjust. Empty metal shelves surround the trees, some at an angle, others knocked over. A wall of glass doors lines the back of the room, most of them spiderwebbed with cracks. There's an alcove off to the right. The only things left that I can see are a stand of clear plastic key fobs, a stack of Styrofoam cups, and a broken analog clock on the wall, its hands frozen at three and six.

Suddenly the roof gives beneath me. My stomach flips, and I tumble down head over heels. I land on my back, the wind knocked out of me. A flurry of dust particles and pollen swirls in the newly opened shaft of sunlight above me.

"Tempest!"

I turn my head and flex my arms and legs. Nothing broken. I sit up carefully and look around. A thick film of dust covers everything, from the counters near the front windows to the darkened track lights hanging from what's left of the ceiling. Something rustles and then scurries by in a gray blur—a rat or a squirrel.

Alder's head appears in the opening above me. "You okay?"

"Yeah." I roll my neck. "Don't come any closer. I think the roof beams are rotten."

"Can you climb out?" He's backlit, but I can hear the frown in his voice.

I look around. The trees are too slender to climb, but I could probably scale one of the metal shelves and use it to boost myself back onto the roof.

"I think so." I squint up at him. "Maybe I should look around a minute, though. See if anything useful's left."

"Hurry," Alder says. "I don't like how open this place is."

I find a single mud-stiffened work glove in the corner and a handful of strawberry-flavored gum packets scattered across the floor behind the counter. I gather them up and toss them in my bag. It might not be food, but it could be enough to trick our stomachs and give us a short burst of sugar.

The door to what might be a utility closet or storage room is locked—something to come back to—but the pair of restroom doors in the back alcove swing open. Nothing but darkness and broken glass fills the women's room. The mirror has been shattered. Bits of it glint on the tile like flecks of mica in the soil. I try the men's room next. Something moves in the dark, and I nearly cry out before I realize it's my own reflection in the mirror above the sink.

I blink and let my eyes acclimate. The air smells like stale earth. I step inside. My foot catches on something, and I throw out a hand to steady myself before I look down. A leg, a shoe. A bundle slumped in the corner. I don't go any closer, but the thing comes into focus as my brain sorts the shapes and shadows into a form. A partly mummified skeleton, skin stretched dry and yellow-brown over the bone, clothes loose over its rib cage and desiccated limbs.

I want to move, but I can't. I want to leave, climb back up into the sunshine with Alder, but I'm frozen. All I can do is shut my eyes. *It's only a body. It can't hurt you. It's just some bones.*

I crack one eye open and make myself look at the scene again. The man—I think it was a man—lies propped with his back to the corner and his legs splayed in front of him. A rusted syringe and a mostly empty bottle rest beside his hand. I pick it up, careful not to brush his skin. Morphine. I shove the bottle in my pocket and scan the room again. One of the soft ceiling panels above the body has been shoved aside, revealing a triangle of darkness and a dangling strap.

I reach up and tug the strap. A shower of rat droppings and dirt falls, along with a backpack. I cough, dust myself off. I start to pull the zipper, but the fabric comes apart in my hands. I reach inside. A handful of loose nine-millimeter rounds. Three clean, plastic-capped syringes. A sweatshirt and a pair of socks. No water. No sat phone.

"Tempest!"

The urgency in Alder's voice snaps me to attention. I race out into the front room, letting the door swing shut behind me, and look up at him through the hole in the ceiling. He points to the road. I hurry to the front windows and look out through a gap in the boards. As I watch, an armored truck, soot black with a golden AgraStar logo on its side, rolls up the off-ramp.

I run back to the gap and look up at Alder.

"Can you climb?" he asks.

I shake my head. Not enough time. "Jump down here."

Alder looks at the road, then back at me, and nods. He sits on the lip of the hole, then pushes himself forward and drops. His feet hit the ground just as brakes squeak to a stop outside, and an engine shifts down to idle.

.16.

FIELD GOLDENROD

SOLIDAGO NEMORALIS

We huddle in the shadows beneath the boarded-up windows. Outside, the engine cuts off and boots fall on the asphalt. Faint voices reach us.

"... still spreading ..."

"... have to call in another strike."

"Aim it right, and we'll get two birds with one stone."

I finger the safety on my pistol. Alder goes up on his knees and peers out.

I remember the man with the machete, the branch snapping, gunfire like rain on the trees. "Are they from the same convoy we saw back in the woods?" I whisper.

"I don't know." Alder narrows his eyes. "Could be. But where are the rest of them?"

Neither of us says anything. Have they run across the Red Hand caravan we saw last night? Is that why there are so few? Or is this a different group, evacuating south in the face of the blight?

"What are they doing?" I ask.

"I think . . . just resting." He presses his lips together, and he swallows. He looks at me. "They have water."

I turn my head away. *Water.* A part of me wants to open the door, raise my hands, identify myself. *Tempest Torres, perimeter patrol, compound SCP-52, sole survivor.* But an undercurrent of doubt runs counter to that. I see my father outside the compound gates in the falling snow, downed by Rosalie's bullet. I rub the twin pink marks on my wrist where my coms anchors used to be. Those pale spots are my only proof of who I am. Any deserter could have them.

And that's the simpler calculation. I can't close my eyes without seeing the jets strafing the compound, lines of fire ripping through the dead fields. I can't sleep without seeing Mr. Kingfisher bloody, hearing Juna whisper, *"I'll never be like you."* If they know who I am, will that save me, or earn me a bullet and an unmarked grave by the roadside?

I look at Alder.

"Don't," he murmurs, his eyes still on the group outside.

I bite the inside of my cheek and look out too. A man and a woman with her hair in a ponytail like mine stand on alert, rifles in hand. The rest of the team sits in a circle in the shade, drinking from canteens and eating what look like dried protein strips from a package. My stomach rumbles.

"I can't take this." I crawl away from the windows, sit back against an empty shelf, and unwrap a piece of gum. It crumbles in my mouth, stale and sweet.

Alder stares at me. I hold out another piece.

He stands to take it. At that moment, a shadow—not his—falls on one of the windows, shuttering out the strip of sunlight between the boards. I freeze, hand outstretched. Alder sees my face and turns slowly.

Outside, someone grunts. The board over the door rattles as someone shakes it, tugs it, tries to pull it loose.

Alder drops and crawls the rest of the way to me. I pull him behind the shelves. The board shrieks.

"I got one!" a man calls—young, maybe Ellison's age.

"Trey, leave it be," a woman shouts back. "Why do you want to go looking in some nasty-ass heap like that, anyway?"

"Go on and laugh," he yells. The board rattles again.

"He wants to earn a commendation for rooting out a jacker stash." An older man's voice this time, raw and broad. "Trey the glory hound."

They laugh, and someone starts baying. The others join in.

"Shut up." Trey lets the board snap back against the window. "Just wait till I get my own team. None of you are getting tapped for it. That's for sure."

Alder lets out a shaky breath. I wipe my hands on my pants.

"Time to roll out anyway." Trey's voice fades as he walks away.

Engines crank and come to life again.

"Load up," the older man shouts over the hum.

Boots clomp and doors slam. Then the pitch of the truck's engine changes, and grit and pebbles scatter as it rolls away.

We wait several minutes and then climb back onto the roof by way of one of the empty shelves. I'm hauling Alder up after me when a sonic boom claps the sky above us. A trio of jets streak by, heading north. I duck instinctively, but as high and fast as they are, we must look like nothing but ants. The planes disappear into the haze at the horizon. Everything is silent and still for a moment, and then fire expands to fill the space between earth and air.

"It's still coming." I stare at the fresh smudge of smoke rising on the wind. "The firebreak—"

"It's not enough," Alder says at my side.

I squeeze my hands into fists. Three times AgraStar has razed the earth, and it still hasn't stopped the blight. What if Alder is right? What if it's not enough? What if it's never enough? What if there's no stopping it?

We sleep through the hottest part of the afternoon in a concrete niche behind the pillars of an overpass. The rumble of thunder wakes me some hours later. I crawl out to prop up our water bottle and then hurry back into our shelter, with its carpet of dry leaves, dirt, and brittle plastic bags. The rain comes fast and hard, borne in by a sudden wind. It flattens the grass and tosses the trees. Lightning flashes, then, a heartbeat later, thunder booms all around us. Alder's lurches up, panting.

"It's all right." I put a hand on his arm. "It's only—"

Another bolt, and the air cracks. The sound echoes through my chest, like an explosion. I can see the R&D facility going up in a bright plume and the shock wave coming at me again, even though my eyes are open.

"Tempest." Alder is shaking me. "Tempest!"

I come to myself again. I have Alder's sleeve in a sweaty grip and I'm doubled over, panting.

"Sorry." I unclench my fingers. They ache, as if they've been locked in that position too long.

"It's okay." Alder hesitates, then reaches for my hand.

I look at our entwined fingers, and then at him. Sweat plasters his dark hair to his forehead. His hand is too hot.

He turns his head away, but he doesn't let go. "It's going to be okay."

The rain keeps up all through the night. We trudge along the edge of the highway, too tired to speak. At least we have enough to drink. Near dawn, we pass an old road sign.

ATLANTA 42

I stop and chew on my lip. Through the mist, I catch glimpses of old housing developments flanking both sides of the road. Their uniform white backs look like ghosts, where they aren't overrun by kudzu vines. The closer we get to Atlanta, the firmer hold AgraStar will have. We'll have to go off-road soon if we want to avoid their patrols. I glance at Alder. He sits by the road, rocking back and forth and shivering. He's past the forty-eight hour mark. Time is running out.

I take a seat beside him.

"I'm not going to make it another day." Alder stares straight ahead, at a tangle of honeysuckle wrapped around an old sign on the opposite side of the road.

I focus on the toes of my boots. "I know."

"I need your help." Alder looks at me. "You promised."

"No, I didn't." I look at the ghost houses and the honeysuckle bobbing in the rain. "But I will now."

I unzip my backpack and hand Alder the tiny bottle of morphine. "I found this back at the station."

Alder turns it over in his hands. A little under a third of the clear liquid is left. "You think that's enough?"

I shrug. "I don't know. Seems like it should at least be enough to put you to sleep. Keep you from feeling it if I have to . . ." I gesture at my gun.

Alder nods and hands the bottle back to me. "Let's do it."

"What, now?"

He leans over his knees. "Why not now?"

"You've still got half a day left, maybe more." I clutch the bottle tight. "We could still find help."

He gestures at the deserted road. "You really think we're going to find anyone but AgraStar patrols and jackers out here?"

I shrug. "It's possible."

He scoffs. "I'm ready, Tempest. You've got to do it before I lose my nerve."

"No." I stand. "Not yet."

"But why? You promised—"

"Because I'm not ready." I turn and start walking, my back to Alder so he won't see the tears brimming in my eyes or the way I'm twisting my face to keep them from falling. It's not so much the thought of doing it. I'm a sniper. I'm trained for this. But I don't want to be alone out here. I don't want to be the only one to remember the place we came from and what the world was like before it ended.

Alder catches up to me. "Tempest . . ."

"Tonight, okay? If we haven't found help by tonight, I'll do it. I swear."

The rain finally slacks off in the afternoon. The thick, sloping stacks of a nuclear power plant appear above the tree line, belching clouds of white steam.

"We should get off the road." Alder nods at the plant. "Lots more roadblocks and patrols whenever those things are nearby."

The ground to our west slopes up to a low ridge covered with trees. We follow it, walking in silence over the damp mulch of old pine needles, the highway visible below us to the left. Alder hums under his breath, a slow, sad tune I can barely hear over our footfalls.

I slow to walk beside him. "What's that song?"

He looks up, as if he's suddenly woken from a reverie. "It's just an old song, something my father would sing. I sang it to Eden once, but she said it was too sad to hear again."

I keep my eyes on the ground. "Will you sing it for me?"

He looks at me sidelong, but then wets his lips. His voice starts low and off-key.

"Cold blows the wind to my true love,
And gently drops the rain
I never had but one true love
And in the greenwood she lies slain . . ."

Alder's voice breaks, but then he finds it again.

"How oft on yonder grave, sweetheart,
Where we were wont to walk,
The fairest flower that I e'er saw
Has withered to a stalk.

"When will we meet again, sweetheart?
When will we meet again?
When the autumn leaves that fall from the trees
Are green and spring up again."

"She's right," I say. "It's too sad."

"Was," Alder corrects. "She was right."

"Let's stop and rest," I say quickly. Better not to dwell on these things. Better to keep our minds on the present, or else Eden and Ellison and all the rest will be there when we close our eyes.

We sleep, and wake, and walk again. Another volley of jets streaks overhead, but we're well hidden by the trees, and we're not their target, anyway. The afternoon thunderstorm rolls in, just as my clothes are finally drying off from the morning's rain. I glance at Alder every few minutes. His pace has slowed, but his expression hasn't altered. He's getting worse. I don't think he's changed his mind.

Sunset comes, then dusk.

Alder stops. "Tempest."

"Not yet," I say. "Another mile or two."

We trudge on through the dark. Fireflies glow among the pine trees, and night insects take up their song.

Ahead, the road straightens, and a steady light breaks the darkness.

I hold out a hand. "Someone's there." Hope and fear fill my heart.

We pick our way forward, moving quietly through the woods. As we close in, I see that the light is coming from flood lamps, dead center in the road, surrounded by vehicles.

"Stay here." I shove the morphine and syringes, and then, after a moment of hesitation, my gun, into Alder's hands. "I'll see what it is. If I don't come back . . ."

Alder nods, his face pale.

I creep forward, heart hammering in my ears, and stop behind the cover of trees a dozen yards away. Two armored trucks block the road on one side, while a personnel carrier does the same on the opposite set of lanes. Five guards kitted out with M4s and body armor mill around behind the floodlights, and a midsize drone circles above, buzzing like a thousand flies. AgraStar.

Bile collects in my throat. I crawl back, deeper into the forest. That drone probably has heat sensors, and I don't want to be in its range when it swings around. When I think I'm safe, I run.

Alder looks up as I crash through the trees. "Is it . . ."

"AgraStar." I drop down beside him, breathing hard. I close my hand over his, the one holding the morphine bottle. "You don't have to . . . We could try turning ourselves over."

Alder shakes his head. "No."

"Will it really be worse than—"

"Yes." He pulls his hand free and pops the plastic cap from the top of the syringe. "You still don't get it."

"Or maybe you're so bent on hating them you don't see that they could save you."

"I wasn't born yesterday," he says. "I don't trust them."

He holds the syringe and morphine bottle out to me, but I hesitate.

"You said you would." He scowls. "You swore."

My hands tremble as I take the vial and fit the tip of the syringe through the hole in the thick metal foil. I draw out everything I can, everything that's left.

"Flick it," Alder says. "Get out the air bubbles."

He holds out his arm, takes a deep, shaky breath, and then looks up and meets my eyes. "I'm ready."

I slide the needle into the soft flesh of his inner arm, close my eyes, and depress the plunger. Alder lets out a breath.

I open my eyes and draw out the needle. "Do you feel anything?"

"Not yet." He leans back against a tree trunk.

I rub at the dirt on my fingers. "Should have washed my hands first, huh?" I joke.

"Doesn't matter."

We sit in silence for a few minutes. I sift through my nearly empty backpack, picking out pieces of the broken sat phone and chucking them into the woods. Even if I could fix it, there's no use for it now.

"Tempest?"

"Hmm?" I look up.

"Will you sing me a song?"

"What kind of song?" I ask.

"Anything," he says. "Something you remember from when you were a kid."

I glance around the woods, as if I'll find one there. "I don't remember any."

"None?"

"Not the kind you mean." All the songs I know are AgraStar training chants or songs the children on the compound were taught about cleaning up or praising sharecroppers. I don't have any from before that, from the white-tiled room, or the flower around my finger, or my father before the neat bullet hole in his forehead.

Alder raises a hand to his eyes. "I think I'm starting to feel it."

I shift closer to him. "We should sing your song again."

He raises an eyebrow, and his head lolls back against the bark. "I thought you said it was too sad."

"I can be sad if it helps," I say.

He nods, and I start, haltingly, unsure of the words.

"Cold blows the wind to my true love . . ."

We sing it through once, and then again, until we reach the autumn leaves.

Alder stops. "Eden," he whispers, and then he is still.

.17.

HEMLOCK

CONIUM MACULATUM

I press my ear to Alder's chest. His heart beats slow and weak, and his breath comes so shallow I can barely feel it. I wait what feels like an hour, but could be ten minutes, then check again. Still beating. Still breathing.

It must not have been enough. I was hoping it would be easy and gentle, that Alder could simply go to sleep in the woods. Now I have to shoot a drugged and sleeping boy.

I stand, put on my backpack, check my rounds. I'll have to run. The gun's report will reach the roadblock, for sure. I flick off the safety, raise my weapon, and brace my arms.

"I'm sorry," I say, and move my finger to the trigger. Ellison's face flashes before mine, then Danica, and Will, and the rest of my team. Eden is on the ground with Rosalie and all those children on the bunker floor. The sky is blood and fire, and the earth is rot, creeping ever closer.

I drop my arms. "Shit."

I turn away, click the safety back on. I walk ten steps into the woods, then back again. *You can do this. It's what he wanted. It's no different from what you've done a hundred times before, guarding the perimeter.*

But it is. Because now I know him. He isn't some shape moving through the grass at night. He's a boy named Alder who fell in love once and sings sad songs, who can catch a rabbit with shoelaces. He may think he's going to heaven, to Eden, but what if he's wrong? What if there's nowhere else after this?

I stare into the darkness. Lightning bugs pulse in and out of view, little flashes of phosphorescence. I wipe my eyes. We hardly ever saw them at the compound. The pesticides kept them away, but sometimes they would blink at us from the forest beyond the perimeter fence. I used to stare at them from up in the guard tower, hungry for some pattern, some Morse code message, but I never saw one.

One of them lands on me, its tiny feet tickling my skin.

"Mira, Papi, luces!"

"Se llaman luciérnagas, cielo. Fireflies."

My father's voice rushes over me like a cool wind. I shiver. What would he tell me if he were here?

"Let the boy die, cielo. It's what he wants."

But my father isn't here. He's gone. He was never the one left behind. If he knew what it has been like for me, alone all these years, would he say the same thing?

I feel for the bag of seeds. If the blight is still spreading, if the firebreaks can't stop it, AgraStar will need them and the information I can give them about what happened back at the compound more than ever. Maybe enough to bargain for a human life or two.

I know what I promised. I know what I decided. But looking down at Alder's broken body, I can't drum up that same feeling of certainty I had at the billboard. How can I balance a life, a boy I know, an ally, against some conviction? He's flesh and bone, solid and lying in front of me, and I can't trade that reality for any belief, any what-might-be. It may not be what Alder wanted, but I can't give him that. I can't pull the trigger. And if I can't do him that mercy, at least I can try to keep him alive. Even if it means betraying him.

I walk down the center of the road, my hands held high. I see the floodlights, and then the trucks and guards. The drone buzzes overhead. A harsh blue-white spotlight surrounds me, brighter and colder than sunshine.

"Unidentified individual," a hollow voice booms from the drone. "Halt. Do not come any closer."

I stop, all my nerve endings crackling with fear.

"I'm Tempest Torres." I shout over the drone's hum. "I survived the attack on compound SCP-52. I have information about blight counteractive measures. Request asylum and medical attention."

The drone hovers silently for a moment. Then a different voice crackles over its speakers, a woman's voice, clipped and rough.

"Place your hands on your head and get on your knees. No sudden movements. We'll come to you."

My stomach flips, but I obey, closing my eyes against the blue light.

Boots approach. I open my eyes and squint into the glare. A team of five stands before me, two of them fixed on me, the others scanning the woods around us with LED beams clipped to their rifles.

"Are you armed?" The guard's voice matches the one from the drone.

I nod. "In my holster."

"Don't move."

A second guard approaches and pulls my nine-millimeter from my hip. He hands it to the older woman. "AgraStar standard issue."

"Anything else?" she asks me.

I shake my head.

She nods. "Pat her down."

The guard briskly runs his hands down my back and legs. I tense as he brushes over the bag of seeds inside my pocket, but he's looking for weapons, not contraband.

He steps back. "She's clean."

"You can get up." The lead guard keeps her weapon trained on me. "Where are your coms?"

"I was captured." I rub my wrist. "They tore it off me."

She nods. "You say you have information about blight countermeasures?"

"I do." I straighten my spine, make myself stand tall. "But I have conditions."

One of the other guards scoffs, and the woman's expression hardens. "Your contract with AgraStar should be all the assurance you need."

"It should be," I say. "But it isn't."

"Captain," the guard who patted me down says. "We're exposed out here, and she's got nothing. We should turn her away or put her down."

"You could do that." I try to keep my voice steady. "But I was there on the ground when the blight released, and I'm still alive."

The guards look at each other.

"What conditions?" the captain finally asks.

I let my breath go. "There's a boy with me, back in the woods. He helped me get out. But now he's sick. Unconscious."

The captain shakes her head. "If you think we're bringing disease back—"

"It's not like that," I say. "The Red Hand had him. They keep rabid dogs. He got bitten while we were trying to escape."

One of the guards whistles, and another sucks in a breath.

"Rabies?" Pity wars with distaste on the captain's face. "How long ago was he bitten?"

"Almost three days," I say. "But there's still time. You have the vaccine."

"And you want us to give it to him?" The captain says. "That's your condition?"

"Yes." I squeeze my hands into fists. "We have seeds from a plant that survived the blight. Cure him, and I'll tell you where they are."

The captain shakes her head. "We'll cure him, but you tell us where the seeds are first. That's the deal."

I stare at her. There's no backing out. She's the one with the guns and the thing I need. Alder is running out of time. She has me, and she knows it. Slowly I reach into my pocket and draw out the plastic bag. One of the guards snatches it from me.

"This is it?" the captain asks.

I nod.

She looks uneasily at the woods, and then at me. "All right. You lead the way to the boy. But anything even feels off, and I'm dropping you. No questions."

"Yes, ma'am," I agree.

I walk a few feet ahead of the AgraStar team, the drone overhead, sweeping its light across the trees. I keep my hands out and to the sides, where the guards can see them.

We find Alder where I left him, lying on his back in a copse of trees several yards off the freeway. One of the guards presses his head to Alder's chest, while another takes his pulse. They look at the captain. She nods, and they roll him over on his stomach, pull his arms behind him, and bind his wrists with zip ties.

"What are you doing?" I push forward. "He's sedated. I used all the mor—"

The guard who frisked me catches me around the stomach, knocking the air from my lungs. He yanks one arm behind my back, and I cry out as I feel it pop out of joint. I blink tears away to see one of the other guards upending the backpack, scattering syringes, our grimy water bottle, and stale gum across the forest floor.

"He's not going to hurt anyone. You don't have to restrain him," I gasp. Then the guard has my other arm behind me, and I feel the bite of the zip tie.

"Stop!" I shrug him off and stumble forward. "You're hurting—"

A buzz close to my ear, a cold burn, and my vision goes white. I catch a glimpse of the treetops illuminated by the drone, pinwheeling, and then the captain's face, and then nothing.

I come to in the back of a covered personnel transport, slumped on a metal bench. My shoulder throbs and my brain feels muzzled. I try to twist into a more comfortable position, but my arms are still tied behind my back. Daylight streams in from the rear of the vehicle, where the road is spooling out behind us in a hot white ribbon. Buildings sprawl on either side, warehouses and cinder-block storefronts, fenced lots and depots filled with armored trucks. We must be entering Atlanta proper—AgraStar's headquarters.

"She's awake."

I sit up. Eight helmeted AgraStar guards sit on the benches around me, but it's the one across from me who spoke, a young man with smooth, dark brown skin and a scar across his chin.

"Where's Alder?" I struggle to make my tongue form the words.

"Who's that?" the guard across from me asks. He looks so familiar, like . . .

"The shirk boy that was with her," the female guard beside him says, turning to me. "He's up in one of the trucks with the medic."

"Why do you care so much?" The guard across from me gives me a curious look, like he might believe me if I could only explain. Even his voice strikes a chord of memory.

One of the other guards snorts. "Because she's a shirk like him. You heard what she said. She's got some miracle cure for fighting the blight, but screw us, she was going to let everyone die unless we saved her boyfriend."

"That's not how it is." I pull at the zip tie. "I'm one of you. Untie me. Look at my wrist."

"Like we're falling for that." The nasty guard shakes his head. "Lie all you like. They'll get the truth out of you once we're back inside the yellow zone."

The guard across from me—the one I could half swear I know—pulls off his helmet and runs a hand over his close-cropped hair. The gesture is so familiar, so . . . His deep brown eyes meet mine.

"Ellison?" I whisper.

He frowns and looks from me to his fellow guards. "What's she talking about?"

"You're not . . ." He looks exactly like Ellison, talks like Ellison, moves like Ellison. But Ellison never had a scar like that, and Ellison is lying beneath three feet of poisoned dirt. I lean forward on the bench, trying to breathe. My vision dims, and I pitch forward onto the floor as I lose consciousness.

I wake in a hospital room. Sunlight pours through the window, sparkling on the pristine white floors. I lift my head, but I can't see any buildings or trees on the other side of the glass, only sky. Where am I? Atlanta? I look down. Someone has undressed me, bathed me, and put me in a cotton gown printed with a pattern of small AgraStar logos. My hands rest at my sides, but something is wrong with them. A thin, rubbery layer of something gray-white covers them from palm to fingertips, as if the inner portion of my hands have been dipped in paint and then dried. I flex my fingers and shiver. I'm cold. So cold.

My heart races, the rhythm matched by the low, frantic beep of the machine to my right. I push myself up, and pain shoots through my elbow. I look down. An IV shunt sticks out of my skin, connected to a bag of saline above the bed. I swallow. There's a pitcher of water on the side table, collecting condensation.

Water. I kick my legs free of the blankets and crawl out of bed. My body moves so slowly. I would think I've been drugged, except my mind feels perfectly clear. I skip the plastic cup and drink straight from the pitcher, gulping down water until my lungs force me to take a breath. I've finished almost half of it when the door chimes, and a pale woman in blue hospital scrubs and a matching cap strolls in, examining a smartboard.

"Miss Salcedo?" She looks up and smiles at me.

I lower the pitcher to the table. "No. Torres. My name is Torres." My voice sounds gravelly, hoarse. I cough.

She frowns at her smartboard, and then her face lights up again. "Ah. I see. How are you feeling, Miss *Torres*?"

The way she says my name puts an uneasy feeling in my stomach. I should be relieved. I don't know where I am, but I'm not in a jail cell. This isn't how we talk to prisoners. AgraStar must have decided I'm valuable if they're giving me medical treatment. I step back toward the window, pulling the IV stand with me. "Fine."

"Are you hungry?" She glances at the water pitcher, then back at me, and laughs. "I can certainly see you were thirsty."

I look at my hospital gown. I've spilled splotches of water down my front. My face burns.

"Where's Alder?"

"The scavenger you brought in?" She raises her eyebrows, as if she's surprised I mentioned him. "I'm not authorized—"

"I only want to know if he's alive. Just tell me that."

"He's being treated in another part of the facility," she says. "He'll recover."

I let out a sigh of relief, and at the same moment, my stomach grumbles.

"Hungry after all!" The woman smiles and turns for the exit. "I'll see if we can't find something in Refectory for you."

"Wait. Why did you . . ." I try to follow her, but the IV stand slows me down. The door closes between us. I tug at its manual grip, wave my hand in front of the motion sensor, bang on the glass. Nothing. It stays calmly and stubbornly closed. A glass antechamber, with nothing in it but a wall of cabinets and a hand-washing station, separates my room from the hall. Everything out there is white and putty gray.

"Hey!" I shout, pounding on the glass. "Come back! Please!"

No one answers. No one comes.

I hit the glass one last time in frustration and storm away, tangling myself in the IV stand as I go.

"Dammit!" I pull the shunt from my arm, grab a handful of tissues to blot up the blood, and kick the stand.

The heart-rate monitor beeps soft and fast. I look inside my robe at the electrodes stuck to my skin. They must be monitoring me remotely. I need to calm down, figure out where I am. I roll my injured shoulder. It doesn't hurt at all. In fact . . . I look down at my hands again. My skin tingles under the stretchy material. I'm almost good as new.

A few flashes of memory skitter by. A dark loading bay, a medic drawing blood, the squeak of stretcher wheels. And a woman on the other side of the glass, shouting. *"You have to let me in! You have to let me see her!"*

I step into the patch of sunshine under the window and immediately reel back. I'm in a skyscraper, dozens of stories in the air—higher than I've ever been. I press my face against the glass and look down on a neat green park trimmed with trees, and across at the neighboring steel-and-chrome towers. None of them are as tall as the one I'm in. Enclosed walkways span the open space between the buildings, connecting them in a crisscrossing pattern. Gray streets jammed with tankers and trucks pass below. Between the towers, I spot stretches of highway wrapping around the western edge of the city, fortified with concrete barriers, concertina wire, and machine-gun nests. Atlanta. I must be in the heart of it. I've heard stories from people stationed here, but they always talked about looking up at the buildings, never down.

The door chimes. An orderly walks in, carrying a gray cafeteria tray, and after him a woman. She's no doctor or medic. It's in the way she walks—confident, but unhurried. She has golden-brown skin and chin-length platinum-blond hair, and wears a white silk pencil skirt and blazer. Her matching heels lend another few inches to her already imposing height. She carries a small gold box.

She stops when she sees me. For a split second, her face registers some emotion I can't name—not surprise, something deeper and more subdued than that. I can't stop looking at her. I don't know if it's just that her walking in is like catching sight of a flash of pyrite on a dull riverbed, or if it's something else. Something familiar, but not.

"Thank you," she says as the orderly sets the tray on the rolling table next to the bed.

I frown. She's older than I first thought, around the same age as the Deacon and Rosalie. I hear it in her voice. We wait in awkward silence until the orderly finishes arranging the tray and leaves.

"They said you were hungry." She gestures to the food—slices of pear with bright yellow skin alongside chunks of a slippery-looking orange fruit, perfectly black coffee with a tiny pitcher of thick cream beside it, fluffy eggs and toast, a still-melting pat of butter on top. "Please, eat."

The smell of bread and coffee pushes all other thoughts from my mind. I temporarily lose all dignity, clamber over the bed, sit on its edge, and dig in, scooping up the eggs with a piece of toast. They're lightly salted and airy, the coffee is smooth, and the orange fruit tastes like syrup in my mouth.

"May I sit?" She gestures to the foot of the bed. Her wrist com catches my eye. It isn't the standard dark green plastic, but a milky mother-of-pearl cuff glowing softly with data.

I stop, mouth full, and nod.

She takes a seat, smooths her skirt, and laughs, a tight, unnatural sound. "I know they said you were hungry. They forgot to tell me you were part horse."

I swallow and blush. Why is some woman dressed like an AgraStar CEO sitting here trying to joke with me? No one brings prisoners trays of fresh breakfast foods and sits next to them while they eat. Does that mean I'm not a prisoner? But then why is my door locked from the outside? I need to be more careful, watch what I give away, try to make sense of all this.

"That would be much easier without those dermagrafts." The woman nods at my hands. "They should have done the trick by now. Would you like some help taking them off?"

I look down at the rubbery coating on my palms and then up at her. As nice as she's being, they could still change their minds any second and decide I'm not worth the security risk. I have to be cooperative, compliant, a model employee, unless I want to end up like everyone else on SCP-52.

"Okay," I say.

"Here." She holds out her hands.

I place one of mine in them. "Who are you?"

"I'm Dr. Orelia Salcedo." She pinches the edge of the dermagraft and begins to peel it up slowly, uncovering the rosy skin of my palm. "You'll have heard of me?"

I stiffen. *Salcedo?*

I realize she's waiting for my answer. "N-no." I make myself blink, try to look natural.

Her face falls, but she tries to cover it by swiping a strand of hair out of her eyes and focusing on the dermagrafts. "I'm the head of AgraStar's research and development department."

I go still as stone, my hand frozen in hers. Research and development? She has to have known about the blight project, then. She has to have known what it did, what it was designed to do. She might even have been the architect behind the whole thing. At the very least, she would have signed off on it.

I straighten my spine. "I appreciate you coming to see me, ma'am," I say. "Whatever you want to know about the seeds or the blight, I'll do my best to tell you."

Dr. Salcedo ignores my offer and pulls the last of the dermagraft from my right hand with a snap. "All done. Now the other one."

I stare at my hand. The skin is as good as new, smooth and perfectly restored, down to the whorls in my fingertips. I've heard about med tech like this, but I've never seen it. I always thought it was reserved for severe cases—whole-body burns and facial mutilations, not cosmetic scarring.

"You might feel some itching for a few days," Dr. Salcedo says, pulling my other dermagraft free. "But don't worry. That means it's healing."

"Ma'am—"

She laughs once, almost a yelp of pain. "Please, you don't need to call me ma'am."

"What do you want me to call you?" I ask.

She glances at her coms, and then up at me. "It's Torres, yes?"

I frown and give a single nod.

"You've brought us something very valuable, Miss Torres." She balls up the used dermagrafts and places them on the bed between us. "Two things, really."

"The seeds?" I say.

"That's right." She looks me in the eye. "AgraStar appreciates your loyalty and all the trouble you went through to bring this information to us. You've saved countless lives."

"What's the other thing?"

She reaches for my hands again. "You've brought my daughter home."

"Your daughter?" I frown. "No, I . . . there was no one else but Alder . . ." And then the pieces come together. *Miss Salcedo.* The tray of exotic fruits and real bread. The top-shelf medical care. The intensity in the way Dr. Salcedo looks at me.

"I'm your mother, Tempest." The head of AgraStar R&D squeezes my hands in hers. "I've been looking for you for fourteen years."

.18.

SWEETBAY MAGNOLIA
MAGNOLIA VIRGINIANA

I study her face, trying to make out some reflection of my own. I think I can see it, if I look past the makeup and dyed hair. The strong jaw; the almond eyes and long, black lashes. Our noses are different—hers aquiline, mine broad—and her eyes are seafoam green, whereas mine are brown. Am I seeing the truth or just random patterns amplified by suggestion?

"How . . . how do you know?" I say. "There must be some mistake. . . ."

"You were missing your coms when you came in," Dr. Salcedo says. "Triage did a blood test to identify you, and it flagged your missing-person report. But the moment I saw you . . . I would have known you anywhere. You look so much like your father."

She reaches out to caress my hair, but I shrink back. This is too much, too strange.

"Forgive me." She draws her hand away. "I look at you, and I still see my baby, my little girl, but this must be difficult for you. They warned me it would be."

"I . . . I'm sorry." I look down at my tray. My mind is reeling, but my body feels still, detached. *Am I really here?* Maybe I'll wake up in the back of the truck any minute, or lying on the asphalt, my hands pinned behind my back.

"Do you remember anything? You were so young, barely three, but . . ."

"I don't know." I rub the bridge of my nose. That moment in the creek comes back to me, the memory of the bathtub and the woman. "Just . . . flashes, I guess. Things that don't—didn't—make sense."

She sighs and sits straight. "It's not your fault."

"You said I looked like my father," I say haltingly. "What I remember . . . it's mainly him. In the forest. We were always walking and he would si—"

"Don't talk about him," Dr. Salcedo snaps. Then she softens. "Please. It's too hard to hear."

I swallow. I'm not dreaming. This woman may be my mother, but she's still AgraStar management. I can't afford to make her angry.

"Can I ask . . ." I hesitate. "What happened? How did . . ."

"He kidnapped you," she says. "He took you from me."

My head swims. My father? The man who ate dandelions

and sang as I rode on his shoulders? "Why would he do that?"

"He met some people who . . ." She presses her lips together and looks away, twisting her com cuff absentmindedly. "They radicalized him. He stopped believing in AgraStar's mission. He wanted us to leave—all three of us—but I didn't think he was serious. Leave a prestigious job at AgraStar? To become a scavenger?" She shakes her head and scoffs.

"But I ended up at the SCP compound," I say, confused.

She frowns, comes back to me. "The security analysts said your father had gone southwest, into Bloom territory. They scoured all their scavenger surrender records and new contracts for three years—believe me, that wasn't easy to arrange." She gives a small, humorless laugh. "We never thought he would stay in AgraStar territory, much less survive off the grid. The facility you turned up at in the SCP region didn't flag your intake record as suspicious, and so they never cross-referenced your DNA."

"And my father was dead." I stare at my half-eaten breakfast, no longer hungry. "So there was no one to question."

"If your facility managers hadn't died in the accident, you can believe there would be an inquest." Her voice ices over. "We're ordering a full audit of intake and security procedures at all compounds. Nothing like this will ever happen again."

Something gnaws at me. *The accident.* Does she know about the Deacon's part in it? Did she know what R&D was making out there? She must have. And that means she must know whether the blight was a simple miscalculation or a weapon all along, like Crake said.

"Could I see the security records?" I say. "Maybe I could help piece together what happened."

"Oh, m'ija, no." She softens. "I don't think that's a good idea."

M'ija. That word clicks home in my brain and sends all the tumblers of my memory turning. *"Put this over your eyes so I don't get soap in them."* Someone pushing me in a swing. *"Higher, Mami, higher!"* Hiding under a table, raised voices in the kitchen, staying quiet so the grown-ups don't notice me. *"Come sit with me, m'ija."* Leaning my head against someone and swiping through the pages of a story on a tablet. Her arms. The gentle press of peace all around me.

And like that, all my walls come down. All my certainties and doubts, plans and strategizing crumble, as if they were tuned to the frequency of that one word. My eyes sting. I want to curl up with my head on my mother's lap and run circles around the city, my hair flapping behind me, blood singing with endorphins, at the same time. That word. It isn't simply some pet name. It's everything I've worked for all my life. That word is belonging.

"Are you okay?" Dr. Salcedo touches my back. *My mother* touches my back.

"I, um . . ." I need to pull myself together, but I feel as if I'm trying to stack bricks in an earthquake. My whole body trembles. I want to laugh. What were we talking about? Does it even matter anymore?

Get it together, Tempest. I draw myself up, try to look

confident, even if I'm still in a hospital robe. "I want to help. I'm a trained perimeter guard. I have the security background."

"I know you do," she says gently. "But you've been through so much. You'll need time to recover and reacclimatize, get used to your old life again."

"I can handle it," I say. "You need everyone you can to help stop the blight, right?"

She strokes my arm. "You've done your part, bringing us those seeds. Everyone on my staff is working on the problem. Now we simply have to wait." She stands. "Why don't we find some real clothes for you? I thought you might like to see our family quarters."

I hesitate. "What about Alder?"

"Who?"

That moment of warm euphoria fades. "Alder. The boy I came in with."

"Oh, yes." My mother waves her hand as if she's swatting away a fly. "He's critical, but stable. He'll recover, but he's not ready for visitors yet. That Red Hand cell you informed us about has been dealt with."

The way she says "dealt with" makes me think of something more final than arrest. Fire on the horizon. The sky darkened by smoke. *Good,* I think, until I remember the children on the Red Hand base. Have they been "dealt with," too? And what about the men out chasing us? Are they still out there? I look at the woman next to me, and a cold feeling creeps up my spine. She isn't just my mother. She's a senior AgraStar official. She's powerful. Dangerous. I wouldn't want to be her enemy.

"I have a surprise for you." My mother smiles and taps her com cuff. "Have them send it in now."

Another orderly backs through the door, pulling a rolling rack stuffed with an entire wardrobe's worth of clothes.

"Choose anything you like." My mother grins. She's clearly been looking forward to this.

I sift through the rack. Every item is some shade of pastel—lilac, butter, lime, rose. I choose a simple, cream-colored shirt and moss-green pants. It's the closest I can find to my old uniform.

"We can do better than that." Dr. Salcedo laughs. "You're in the city now. You don't have to dress like a drone anymore."

A drone? I bristle, but she doesn't seem to notice. She picks out a baby-blue skirt with a band of navy around the hem and a pair of low, sparkly heels that change color as the light hits them from different angles.

"Come on. Give these a try."

Keep her happy, I remind myself. Despite all the emotions flooding me, my mother and I are strangers to each other. It doesn't change the fact that she needs to like me. She needs to think I'm pleasant and compliant. The model employee, the perfect daughter. I can still feel the ghost of the zip ties around my wrists.

I put on the new clothes. They fit well. The skirt, lined with cool satin, floats around my knees, and even the plain V-neck shirt has a subtle sheen worked into its thread, like white morning light refracting through mist. Another fragment of memory—spinning around and around under the sunshine so my dress will catch the air and billow out around me. My favorite dress, with a print of blue chickens and yellow cornstalks. Was that me? A carefree little girl in a dress? *"Fancy-ass princess shit,"* Seth would say. But Seth's dead. There's no one to judge me but myself.

"Better?" I ask my mother.

"Better." She beams.

The wall I've begun to rebuild cracks again. Maybe she feels as uncertain and awkward around me as I do around her. And maybe it's weakness, but I want to be liked—no, loved. To be comforted. To know, after all these years on the margins, that I fully belong. Whoever that little girl was, whoever that woman was before her daughter was taken from her, I want us to be that again.

"One more thing." My mother picks up the gold box and opens it. Inside rests a com cuff, exactly like hers, on a bed of blue velvet. She clips it around my wrist. It activates with a soft glow. The hinges seal themselves.

WELCOME, ADELA SALCEDO. The message scrolls across the device's surface. PLEASE ENTER USER PREFERENCES.

I frown at the cuff. "Was that . . . is that my real name?"

My mother winces. "Your father told you your name was Tempest?"

I nod.

"We had a friend with that name who died on a transport

mission." She shakes her head. "We can still call you that, if you prefer."

I can tell by the tightness in her jaw that she hopes I'll say no. But this, I can't fake or grow accustomed to, like skirts or glittery shoes. A new last name is weird enough, but Tempest is mine. I can't give it up, even if the man who gave it to me and the woman it belonged to are both dead.

"I'm used to Tempest," I say. And then, because she looks so sad, "I'm sorry."

My mother shakes her head. "It's not your fault. Your father's the only one to blame. The rest of us have to deal with the consequences as best we can."

I look down at my com cuff again. It's already monitoring my heart rate and temperature, pinpointing my location and giving me the time and weather forecasts.

"Come on," my mother says. "I, for one, am sick of hospital rooms. Let me show you your new home."

We take a skywalk from the hospital to another building, and then a private elevator up to my mother's apartment. The hall outside is a windowless beige tunnel, but then she keys us through a set of double doors, and we're in a different world. An enormous room backed by a wall of windows looking out on the city stretches before us. There's a sunken sitting area with a long white sofa and two chairs directly in front of me, and off to the left, blond wood floors lead to a dining table and a kitchen. A floor-to-ceiling birdcage takes up the right-hand corner of the open space. Inside sits a snow-white cockatoo. It ruffles its feathers and eyes me silently.

"What do you think?" My mother sounds nervous, if such a thing is possible.

It's like something out of an AgraStar PSA, where they show a woman in an enormous, too-perfect kitchen, talking to the camera about the importance of updating your coms software or how the newest crops are so nutritious and high yield, you no longer have to worry about rationing. I always thought those were sets. I never thought anyone really lived in a place like that.

But I don't say so. "It's like walking into a cloud," I say instead.

I step down into the sitting area and approach the smartwall facing the sofa. A series of photographs cycle in and out of view. They have an old look to them, the resolution not quite as crisp as modern shots. In one, a family of five stands posed in matching white shirts—a man and woman, and three young girls, all with perfectly styled hair, straight white teeth, and clear brown skin. In another, a young woman in a green-and-gold graduation robe holds out a contract certificate for genetic research, grinning shyly. My mother, I realize. In a third, an old woman sits with a little girl in her lap, a smile of delight on her face as the child leans forward to blow out five candles on a cake.

"Who are these people?" I ask. "Are they your family?"

"They're *our* family." My mother joins me, facing the wall. "Your grandmother and grandfather, your aunts Evelyn and Valeria, and that's your great-grandmother Zamira holding me."

I squint at the last picture. There's writing on the cake, but words I don't recognize. ¡FELIZ CUMPLEAÑOS! "What's that say?"

"Oh, it's only 'happy birthday.' Your great-grandmother was always trying to push us to use Spanish around the house." My mother smiles and shakes her head. "She was already a young woman when AgraStar stepped in to bring order to things. She was so stubborn. She could never get used to the new ways."

I bite my lip and stare at the woman in the photo. Was that the language my father spoke? Was that what he sang to me in as we walked through the forest?

I lean closer to the photo. The woman—my great-grandmother—wears a mischievous smile and a little silver necklace around her neck. A cross. A bolt of shock runs through me. That's the same symbol Eden and some of the other scavengers wore. Why is my great-grandmother wearing it? Does that mean she believed what they do?

"Where is she now?" I ask. "Does she live here?"

My mother shakes her head. "She died when you were a year old. I doubt you remember her."

"Oh." Grief stirs in me. Or maybe it's not grief but some cousin to it. Longing. I know it doesn't make sense to feel like I've lost something, when I never had it to begin with. It's just for a few seconds; I wasn't being careful and started imagining what it would be like. Not only having a mother, but a whole family history. And someone who might understand how mixed-up all of this is making me feel. Someone who knew who we were before AgraStar. It's the same feeling I get when I try to remember the words to my father's songs—as if I'm touching a hole in myself where they used to be. I can hear the melody, but it's not the same.

I frown. "Why didn't you want to speak Spanish with her?"

"AgraStar management speaks English. It's easier if we all use the same language. We wouldn't want anyone to feel uncomfortable, wouldn't want people not being able to understand each other, would we?"

Part of me believes what she says—the part that wanted to hit all my marks and prove myself to AgraStar. But another part of me—the part of me that hid in the woods with Alder and saw the people in his camp mourning Eden the way no one will ever mourn Ellison or any of the other people who died on SCP-52—that part throbs *wrong, wrong, wrong.*

A memory rises up at me. I'm small, in the play yard at the compound, the sun hot on my head. I'm playing tag with the other kids, and one of them grabs me by the ponytail. She won't let go. "¡Suéltame! ¡Suélltame!" I scream, until our minder comes running and separates us. The other girl gets her hands slapped, but the minder marches me into the washroom and sticks a bar of soap in my mouth. *"You don't talk like that, you hear? English only. You talk like a shirk, you get treated like a shirk."* I taste the soap mixing with my tears, and I nod.

My mother touches my shoulder. "Tempest? Are you all right?"

My voice won't come out. My body feels feverish, as if it's rejecting the memory, rejecting what my mother said. Why can't people speak more than one language? Why should we be the ones who have to change to make everyone comfortable? Who decided all this? I feel the words on the tip of my tongue, dangerously close to coming out.

Get control of yourself, I order. *You don't want to upset her. You don't want her thinking you aren't company-compliant anymore.*

"You call me *m'ija*." The word sticks in my throat. "Isn't that . . . that's Spanish, right?"

"It's only a little family nickname." My mother looks uncomfortable. "Just between us, at home, it won't bother anyone. My mother and grandmother used to call me that. Do you mind?"

A small part of me settles, pulls back from the brink. Maybe she isn't all perfect AgraStar etiquette and regulations. Maybe there's some part of my great-grandmother in her still.

"No," I say. "I like it."

She smiles. "Good. Would you like to see your room?"

I start. "My room?" I know this is a thing people who have earned out their contract do, keep a separate, private space for themselves, but I'm several years away from even signing my own contract.

"We can't have the head of R and D's daughter sleeping in

the barracks," my mother says. "Can you imagine?"

"Oh." Of course. I'm not Tempest Torres, still earning out her contract. I'm Adela Salcedo, born with parents who could buy out the contract.

"Did I . . . did we live here before?" I ask. Nothing about this place is remotely familiar.

"No. I couldn't stay in our old apartment after your father . . . well . . ." My mother closes her eyes and smooths her skirt. "I wasn't the head of R and D then. Promotion has its perks."

I wince. "Sorry."

"That's all past now," she says brightly. "Let's finish our tour."

I follow her down a hallway. The only illumination comes from a long aquarium built into one wall. Brilliant purple jellyfish, each with a ridge of frills along its top, drift in the water, their tendrils glowing lavender and white in the underwater lights.

"Portuguese man-of-war," my mother says. "Beautiful, but toxic."

We arrive at a bedroom, smaller than the vast living room, but still much larger than any sleeping quarters I've seen. Almost the size of the women's barracks at my compound.

"Here it is. I know it's a bit bare, but I didn't know what kind of things you liked, and well . . . I thought you might like to decorate it yourself."

My feet sink into the carpet. The room is another PSA set, in green-and-rose tones. Gauzy pink fabric covers the windows and the top of the four-poster bed. A mint-green cover lies over the high mattress and fluffy pillows, and a shaded lamp casts a soft coral glow throughout the space. There's a built-in bookshelf next to a set of closet doors on the left wall, but the only things on it are several decorative ceramic balls and a white picture frame playing the same set of photos as the smartwall in the living room. It looks like no one has ever walked in this room, much less slept in it.

"Do you like it?" My mother asks. "It used to be the guest room."

I turn in a slow circle, taking it all in. "It's just me in this room? I'm not supposed to share with anybody?"

This much space for one person seems a waste, but between the soft light and the fact that whatever painkillers they had me on are wearing off, part of me wants to lose myself in that oversized bed.

"It's just you." My mother takes a hesitant step toward me. "I know maybe you aren't ready—it's a lot to take in—but . . . may I hug you?"

I freeze. She looks at me expectantly. The last time anyone hugged me was . . . I think back over the back slaps from my trainers and casual half hugs from my teammates when we did well on an exercise. It was Rosalie, and I was nine. She would check in on me sometimes, bring me a little extra something, like an apple or a small bag of caramel corn. When I heard her in the hall outside the children's quarters, I would race to her and throw my arms and legs around her like a monkey. Until that day when I was nine.

That day, she caught me under the arms and stopped me. "You're too big for that now." She knelt down so that she was eye level with me. "I can't be showing favoritism. You understand that word?"

I nodded, even though I didn't, not entirely. I knew it had something to do with favorites, and Rosalie didn't want anyone to think I was hers.

Later I understood, and I knew Rosalie was right. I wouldn't have wanted anyone giving me something I hadn't earned, especially if it was because they felt sorry for me. I wanted to prove I wasn't some shirk like my father.

Except that wasn't who he was. He was something else entirely, something like Deacon Ward. A defector. A kidnapper.

"Ade—I mean, Tempest?"

"I . . ." I waver, caught in a swirl of memories. Rosalie's hands gripping my arms. The clover ring. The white-tiled bath. The twirling dress.

A chime sounds throughout the apartment. "Mami!" a girl's voice calls from the living room. "I'm home."

My mother stiffens and purses her lips. "I thought we'd have a little more time to talk, but . . ."

Footsteps tromp closer. "Mami, I think we're out of—"

The girl stops cold in the doorway, staring at me. I stare back.

My mother clears her throat. "Tempest, this is Isabel, your sister."

CHOKEBERRY
ARONIA MELANOCARPA

The girl facing us looks exactly like me, minus a handful of years. Same light brown skin, broad jaw, hair pulled back in a glossy dark ponytail. She wears a khaki skirt, white sneakers, and a green shirt with the AgraStar logo embroidered over her heart.

"Isabel, this is your sister Adela . . . Tempest." My mother corrects herself. "You remember we talked about her?"

"Yeah." Isabel goggles at me. "I thought you were supposed to be dead."

"Isabel!"

"What?" She arches an eyebrow at her—our—mother. "That's what you said."

My mother sighs.

"It's okay. This is pretty weird for me, too." I smile

awkwardly at them, even though my heart is stinging. A sister. What the hell? I know that shouldn't bother me. People get on with their lives. It's normal.

"Isabel, why don't you go fix yourself a snack?" my mother says. "Tempest and I will be along in a minute."

As soon as Isabel is out of sight, she sighs again. "Eleven years old and still putting her foot in her mouth."

"She looks like me." I stare at the floor. "Like my father."

My mother nods. "He was her father, too."

"What?" My head snaps up. "How?"

"Your father and I had our embryos frozen." She looks at me, and then quickly looks away. "You'd been gone so long . . . I had given you up for dead, m'ija. And your father . . . I didn't want to be alone anymore."

My mind tumbles back to the forest, to Alder dying in the wet pine needles. *Of course.* Of course she didn't.

I take a tentative step forward and put one arm around her.

She lets out a little sob, drawing me closer and wrapping me up in both arms. "I missed you so much, m'ija."

I don't expect it, but suddenly my eyes sting and blur, and my throat feels like someone is holding it in a fist. I squeeze her tighter. We stand together in the petal-soft light, crying quietly and hugging each other until I forget everything else.

I dream I'm walking in the forest. A branch cracks behind me, and I spin around. Nothing. But then I notice the ground is alive with snakes. Copperheads and water moccasins. Black rat snakes and timber rattlers. All coiled together and writhing where the dirt should be. I turn back, but the path behind me is covered in snakes, too. I can't move either way. My throat spasms. I double over to retch, but what comes out is another snake, golden brown and mottled, with an arrow-shaped head.

I wake with a strangled shout, kicking the sheets from my legs. I sit on the edge of my new bed, gasping until my heart rate returns to normal. *Shit.* My skin prickles. I look at the untouched sleeping pills and glass of water my mother left by the bedside. Maybe I should have taken them, after all.

My head swims. I walk to the window and pull back the curtains. It's night, and the streets far below are deserted, except for the odd patrol car slowly winding its way between the buildings. Red and blue signal lights pulse and dim along the spire of the neighboring skyscraper. Floodlights shine out along the highway barricades. I've always liked being up high—in a tree or the guard lookout—but this is too high. I keep imagining myself falling.

I make my way to the bathroom and splash cold water on my face, then wander down the hallway, past the jellyfish, into the living room. A light is on in the kitchen. Isabel sits on the counter, swinging her legs and eating from a tub of yogurt. She pauses with the spoon in her mouth to tap at her com cuff, and it emits a burbling sound and a flash of pink light.

I stop short. "Hi."

Isabel pulls the spoon from her mouth. "What are you doing here?"

"I . . . um . . . I had a nightmare." I step closer, into the isolated glow of the kitchen. The refrigerator senses me, and its glass doors light up from within, showing me its contents.

Isabel holds out the yogurt container. "Want some?"

The memory of my dream tightens my stomach. "Nah. I think I'll just get some water."

Isabel shrugs and goes back to tapping and swiping at her cuff.

I stare at the cabinets lining the kitchen walls. Which one has cups? I peek in one, then another. Jars of olives and tiny onions, spices, oils, syrups, and dried peppers, then boxes of crackers and bags of puffed corn dyed orange, green, and purple. I glance over at Isabel and find her watching me, one side of her mouth pulled up in a smirk.

"Um . . ." Why is this kid making me feel so nervous? "Where do you keep . . ."

"Glasses?" Isabel points to a cabinet to the left of the sink. "There."

"Thanks," I mutter. I pull open the door and stop short. Crystal goblets and tumblers fill the shelves, top to bottom. I glance at Isabel to see if this is some kind of joke, but she gives me a confused look and takes another bite of yogurt. Her com cuff tinkles and sends up a cascade of blue light.

"What are you doing?" I look at her cuff.

"Bubblebop," she says, her mouth half full.

"What's that?" I ask.

She swallows and gives me a look that says she thinks I'm dumb. "A game."

I fill one of the heavy glasses with water from the sink and lean against the counter opposite her.

"Won't you get in trouble for eating all that?" I nod at the yogurt.

She freezes with the spoon halfway to her mouth. A small glob of yogurt falls back into the tub. "Huh?"

"Isn't it . . . I mean . . ." I flush. "I'm not going to tell on you or anything. I only . . . isn't it rationed?"

"Rationed?" Isabel looks at me like I've grown another head. "Nooo?"

"Oh. I thought Dr. Salcedo . . . I mean, your mother . . . might get angry." I look down at the water glass.

Isabel sets the nearly empty carton on the counter and drops the spoon into it. "Mami doesn't care if I snack as long as it's healthy."

"Oh." Of course. They have cabinets full of food and spices, all to themselves. If they have rations, those must be so generous they don't notice. Those PSAs are real for them. "Right. Okay."

"You're weird." Isabel hops down from the counter and silences her cuff. "Are you really going to live with us?"

"Is that what your mom says?" I ask.

"Yeah," Isabel says.

"Then I guess so." I gesture at the yogurt. "Are you going to finish that?"

"No." She folds her arms. "And I'm telling Mami if you don't stop picking on me about food."

I blink. "I'm not trying to pick on you, I just—"

"Whatever." Isabel turns and stalks toward the hall leading back to the bedrooms.

"Watch out for the jellyfish," I joke lamely.

She stops and rolls her eyes at me. "Portuguese men-of-war aren't jellyfish. They're a colony of smaller creatures that look like jellyfish."

"Oh," I say.

"Maybe you should go back to school instead of hanging around here bothering me," Isabel says, then spins on her heel and disappears.

I stand staring at the empty doorway for a moment, then turn back to the yogurt container. There's barely any left, but it seems a shame to waste it. I scrape it out and bolt it down, not really tasting it. Then I rinse the container and spoon and start back to bed.

I stop in the middle of the living room, caught by the soft glow of the family pictures slowly cycling on the wall. My great-grandmother smiles out at me from one of them. She's still gray-haired, but slightly younger in this one, with a man around the same age sitting beside her on a dock. My great-grandfather? My great-grandmother is holding up a fish as big as her forearm, pretending to kiss it. Her eyes gleam with mischief.

I don't think I've ever smiled like that. I doubt my mother has, either. I wonder what else she could have passed on if our family hadn't chosen to fall in line with AgraStar. If we'd kept to the outskirts like Alder's family, would I know the story of how she caught that big fish or what things were like when she was a girl, before the company-states? Did we have rituals for when someone died, like the Deacon did? For some reason, I find myself thinking about the Kingfishers' contraband tomatoes. There are a million reasons AgraStar didn't grow that variety. It tasted strange, but that was because it tasted so much more than the approved strains. It survived when those other strains didn't. And it might save us. What if the Kingfishers hadn't preserved it and passed it down all these years? What if they'd given in and only planted what AgraStar decided was best?

I step back. What am I saying? I shouldn't be questioning the company, not even in the privacy of my own head. That's how treason starts. *You're just exhausted*, I tell myself. *Your thoughts won't go to wild places like this in the morning.*

I go back to my room. Before I lie down, I take the sleeping pills and hold them in my mouth, feeling their shape with my tongue. I look out at the night, at the blinking lights atop the buildings and the pavement far below, and swallow.

Morning comes out of nowhere. I get up and peek out the window. The sun is high, glimmering on the neighboring buildings. I've slept late, too late. *Way to start off on the right foot, Tempest.* I shower quickly and pick through the collection of clothes in my closet. I need something my mother will like.

Something that will say, *See how well I'm acclimating?* I decide on the saffron dress with buttons all the way down the front. It reminds me of the sun and red clay. I feel strong in it, grown-up, like someone who can be trusted to look at security records and maybe even visit a sick scavenger boy.

I find my mother at a round breakfast table in a glassed-in patio beside the kitchen, scrolling idly through a tablet. She's as perfectly put together as the day before, only in a powder-blue suit this time.

"There you are!" She looks up and smiles at me. "I like the dress."

"Where's Isabel?"

"At school." My mother folds her hands across her lap. "I thought we could spend the day together."

School. Right. Of course. I take a seat next to her. "I'm sorry about the yogurt."

"Oh, was that you who ate it?" My mother laughs. "I thought Isabel was finally learning to clean up after herself."

"Yeah." I laugh along with her, but I sound nervous.

"What would you like to do today?" she asks. "I thought maybe we could go shopping. I had some points transferred to your cuff, in case you want to buy something."

Points. Another weird city quirk. All AgraStar contractors earn a monthly point allowance for extras like alcohol or sunglasses, but hardly anyone bothered with them back at the compound. There wasn't much to spend them on, so we mostly traded favors and food instead.

"Actually." I rub the back of my neck. "I was hoping maybe I could see Alder."

"I'm afraid he's still not well enough for visitors." My mother answers too quickly, as if she already has the words planned out. She glances at her com, not meeting my eyes. "Isn't there anything else you'd like to do?"

"Maybe . . ." I look at her cautiously. What I really want to do is sit in on a status update about the spread of the blight, or spend the day poring over my own files, trying to make sense of everything. But I don't think she'd allow that. Not yet.

"Could I see where you work?" I ask instead.

She frowns. "Wouldn't you rather go out and see the city? There are parks and malls. Isabel always wants to go to the aquarium. There's even a Ferris wheel. Have you ever been on one of those?"

I shake my head. I'm not a child. I can't go skipping around some park when I know how much danger all of us are in.

My mother stands. "We should go to lunch. There's a rooftop bistro upstairs. You're hungry, aren't you?"

I nod, despite myself.

"After that, I'll take you for a manicure." She beams. "And a pedicure, too. That will help you relax."

I stiffen in my chair. I don't know exactly what's involved in either of those things, but they have something to do with painting your fingernails and toenails, I think. The corpses of all the people at my compound crawl across my vision. I feel sick, like I'm going to vomit up that snake again.

I shake my head. "I don't think I want to—"

My mother's face is . . . crestfallen. That's the word for the way she looks.

"I mean . . . could we do that another time? I'm still real tired," I say.

"Very tired," my mother says.

"Huh?"

"You're *very* tired, not *real* tired," she corrects. "You're my daughter. You have to learn to speak properly."

"Oh." My face goes hot. I twist one of the buttons on my dress. "Right. Sorry."

"Tempest." She places a hand on my arm, suddenly all warmth again. "It's not your fault, m'ija. You didn't have the opportunities you could have had if you'd grown up here in the city with me."

"I went to school," I say. "Till I was twelve, same as everyone else."

"The same as all the sharecroppers and rig drivers." She cocks her head to the side and raises her eyebrows. "Didn't you ever think about doing something else? Working in R and D or, I don't know . . . strategic defense, since you seem fond of the security field? I saw your aptitude tests. You're as smart as your father was."

I give her a half smile. I can tell from her face how much it costs her to say something nice about the man who took me from her. It's an apology, of sorts, for snapping at me when I mentioned him yesterday.

"So, not so smart, huh?" I joke.

"Your father was incredibly intelligent." My mother squeezes my arm. "All the irrigation systems we use from here to the Gulf are based on his designs. That wasn't his problem. He simply couldn't deal with the kind of compromises you have to make in the real world." She pulls away and looks out at the city below me.

My stomach twists. *What kind of compromises? The kind that mean forgetting where your family came from? The kind that lead to developing a weaponized blight?* The knowledge of who my mother is, what she does, rolls over me again.

"I'm sorry," I say, for what feels like the millionth time.

"I'm the one who brought him up." She shakes her head, and when she turns back to me, her smile is bright as ever. "Let's forget about all of this and go have lunch."

We eat at a poolside café on the roof of her building, shaded by a red umbrella. Waiters keep bringing us fruit juices, fresh vegetables cut into roses and other shapes, and then chunks of raw fish rolled up in rice and seaweed.

"Sushi," my mother says, lifting a piece delicately with a pair of tapered sticks. The other tables, with their red umbrellas, and the impossibly blue pool reflect in her sunglasses. "So refreshing on a hot day."

I look at my plate and try to fight down the heat rushing my face. Everyone else around us is using the sticks, but I don't know how, and I'm too ashamed to ask for a fork.

"Is it really okay to eat?" I ask quietly. I'm starving, but everyone knows you should never eat uncooked meat.

"Of course!" She laughs. "You'll develop a taste for it."

I try to pick up my food, but I fumble, and the sushi plops back onto my plate. My mother stops eating and stares at me, lips pursed.

I look down. Flecks of rice and sauce dot my new dress. I am hopeless, like a freaking toddler.

"Here." My mother reaches over and positions my hands on the sticks. "Like this."

"Thank you." I am going to burst into flames. I don't dare look up at the people at the surrounding tables. "Why do we have to use these things anyway?"

My mother gives me a funny look. "It's just the way it's done. You wouldn't use a dessert fork for your salad, would you?"

I don't know how to answer that. I didn't know there were different kinds of forks for particular foods. I want to put my head down on the table, but I'm pretty sure that would make things worse.

"It's not your fault." My mother pats my arm. "If you'd grown up here . . ."

But I didn't. None of the things I've spent my life learning seem to matter here. It's as if the top of this building and the compound that was my whole world until a week ago are in different universes.

I look at the other diners. Two middle-aged women, both wearing pearls around their necks and a ring on each finger, sit at the table beside us. A man and woman in business suits have the table behind them. Two children splash in the shallow end of the pool while their mother reclines on a chaise, flicking through pages on a tablet. They all seem relaxed. None of them are acting like a wave of blight and death is swallowing up the compounds to the north. If I were them, I would be frantically packing my things or, better yet, lining up to volunteer to save my company.

Don't they care? Or—another possibility strikes me—do they even know? Has AgraStar told them the same thing my mother told me, that the crisis is in hand, that everything will be fine? Are they distracted by PSA-perfect apartments and a never-ending supply of food?

I look at my mother, and something cold settles in my gut. The more I get to know her, the more I don't want to believe that she knew what the blight was, that she could have ordered it created. But how much do I really know her? How do I trust anything she says is the truth?

I let my mother take me downstairs to get my hair cut after lunch. *Haircuts are normal*, I reason as the doors to the salon slide open and a waft of jasmine-scented air greets us. *Everyone gets haircuts.*

The salon stretches out before me, a long expanse of blond wood floors and plump barber chairs separated by gauzy curtains. There's a pond in the middle of the room, cut right into the floor, full of lily pads and the muted orange flash of enormous goldfish.

A tall, dark-skinned woman with braids piled in an elegant twist on top of her head hurries to us. "Dr. Salcedo." She smiles, but I hear the tension in her voice. "We weren't expecting you until Wednesday."

"Margit," my mother says. The two of them kiss the air beside each other's cheeks. My mother places a hand on my back, urging me forward. "I've brought my daughter. I thought you could squeeze us in."

"Of course." Margit shoots a look at her colleague, a mouse-boned woman with short blond curls sweeping hair clippings from the floor. Their look says it all. They know who I am. They've heard what happened.

Margit turns back to us. "Will you have the usual?"

"Not me today." My mother smiles at me. "Just Tempest."

"Tempest!" Margit beams. "Don't you look exactly like little Isa? Doesn't she, Lally?" She looks over her shoulder at the other woman.

Lally nods. "Spitting image. Two peas in a pod."

I squirm in my skin. They're being so nice, but it feels like pity.

"What shall we do with her?" Margit walks behind me and combs her fingers through my hair. It takes everything I have to fight my instincts and not flip her over my shoulder and then run out into the street. Except we're still several dozen stories in the air.

"So many split ends." She *tsks*. "What have you been washing your hair with, child?"

I don't answer. Back on the compound, we all used the same gel soap for our hair and bodies. There were specialty shampoos and conditioners you could buy at the commissary, but hardly anyone ever wasted credits on those, so they sat on the shelves, gathering dust. I never really thought about my hair before, except as a nuisance when it got in my face.

"Let's do the full treatment." My mother reaches forward and fingers a strand of my hair, too. "Straightened, same as mine. Maybe some highlights."

I don't know if I want my hair straightened, or what *highlights* means, but she's smiling, and Margit and Lally are smiling, so it seems best to grit my teeth and let them do whatever it is they want. Pleasant. Compliant. Unthreatening.

Lally sits me in a reclining chair and tips my head back into a sink. She runs warm water over my scalp, then lathers strawberry-scented shampoo into my hair. I close my eyes. Her fingertips circle around, massaging my scalp, and some of the muscles in my shoulders unknot. My mother or father must have washed my hair when I was little, but I don't have any memory of it. All I remember are the timed showers in the girls' dormitory.

Lally rinses my hair, works some sort of peppermint-smelling cream into it, and then rinses it again. My scalp tingles, but in a nice way. She takes me to one of the plush barber chairs and turns me over to Margit. My mother sits on a corner bench, checking something on her wrist com. She looks up as I enter.

"Better?" she says.

"Yes," I say. "Thank you."

Margit runs her fingers through my wet hair, letting it fall back around my shoulders. "You like to keep it long?" she asks.

I start to nod and then stop myself. "Yes." I like to be able to pull it up off my neck when I'm patrolling. Except now there's nothing to patrol.

"But not too long," my mother adds. "We don't want her to look like a shirk queen."

She and Margit laugh, and I make myself smile, but my chest feels full of stones. *Shirk queen?* So, my mother calls them that, too. I didn't expect that. I thought she was better, more refined.

Margit paints pieces of my hair with sharp-smelling gel, then wraps them in foil. She asks me about what I want to study and what I do for fun, but I don't have answers for either of those things, so she chats with my mother instead.

"Does Isabel have a new favorite animal this week?"

"Ugh." My mother leans back against the cushions. "She's trying to convince me to let her breed mice so we don't have to requisition them for Rene, but I told her I'd rather fill out all the paperwork in the world than chance a bunch of rodents running loose in the apartment."

I peek out from underneath the mass of foil. "Who's Rene?"

"Your sister's Burmese python." My mother rubs her forehead, and then looks up suddenly. "I hope you don't mind snakes. She's supposed to keep him in his cage, but you know Isabel."

I nod. Even though I've only just met Isabel, I think I know what she means. I decide not to tell her that my experience with snakes is limited to killing copperheads and relocating black rat snakes with a shovel. Or coughing them up in my dreams.

"Honestly, I keep telling her she'd have a much easier time if she took an interest in robotics or gene manipulation. There aren't that many positions available working with animals, unless she wants to work with the canine guard units." My mother says this like it's a bad thing, a failure.

"She'll come around," Margit says.

Lally reappears, trailed by a girl around my age with streaks of cherry red in her straight black hair.

"I thought we could give Miki a chance to practice applying a face mask." She looks at my mother. "If that's all right with you, ma'am."

"Of course." My mother waves a hand. "We might as well while the dye sets. Right, Tempest?"

"Right," I say, even as I grip the chair arms. Why do they want to make a mask of my face? There is no part of this that is not weird.

Miki stands by my side, stirring a green mixture in a bowl.

"What is that?" I ask.

"Avocado, oatmeal, yogurt," she answers. "Don't worry, it's all natural."

"Yogurt?" I draw back. She's going to put food on my face? I cut my eyes to my mother. This can't be right. But she's deep in conversation with Margit, both of them turned away.

"Hold still." Miki daubs the light green paste onto my forehead and then down around my eyes.

"Shouldn't . . . shouldn't someone be eating that?" I glance at the bowl.

Miki laughs and sticks out her tongue. "Yuck! I guess you could, but who'd want to?"

I frown. "We never did this kind of thing at my compound."

"Ugh, I know." Miki smears the paste down my nose. "After I earn my contract, I want to spend some time going around to the compounds and teaching beauty and relaxation techniques. Those assignments are so stressful—and the sun damage your skin is getting!"

I swallow. "Have you heard anything from the compounds?" I ask. "Did the firebreaks work?"

"Firebreaks?" She steps back. "You mean the forest fire to the north?"

"Tempest!" my mother says sharply, then softens her tone. "Let Miki do her work."

I sit uneasy in my skin as the paste dries. *Forest fire.* Why doesn't my mother want me talking about it what it really is? Is that why no one is afraid, no one is panicking, trying to leave the city? They think it's only a forest fire? I glance at my mother, bent over her com cuff, frowning. How much more does she know? Will the firebreak be enough to stop the blight, or will it keep spreading? Will the seeds Alder and I brought make a difference? Or will we never be able to plant again where the blight has blown through?

I need to find Alder. Not only to make sure he's okay. I need to talk to him, work out what's real and what's not. Our time together is starting to feel like a distant nightmare, a hallucination. How could all of that have been real, and this too?

After the paste has been washed off, after the foils are removed and my hair clipped and blown straight, my mother and I stand in the elevator.

"You shouldn't talk about the blight, Tempest," she says.

"Why not?"

She presses her lips into a thin line. "We don't want to alarm the general population when there's no need. The situation will be under control soon enough. Your actions have seen to that. It's best to let everyone keep living their lives without fear."

I stare at myself in the mirrored surface of the elevator doors. A stranger looks back at me. Her skin is smooth and clear, and her hair hangs to her collar-bone in layers, with subtle caramel streaks running through it. She looks beautiful. She looks like she belongs to the city, as if her father didn't kidnap her and she grew up in a picture-perfect world with everything she ever needed. But she doesn't look like me. I didn't think it would bother me to see all the frizzy curls gone from my hair, but there's something unnerving about it. I feel like some part of me is gone, replaced by an illusion. Can I be this girl? Or at least, can I wear her mask long enough to find out the truth?

.20.

DANDELION
TARAXACUM OFFICINALE

On the third morning in my new home, my mother walks
into the sunroom wearing a white lab coat over her yellow
chiffon blouse and tailored skirt.

"I thought I might go into work for a few hours today."
She adjusts her sleeves and checks her wrist com. "Will you
be all right here?"

"Can I go with you?" I fold my hands on the glass tabletop.
I need information, and I won't get it here. There's a tablet in
every room of the apartment, but they access only AgraStar's
preapproved sites—gossip about singing-competition winners
and new restaurants opening, games like that one Isabel was
playing, updates on the "forest fire." I need internal files,
security records.

"Oh, Tempest. I don't know." My mother frowns. "Wouldn't you be bored?"

"No." I look down at my hands and then up at her. Will she buy this? "I like to be busy. And now, you know, I have all these opportunities I didn't before, yeah?"

"Of course." Her voice softens. "You can do anything you want now."

"I was thinking, I want to see what it's like to work in R and D. I want to help figure out how to end the blight," I say.

My mother sighs. "I understand you're concerned, but I keep telling you, you don't need to worry about the blight anymore."

"The next problem, then," I say. "Like, what if one of our rivals decides to weaponize their herbicides?"

She stares at me, expressionless. "I doubt anyone would risk it. Anyone who did that would void their trade agreements with the other company-states."

Stupid, stupid, Tempest. Why did I say that? I can't push her, even if every time she tells me not to worry about the blight, it makes me more certain it's creeping closer. The only way I'm going to find out the truth about anything is if I get out of this apartment, out from under her watchful eye.

"We got to learn some science in school, before I signed up for perimeter defense. I liked it. I always wished I could've learned more," I lie. And now for the knife twist. "Do you think it's too late for me?"

Her face crumples. "Of course not, m'ija." She tucks a newly dyed piece of hair behind my ear. "But just a quick tour, okay? I have a few things to attend to today."

"Thank you!" I smile and make sure to crinkle up the corners of my eyes so it seems more genuine. A small pang of guilt tugs at my stomach, but I push it away. I need to find out where Alder is. I need to know what's really happening with the blight. And if no one will tell me, I'll have to find out on my own.

My mother and I stop in the R&D reception area. Behind the receptionist, the wall plays footage of a cheery farmer leaning against a combine, and then a young scientist staring intently at something in a beaker. "At AgraStar Conglomerate, we are always pushing the bounds of innovation," a man's voice narrates.

The young man behind the desk looks up. "Dr. Salcedo! Aren't you still on family leave?"

"I am," she says coolly. "I've brought my daughter to tour the facility. Would you set up visitor security status for her?"

"Of course, ma'am." He gestures at a scanner built into the counter. "If you'll place your wrist com here, please, miss."

I hold my cuff under the red lights. It chimes softly, and he smiles up at me. "All done."

I follow my mother through a bank of turnstiles, stopping to scan my wrist com, and then waiting as she places her eye up to a biometric scanner outside a pair of glass doors. Beyond, tables upon tables of potted seedlings stretch out across a white-walled lab, lit by hanging heat lamps. People in lab coats walk between the rows, stopping to inspect the plants or peer through the microscopes stationed along the sides of the room.

The doors chime and glide open. A wave of warm air rolls over me, along with the smell of earth and green. I breathe in deep, and instantly, homesickness hits me. *Dew on the corn and the first hint of light on the horizon as my shift in the guard tower ends, crickets turning over their song to the birds. Red clay on my boots and the younger children filing by hand in hand on the way to the mess hall . . .*

My mother stops and looks back at me. "Are you all right?"

I blink myself back to the present. "Yes." I clear my throat. "I'm fine."

"These are the upcoming strains of corn for the next growing season." My mother waves at the plants spread out before us. "First we run the constructs through a genetic viability simulation module. After that, we test them for soil acidity resistance and success across climatological variation. Then the variants that thrive across multiple parameters are slated for distribution."

I stare at her. I know most of those words, but not necessarily when they're thrown together like that.

Her face falls, but then she rallies and smiles sheepishly. "I get excited. Would you like to see the herbicide and biological agent resistance lab? Or maybe the genetic modeling center?"

"Sure." I wish I'd opted for more schooling instead of guard training. If I keep giving my mother blank looks, she's going to catch on that it's not R&D itself that I'm interested in.

We pass through another set of glass doors that require both my mother's eye scan and her cuff, and start down a hall lined with framed photographs of cornstalks. A pink-faced, barrel-chested man in a security forces dress uniform stalks toward us.

"Director Salcedo." He smiles, and I notice his teeth are unnaturally small and even. "Will I be seeing you at the security forces appreciation gala tonight?"

"I'm afraid not, Mr. Kurich." She smiles apologetically and glances at me. "I'm sure you've heard I'm taking some leave to attend to family matters."

"Yet here you are." He follows her gaze. "Who's this you have with you, now? Is that who I think it is?"

My mother stiffens, almost imperceptibly. "This is my daughter Tempest. Tempest, Mr. Kurich is our director of security forces."

"Tempest. I've been itching for a word with you," Mr. Kurich says. "You're a hard young lady to find. Your mother tells me you've been too ill for a little chat."

I glance at her. He says "little chat" the same way she said "dealt with." My skin starts to crawl.

"Yes," I say.

"Well, I'm glad to see you up and about." He smiles again, but there's a sharpness to it. "Maybe now we can find the time for a conversation."

My mother steps between us. "I told you, Mr. Kurich, I don't believe that will be necessary."

His eyes glitter. "I'm the director of security forces. Any potential security matter falls under my direction. That includes Miss Torres."

"Miss *Salcedo* is my daughter." My mother's sharpness matches his. "She's no longer under your command. I'm sure you'll respect my judgment in this matter."

His face reddens. "Of course." Those teeth again. He looks at me. "I wish you a speedy recovery, Miss *Salcedo*."

He turns to my mother. "I hope you'll change your mind about tonight, Orelia. Security forces could use your support." I hear the quid pro quo in his words. It's not an invitation, it's a warning.

"I'll try," my mother says stiffly.

Kurich nods and stalks away. We watch him disappear through the doors. My mother lets out a breath.

"What was that about?" I ask.

"Nothing. Office politics. Nothing for you to worry about."

I want to reach out and squeeze her arm, tell her thank you. I'm not sure exactly what she just did, but she did it for me, and it cost her something.

But before I can open my mouth, she pastes a smile back on her face. "Shall we continue?"

We reach the end of the hall and enter a room full of softly humming screens. A young man with thick, wavy, black hair is hunched next to one of them, tapping and zooming in on a series of colorful bars stacked one on top of the other.

"Dr. Mitra," my mother says.

He swivels in his chair. His eyes widen, and he shoots to his feet. "Director Salcedo." He wipes his hands on his lab coat. "I didn't hear you come in."

"I'm showing my daughter the facility." She puts a hand on my shoulder. "Tempest, this is Dr. Mitra. He's one of the best geneticists in our modeling division."

"Pleased to meet you, Miss Salcedo." He holds out his hand, and I notice he's decorated his com cuff with several layers of fruit and vegetable stickers, like the ones I used to peel off my apples at breakfast each morning.

"Just Tempest." I shake his hand and then quickly look at the floor. He's distractingly handsome, with buttery brown skin and long eyelashes.

"Hello, Just Tempest." He winks at me.

I shove my hands in my pockets, unsure of what to do with them and glad I managed to find a pair of pants to wear, even if they are the color of honeyed cream and likely to stain if I do more than sit around the apartment.

"I thought you could run us through the analysis you're conducting on the seed sample Tempest brought in from the field," my mother says.

"Of course." He turns back to his screen, excitement surging in his voice as he pulls up a different set of multicolored bars. "It's an incredibly rare genotype. All the models show excellently low risk ratios if we insert this portion of coding into next year's corn strains." He points to a cluster of yellow hash marks on one of the bars.

"You've saved next year's harvest, Tempest," my mother says quietly.

"What about . . ." I look between the two of them. "What

about the other plants? The trees and things? And the people?"

They exchange a look.

"Corn production is the first priority," Dr. Mitra says hesitantly. "Then we'll look at the citrus crop and other fruit products. As for people, I don't know what we can do, aside from vacate the affected areas."

My mother nods. "We've already sent out evacuation orders to all AgraStar compounds within a hundred-mile radius of the detonation site. Everyone is safe. They've been relocated farther south or west."

"But what about the scavengers?" I frown. "Has anyone warned them?"

"They're on the land illegally." My mother's voice hardens. "We can hardly be held responsible for them, even if we knew how to get in touch with them in the first place."

"But they could die," I say. "If the firebreaks don't hold, if they breathe in the blight. And even if they do run, everything around them is dead for several hundred miles. They'll starve." Alder said some of the scavenger camps might get word through the Latebra Congress and reach safety, but not all of them.

"I won't shed any tears over a few shirks," my mother murmurs.

I suck in a breath. That could have been me. I could have been one of them.

Dr. Mitra looks uncomfortable. "I'm sure they'll see the evacuations in progress and put two and two together."

My mother's wrist com spits out an urgent, four-note tone.

She glances down and furrows her brow. "Hmph. I need to . . . excuse me." She turns and starts to walk away, then stops. "Oh, Tempest . . . Dr. Mitra, could Tempest stay here with you for fifteen, twenty minutes?"

"Of course." He nods. "I can show her my genetic duplication research."

My mother makes a face. "Maybe not that."

"Oh." His shoulders stiffen. "Of course. Maybe transgenics, then."

"Excellent." She gives him a brief smile and disappears.

"Do you really think they'll survive?" I ask.

Dr. Mitra shrugs. "They might. But we have to take care of ourselves before we can help anyone else, and we still have a long way to go."

I look the doctor in the eye. "Has the blight stopped spreading?"

A flash of alarm crosses his face. He opens his mouth as if to speak, then hangs his head.

"It hasn't, has it?"

His head snaps up. "It isn't all as bad as that." He checks over his shoulder, and then turns back to me. "Don't let your mother know I told you this, but it's almost contained along all borders except the east, and then there's the sea to stop it, if it gets that far."

The children's bodies on the bunker floor flash before my eyes, and then the gray trees with their shriveled leaves. I see the creeks and rivers branching across the land like a circulatory system. Purposeful or not, the blight is a weapon, engineered to kill anything and everything. "What makes you think it will stop at the sea?"

He looks from his computer to the door, and then back again, his eyes widening. "I hadn't . . . uh, excuse me. Could you stay here a moment? I'll be five minutes, no more."

"Okay." I point to his screen. "Could I look at the blight resistance data?"

"Of course." He pats his pockets, looking distracted. "I have some games on there, too, if you want. Harvest Town. Bubblebop. MoleMaze."

I raise an eyebrow at him. Does he think I'm a little kid?

"I'll be right back." He runs out, tapping something into his com cuff.

I take Dr. Mitra's seat and minimize the file he had pulled up. *Yes.* He's left himself signed into AgraStar's internal network. I check over my shoulder. His screen faces outward, so anyone walking in will immediately see what I'm up to.

My heart beats fast and tight. If Kurich is still around and walks in on me doing this, I have a feeling things are going to escalate beyond a "little chat." I open the link to the security division's intranet and page through. Building evacuation procedures, incident reports, transport guard rosters, patrol rotations, and—there! Protective Custody Database. Even if Alder is in the hospital, they'll still have him under guard.

I click to open the database, but the screen flashes red and a password box pops up. I try my old code from the compound.

INVALID ENTRY.

I drum my fingers on the lip of the desk. Dammit. I look behind me again. Any minute, my mother is going to come back or the doctor is going to realize he's left me with open access to the network and rush back in. If only Crake were here. He could hack past this, no problem. But he isn't. He won't ever be.

Crake. I must have watched him log into the security databases in the Eye a thousand times. With so many dead, will they have had time to update his records and erase his access codes yet? I close my eyes and move my fingers. Yes. I still remember it. I tap in the code.

The password box clears, and the screen fills with names. I let out a breath and then lean forward. *Where is he?* I scan the list, but there are too many entries, and I don't have any clue what security would have put down for Alder's last name. Does he even have one? Eden did, and Deacon Ward, but Alder's parents died along the road, so maybe he never even learned what it was. I re-sort the list by intake date. There. Four days ago.

Company-State: Unaffiliated
Sex: Male
Given name: Alder
Surname: N/A
Status: Medical detention, stable
ID Assigned: 02477193-S

Location: Complex MA, security sublevel 2, cell 2-020

Note: Self-surrender. Found incapacitated near roadblock 73-Outer, southbound. Treated for rabies, infection, severe dehydration. Recommend transfer after completion of observation period

I let my hand fall away from the screen. He's stable. Not too sick for visitors. My mother lied.

Maybe I shouldn't be surprised. But why would she care so much if I want to check in on him? Is she afraid he's going to . . . what did she call it? *Radicalize* me, like my father. Maybe he already has. Thinking scavengers' lives are worth saving seems to be a radical idea around here.

I hear someone coming. I quickly log out and pull up the genetics data again. I prop my elbows on my knees and lean toward the screen, trying to look engrossed.

Dr. Mitra appears in the doorway. "Ah . . . um, excuse me. I forgot . . ." He leans over me, and with a few taps and swipes, logs out of the network so all I can see are the files he's opened for me, the data on the blight-resistant tomato seeds. "There. Be right back."

He disappears again, and I'm left with nothing to look at but the color-coded bars on the screen. I fiddle with my com bracelet and tap open the heart-rate tracker. It shows a series of steep spikes from the past few minutes. I have to do a better job of keeping my pulse steady, so I don't leave a record of my wrongdoing.

"Hey!"

I jump. The guy from the transport, the one with the scar—Ellison, but not Ellison—stands behind me, dressed in pressed dark green fatigues and buffed black boots. He looks like a security forces recruitment poster.

"What are you doing here?" I blurt out.

He's not Ellison, I remind myself. *It's only a coincidence. An extremely fucked-up coincidence.*

"I was going to ask you the same thing." He smiles at me, that teasing grin I know so well, but on a living man, not a dead one. I feel dizzy.

"You're the Salcedo girl," he says. "Adela, right?"

"Tempest," I say. "But yeah. That's me."

"I'm sorry we were so rough on you during the drive in." He shrugs. "We didn't know who you were."

"Neither did I," I say quietly, and then look up at him. "Besides, you weren't the one being rough on me."

"Aw, well." He hangs his head slightly. "I didn't stop them, either."

I lean back in the chair and wave away his words. "I know how it is on patrol. I could have been anybody. A scavenger, or a spy for one of our competitors—"

"That's right. You were on security up at SCP." He smiles broadly. "Man, everyone in our unit went insane when they heard that. Director Salcedo's daughter, a perimeter guard, like us."

My whole body warms, and then my stomach drops. *He's*

not Ellison. As much as he moves and looks and sounds like him, he's a stranger.

"I know this sounds weird, but . . ." I twist my com cuff. "Did you have, like, a brother or a cousin at my facility?"

He frowns. "No. I'm an only child. My parents wanted more, but it wasn't in the cards."

"Are you sure?" I raise my eyebrows.

He nods. "Unless my dad is keeping a second, secret family on a mechanic's allotment."

I snort and cover my mouth. "Sorry."

He grins. "So, what are you doing up here?"

"Dr. Salcedo—I mean, my mother was giving me a tour."

He straightens his back and looks around. "Where is she?"

I shrug. "She got called away and left me with Dr. Mitra. Then he had to leave, too." I cock my head to the side. "What about you?"

"I'm on security transport duty," he says. "For the H-BAR."

"The what?"

"The herbicide and biological agent resistance lab." He nods to his right.

"Oh. What are you transporting?" I ask.

He shakes a finger at me mock-menacingly. "I could tell you, but I'd have to kill you."

I laugh again, despite myself.

"My unit's off tonight. Some of us are going out," he says. "You should come."

My smile falls away. It's not this guy's fault he looks like Ellison. He's nice. Has that same kind of gallows humor all of us on guard duty have. Any other time, I'd say, "Yes, sir, present for duty." But what about Alder? How can I go out when he's in a detention cell somewhere? And with Ellison's ghost?

I glance at the deserted hall behind him. "I don't know. My mother might not let me."

He nods. "I guess my mom would keep me on a pretty tight leash if I'd been missing for fourteen years, too."

I look down at my com cuff. "Yeah."

He stuffs his hands in his pockets. "Well, if you're able to get off daughter duty, we're meeting at the Ferris wheel at nine."

"Okay," I say, my heart beating faster despite myself. "I'll try."

He steps back and waves. "See you, Salcedo."

Salcedo. Homesickness washes over me. I push myself out of the chair. "Wait!"

He stops midway down the hall and turns. "Yeah?"

"You didn't tell me. What's your name?"

"Byrd," he says. "Eli."

I put my hand on the wall to steady myself.

"See you tonight." He smiles again, just like I remember, and with that, he's gone.

.21.

BUTTERFLY MILKWEED
ASCLEPIAS TUBEROSA

I sit at the sunroom table, studying the map of AgraStar headquarters. We're in the R&D building, full of labs and offices on the lower floors, and residences for the senior administrators and scientists above, as well as a health club, spa, and that pool and restaurant on the roof. MA, where Alder is being held, is two blocks over, near the security forces barracks. HEALTH CLINIC, INPATIENT WARDS, ADMINISTRATIVE OFFICES, the building key reads.

Isabel drops her schoolbag in the chair next to me and leans over my shoulder. "Whatcha looking at?"

I tap out of the screen. "Nothing." My voice sounds all wrong. Guilty. Defensive. And for no reason. The map is one of the unrestricted pages on the AgraStar network. No one would think I was trying to find a way to Alder by simply looking at it. "Just a map of downtown."

She folds her arms. "Are you actually leaving the apartment?"

"Maybe. I—"

My mother breezes through, carrying a tray of sliced vegetables. "What's this I hear? Going somewhere?"

I look down at the tablet, mind racing. "I ran into someone from security detail at the lab this morning," I blurt. "He invited me out with his unit this evening."

"He?" My mother raises an eyebrow and sets the tray down. "What's his name?"

"Eli Byrd," I say, dying a little bit. "But it's not like that. I only . . . I thought it'd be nice to meet some people my own age."

She frowns. "I'm sure I could invite my colleague Sonja's daughter and some of her friends over, if you're feeling lonely."

"No, that's not . . ." Why does she care? And why am I asking her in the first place? I've always been free to wander the open zones whenever I wasn't on duty—jog the track around the substation, visit the firing range, hang around the Eye or the motor-pool garage, listening for gossip. "I'm used to how things are in a security unit. I just want to feel, I don't know . . . normal for a little."

My mother's face relaxes. "I see. Where would you be going?"

"He said to meet at the Ferris wheel at nine o'clock." I look at Isabel, who's slumped in a chair and scowling.

"So late," my mother says.

"I guess my mom would keep me on a pretty tight leash if I'd been missing for fourteen years, too."

"I used to do midnight to six a.m. patrols," I say. "Besides, I'd be with a whole security team. Nothing's going to happen to me."

My mother purses her lips.

"And this way, you could go to that gala thing," I add, and smile. She was going to anyway; I'm sure of it. But now she doesn't have to feel guilty. "You don't have to hang around here keeping me company all the time."

"It would be good to put in an appearance." She stares out at the city, and then nods. "I'll have my people conduct a security audit."

"Does that mean yes?" I ask.

"Tentatively." She smiles. "And you have to be back before the midnight civilian curfew."

Yes! I mentally pump my fist. "Thank you." If nothing else, I can recon the MA building, see how difficult it would be to get in.

"Do you have enough points?" she asks.

I nod. Of course I do. I haven't spent any of the ones she transferred to me, and even if I had, she gave me enough to last an entire year.

She clears her throat. "In the meantime, I have something

for you." She sits on the opposite side of the table and nods at the tablet in my hands.

"What's this?" I look down. A new icon flashes on the screen. A security file. I tap to open it. *My* security file. I look up at her, wide-eyed. I had thought she was brushing me off when I asked to look at it.

"You said you wanted to see it." She reaches across the table and lays a hand over mine. I look at it. The tendons and veins stand out beneath her skin, but her fingernails are perfect, delicate ovals. *Tracing the elegant lines of my mother's fingers with my own chubby child's hand. Up and down, like a sound wave. Studying the folds of her knuckles and the lines on her palms.*

I draw back sharply and look up, meeting her eyes.

"I'm sorry," she says. "I should have asked. I—"

"No." I shake my head, guilt overwhelming me. Here I am, plotting ways to work around her, and she's trusting me with the information I asked for. "It's only . . . you asked me if I remembered anything, and I think I do. Just a little piece."

She stills. "What was it?"

"We were at a meeting, maybe. Some kind of place where I had to stay quiet and sit in my chair." I study her expression. Soft and open. Wanting. "And I was looking at your hand."

She looks away and smiles. "You were always doing that. I showed you how to trace our hands with a pen one time, and you liked it so much, you used to pretend to trace them even when we didn't have any paper."

Isabel lets out a huff, grabs her bag, and storms out of the sunroom.

My mother and I exchange a surprised look.

"What was that?" I say.

She shakes her head and pushes herself up. "I'll go talk to her. Don't worry about it." She points at the tablet. "Just read over that, whenever you're ready. And if there's anything you'd like to discuss . . ."

I nod and hug the tablet to my chest. "I'll let you know."

"Good," she says, and then sweeps away, calling Isabel's name.

I gaze down at the screen, but my eyes won't focus. How can my mother be so soft and kind one minute, then so businesslike and calculating the next? The unpredictability makes me uneasy. But she cares about me. I don't think she's faking that. It would be so much easier to trust her and forget about everything that happened before, to lean back into all this luxury and opportunity, and never worry again. She'll take care of me. She trusts me. With her behind me, I could be more than a loyal AgraStar employee, I could be someone important. I could truly belong.

But Alder . . . Even if she gave me my security files, she lied about Alder. And she lied about the blight. Or at least, she didn't want me talking about the truth. I look through the doorway into the living room, where she stands talking to Isabel. I can't hear what they're saying, but I can see my mother gesturing, pleading. What else could she be hiding?

✸ ✸ ✸

I stand on the brick pavers beneath the lights of the Ferris wheel, a warm August breeze ruffling my hair. It isn't what I expected, looking down from my window several days ago. The skeleton of a larger wheel stands still and dark behind the lighted one. Most of its cars are missing, but the remaining ones are sleek, glass-enclosed pods, big enough for six people, easy. I crane my neck to look all the way up at it. That's what I saw from the window. I didn't even notice the smaller one in its shadow.

The sun has gone down, but the streetlamps and colored bulbs strung over the entrance to the ride give the plaza the feeling of dusk. Couples and families with small children breeze by, hand in hand, and a group of kids Isabel's age screams in delight from the top car. The smell of sizzling meat and popcorn wafts from the food cart vendors parked on the sidewalks. Several kids fly small radio-controlled drones with neon colors and flashing lights above our heads. The kids shriek when their toys nearly collide and then pivot them to chase one another.

Eli emerges from the crowd, wearing a plain black T-shirt and his green fatigue pants. He raises his hand in greeting. I'm braced to see him this time, and the shock is a little less. I wave back.

He stops in front of me. "Hey."

"Hey." I smile back.

"So, what do you think?" He looks up at the Ferris wheel and the skyscrapers beyond it.

I follow his gaze. "Everything's so tall."

He grins. "Spoken like a true country girl."

I roll my eyes at him. "Didn't you think the same thing the first time you saw the city?"

"I grew up here," he says. "It's just part of the landscape to me. I guess you stop noticing after a while."

"Yeah," I say softly. "It must be you can get used to anything if you grow up with it."

Suddenly it dawns on me—he's come alone. "Where are your friends?"

"They went to grab a drink," he says. "I told them we'd come find them after I introduced you to the Ferris wheel. I figured, she's never been to Atlanta, she probably hasn't crossed paths with too many amusement-park rides."

"I haven't." A giddy feeling starts in my stomach. I know I ought to be all business and gather as much information as I can, but I can't keep down a burst of excitement. "They won't mind if we go without them?"

"Nah." Eli waves a hand. "They're tired of it. They've been on it a million times."

"But not you?" We start toward the low metal entrance gates.

"I never get tired of Ferris wheels." He gives me a sly look. "Or pretty girls."

I stop, face flaming. Is that what this is about? My body is giving all the signs that's what I want, but my brain feels fuzzy, like I'm not getting enough oxygen. He's not Ellison.

He might sound and look and move like Ellison, but he isn't. And I'm not here for him, anyway. He's only my cover for reconning the MA building.

"Hey." He stops beside me. "Are you all right? I can't be that bad looking, can I?"

I force a laugh. "No, it's not that. It's just . . ." I stare up at the R&D building and the lights on its top floors.

"What?" he says. "Your mom doesn't want you fraternizing with lowly security forces now that you're one of the elite?"

"No," I snap, more sharply than I mean to. Although . . . does she? She didn't want me going out tonight, but that could have been for a million other reasons. "I'm sorry." I run a hand through my hair. "You look like someone I knew back home. Someone who died."

"Oh."

The lights and sounds of the plaza swirl around us, but we stand in silence.

"Did you . . ." He shifts from one foot to the other. "Were you two, you know . . ."

"No," I say. "But we might have been. I liked him. I think he liked me."

He nods. "That's why you were asking if I had a brother or a cousin."

"Yeah," I agree.

"I'm sorry," he says. "I had a teammate die on clearing duty last year. I know how it is."

I wave it away. "Not your fault."

"Okay, then." He draws himself up and shakes off the heaviness that's fallen between us. "We have a Ferris wheel to ride."

We climb into one of the seats, and the operator lowers a bar over our laps. My stomach tightens in anticipation as our car glides backward to let more riders on, and then lifts up into the air.

"What happened to the big one?" I nod up at the towering frame.

Eli shrugs. "Some relic from back in the tourist days, before AgraStar took over. My dad says it'd be a fuel hog if they got it running again."

"And this one isn't?" I say. We've reached the apex of the wheel, but its larger sister still towers four or five stories above us, the city's lights shining through its beams.

"This one's sweat powered," Alder says.

"Sweat powered?"

"Yeah." He points down. "Didn't you see the guys turning the cranks?"

"What? No." I grip the lap bar and lean forward. Far below, I catch sight of two bare-chested men turning a pair of cranks built into some kind of machine. A generator? I lean out farther to get a better view. The car pitches under me.

"Whoa!" Eli throws out an arm to catch me.

A half laugh, half shriek pipes out of me. "Shit!" I scramble back into the seat, giggling nervously.

"Not enough excitement for you, Salcedo?" Eli teases. He

leans forward and then back, making the whole car swing on its pivot bars. I laugh and join him.

"Hey, you two! Cut it out!" the operator shouts. "We're starting."

Eli stops rocking, and I go still beside him. The ride finishes loading and starts to move, slowly at first, circling down and then lifting us up and up above the streetlights, into the night. Our car reaches the top of the Ferris wheel, and our legs swing out over the empty space above the plaza. I yelp with delight. Adrenaline rushes through me as we swoop down toward the pavement, then circle back to begin the climb again. It's delicious. Like a runner's high, but without the effort.

I'm out of breath and grinning ear to ear when the ride finally stops.

Eli stares at me.

"What?"

He shakes his head. "Who'd have thought the director's daughter was a danger junkie?"

I elbow him. "Am not."

We step off the ride and wander out into the plaza.

"You hungry?" Eli says. "I'm hungry."

I'm not, but it's still early. I have plenty of time. And maybe I'm not in a big hurry to get away from him. Being with Eli is nice. Normal. The most like myself I've felt since I woke up in that hospital bed.

"Sure," I say.

"Scorpion cheese bombs?" Eli says.

I grin. "That sounds . . . terrifying?"

"I think you mean amazing," Eli says, taking my hand. "Come on."

He starts for the freestanding archway above what looks like a hole in the ground. As we get closer, I see it's an escalator ferrying a line of people down below the street.

I pull back. "What, down?"

"What's wrong with down?" Eli says.

"Nothing." I tilt my head back to look at the perfectly cylindrical skyscraper beside us. "I guess I'm just used to *up* now."

"There's more to the city than what's up there." Eli steps backward onto the escalator, and it starts to carry him down, away from me. "Don't make me eat those cheese bombs all by myself."

I laugh and step on after him. We come out at the bottom in a crowded concourse of glass-fronted shops. Handbags, shoes, and com cuffs in all colors rest on frosted-glass pedestals inside. Shop assistants stand by the entrances, pushing perfume, cooling gel packs, and color-changing fingernail tape at us as we pass.

"New com skins?" A woman steps into my path, completely ignoring Eli. "We have fresh releases this month, Raspberry Fade and a Bubblebop theme!"

"Um . . . no thanks." I step around her and frown at Eli. "What was that?"

"You're civilian. And fancy." Eli looks my outfit up and down. "You look like you have points to spare."

I want to shrink down in my skin. This isn't me. I'm used to fading into a crowd, being no one.

Bright lights shine overhead, and the chatter of voices and shouts of delight echo all around. Eli threads us through the press of people and over into an area full of tables and chairs. The smell of frying meat and corn oil swirls around me, and my stomach grumbles. Maybe I am hungry after all.

Eli gestures to one of the cafeteria-style food shops. "I'll be right back. Find us a seat?"

"I can get it." I hold up my cuff. Eli shouldn't have to use his hard-earned security detail allowance when my mother is drowning in company points.

Eli shakes his head. "No way."

I cock an eyebrow. "Because I'm a girl?"

"Because I'm the one who asked you out." He shrugs and grins. "Besides, it's only cheese bombs. I promise you can pay when we're dining on steak and buttered parsnips or whatever."

I wrinkle my nose. "What the hell is a parsnip?"

"Wouldn't you like to know," Eli lifts his eyebrows mysteriously.

I grab a table for us and check my data cuff . . . 9:40. Still enough time.

I stare across the cafeteria at a wall screen playing footage of the AgraStar board of directors and their spouses arriving at the security forces appreciation gala. One of the guests of honor climbs out of a shiny black Humvee, a clean-shaven young man with fair skin and a stiff limp. As he smiles and waves to the crowd, data points about AgraStar's latest achievements in prosthetics and cloned blood transfusions pop up beside him. Kurich steps out after him. Medals wink on the front of his uniform, and he smiles that awful, sharp smile. I stiffen. My mother is there somewhere. Will the camera pan to her? When I left, she was sponging makeup onto her cheeks, a silk dress the purple-red of blackberry stains laid out on her bed.

The footage cuts to a rotating ad—the same company slogans and pictures of happy people at work that used to hang on my old compound's walls. AGRASTAR CONGLOMERATE— COME GROW WITH US. I look away.

Kids' drones whiz overhead, beeping and flashing. A pair of children giggle and shriek as one of them pilots the drone and the other aims a plastic laser gun at its underside. The drone lights up red when the laser hits it.

"Got you!" the little girl yells. "You're crashed!"

Eli returns with a cardboard tub in one arm. "Nice shot," he calls to her, then takes a seat across from me. "We've got some future drone pilots on our hands here."

My stomach churns. The lights flashing on the toys above us are too bright. I close my eyes, and I'm in the dirt yard behind the children's barracks, playing guards and shirks with Seth and a bunch of the other kids. Seth goes down hard on one knee. I run at him and point a broken rake handle at his head. *"Pow, pow. You're dead, shirk."*

"Hey." Eli jostles my hand gently. "You okay?"

"Yeah." I shake my head. *You can get used to anything if you grow up with it.*

"You ready to try these?" Eli tips the tub toward me. A collection of neon-orange corn puffs flecked with green tumble to the edge.

I take one and raise an eyebrow at Eli, hesitating.

"What, are you chicken now?" His grin turns devilish. *"Bok bok bok."*

I roll my eyes and crunch down on the cheese bomb. A chemical burn immediately fills my mouth and shoots up my sinuses. "Holy—" I pound the table with my fist and wipe tears from my eyes.

Eli doubles over laughing and takes one for himself. "We used to bet each other how many of these we could eat in a row without going for water." He pops it in his mouth and shudders.

"Ugh." I wipe my hands on my pants. "I'm glad you didn't let me pay for those."

"They kind of grow on you." Eli eats another. "You've got to lean in to the burn."

"You're sick." I laugh. "They're all yours."

He dusts off his hands. "You still want to come have a few drinks with my unit?"

I check the time again. It's 10:06. I'm pushing it if I want to recon the MA building, then be back by midnight. But will it look suspicious if I don't go? Eli seems like the type who might insist on walking me home. The MA building is right near the barracks. Maybe I should go and then beg off after half an hour. . . .

"Okay," I say.

Eli leads the way back to the surface and over to the security forces barracks, a plain, five-story concrete building beside a fenced lot. Transport vehicles and tanker trucks sit darkened behind the chain link. He swipes us in at the front door, and we step into a lobby.

At once, I feel as if I'm back in the substation at my old compound—the close, warm air, the yellow fluorescent lights, the low ceilings, and the smell of cleaning products competing with so many bodies packed into one place. Even the same motivational posters hang on the cinder-block walls, though someone has drawn a mustache on the young woman balancing a basket of corn against her hip. A screen displaying a rotating list of the next day's duty rosters fills most of one wall.

Two identical corridors branch off from the lobby. We take the left one, passing a series of scuffed gray doors along both sides. Some of them are open, revealing cramped rooms with steel bunks. Shouts and music ring up and down the halls, and a group of young men with identical black T-shirts and cropped hair jog by us, carrying rolls of toilet paper. I stare after them.

"What?" Eli says.

"It's so loud here." The barracks at my substation were just one long room, women of all ages and duty rotations bunked together. No one ever made much noise. We were all too tired.

"Ground floor's always crazy." Eli hangs a right into a stairwell marked BASEMENT. "Full of new blood."

I follow him. "When did you sign on?"

"Four years ago," he says. "Fourteen."

"You studied some, then?" I trail him down the flight of stairs.

"A little. My dad wanted me to go into the mechanics' pool, like him, but, you know . . ." He shrugs and jumps the last few steps down to the floor. "No glory there."

Glory. My body goes cold, and suddenly, I feel tired. Is there glory in any of this?

"I'm up for unit captain this quarter," Eli says. "My own team."

I stop on the last step. I'm looking at him, but it's like looking at a reflection in a poorly made mirror, as if his every movement has a shadow and a blur.

He pauses with his hand on the door handle. "You okay?"

"Fine." I shake away Ellison's ghost. "I just . . . I think I'm not all the way back in shape yet. I keep getting tired easy."

"I hate that." Eli makes a show of slumping his shoulders. "I got the flu last winter, and it was such bullshit. I couldn't do anything for two weeks."

"At least I'm not contagious," I say.

He laughs. "Come on. They're waiting for us."

We push through the door and into a windowless basement room. A roar of laughter bursts out as it swings open. A dozen or so people our age sit at a trio of mismatched tables.

"I told you!" A girl with short black hair points at one of the boys. "I told you he would!"

The room smells sour, like dried sweat and old food. *Like the Eye*, I think. This is exactly how it was after shift change, when the pile of dirty uniforms hadn't been collected and Crake hadn't thrown away the protein bars and cheese corn bags he'd been snacking on all night. I can see him, his head backlit by the screens, blood on his teeth—

The door slams behind us.

One of the boys turns at the sound. "Byrd! Hey, you made it." His eyes skip to me. "Who's this?"

"Tempest," Eli says. "Salcedo."

"No way!" he says. "She looks like a civilian."

The girl elbows him. "She *is* a civilian now, dumbass." She slides her chair back and walks to me, hand outstretched. "Hey, I'm Garin."

"Hey," I say faintly. Half of me is still back in the Eye. I look past her to all the faces turned in our direction. One of the other boys glares at me from the far end of the table. I recognize him—he's the one who accused me of being a shirk on the transport ride into the city.

"So, you liking Atlanta?" Garin says. "Did Eli trick you into eating those scorpion things yet?"

I try to focus on the girl. Behind her, another boy leans against the wall. For a brief moment, his face shifts, and he looks exactly like Marco Etowah. Marco, his body still warm, his eyes glassy, hanging against his restraint in the back of the flipped jeep.

"Um . . . yeah . . ." I look over at Eli. A raw red hole has opened in the center of his forehead. He smiles questioningly, but then tendrils of blighted kudzu begin to circle his legs, creeping up his body, rotting the skin everywhere they touch. The room tilts like the Ferris wheel car.

"I . . . I'm sorry." I step back. The vine is climbing the corners of the room, withering as fast as it grows. My head is filling up with ghosts. "I can't . . ."

"Salcedo?" Eli's voice sounds far away. "What's wrong? Are you—"

I don't stay to hear the end. I bolt out the door, up the stairs, and down the hall, and burst out into the humid city night.

.22.

RATTLESNAKE FERN
BOTRYCHIUM VIRGINIANUM

"Salcedo!" Eli's voice rings out behind me.

I keep walking. I don't know where I'm going. I can't tell the buildings apart, even lit up like they are. I can't get Marco's eyes out of my mind, the way his pupils were dilated, big black pools of nothing. I can't stop seeing the kudzu engulfing Eli's body, his skin sloughing away as the rot touches him. He's dead. Him, Crake, Danica, Will, Ellison—

"Salcedo." Eli grabs my arm. "Tempest—"

I whirl on him. "You can't be here. You're dead. They're all dead!" How could I forget, even for a little while? How could I let myself try on pretty clothes, ride a Ferris wheel, flirt with a ghost?

"Tempest, what are you talking about?" He stares at me, eyes wide. "It's Eli. Remember?"

I laugh. "Are you? Are you even here? Are you real?" I hit him in the chest.

He winces. "Tempest, stop."

"Why?" I hit him again, harder. "You're not real. You're dead."

He tries to catch my hand, but I'm too fast.

"You're dead!" I shout, pummeling his chest. My eyes blur, and I don't care if I'm on a city street, or if anyone is watching. "You're dead! You're dead! You're dead!"

"Hey." Eli grabs my wrist, making me look at him. His scar is back. The vines are gone. "Hey, it's okay."

I try to speak, but all that comes out is a sob. He isn't Ellison. My mind keeps tricking me, making me think he's here in front of me, but he's not.

"Come on," Eli says.

He guides me down the street, one arm around my shoulders. I walk numbly beside him until we come to a pair of sliding doors awash in light. A woman in medical scrubs sits at the circular desk in the middle of the reception room, surrounded by several dozen people waiting in chairs.

"Where are we?" I ask.

"You don't need to be ashamed," he murmurs. "This kind of thing happened to my friend Jens when he had guard duty for a transport run to OBX compound."

The triage nurse looks up at us. "Who's hurt?"

Eli points to me.

"Bleeding?" she says. "Pain? Shortness of breath?"

I shake my head.

"Scan your wrist and take a seat." She points to a scanner on the counter, and then to the waiting room.

I do as she says and take a seat beside Eli. "What happened to him?" I say quietly, the fight gone out of me. "Jens."

"They gave him some pills and he was on light duty for a few weeks," Eli says. "That's all."

I stare at my feet. "No, I mean, what happened to him on the road?"

"One of the jacker gangs tried to steal their cargo. They drove them off, but the driver got shot."

Pills. Light duty. The waiting room starts to solidify around me. The flecks of mica in the tiles, the scratchy green fabric covering the seats, a wall screen cooing at low volume about AgraStar's latest advancements in gene therapy and what guests wore to the appreciation gala. My heart slows to something approaching normal.

"I'm sorry." I look up from the floor. "I don't know what happened to me. I shouldn't have hit you."

"It's okay." Eli stretches his arm across the back of the chairs. "You didn't hurt me any."

I smile. "Liar."

Eli studies me. "I really look like him, huh?"

I nod. "Exactly like him."

He shifts in his chair and frowns. "But it was something else that set you off."

I pause. "Yes."

"You want to tell me what?"

I rub my fingers over my palm and shake my head. We sit in silence for several minutes.

"You don't have to stay with me," I say. "I'm fine. It's your night off."

"More reason to keep you company," he says. "The health clinic's dead boring."

Suddenly my head clears. I sit up straight. This is it. The MA building. Alder is somewhere nearby.

"You want something to eat or drink while we wait?" Eli asks. "The cafeteria upstairs is open all night."

I glance around at the triage nurse and the other patients. No one seems to be paying any attention to us. "Um . . . yeah. Okay." I try to smile. "As long as it's not more scorpion bombs."

Eli winks at me. "Back in ten."

I watch him disappear into the elevator at the far end of the room, then count to twenty and stand.

"Bathroom?" I ask the triage nurse.

She points down the hall to the left, without looking up.

I walk quickly, trying to look casual. A set of double doors with a scanner lock closes off the rest of the floor from the waiting area. I try my com bracelet, but the lock flashes red and beeps unhappily. *Damn.* I stand back and wait, pretending to look something up on my com. A minute later, the door opens, and a young man in scrubs breezes past. I catch the door an inch before it swings shut and slip through. What was it Crake always said? *"The majority of system failures are the result of human error."*

Exam rooms line the broad hallway. I keep close to the

wall, ready to duck into one. The corridor Ts, and I stop. Which way? I close my eyes, calling up the floor plan in my memory. Right should take me deeper into the building, left toward the exterior. I turn right. I need a service elevator. And a disguise.

I scan the signs. EXAM 1017. EXAM 1019. SUPPLIES. MAINTENANCE. LAUNDRY.

Laundry. I stop and glance up and down the hallway. At the far end, an orderly pushing a patient on a gurney rolls in my direction, but I don't think they've seen me yet. I try the handle. Unlocked. I slip into the laundry room and push the door closed behind me.

Lights stagger on, sensing my movement. Huge rolling bins with black biohazard symbols stenciled across their sides fill the room, parked in crooked lines. I peer into one. Bloodstained and dirty scrubs, soiled sheets and pillowcases.

I grimace and pick through the bin. Halfway down, I find a pair of teal scrubs, wrinkled, but mostly clean. I ball up my own clothes, stuff them under one of the bins in the corner of the room, and pull on the scrubs. They smell faintly of someone else's sweat and deodorant, but no one will know it but me.

I take a deep breath, pull open the door, and step back out into the hall as if I belong there. The pair of nurses passing by don't so much as glance at me. I fall in behind them, walking purposefully, keeping my head up, searching for an elevator or a stairwell.

The nurses veer right and stop in front of an exam room. I curse silently, then keep walking. This building is thirty stories tall. If there's a way up, there has to be a way down to the sublevels, too. I check the time on my coms. Four minutes since Eli left for the cafeteria. He'll be back soon.

I spot a janitor's cart outside a lab, grab it, and keep moving. Every floor might not need a doctor or an orderly, but every floor has to be cleaned. I find a handful of disposable paper caps with elastic bands in one of the boxes on my cart and pull one over my hair.

The hall ends at a bank of elevators, with a cluster of hospital personnel waiting for one to arrive. I linger at the back of the crowd. The minute marker on my com ticks over. Five minutes gone. I jiggle my foot. *Come on.*

The elevator dings and its doors slide open. I follow the rest of the workers into the car, pulling my cart after me.

A woman in a white lab coat waves her wrist com over the elevator's security scanner and pushes the button for level five.

"Hit seven for me?" The man behind her says.

She does. "Anyone else?"

"Three," says a woman in scrubs beside me.

I swallow. "Sublevel two?"

I expect them to turn and stare, to be caught out, but none of them do. She presses the button for sublevel two, and the doors close. We ride up first, dropping off passengers and picking up others, then back down. I check my coms again. Seven minutes. The elevator empties on level three, and then I'm alone.

The elevator doors open. Dim track lights run along the ceiling. The walls are dingy gray-green, the floors dull beige. A plexiglass guard station stands directly across from the elevator.

"You're early tonight," says a staticky voice.

I jump, and then spot the guard on the other side of the glass, his feet up on his desk and a tablet open in his lap.

"Um . . . I got done early upstairs." I roll the cart forward, trying to look bored, but my hands are sweating like crazy.

He glances up at me. "You're new."

"Yeah?" I say.

He drops his eyes back to his tablet and shakes his head. "New meat. You won't win any friends by overachieving."

"Thanks," I mutter.

He looks up at me again and gestures to the door. "Well, get on with it. Wouldn't want you ruining your winning streak."

Shit. I approach the door scanner hesitantly and eye the guard. He's going to figure it out. He'll know. Why won't my palms stop sweating?

"What's the matter?" he calls.

I raise my wrist com and pretend to swipe it across the scanner, sweeping wide of the beams' focal point.

"It's not working," I call back.

He drops his feet and leans up to the glass. "That one's tricky. You've got to hit it just right."

I pretend to swipe again. "I . . . uh . . . I think it's broken."

He sighs. "Goddamn piece of shit. Here."

A buzzer sounds. The lock mechanism clacks open.

"Thanks!" I wipe my hands on my shirt and push my cart through the door.

A dim hallway lined by glass-faced cells stretches before

me. I check my coms again. Eleven minutes. Eli is surely back now, wondering where I am. Bulbous security camera eyes dot the ceiling at regular intervals. I'll have to be fast, hope no one is watching on the other end of those feeds. I scan the cell numbers as I roll past. S2-010, S2-012, S2-014. S2-016. S2-018. I stop. There it is. S2-020.

I peer inside. Someone is lying on the narrow bunk, under a thin gray blanket. I tap on the scuffed glass, but the figure doesn't stir. There's a narrow rectangular hole cut into the door, barely big enough to slip a meal tray through.

"Alder," I whisper, kneeling beside it.

He still doesn't move.

I clear my throat. "Alder."

He lifts his head.

"It's me," I say. "It's Tempest."

"Tempest?" He sits up.

The blanket falls away, and I gasp. He looks so thin. His skin is sallow and bruised, and his eyes bloodshot. A thick white bandage covers his forearm. It was real, all of it. It's written on Alder's body.

"What did they do to you?"

"Nothing." He grimaces as he eases his feet to the floor. "What are you doing here?"

"I had to make sure you were okay." I press a hand to the glass. "They wouldn't let me see you."

He shrugs. "Well." He looks me in the eye, the accusation plain in his voice. "I'm here."

"I'm . . . I'm sorry," I say. "The morphine, it wasn't enough, and then . . . you were lying there, and . . ."

"You promised," Alder says.

"I know," I say. "But I couldn't do it. Not after everything."

Alder shakes his head and looks away. "You know what they're going to do with me now, right?"

I don't answer. I can't talk around the lump in my throat.

"They're sending me to an assimilation camp. They're transferring me in two days."

Assimilation camp. A place hardly ever mentioned, except as a threat or a punishment. *If you can't walk in line, I'm sending all of you to assimilation camp.* Or, *"Damn, I heard he got picked for assimilation camp duty."* It was somewhere far away. Somewhere harsh, somewhere you had to go if you weren't behaving like a loyal employee. Now it sounds even more sinister.

"Listen." I clear my throat. "I'm going to try to get you out, okay? But I need your help. Is there any way to get word to the other scavenger settlements? The blight is only partially contained. It's still spreading east past the firebreaks. AgraStar is evacuating all its personnel."

Alder stares at me, then narrows his eyes. "Did they send you here to question me?"

"What?" I blink.

He stands and limps closer. "I see you. You come here looking all clean and rested. I thought you'd changed, but you're still one of them. Cog, through and through."

"No!" I catch myself and lower my voice. "I'm your friend. I'm not—"

"I'm not falling for it," he shouts at the ceiling. "Do you hear that?"

I glance nervously at the security camera. "Alder, stop—"

"I don't know where anyone is, and even if I did, I'd never tell you!"

"Goddamn it, Alder!" I say through gritted teeth. "Will you shut up? I'm trying to help you."

"Help me." He scoffs.

"Yes," I say. "AgraStar was able to use the seeds. They can splice the genes together with ones from other plants, make them blight resistant. We'll be able to plant again, but first we have to get everyone out of harm's way."

Alder shakes his head. "You really think AgraStar is going to share that information? You think they're going to let a bunch of scavengers have their *intellectual property*, no strings attached?"

"No, but . . ." Of course they won't. It doesn't matter that the seeds that will save us came from the scavengers in the first place. They're AgraStar property now.

"I'll tell you what'll happen," Alder says. "The same thing that always happens. AgraStar will be the savior. They'll have the only seeds that will grow in the blighted areas. And all those free people living outside the compounds? Those scavengers and uncontracted farmers? They'll have to sign on with AgraStar or starve."

I don't say anything. He's right. I'm an idiot. That's exactly how this will play out.

"And you know," he says, his eyes sunken and half wild, "now that they have the key to developing blight-resistant crops, what's going to stop them from letting the blight spread so they can bring more people under their control? Maybe next there'll be an outbreak down in Tallahassee or Shreveport. Or up in Richmond. Or out in Bloom."

A chill runs through me. If AgraStar releases the blight outside our territory, what choice would the other companies have but to create their own biological weapons? Their own proprietary strain of resistant seeds? How long before we can't out-design one another anymore, before nothing will grow and everyone is dead?

"It doesn't matter if you get me out," Alder says. "If they're the only ones with the seeds, nothing matters."

"What about the Latebra Congress?" I whisper. "If we can contact them—"

"Shh," Alder hisses. "Not in here."

"If they're listening, we're already screwed," I say. "Let me help. How do I get the word out?"

He stares at the floor, chewing his lip, but says nothing.

"You have to trust me," I whisper. "I'm running out of time. They'll notice I'm not where I'm supposed to be any minute and run a trace on my com cuff."

He looks at me, his expression unreadable. "There's a game," he says slowly. "MoleMaze. You play it on your coms or a tablet."

I screw up my face. MoleMaze? Isn't that one of the games Dr. Mitra tried to get me to play? "And that's supposed to help us . . . how?"

Alder rolls his eyes, and for a second I see the boy I knew on the road. "It's not the game itself you want. That's a cover. There's a link where you can submit fan art or a picture of a mole you spot in the wild. You go there, and it'll let you upload anything you want—a tip, a file, whatever."

"And the filters won't block it?" I say. "They have me locked out of any sites that aren't AgraStar approved."

"I don't think so," Alder says. "We couldn't get a network signal out at our camp, so we only ever used the satellite phone to call in tips and check for any warnings. The game's more for city dwellers and informants inside the compounds. You know—"

"Moles," I finish, and close my eyes. "Got it." At least someone in their resistance movement has a sense of humor.

"Get out of here, Tempest." Alder moves back. "Before they realize you're not supposed to be here."

"I'm coming back for you."

"Don't," Alder says. "Get the data out. That's all that matters."

"Not to me," I say.

"Then you're an idiot," Alder says.

"Lucky for you, then," I say, and before he can answer, I slip away.

.23.

BLOODROOT

SANGUINARIA CANADENSIS

I take the elevator to the ground floor and find my clothes. Is this what I am now—a mole? A spy? I follow a group of doctors and nurses to the cafeteria and scan the crowd for Eli. No sign of him. Relieved, I step inside the public elevator to ride back down to the main floor.

"Tempest!" My mother, still in her gown, flies across the waiting room and grabs me. "Where have you been?"

I freeze under her touch. *Shit.* What is she doing here? She must have come straight from the gala. Did Eli call her? I spot him, standing behind her near a row of seats. He shrugs and grimaces. *Sorry.*

"I . . . I went upstairs to find Eli." I meet her eyes and then look over to him. "I'm feeling better. I was thinking I'd go home, but I wanted to tell you before I left."

My mother glances over her shoulder at Eli.

He gives her a sheepish look. "We must have missed each other."

"You had me so worried." Her fingers dig into my arms.

"How did you know I was here?" I step back and look at Eli. "Did you call her?"

He shakes his head.

"I have your security settings programmed to alert me if you're scanned at any medical center," my mother says. "Same as Isabel."

My cuff. I twist it. I'm lucky she didn't activate its tracking function.

"I'm fine," I say. "Eli was with me."

"He said you had some kind of attack." She frowns.

"I just . . ." I glance at Eli. "I saw something that reminded me of being out there on the road."

"Oh, m'ija." She buries me in a hug. I smell her perfume, like honeysuckle and oranges, and I realize she must be truly rattled if she used that name for me with other people nearby. "You've been through so much. You see, this is why I didn't want you going out yet. You need more time to heal. We'll set up an appointment with a trauma therapist first thing tomorrow."

Out of nowhere, tears spring to my eyes. "You don't need to worry about me," I say into her shoulder.

But that isn't true. Guilt swells in me. If I'm caught, she might be able to save me from the worst fate. But what will happen to her if I succeed? First her husband, and then her daughter turned traitor? What will Kurich and the board of directors have to say about that?

She steps back and cups my face. "My brave, tough daughter. I don't want to lose you again."

Eli clears his throat. "I should go. Tempest." He nods at me, and then turns to my mother. "Ma'am."

"Oh!" My mother holds out a hand to him. "Young man . . ."

"Eli," I say.

"Eli." She smiles at him. "Thank you for looking after my daughter. Please come to dinner at our house tomorrow, if you're free. Wouldn't that be lovely, Tempest?"

I want to sink into the floor. "I don't know." I look at Eli. "Don't you . . . I mean, you must be on duty."

"I think we can work around that." My mother winks at me. "There are a few perks that come with my position."

"Do you want to come?" I ask Eli. *Please say no. Please say no.* There's so much to do, and when Eli is in the room, it's all I can do to fight off the flashbacks and memories.

"It'd be an honor," Eli says.

"Seven o'clock?" my mother says.

Eli nods. "Thank you, ma'am." He looks to me, and some of his soldier-boy rigidness melts away. "See you then, Tempest."

I stand watching him, openmouthed, as he walks out the front doors of the clinic, and then I turn on my mother. "Why did you do that?"

"Well, you like him, don't you?" She smiles and raises an eyebrow. "His record is top-notch. He's on a leadership track within Security. He's an excellent match for you."

"I don't want a match," I say.

"It's perfectly normal at your age," my mother says. "That's what you need right now. Normal. Routine. A chance to recover."

I look at my feet and swallow the scream building inside my chest.

"You're tired," my mother says. "Let's go home."

"Okay." I head for the door, but my mother catches me with a laugh.

"Oh, no. We don't have to go by street."

"Huh?"

"Come along." She gathers me under her arm. "This way."

She leads me down a corridor to a small elevator with buffed steel doors. It's scanner-locked and, inside, tiled in white marble.

"Executive elevator," my mother explains. "For security reasons, of course, but sometimes it's nice not to have to fight your way through the hoi polloi. I'll arrange for you to have clearance for it, too."

"Oh." I'm too wrung out to protest or ask what those strange words mean. "Thanks."

I watch the elevator's readout as it rises. Level twenty, twenty-one, twenty-two . . . we stop at the thirtieth floor and step out directly onto a skywalk. Beyond the glass, the city is beautiful—headlights crossing the street below us, streetlamps bathing the buildings in warm orange, a slice of the Ferris wheel glittering between the skyscrapers. I pause and take it in. All that glittering night moves me and makes me feel lonely at the same time.

My mother steps up beside me. "Sometimes I forget how pretty it is." She wraps an arm around me and squeezes me against her side. "You don't know how lucky I am to have you back. There's so much I want to show you, Tempest."

I want to step out from under her arm. She's too close, too much. But guilt keeps me still. This woman has been missing her daughter for so long, and now what she has is me. Rough-edged, shell-shocked, traitorous. If I go through with Alder's plan, I'm going to break her heart all over again, exactly like my father did. Can I live with that?

I look at her. Betray my mother and AgraStar. Betray Alder and everyone living free. Suddenly I see the terrible choice my father had to make. There's no escaping it. No matter what I choose, someone is going to suffer.

I try to sleep, but I can't. Images of Ellison and Eli circle through my head. Ellison smiling at me as he steers the jeep down a dirt road. Mischief in Eli's grin as he rocks the Ferris wheel car. Ellison crumpling to the dirt. His ghost in Eli's eyes. The blight crawling over both of them. I get up and make my way into the living room. The cockatoo stirs and squawks lowly when I grab the tablet my mother left for me on the coffee table, then settles back down with its head under its wing.

I perch on the couch and tap the screen to life. A blue glow surrounds me, an eerie bubble in the darkness. I wasn't ready to look at my files before, but now I need answers. I need context. Why did my father do what he did? What made him decide?

I skim through my health and performance records from the SCP compound. Notations on height and weight, merits for sharpshooting, records of my volunteering for clearing and eradication missions and completing basic wilderness training. The last entry on the page catches my eye:

Request for trial period of inclusion on special operations team by Long, Ellison.

I trace his name. Eli is never going to be Ellison, no matter how their smiles match, no matter how their voices lilt and drop, no matter how easy Eli makes me feel. I can't simply substitute one for the other and go on like everything is normal. *Normal.*

I press my hands over my eyes and lean back against the couch. Maybe I should tell my mother about my waking nightmares, why I can't see Eli tomorrow, or any other night. I should never have gone out with him last night. I should have found another excuse to get into the MA building.

I shake my head. *Focus.* I know everything I've read already, my life at SCP, or at least the broad strokes of it. I open an older file. A birth certificate for Adela Beatriz Salcedo

and a DNA chart. I run my finger down to the parents section
of the certificate.

Mother: Orelia Isbet Salcedo Pallares
Age: 28
Location of Birth: Port Miami Compound, South FL Coastal Territory
Current Residence: administrative apartments, green zone, Atlanta headquarters

Father: Daniel Omar Duarte Lacayo
Age: 31
Location of Birth: Matagalpa, Nicaragua*
Current Residence: administrative apartments, green zone, Atlanta headquarters
*Contract transfer 08-02-44

My father wasn't born here? I scratch back through my
patchy knowledge of life outside AgraStar's borders. Nicaragua
isn't a company-state, it's one of the old-fashioned countries.
Most of those are across the ocean, but I think Nicaragua is
south of us, somewhere. Is that why he was willing to break
his contract and flee? Did he want to go home? But if that
was the case, how did we end up north of Atlanta, not south,
closer to his country?

I open another file, and a series of pictures rotates in and
out of view. My mother, younger and with dark hair like mine,
smiling at the camera as she holds up my hands to help me
walk in little sock feet. My mother and a man with a neat beard
and slightly scruffy black hair, holding me between them. My

father? It must be. He has my nose, or I have his. I stare at his face, hoping for some spark of recognition, some new memory, but nothing comes. Next, a picture of me playing in a bathtub, surrounded by mountains of bubbles, my hair wet, and my mouth open in a snaggle-toothed grin. Like my memory. Why did my mind hold on to such a small, stupid detail and forget anything that might answer some of my million questions?

I tap on a file labeled SECURITY FOOTAGE RECONSTRUCTION. A video begins to play, soundless, with all but a hint of color washed out. A man with a knapsack and a little girl asleep in his arms steps onto an elevator. He looks around, then reaches up, and the picture goes black. It skips to another view—a parking deck, the same man hurrying across the frame, disappearing, then getting picked up by another camera out on the street. Skip again, and a shadowed figure ducks through a hole in a line of fence, then helps a smaller shadow through. I back up the footage. That's my father, and me. That's him abducting me, or escaping with me, depending on how you look at it.

The lights snap on.

"What are you doing?"

I nearly drop the tablet. "Isabel." I turn. "Nothing. I was just looking at these files your—our mother gave me."

She peers at me. "Mami says you don't sleep enough. Is that why you're having a breakdown?"

A short bark of laughter escapes me. "I'm not having a breakdown."

"Then why were you at the clinic?"

I set the tablet down. "You heard about that, huh?"

She wanders closer and leans against the back of the couch. "I hear a lot of stuff. Mami doesn't trust me enough to tell me. She thinks she can hide things from me, but I find out anyway."

"Don't you have school in the morning?" I ask.

"So?" She cocks her head.

I shrug. Fair enough. "Do you want to look at this stuff with me?"

She frowns and examines me through narrowed eyes. "Yeah. Okay," she says, dropping down next to me and leaning over to look at the screen. "What's that?"

The blurred image of my father helping me through the fence is frozen midframe. "Security footage," I say. "That's my . . . our dad. And that's me."

Isabel's eyes widen. "That's him kidnapping you?"

"I think so." I touch play, and we watch the entire thing again—the elevator ride, the grainy street views, and then the fence.

"Creepy," Isabel says.

I nod. I understand my father wanting to leave AgraStar, but why'd he take me with him? He must have known what it would do to my mother, yet something made him do it anyway. All of a sudden, I'm angry. I could have grown up like Isabel—clean and well-fed, studying whatever I wanted.

But then I never would have met Ellison or Alder. I

never would have questioned what AgraStar does.

"Do you remember him?" Isabel interrupts my thoughts. "Our dad?"

I shake my head. "Not very much. I was really young when he died."

"Oh," Isabel says. "I always thought you were lucky, getting to know him."

I stare at her. Lucky? Is that really what she thinks?

"I remember his hands," I say slowly. "He always had dirt under his fingernails. One time we found this whole bush of honeysuckle, and he showed me how to eat the flowers." I close my eyes and see him pinching off the back end of a bud, drawing the pistil out with a single gleaming drop of nectar on its end.

Isabel makes a gagging noise. "Gross."

I open my eyes. "It wasn't. Haven't you ever tried it?"

Isabel shakes her head.

"Sometime I'll show you." I say. "If we're ever out of the city."

"Mami would never let me out of the city." Isabel rolls her eyes. "Too dangerous."

"Don't you want to see other parts of the territory?" My mouth is dry. Two weeks ago, I never even would have thought of this question, much less asked it aloud. "See how other people get by?"

Isabel shrugs and cuts her eyes back to the tablet. "What else have you got on there?"

"Pictures." I open the gallery of photos. "Me when I was little."

Isabel watches them cycle through. "Wait." She points at the picture of me with the bubbles. "That's not you, it's me!"

"Are you sure?"

"Yeah." Isabel grabs the tablet. "Mami's always getting them mixed up. Look."

She spins the screen around. A whole new set of files have appeared. More pictures, but also CONTACTS, ALERTS, CALENDAR, INTRANET, SPREADSHEETS, CONTRACTS.

"Isabel," I say cautiously, taking the tablet from her. "Did you just hack into your mother's profile?"

"Yeah." Isabel smiles. "I told you, she thinks I don't know about stuff, but I do."

I stare at the screen. This is it. Her access codes will be somewhere in these files, or maybe even the genetic data itself.

Isabel grabs the tablet. "You won't tell her, will you?"

"No," I say. "Of course not. But . . . do you think you could show me how to do it?"

"Sure," she says. "It's easy."

She walks me through signing out of my own profile, disabling filters, bypassing the biometric scans with security questions, and signing in as our mother.

"I can almost do her voice for the biometric lock," Isabel says. "I bet you could do it. Try saying her name." She holds up the tablet.

I hesitate and clear my throat. "Orelia Salcedo."

The screen flashes red. Denied.

"Try again," Isabel says. "But with your nose in the air. You know."

I laugh, and do my best impression of our mother, confident and imperious. "Orelia Salcedo."

A pause, and then the screen flashes green.

"Yes!" Isabel laughs. "That's the best. It only lets you do the biometrics bypass once a day, but if you can do the voice, you can get in anytime."

"See?" I say. "I have hidden talents."

"Copycat talents," Isabel says, but without any bite. She stretches her arms over her head and yawns. "I'm gonna go back to bed."

I stop, my eyes frozen on a spot on her forearm. Isabel has a small mark an inch below her elbow, in exactly the same spot where I have a matching mole. My scalp prickles.

"Isabel . . ."

"What?"

She faces me. Another mole to the left of her chin, along the jawline. The exact same spot as mine.

"Nothing." I look down at the tablet, thoughts and heart racing in tandem.

"Oookay. Good night, weirdo."

"Good night," I say absently.

I'm already flipping through the pictures Isabel pulled up, comparing the images of the two of us as babies and toddlers. Same face, same hair. Same moles, same slightly bent pinkie toe on our left feet. The only way to tell us apart is the original time stamp on the files. Ellison and Eli . . . me and Isabel . . . it all starts swirling together in my head. It can't be a coincidence. Something Dr. Mitra said bubbles up in the back of my mind. *"Genetic duplication research."* Does that mean what I think it means?

I enter a search for the words in my mother's files. Several dozen files pop up. I choose the most recent one and click it open.

Report on Health and Social Integration of Genetic Optimization and Duplication Pilot Project Subjects

Author: Mitra, Yves, PhD

Abstract: Genetic Optimization and Duplication Pilot Project (GODPP) subjects continue to perform admirably across all monitored health and social criteria, exceeding their random-born donors and peers in disease resistance and other physical measures. In subjects without neurological optimization, social integration proceeds largely concurrent with donors and peers. Neurologically optimized subjects show increased success in social integration, but without the magnitude of extraordinary success observed in the physical sphere, perhaps due to uncontrolled variables in the home environment. Continued neurological optimization and greater environmental regulation are suggested as avenues for future research.

The words are a thicket, as impenetrable as the briars that forced Alder and me onto the road so many days ago. But there are a few I understand. Random-born donors. Disease resistance. Optimization. They're experimenting on *people*. Copying and improving on their genetic codes. Making them better able to thrive in the world, exactly like the corn-seed variants. I skim through the rest of the document, unsure what I'm looking for. A name jumps out at me.

Subject: Byrd, Eli Amari

Age: 18

Location: yellow zone, Atlanta headquarters

Donor: unidentified infant, SCP-52

I start to shake. I page faster, eyes out for a specific name this time. And then I find it.

Subject: Salcedo, Isabel Adela

Age: 11

Location: green zone, Atlanta headquarters

Donor: Salcedo, Adela Beatriz

There are other names, too. Two dozen or so, spread throughout AgraStar's territory, all of them under twenty years old. It's *not* a coincidence. Eli isn't some long-lost relative of Ellison's. And Isabel isn't just my sister.

They're clones.

.24.

OCONEE BELLS
SHORTIA GALACIFOLIA

I'm still awake when the first blue light of dawn touches the windows and my mother clicks into the living room, already dressed for the day.

"Were you going to tell me?" I say from the shadows of the couch.

She gasps. "Tempest! You startled me." She takes a few hesitant steps closer. "Tell you what?"

I glare at her. "About me and Isabel."

A brief look of horror crosses her face before she masks it with her usual stony professionalism. "I don't know what you—"

"Don't lie to me!" It comes out louder than I meant, and I lower my voice. I don't want Isabel waking up. "Did you think I wouldn't notice? We're exactly the same, just like Eli and my friend Ellison—perfect copies."

"You and Isabel are sisters." My mother sinks gracefully onto the far end of the couch. "And your friend, I'm sure that's only a coincidence."

I stare at her, boiling.

"You've had a difficult night, Tempest," she says. "You're seeing things that aren't there."

Not there. I clench my fists to keep from shaking. They took a baby and used him for an experiment. Ellison never had a say in what they did. He was alone in the world, so AgraStar decided they could do whatever they wanted, as if they owned him. The same with the rest of us—Eli, me, Isabel, and all the other people in that file. Do they even think of us as human? Or are we just pawns—*assets*, the way I used to think of myself?

I bite my tongue. If I say any of that, she'll know I read Dr. Mitra's report. I need to get back into her files, and if she knows what I've seen, she'll lock me out for good. Or worse, she might stop protecting me from Kurich.

"Why don't we discuss this with the counselor tomorrow?" she suggests. "He can help you work through whatever it is that's making you think this way."

"You want me to feel at home here, right?" I say, twisting the knife. I need to know the truth. "You want me to get better, to be normal?"

"Of course I do." She reaches out to touch my shoulder, but I pull away.

"Then why are you trying to make me think I'm crazy?"

"I'm not," she says. "I only want to protect you. I wasn't able to when you were younger, but now—"

"I'm a soldier." I sit up straight. "You don't need to protect me. I can take it."

"Of course you are." She stands and walks to the window, gazing out at the city.

There's only one thing that might make her break. I have to try it.

"I know you don't know me," I say to her back. "But you've read my files. You know I've given everything I have to AgraStar. Why can't you trust me?"

She turns. "It's not that I can't trust you."

"Then tell me what's going on." I try to ignore the sick feeling in my gut and put an extra burst of confidence behind my voice. "Bring me in. Make me part of it."

She hesitates.

I hold my breath and bite down on my tongue. Was it enough? How much will she give away to keep me happy?

My mother raises a hand to her brow. "It isn't the same. You and Isabel," she says in a quiet voice.

I sink down on the couch. "What is it, then?"

She locks eyes with me. "This is confidential, Tempest. You understand?"

My throat feels dry. "Yes."

"Good." She takes a seat in the chair across from me. "I'm telling you this because you're loyal. You understand how important AgraStar's work is. There are a lot of variables when it comes to AgraStar's human assets—health conditions, longevity, temperament. A little over twenty years ago, we started asking, what if we could control those variables? What if we could strengthen the company and increase production by introducing a standardizing element into our population?"

Assets. I shake my head. "You mean cloning?"

"Yes," she says. "And it's been very successful, especially when it comes to staffing security forces. Of course, you can't control for accidents and variations in environment as the child is growing up, but physical build, disease resistance . . . and if conditions are right, the combination of intelligence and loyalty that makes a good soldier."

I lean away. "You mean . . . you can control how they think?"

"No, no," my mother says. "But we can give them an innate predisposition to certain characteristics that will come forward with the right training."

"Like compliance," I say.

My mother makes a face. "I would call it a desire to cooperate. These aren't automatons we're talking about, Tempest. They're people like you and me."

"But more like me," I say. "And Isabel."

My mother smooths her skirt. "As I said, you two are a different matter. Your father and I conceived you the natural way, Tempest. No genetic interventions."

I frown, puzzled. "Me, but not Isabel?"

My mother looks up. "I was so alone, m'ija. You were gone. Your father was gone. I thought you were both dead. But I had a record of your DNA, and the technology was there."

"So you made a copy of me?" I know I need to stay calm, but I feel as if electricity is shooting through all my nerve endings. "You just . . . replaced me?"

Anger flashes across her face. "I never replaced you. It wasn't simple for me, Tempest. It wasn't easy."

"Oh, God." I rake a hand through my hair. "Does Isabel know?"

"Know what?" Isabel stands in the doorway in her pajamas, hairy messy from sleep.

"Nothing, m'ija." My mother jumps up and hurries to her, shooting a warning glance at me over her shoulder. "Go on, get into your school clothes and I'll make some breakfast."

Isabel looks between the two of us, and then turns and trudges back down the hallway.

"She's going to find out," I say quietly as soon as she's gone. "She picks up on more than you know."

My mother's mouth tightens into a line. "And you're an expert, after knowing her for a week?"

I stand. Any guilt I had about manipulating her into telling me the truth evaporates.

"I know I don't like being lied to, so if she's my clone, I imagine she doesn't either."

"Tempest . . ."

I brush past her and storm down the hall, into my room. I want to slam the door, but it will only hush closed, so I punch the wall and scream, instead. Altering our seeds, *optimizing* them, never really bothered me, but . . . human beings? Are they AgraStar's intellectual property the same way the seeds are? If they run away, does the company have the right to hunt them down, reclaim them? And who decides what's optimal? Resistance to common diseases, obviously, but what about height, build, skin color? They've already decided which languages we should speak and which we should forget. What if they decide hair like mine is too much trouble, and instead of making me straighten it in a salon, they go a step further and write it out of the genetic code altogether? What if they perfect us so narrowly that we're like our crops, all wiped out by a single agent?

A few moments later, there's a soft knock at the door. "Tempest?" my mother says.

"What?" I snap.

"I have to go to work and get Isabel off to school, but I'll be home by three. We can talk more about this then, okay?"

"Fine." I'm already restarting the tablet, going through the commands Isabel taught me. I'm going to make use of every minute my mother is gone, pull every piece of information I can from her files. I'm done being lied to. It's time to extract the truth.

My mother's files are a maze of information. I try searching her hard drive for "blight resistance" and "seeds," but nothing turns up on the first search, and the second generates thousands of results. The sheer volume of documents might be a better security measure than her passwords and biometric lockouts.

I enter a search for my name, and along with the photos she already gave me, I find a log of my internet activity—all the searches I did and sites I visited under my own profile. Fortunately, there's nothing more incriminating than maps of the city and me looking for updates on the spread of the "forest fire." I find a similar log for Isabel. It's equally clean, but that isn't surprising. Isabel is smart enough to work around the invisible eyes everywhere.

Inspiration strikes me. "Adela," I type into the search bar. My security profile springs up. Only it isn't simply static files like the ones my mother gave me to look through. This is active, monitoring my heartbeat and location, displaying a photograph of me, and listing my security clearances. I tap the edit button, and it responds. Holding my breath, I flip over my settings, giving my com cuff access to the detention levels of the MA buildings, the R&D labs, and all the executive-level doors and elevators.

"Yes!" I smile. But what I really need is the data on the blight resistance genes. Without that, all the open doors in the world mean nothing.

I work through the morning, digging through file after file, all of them with meaningless alphanumerical names— MX33-18, H1-L25, P92-IL1. Spreadsheets and database files I can't parse, project summaries that aren't much clearer. I sigh and rub my forehead. My exhaustion headache is coming back, creeping along the base of my head and into my jaw. *If I lie down for a few minutes . . .*

No. I blink furiously and sit up straight. I can't fall asleep right now. There's a mountain of data to sift through, and I have only a handful of hours until my mother comes back.

I page through another set of files—all color-coded columns of numbers. Nothing that looks like the bar graphics Dr. Mitra showed me. Nothing like the DNA record in my files. I groan and flop against my pillow. Will I even recognize the data when I see it? What if my mother has it encoded somehow?

I rub my eyes and pick up the tablet again. I open another set of files. The screen is so bright, the light stabbing at the back of my eyes, pouring pain into my skull. I squeeze my eyelids shut. *Just for a moment . . .*

The sound of the door chime startles me awake. I sit up quickly, dazed. Footsteps in the hall. I look at the tablet open in front of me. No time to log out. I slide it under my pillow just as my mother appears in the doorway.

"Tempest?" She frowns at me from the doorway. "Are you okay, m'ija?"

"Yeah." I rub the grit from my eyes. "I fell asleep."

"That's understandable. You were up all night." She sits down next to me on the bed. "Are you still angry with me?"

I check myself. I feel quieter after sleeping, less jagged. "No."

"I was having a chat with Dr. Lefebvre today." She runs her hand over the bedspread, smoothing out the wrinkles, studiously not making eye contact. "I know that was a lot to take in this morning. I was thinking . . . perhaps you, Isabel, and I should speak to one of the family counselors. This is a big adjustment for everyone. We have a lot to work through."

"Okay," I say. Getting angry with her was the wrong tack. I can't do anything for Alder if she has me under a microscope.

"Yes?" My mother brightens. "Good. I'll make an appointment."

"Great." I make myself look at her and work up a small smile. No threat, no security risk. Only an emotional teenager.

She stands and walks to the closet. "We should pick out something nice for you to wear tonight. Your young man will be here in a few hours."

"Are we still doing that?" I frown.

"Well, yes." She stops and turns to me. "Unless you don't want to. Dr. Lefebvre agreed it would be good for you to socialize in a familiar environment."

Socialize in a familiar environment? She sounds like Dr. Mitra's report. I bite back my anger. "No, it's fine. We should still do it."

"Excellent." She spins back to the closet. "Maybe something blue. Cool colors look so pretty against a warm skin tone like yours."

While her back is turned, I scoot forward on the bed and slip my hand beneath the pillow, feeling for the manual OFF button. I find it and press it down just as she turns back to me, holding out a cornflower-blue dress cut to knee length.

"This will do nicely, don't you think?" she says.

I nod and fake a yawn, withdrawing my hand from beneath the pillow in a way I hope looks natural.

"Poor thing. You should go back to sleep," my mother says. "I'll come wake you an hour before dinner so you can get ready."

"Thanks." I lay my head down on the pillow.

"I love you, m'ija." My mother bends over and presses a quick kiss against my forehead. "We're going to get through this together, okay?"

I nod, holding my breath. I wait until the door closes softly behind her and her steps recede down the hall before I let it out. My whole body is shaking like the aftershock of an earthquake. I've called out my mother for lying to me, shouted at her, slammed doors, when I'm the liar. I'm the one who's planning to betray her.

The blue dress is silky on my skin, like fine fescue grass. My mother has piled my hair on top of my head in glossy waves and is trying to convince me to let her apply makeup to my face.

"Just a little shimmer on the lips and some blush," she says.

I shake my head. Having Eli over for dinner is bad enough, but me looking shined up and fancy? It's only dragging out the inevitable, setting us both up for more pain.

"I'm not used to it," I say. "It doesn't feel like me."

"You won't say that when you're older." My mother waves a lip-gloss tube at me. "In ten years, you'll be swearing foundation is your best friend."

There's no point in fighting her. She's determined.

"Fine." I close my eyes and screw up my face. "Do it."

My mother laughs. "You'd think you were going to your execution."

My stomach turns. I know it's a joke, but AgraStar has been known to execute traitors. Not often, and not recently, but it's happened. And I'm dangerously close to becoming exactly that.

"What about me?" Isabel pokes her head into the bathroom. "Can I put on makeup?"

"You can paint your nails," my mother says, not breaking her concentration on the line she's drawing on my eyelid.

Isabel scowls. "Tempest gets to, and she doesn't even want to wear it."

"Tempest is a young woman," she says, uncapping the lip gloss. "When you're done with your primary studies, you can wear it too."

"Ugh!" Isabel slouches away.

"None of that at dinner!" My mother calls after her. "We have a guest."

My mother steps back, letting me see my reflection in the mirror. "What do you think?"

I stare at myself. "It's . . . pretty." My eyes look bigger and brighter, more alert. The girl in the mirror doesn't exactly look like me, but she doesn't *not* look like me, either. Or maybe I'm just getting used to who I am here. A different version of the AgraStar ideal, but still something created by them. The thought makes me uneasy.

The door chimes. Eli's arrived.

My mother clicks down the hall. I hear the door open, and follow her.

"Specialist Byrd." She gives Eli a brief, airy hug. "So glad you could come."

"Thanks for inviting me." He spots me lurking in the hall. "Hey, Tempest."

My heart lunges the way it always does when I first see him. *Ellison.* And then the aftershock a split second later. *Not Ellison. Eli.*

"You look nice," he says.

I flush. "You, too."

He's wearing a dark green dress uniform with brass buttons. It makes him look more slender than he did in his fatigues and T-shirt. His hair is freshly trimmed, and he smells like shaving cream and pine. Suddenly my dress and makeup feel less out of place.

"Why don't you two sit down?" my mother says. She's grinning like a cat that's caught the plumpest, juiciest bird in the nest. "I'll let them know we're ready."

"So." Eli takes a seat on the couch and rests his elbows on his knees.

I join him. "Yeah."

"You didn't have to dress up for me." He gives me a sidelong smile.

"I didn't," I say. "I did this for my mother."

"Yeah." He looks down at his dress uniform. "Same here."

I laugh. "I guess she has that effect on people."

The door chimes again, and servers in white aprons wheel carts bearing covered platters into the dining room. A light, buttery smell fills the air, making my mouth water.

I look at Eli. He nods mock-knowingly and mouths, "Parsnips."

I suppress a snort. "Definitely."

We take our seats—Eli and I across from each other, Isabel at my side, and our mother at the head of the table. She lifts the cover from the largest platter with a flourish.

"Crab cakes Benedict with a lemon hollandaise sauce and roasted asparagus." She smiles. "A little treat for us."

Eli's eyes go wide. We look at each other. I know what he's thinking. Seafood, this far inland? She must have had it specially shipped from the coast, maybe the Charleston port facility. And asparagus is a specialty crop, slow to grow and not practical for mass production. How much did this dinner cost?

"I don't like asparagus." Isabel sticks out her tongue. "It makes your pee smell funny."

"Isabel!" my mother says. "Not at the table."

"What?" Isabel says. "It's true."

"It's okay," Eli says. "Thanks for the warning." He winks at Isabel.

My mother passes around a bottle of spring water and another of white wine. Once our glasses are full, she raises hers.

"To new friends." She beams from Eli to me. "And new beginnings."

I smile back, but I feel sick. Every second I sit here binds me closer to my mother, to Isabel, to this whole life. The idea of betraying them . . . my throat knots. I have to. I have to save everyone living outside AgraStar's protection, even if it means I might lose this family and the glimpses of belonging I've been chasing for the last fourteen years. I have to make sure the earth doesn't rot out from beneath us. The thought of ignoring everything I've learned and going on like none of it happened, like Alder's body isn't covered with bruises and my mother didn't call us *assets*, and the blight isn't still creeping toward the coast, makes my stomach ache, too.

"So, Eli." My mother sets down her glass. "Tell us about yourself. Are you hoping to make captain?"

I stop cutting into my crab cakes. Why is she asking him that? She knows he's on the leadership track. She's read his entire file. She as much as created him.

Eli swallows and sets his fork beside the plate. "Actually." He wipes his mouth with a napkin. "I just found out I have charge of a transport tomorrow. It's sort of a test to see if I'm ready for my own team."

"Corn diesel?" I say, remembering what he told me about his last transport duty. "Are you nervous?"

"Prisoner transport," he says. "And yes. I'd be crazy if I wasn't."

I freeze. *Prisoner transport.* "Where to?"

"An assimilation camp down near Valdosta." He slices a piece of asparagus in half. "This food is amazing."

"Thank you," my mother says. "I'm sure you'll perform beautifully tomorrow. We'll be calling you captain in no time." She grins and winks at him.

I stare at her, and then catch myself and quickly drop my eyes to my plate. *Assimilation camp . . . Alder.* Tomorrow. They're moving him tomorrow. Did she know Eli would draw this duty? Did she engineer it?

"Is everything all right, Tempest?" my mother asks. "You've barely touched your food."

"It's so rich." I hurriedly spear a chunk of crab cake and stuff it in my mouth.

"Well, leave room for dessert," my mother says. "We have Black Forest gâteaux to look forward to."

I eat, not tasting anything, while my mother makes small talk with Eli, and then Isabel takes over and starts telling him about her snake. An idea is forming in my brain. I think I know how I can rescue Alder. But it means not just risking this new life; it means giving it up entirely. And first I have to find the blight resistance data. I have to make sure that if I free Alder, there's something for him to escape to in the end.

.25.

HONEY LOCUST

GLEDITSIA TRIACANTHOS

I huddle beneath the covers in the glow of the tablet screen. It's past midnight, and I've gone through half of my mother's files. I rub my forehead and sigh. A few more hours, and my window to rescue Alder will be gone. He'll be on his way to the assimilation camp.

I skim through the remaining file names, hoping something will catch my eye, but it's all meaningless to me. Suddenly it occurs to me—*time.* I sort the files by most recently modified. The tablet screen blinks and rearranges the list. The top three files have been created in the past week. It has to be one of those.

I open the first one. Genetic charts! But no . . . I look closer. This is a proposal for a new corn strain, not a genetic analysis of tomato seed. I click on the second file. Financial reports, detailing the lost revenue from the spread of the blight and the evacuations, as well as projected earnings and territory expansion from the sale of the blight-resistant seeds to the sharecroppers and new contracts signed by unaffiliated farmers desperate for the company's protection. AgraStar is going to lose money short-term but gain it in the long run. I chew on a hangnail and open the last set of files. This has to be it. It has to be.

A grainy image pops up—an overhead shot of a young man with dark hair and pale skin handcuffed to a desk. Alder. Another man steps into the frame, also pale, but bald and heavyset, wearing security forces fatigues. My heart stops. Kurich.

"Did you turn her?" Kurich asks.

Alder shakes his head. "I told you. We took her prisoner in the confusion after the explosion. You saw—she turned me in at the first opportunity."

"She was pretty worked up over you." I can't see Kurich's face, but his voice is firm. "Screaming and ranting at the checkpoint guards."

Alder looks up at him. "We'd just escaped the Red Hand. You would have been screaming and ranting, too, if you'd seen what we saw."

She. That's me they're talking about. Does he really think I turned him in at the first chance, or is he lying for me?

Kurich slams the table. "Don't get smart with me, shirk."

I look at the time stamp on the video. Two days after we arrived at the checkpoint. I was having my hair washed and styled while Alder was chained to a table. How is he even upright? The video is too blurry for me to see whether he already had the bruises I saw in the basement of the MA building.

"Let's go back," Kurich says. "You say you headed southeast on foot after the explosion, but you didn't encounter any patrols?"

"No."

But we did. That first night. He's lying. But why? They wouldn't care if Alder ran from a patrol. The only person that would reflect badly on would be me. I suck in a breath. He's trying to cover for me.

"You're sure?" Kurich says. "Our records indicate there was a patrol in the area less than thirty-six hours after the incident."

"We went off-road," Alder says. "We didn't want to run across any jackers."

He sounds so tired, and my heart breaks a little bit. What will happen to him? What will they do to him at the assimilation camp?

I stop the recording and knead my forehead. Dr. Mitra would have the answer in his files, but his lab is closed now, and I don't have his log-in credentials. If I could find a way . . . wait. Who wrote the proposal for the new strain of corn? Dr. Mitra? I go back to the first file and open it again.

There, at the top of the page, along with the names of three other scientists—Dr. Yves Mitra. I scroll down past the abstract, past the introduction, to the section on methodology. There.

On the third attempt, the authors successfully isolated the genes responsible for the resistance trait and transferred them to the proposed corn strain, iteration ZM112-864. (See appendix B for a detailed analysis of the resistance gene.)

I flip to the appendix. A detailed genetic graph and notes. It was here. It was here the whole time. I check my cuff . . . 2:43 a.m. I don't know exactly when the transport carrying Eli will leave, but at the compound, caravans usually set off before dawn. I have a few hours, at most.

I open the internet and pause, my fingers hovering over the keys. Once I do this, all the pieces will start to fall. No more plentiful food and soft bed. No more chance at a future inside AgraStar. No more family, no more belonging. I hesitate. My whole body feels cold. Some small part of me hangs back, clinging to the image of my mother smiling, to Isabel needling her with talk about Rene and asparagus pee.

I stand and push back the curtains over my window. The city glitters beneath me. Will I ever really belong here? No matter how long I live in this high-rise and dress the part, will there always be something off about me, some stigma, the same as there was back at my old compound? Will I ever really be a human being in the company's eyes, or just a resource to use?

But if I go through with this, what's the alternative? Alder's people would kill me on sight, and any other scavenger band would always look at me sideways, knowing where I come from. Defecting to another company wouldn't be any better than staying with AgraStar. Maybe no matter where I go, I'll never truly belong. Here I have a future, a family, even if that family doesn't have a past. Even if I don't exactly fit, even if it feels like something's missing, at least things could be easy.

But do I want that? Can I live with that, knowing what will happen to all the scavengers, to anyone who resists AgraStar? The memory of Alder, bruised and weak in his cell, rises up at me. Then the image of the clearer that haunts my nightmares, blight spreading wherever her feet touch the ground. An orphaned baby, scrunch-faced and squalling as his blood is taken. Maybe this is the price—that I'll never have a place of my own, that I'll never belong. I'll always be someone who exists between worlds. But aren't tens of thousands of lives worth that much? Aren't they worth more than some shadow of belonging? I think of my great-grandmother trying so hard to pass on who our family was, that common language, the things that made us *us*. And then of AgraStar draining it all away. Our roots drying up until they're nothing but dust.

I pick up the computer again. MoleMaze, I type.

A brightly colored site with a grass-green background and a cartoon of a mole emerging from the dirt pops up.

MOLEMAZE—ESCAPE THE MAZE! DIG YOUR OWN! it says in rounded brown-and-yellow letters.

I scan the page. GALLERY—FAN ART AND PHOTOS! one of the links reads. I open it and scroll past dozens of photos of moles and drawings, until I reach the submission box. It's exactly what Alder described, but it looks so real, like nothing more than an innocent game about garden pests. Is this really it?

Alder trusted me. He covered for me. I have to trust him. Quickly, before I can change my mind, I upload Dr. Mitra's proposal and click submit. A cartoon mole appears, holding a placard. CONGRATULATIONS! YOUR FILE WAS SUCCESSFULLY UPLOADED.

I have to move. I have to go. But all I can do is stare at the screen. Everything feels surreal. Like I could delete my browsing history, go to bed, and in the morning, everything would go on like before. I could keep feeding information to the Latebra Congress. That's what Alder would tell me to do. Forget him, and do whatever I can from the inside.

Except, eventually, AgraStar will figure it out. Kurich will trace the source of the leak. He'll narrow in on my mother, and Alder will disappear into the assimilation camp. But if I go, if I disappear tonight, they'll know it was me, not her, and I'll have a chance to repay Alder, to make it up to him.

I open the closet and rifle through the collection of purses hanging from hooks along the back wall. Most of them are delicate beaded things or silk pouches no bigger than my hand. I push them aside and grab a black leather bag with a silver clasp, not anywhere near the size of my long-lost backpack, but bigger than the rest. It will have to do.

I dress quickly, in the darkest, plainest clothes I have— navy jeans and a black dry-wick shirt with long sleeves— and walk softly to the kitchen, carrying my shoes. I open the cabinets and start stuffing the bag full of food. Almonds, olives, peanut butter. Anything shelf stable. Anything with protein.

"What are you doing?"

I nearly drop a packet of dried pineapple. "Isabel," I gulp. "Nothing. I was just going out."

"No you're not." Isabel looks at my bulging purse, and then glares at me. "You're leaving, aren't you?"

"No." The look on her face tells me there's no point in lying. "Yes."

"Why?" she asks.

"They're sending my friend to an assimilation camp. I've got to stop them."

Isabel's eyes widen. "That shirk boy? The one that was with you at the checkpoint?"

"Yes."

"But I thought you liked Eli."

"I do." Suddenly my whole body feels heavy. "It's not like that, though. Alder and me, we owe each other."

"What about me?" Isabel frowns.

"What do you mean?"

Isabel fidgets with her nightgown. "I want to go with you."

"Isabel," I say gently. "You can't. It's too dangerous.

Besides, when I'm gone, our mother's going to need you even more." I'm not going to repeat what my father did. I'm not going to whisk Isabel away in the middle of the night. I can make this choice for myself, but not for her.

"She's much nicer when you're here," Isabel says. "If you go, she'll turn witchy again."

"I'm sorry." My chest aches and my throat feels tight. "But I have to do this."

Isabel stares at the floor. I recognize that look. She's trying to fight back tears.

"You won't tell her," I say. "Will you?"

She looks up at me, chin trembling slightly and eyes defiant. "No. I won't."

"Thank you," I say.

I zip my bag closed and head for the door.

"Tempest?"

"Yeah?"

"I liked having you as a sister."

I stop, staring at the scanner lock on the door.

"I'll always be your sister," I say. "No matter where I am."

Then I open the door, and I'm gone.

I sidle around the back of the security forces dormitory and let myself in by the stairwell. First things first. I need a disguise. I hurry down the stairs to the basement laundry. The lights shine bright over the rows of washers and dryers. Some of the machines are on, but the only sound is the low tumbling of clothes spinning. I look left, then right. No one.

I check a dryer. All men's clothes, too big for me. I try the next one. Jackpot. Plain green coveralls, like the ones drivers wear. They may be a little big and slightly damp, but they'll do. I had thought about disguising myself as a guard, which would mean finding a sidearm and body armor, but maybe a driver is better. No one pays much attention to the driver, and I won't have to risk finding and breaking into a weapons locker. My eyes go to my bulging purse. I still have the tablet. I can alter one of the other drivers' schedules, slip into her place. I find a matching green cap in the same machine and pull it low over my brow. The only things that look out of place are my feet. I'll have to hope I can find some boots before anyone notices.

I race up the stairs to the main level, suddenly much more aware of the black security camera bulbs studding the ceiling. My skin crawls, and I duck my head. They'll realize it's me later, when they analyze the recordings, but I don't think they'll recognize me now.

The corridors are quiet, the lights set to motion-sensor mode so that they stagger on as I approach, and slowly click off behind me. I check the time—4:51. Sunrise is at 6:37. I pass a girl headed in the opposite direction. I hold my breath, but she nods sleepily at me and pads past in sock feet.

The duty roster screen glows electric blue in the dim light of the lobby. I stand watching it until Eli's name cycles into view.

Name: Byrd
ID: BE20780115
Duty: prisoner transport
Report to: East Vehicle Lot
Time: 0600

0600. Six a.m. I look at the time again. A little over an hour before Eli and everyone under his command reports for duty. I have to be in that caravan.

I pull at my too-big sleeves. I need to be out in the lot early, but not too early. Until then, I need a place to stay out of sight and make room for myself on the caravan. *The basement,* I think, but then immediately feel sick. There may not be any security cameras down there, but that's where I saw the ghosts of my old teammates, where the blight and kudzu came creeping over my vision. Will it all still be there, waiting for me?

I take the stairs down and stand outside the door. I will not hyperventilate. I outran firebombs, escaped the Red Hand, survived the blight. I'm not going to let a stupid empty room defeat me. I push open the door and flip on the lights. The lounge smells even mustier after the clean scent of drying laundry. There's a half-eaten bag of corn chips in the center of the table, and a pair of abandoned boots flopped over in the corner. Boots! They're a size too large and the laces are frayed, but they'll work. I dump out the chips, rip the bag in half, and stuff the toes with it.

I turn on the tablet and find the list of drivers and vehicles slated for 0600 transport duty. I have my choice—a huge personnel carrier on eighteen wheels, several fuel trucks, armored cars, pickups, jeeps, and motorcycles. Not the eighteen-wheeler. That and the fuel truck will be closely watched, if they're assigned to the caravan. Same with the armored car—that's likely what they'll use to transport Alder and any other prisoners. A motorcycle would be excellent for agility, but guards usually take those, and I'm dressed as a driver. A jeep, then. It'll be better on rough terrain than the truck, and if I'm lucky, no one will notice a new driver.

I scroll over to the current driver's name. One Padma Black. I open her schedule detail and change her departure time to 0730. Her com cuff will alert her, and if I'm lucky, she'll think it's only a simple schedule change, until she arrives at the lot and discovers everyone is already gone. By the time she and her supervisors work it out, we'll be well outside Atlanta.

I jiggle my foot. What is Eli doing now? Did he just roll out of bed, or has he been up all night like me, nervous about the transport? And Alder? Do they let him sleep? Have they fed him? Does he have more bruises purpling his arms?

I check the time again . . . 0537. I can't dwell on these things. I've made my decision, and now it's time. I make my way up the stairs and down the left wing of the barracks. This side of the building is flush with the vehicle lot, so there must be a door that opens directly onto it. The sound of showers running and the mumble of voices behind closed doors reaches out into the hall. The barracks is waking. Soon I'll have company.

Out in the lot, the dark, humid morning clings to my skin. The transport duty vehicles are lined up in front of the gate. I locate Padma's jeep, J-195. The door opens easily, but the keys aren't in the ignition. *Dammit.* I check the dash, the glove box, the sun visor. Nothing. Or no keys, anyway. I sigh in frustration. I'll have to hot-wire it. I check the time—0548. The other drivers will be arriving soon to do safety checks and prep for the journey.

I grope under the passenger seat, then the driver's. My fingers brush something hard and plastic. I pull it out. A small emergency kit, full of flares, water purification tablets, a flat-head screwdriver, electrical tape, and a slim nine-millimeter with a full ammo magazine. *Yes.*

I glance out the window. The distant hum of an air conditioner fills the air, and the streetlamps cast pools of yellow light onto the asphalt, but nothing moves. I wrap each of my fingertips in electrical tape, kick loose the panel beneath the steering column, and pull out a fistful of multicolored wires. Red to yellow, power to engine. I use the screwdriver to strip the wires and touch the exposed ends together. The jeep sparks to life.

The door to the barracks squeaks open, and a pair of drivers walks out onto the lot. *Act normal, act normal.* I nod to them as they pass and pretend to adjust something on the navigation and communications screen built into the dashboard. All it shows is a rotating image of AgraStar's logo, but at my touch, the short-range radio crackles to life, broadcasting a low line of static. An aerial map of the route from Atlanta south to the assimilation camp appears on the screen.

More drivers and the first of the security teams file out. I check my fuel gauge. Full. I check the time again—0556. This is the hard part, the waiting. I keep my eye on the door, watching for Eli. Will he recognize me? My heart feels like it's slowly crawling up my chest. *Call roll out, call roll out,* I plead silently. What if I fail? What if I'm caught before I can reach Alder?

The short-wave radio spits to life. "Drivers, preliminary safety check report."

"J-212, go," a woman's voice comes back.

"A-134, go," a man says.

"J-195, go." *Please, don't let anyone have noticed the tremor in my voice.*

The callback continues. Thirteen vehicles in total.

"Roll out," comes the command.

I put the jeep into gear and pull behind the fuel tanker. Two motorcycles peel past me on the left. We circle around the far side of the barracks, and then roll to a stop on the main road, the skyscrapers towering around us . . . 0604. The sky is still dark as night.

"Stand by for detention transport," the radio says.

I look up and down the length of the caravan. That's the

MA building ahead of us, to our right. Another jeep, four guards on motorcycles, and the fuel tanker stand between it and me. Behind me, the armored car, four more motorcycles, and two pickups. A short line of people files out of the building, cast in blue by the streetlights. As they come closer, I make them out. Five prisoners shuffle forward in loose gray jumpsuits, flanked by guards.

A man in fatigues and a helmet walks out to meet them and follows along beside the lead guard, leaning close to speak to her. *Eli*. I tighten my fingers on the steering wheel. I'm not only ruining my mother's life. If I succeed, I'm going to ruin his as well. They'll think he was in on this in some way. And even if they decide he wasn't, he'll always have that cloud of suspicion hanging over him. Was he? Wasn't he?

He's not Ellison, I remind myself. *You don't owe him anything. You barely know him.*

But he was kind to you, I argue back. *He made you laugh. He doesn't know what AgraStar has done.*

The prisoners walk past my window, and I fight to keep my gaze straight ahead. The second they're past, I lift my eyes to the rearview mirror. A short, overweight girl. A pale man with thinning hair. A middle-aged woman. Two boys. I zero in on the one with a head of unruly black hair. *Alder.* They stop on the sidewalk beside the armored car, waiting to be loaded into the back of the vehicle. For a moment, he looks my way, and I think our eyes meet in the mirror—but then he drops his head and steps off the curb.

"All vehicles, roll out." The order comes over the radio.

We pass the darkened Ferris wheel and crawl out onto the raised, fortified highway hugging one side of the inner city. NOW ENTERING YELLOW ZONE, a sign above the road reads. The buildings around us drop in height and move back from the road—low, windowless warehouses, a cinder-block mechanic's shop, a tumbledown brick building with a single light shining eerily in one of the upper rooms. A bus trundles past us, heading into the city. Against the lightening horizon, I can make out boxy apartment buildings.

Ahead, the other vehicles slow, and then come to a stop. I crane my neck to see what's happening at the head of the caravan. A gate and two trucks block the road. A checkpoint. *Dammit.* I look down at my com cuff, and then at the dashboard clock . . . 0633. Is my mother still asleep? I picture her waking up, fixing coffee, knocking on my door, softly at first—and then pushing it open to find my bed empty. Isabel lying in her room, feigning sleep.

A cold, electric thought passes through me. How long before my mother finds me truly gone and activates my tracker? And what if the checkpoint guard sees my wrist com? A driver would have a dark green utility cuff, like Eli's or my old one, not one disguising itself as a piece of jewelry. I should have thought of this before now. I'm so used to the weight of a com cuff on my wrist, I forgot about it in the rush to plan Alder's escape.

One of the checkpoint guards moves down the line,

a clipboard and scanner in her hand. I tug at my com cuff, trying to pull it off. No luck. I pull harder, gritting my teeth as the cuff grinds against my bones. *Dammit.* I stop, panting. All I'm doing is making my hand swell.

The guard taps something into her clipboard and moves to the car two ahead of me. *There must be a way to get this thing off.* I hold my thumb down over the settings feature and select maintenance mode. The cuff makes a tiny buzzing noise, and a pinhole the size of a paper clip head opens in its side. *Dammit.* I must need a special tool to remove it altogether. I look around the cab of the jeep. Nothing.

The guard approaches the fuel truck's window. *What am I going to do?* I glance down at the wires hanging loose beneath the steering column. Maybe . . . I pull out the power wire, and immediately the engine gutters out. I glance up at the guard. She smiles at the fuel truck driver, steps back. I straighten out the power wire and thread its bare end into the hole in the cuff, then do the same with the starter wire. The live ends touch.

Snap. An icy current zips through my body, and the smell of burned plastic fills the air. I let go of the wires and look down. My com cuff still hangs around my wrist, but it's lost its pearlescent sheen. Faint gray lines spider under its surface, along the path of its circuits. I turn it over. The readout screen has gone flat and dull. I've disabled it.

"You okay?"

I jump.

The guard stands at my window. "Why're you sitting here with your engine off?"

"I'm fine." I manage a smile that I hope doesn't look half crazed and tug my sleeve down over the com cuff. "Trying to conserve fuel."

The guard shakes her head, raises her scanner, and runs it across the bar code etched into the jeep's windshield. I hold my breath.

She raises an eyebrow at me. "This your first caravan?"

"Yeah," I say tightly.

"Figures." She pats the truck's hood and steps back. "Don't sit there without any AC on, huh? You'll get heatstroke and then nobody will be impressed you saved a few ounces of fuel."

She moves on to the next vehicle, and I let out the breath I've been holding. I restart the engine. We sit for a few minutes more, and then the command comes over the radio again. "Roll out."

As the sun breaks over the horizon, we pull out past the checkpoint, onto the open road.

.26.

IRONWEED

VERNONIA GIGANTEA

The fuel truck kicks up dust on my windshield. I flick on my wipers and glance left as one of the motorcycle guards roars up from the back of the caravan. The landscape on either side of the highway alternates between overgrown fields of Bermuda grass and stands of pine.

I spare a look at the emergency kit on the passenger seat beside me. I may have a gun, but I can't take on the whole caravan with a single mag of ammo. If I'd had more time, maybe I could have orchestrated something neater and less risky, but so far, my plan is to wait until the caravan stops for its scheduled refueling break in an hour, and then make my move. Volunteer to guard Alder and the other prisoners while someone takes a piss break. Get him to recognize me, so he can help. Let them out and then get off the road, into the backwoods, where the AgraStar vehicles can't follow.

I look at the time—0744. The driver whose spot I stole is probably in her supervisor's office, getting chewed out for missing her departure time. On the other side of the city, my mother is activating my tracker, finding no trace of me. She might be panicking now, but she'll get herself under control, call in security forces, start reconstructing my movements from the night before. Maybe they'll put together a composite feed of me slinking out of my mother's residence, stealing clothes from the dryer, walking the halls of the security forces barracks, the same way they did for my father.

I imagine her watching the footage, and a lump rises in my throat. I wish I could explain, make her understand. I know there's a part of her that might—the part that called me m'ija despite the stigma of Spanish words, and stood up to Kurich for me. But then there's the part of her that jokes about shirk queens and doesn't care if the blight kills thousands of scavengers. There's the part of her that believes so deeply in AgraStar's mission that she would do anything—denounce her own husband or engineer a bioweapon—if it meant strengthening the company. Nothing I could say would make that part of her understand.

The radio beeps on. "Caravan status check. Lead vehicle, repor—"

Something moves in my peripheral vision. I jerk the wheel right. An eighteen-wheeler, its cab aflame, plows out of the overgrown brush along the side of the road and collides with the fuel tanker in a terrible, screeching boom. My jeep pitches and tips as it hits the ditch at the side of the road. An enormous wave of heat, light, and sound washes over me. It's all I can do to hold on as the jeep rolls.

It comes to a stop upside down in the grass. Outside, shouts and gunshots punctuate a static roar, but I can't see through the film of black soot covering the windshield and driver's side window. I brace myself so I won't fall and break my neck, then release the seat belt. I tumble against the roof of the car and right myself. The emergency kit has skidded to the back and broken open. I grab the pistol and kick open the driver's-side door, so the body of the jeep stands between me and the chaos on the road.

I peer over the front wheels. The fuel truck is a tower of flame, oily black smoke billowing into the sky. The smell of burning rubber and corn diesel hangs thick in the air. I see movement through the haze, muzzle flashes briefly illuminating human shapes as they advance on the armored car. Distantly, I hear the sound of gunfire on the other side of the blaze, and the motorcycle engines revving. Whoever this is, they're organized, splitting the caravan and coming at us from both ends.

I move out from behind the jeep, staying low in the overgrown grass. The ground slopes up to the road, affording me a little cover. I drop to my stomach and crawl on my elbows. The other jeep and pickup have pulled up to flank the armored car, and all of the AgraStar forces on this side of the explosion have taken up positions behind the vehicles, firing on the people walking toward them. I squint through the smoke. Every person advancing on them is a man, with goggles over his eyes, a bandanna covering his nose and mouth, and a shaved head. Some of them wear body armor vests instead of shirts. I catch a flash of an arm, and the bold black tattoo on the bicep. Double lightning bolts . . . 88. The Red Hand. AgraStar hit their base. Now they're hitting back.

A burst of gunfire lights up the smoke. One of the Red Hand soldiers has a modded AR-15, set to full auto. Bullets spray across the AgraStar line, shattering the windshields of the jeep and pickup and glancing off the armored car. The AgraStar guards return fire. One Red Hand fighter drops, but the smoke is thickening, and the wind is against AgraStar. Most of the shots go wide.

I raise my pistol and take aim. Like hell is anyone I know going to be taken by the Red Hand again. I single out the man with the AR-15, line him up in my sights, brace, and fire. He falls, one hand flying to his neck, the other spasming on the trigger. A wild arc of bullets fly, puncturing one of the armored truck's wheels. I flatten myself against the ground as the remaining Red Hand men wheel on my position and fire.

A bullet rips open the heel of my boot, grazing my foot. Other shots thud in the dirt beside me. I cover my head. The smoke seems to be working against them, too, but I'm pinned down.

The sound of gunshots intensifies on the road above me, and the rain of bullets stops. I look up. The wind has shifted. AgraStar opens fire on the Red Hand, driving them back toward the burning fuel truck. I jump up and run for the shelter of the AgraStar vehicles. I spot Eli, steadying his rifle over the hood of a pickup. He sees me running and lays down covering fire so I can make it across the open space.

I skid to a stop beside him, heart thumping, ears ringing. Several AgraStar guards and one of the drivers lie on the asphalt, bleeding or dead.

"You hit?" he asks over his shoulder.

I don't think he's recognized me. In the chaos, in my hat and jumpsuit, I'm just another soldier.

"Only grazed," I say.

"You still have ammo?"

"Yes," I say.

"Then use it," Eli says.

I take up a position beside Eli, firing over the hood. The smoke is still thick, but the inferno lights up the Red Hand from behind, turning them into silhouettes wavering in the heat. My training tells me to aim for the center mass, but that isn't much use when my opponents are kitted out in armor. Head and legs, then. Most of my shots disappear into the flames, but I think I clip one Red Hand man on the ear. Another falls, clutching his leg. And then my pistol clicks. I'm out of rounds.

"Get back!" Eli shouts. "Help the wounded."

I drop down and crawl to the closest injured guard. She lies beside her motorcycle, her uniform dark with blood. I push back the visor of her helmet, and for a split second, her face morphs into Danica's. *No.* I squeeze my eyes shut and open them again. This isn't Danica. This is another girl, no less real, bleeding out on the highway. Her breath comes hard and fast.

"Hey," I say. "Stay with me, okay? I'm going to take care of you."

"I think it went through." She pants and looks down at herself, eyes wide. "I'm bleeding."

"We need to put some pressure on it." I cover the wound with my hands and look around wildly for something, anything to staunch the bleeding.

She groans. Her skin is clammy and ashen. *Not again. This can't happen again.*

My coveralls have a tear at the knee. I rip it wider, strip off the fabric covering my calf, and press it against the girl's stomach. Everything is filthy, but if she doesn't bleed out, AgraStar's doctors can pump her full of antibiotics to kill any infection.

Shouting and engines rumbling rise above the tumult. I look up. Two of the motorcycles from the front end of our convoy fly alongside the burning truck, firing at the Red Hand guards. The AgraStar line lets out a ragged cheer.

At that moment, a second explosion rocks the air. A ball of fire blossoms under the fuel truck as its own gas tank catches, engulfing one of the motorcycles and throwing Eli against the pavement. The remaining windows on the pickup blow out, scattering shards of glass over us.

"Eli!" I run to him.

Dozens of small cuts cover his face. He opens his eyes. They take a moment to focus, but when they do, they fill with confusion and horror. "Tempest? What the hell are you doing here?"

I help him up. "We have to fall back."

He looks over the remaining AgraStar guards, the ruined pickup, and the bodies on the ground.

"Fall back!" he shouts into his shortwave radio. "Fifty yards. Regroup."

I run to the wounded girl and lift one of her arms around my shoulder.

She cries out, and then bites down. "Leave me here."

"Not a chance," I grunt as I lift her to her feet. She sags against me.

"Eli!" I shout.

He hurries to us, ducks his shoulders under the girl's other arm, and holds the compress to her middle. I grab her rifle. Together, we drag her back along the highway, the armored car slowly rolling in reverse alongside us, giving us cover.

Fifty yards back, we stop and lay the wounded girl down. Eli and I survey what's left of our group. We have three AgraStar guards still in fighting shape, plus the two of us and the armored-car driver. The sound of engines and whoops reaches us from ahead. The Red Hand is regrouping.

I grab Eli's arm. "The prisoners. Let them out. They can fight with us."

Eli pulls away. "You want me to arm them?"

"Yes," I say.

He shakes his head. "How do we know they won't turn on us and join the jackers?"

"Because the boy who came south with me is one of your prisoners," I say. "These assholes killed his parents and tortured him. He'll fight with us, and if he will, the others might, too. Let me talk to him. Please."

He looks at the back doors of the armored car. "The boy you were on the road with."

"Yes," I say. "Alder."

Eli licks his lips. I know the math he's doing. He may have sent out a distress call when the gunfire started, but we're in the middle of nowhere. Help is at least thirty minutes out, and we won't last that long. He closes his eyes, wipes the blood from his face, and nods. He walks to the side of the armored car and taps the window. The driver steps out. Eli leans close. The man shakes his head, then stares at Eli, then nods. They walk to the back of the vehicle. The driver unloops a key from his neck and inserts it in the door, while Eli holds his com cuff to the scanner. He motions to me, and we stand in front of the double doors, ready to pull them open.

As one, he and the driver each turn a handle and step back. Alder and the other prisoners stand in the compartment, braced and ready to fight. A flash of shock travels over Alder's face as he sees me. He holds out a hand, signaling to the others to wait.

"Tempest." Alder's eyes travel over the blood and dirt on my clothes, and then widen when he sees Eli. "What—"

"We need your help." I step close. "That's the Red Hand blocking the road ahead. If we give you weapons, will you fight with us?"

The older man looks over Eli and the other AgraStar guards. "So you can carry us on to your assimilation camp?"

Eli stands beside me. "Would you rather be captured by the Red Hand? Because we're outnumbered."

"It's a trick," he says. "You get us holding rifles and then you gun us down and say it was justified."

Eli clenches his jaw and turns to the bleeding guard on the road behind us. "Does this look like a trick?" He looks at me. "We don't have time for this."

I lock eyes with Alder and hold out the rifle. "Please. I'm not your enemy. Neither is Eli."

He opens his mouth to answer, but the girl at the back of the compartment pushes past him. "Give it to me. The Red Hand took my sister. I'm not letting them take me."

I hand over the rifle and raise my eyebrows at Alder.

"Okay." He hops down onto the pavement. "If Tempest gives her word, I'm in."

Now it's just three—the old man, the woman, and a boy a little younger than Alder.

"If you're not going to help, then run." Eli jerks his head at the road. "Get out of here."

The boy swallows. "They'll gun us down."

"Then stay and fight," I say.

The three remaining prisoners glance at one another.

"Fair enough." The woman sighs. "Shouldn't always be the young people dying. I'll stay."

"I'm out," the man says. "I'm not getting killed for a bunch of cogs."

We all look at the boy. His Adam's apple bobs, and his eyes flit between all of us. His gaze comes to rest on Alder, then on me.

"I . . ." His voice cracks. "I'm in."

Alder and I lie side by side beneath the armored car, rifles at the ready. Above us, Eli, the other scavengers, and the AgraStar guards stand with their weapons drawn, aiming at the tower of fire where the fuel truck once was. Shouts and starting engines echo down the blacktop.

"Hold steady," Eli says. "They're trying to scare us, that's all. We can take them."

I lick my lips and taste blood and sweat.

"I told you to forget about me," Alder murmurs.

"And I told you I was coming for you." I look at him. "No matter what happens to us, the data is out. I uploaded it, exactly like you said. I keep my word."

Alder turns his attention back to the road. "I guess you do."

The clamor of a dozen engines gunning rips through the air. Ninety feet down the road, the Red Hand have staggered their vehicles in a rough V formation, a reinforced tow truck with a low-set metal plow welded to the chassis at the front, and a collection of pickups and motorcycles flanking it. They lurch forward.

The Red Hand men open fire, and we answer. I take aim at one of the motorcycles with two riders, a driver and a man with an AR-15, and fire. The front wheel blows out. The driver flips over the handlebars, and the gunman flies off to the side, colliding with the back end of the tow truck.

Eighty feet.

A fresh hail of bullets patters against the armored car. One of the other wheels pops, sinking the undercarriage lower above our heads. Alder lets off five shots in quick succession, partially shattering the windshield of one of the pickups on the right flank. It veers off to the side of the road, plowing into a motorcycle.

Sixty-five.

I try the same on the left flank, but they're on to our trick. The pickup pulls forward and weaves, so my shots ricochet off the grill. The tow truck picks up speed, barreling down on us, its plow glinting in the sun.

"Fire on the lead truck!" Eli shouts.

We pepper the truck with shots, but it doesn't slow. I try for the tires, but the plow sits too low for me to hit them.

Fifty.

"Alder!" I shout. "The pickup! Force it into the lead truck."

We concentrate fire on the pickup. Above us, the others seem to catch on to our plan, and redirect their shots.

Thirty.

The pickup's tires blow, and then a bullet strikes the driver. The vehicle veers hard to the left, wedging its front end beneath the tow truck's undercarriage. Time slows. The tow truck shudders, then tilts up on two wheels. Ten feet, nine, eight . . . The tow truck crashes to its side and skids, sparks flying across the pavement as it rushes toward us. I grab Alder, but there's no time to move. I squeeze my eyes shut.

The truck flies past, barely missing us, and grinds to a stop forty feet behind us. For a moment, the only sound is the rush of the flames. Then coughing. Voices.

I crawl out from beneath the armored car and stand unsteadily. All but two of us have survived the fight; we lost the scavenger woman and the armored-car driver.

Eli aims his weapon at the remaining Red Hand men, idling their bikes and staring at the wrecked tow truck.

"You've got five seconds!" he shouts, his voice hoarse. "Then we fire."

I bring up my rifle beside his. Alder does the same, and the rest of the survivors follow his lead. The Red Hand men exchange a look. One of them spits on the ground between us, but then he turns on his bike and tears away. The others flee after him.

"Means. Wolff. Ortiz." Eli points at the last three AgraStar guards and gestures at the wrecked Red Hand truck. "Pull out any survivors and place them in custody."

"Yes, sir." They run to the truck, weapons drawn.

Eli turns to me and holsters his weapon. "You came for him." He glances at Alder, and then back at me.

"I did," I say.

"He turned you?" His eyes search mine.

"No one turned me," I say. "I made up my own mind."

Eli looks down. His jaw works as he studies the asphalt. "Backup will be here soon. None of you should be here when they arrive."

"What—"

His face is fierce. "I don't know why you did what you did, but I'm not going to turn over people who've fought by my side."

I stare at Eli. What he's doing? He could be put before the disciplinary committee. At the very least, he'll be taken out of the running for any future promotions if he loses all of his prisoners on the very first mission he's charged to lead.

"What about you?" I ask. "Will you be okay?"

"Don't worry about me." He smiles, and there is the ghost of Ellison again. "I'm too handsome to get in much trouble."

My eyes sting, but I smile back. "Liar."

"You don't have to run." Eli glances at the side of the road, where Alder and the other freed prisoners have righted the overturned jeep and are pushing it up out of the ditch. "I'll stand for you. Your mom will, too. I know it."

I shake my head. It's too late. He doesn't know the half of what I've done. Or how dangerous it is to know what I do about AgraStar.

"The boy I knew back at my old compound . . ." I look up at him, struggling to explain. "It wasn't a coincidence he looked like you."

Eli's smile disappears. "What does that mean?"

"When I went through my mother's files . . ." I swallow. Whatever I say now, he's duty bound to report back to the company. Telling him too much will only put him in more danger. "There are things AgraStar isn't telling you. Not just about crops. About you."

Eli looks doubtful, wary.

"You don't have to believe me," I say. "Only promise me you'll keep your eyes open."

He half smiles. "Make up my own mind, huh?"

"Right."

He nods. "If you say so, Salcedo."

I grin. "Thank you." I hesitate, and then place a gentle kiss on his cheek. "For everything."

I back away, even though it's breaking my heart. Alder is waiting for me at the side of the road, holding an AgraStar rifle at his side.

He squints as I approach. "You coming with us?"

"Where are you headed?" I ask.

"South till we find a crossroad, then west," he says. "Nina knows of a free settlement near Mount Cheaha. And then . . . I don't know. I might go north again. See if I can get lost in the Smoky Mountains, like I always talked about with Eden."

"You won't go looking for the Deacon?"

"It won't be the same without Eden," he says. "Nothing will be."

I look past him. The others have gotten the jeep's engine running and are scrubbing at the soot on the windshield. He's right. Nothing will be the same. Not me. Not him. Not the earth beneath our feet.

"So, are you coming?" Alder asks.

I resist the pull to turn around, to look at Eli and everything my life could have been one last time. I made my choice, for good or bad, just like my father did. I know the hurt it will cause, for me, for my mother and Isabel, for Eli, but I can't undo it. And I wouldn't.

"I am."

We pile into the jeep and pull out onto the road, heading south. I watch over the backseat as Eli and the caravan slowly shrink on the horizon. I watch and watch until there's nothing around us but the road and the sky and the riot of unbound life beyond the verges.

ACKNOWLEDGMENTS

I'm constantly amazed looking back at the community of support that contributes to writing a book, at every stage from inspiration to polishing the manuscript.

In 2011, writers Nathan Ballingrud, Theodora Goss, and I challenged each other to write a novel over the course of one summer. I'm a slow writer and didn't quite hit that goal, but I did write the first 20,000 words of the book you are currently holding in your hands, thanks in large part to Nathan and Dora's feedback and encouragement. Without them, *Blight* would not exist.

Another crucial component of *Blight* came from readers Anna-Marie McLemore and Yamile Said Mendez, who discussed the difficult topic of cultural erasure with me and shared their wisdom. Their help took this book to a level I couldn't have reached on my own. I hope I have done justice to their words and advice.

Thanks are also due to the Bat Cave writers who read an early draft of *Blight* and gave so much helpful advice on Tempest's story. Also to the Asheville writing community, particularly Beth Revis (to whom all the explosions in this book are dedicated), Stephanie Perkins, Meagan Spooner, Megan Shepherd, Amy Reed, and Jaye Robin Brown.

Another huge thank-you goes to my editor, Virginia Duncan, for all the phone calls, emails, and time spent helping me make this book what I wanted it to be. To Lois Adams and Sylvie Le Floc'h, and all the people at Greenwillow Books and HarperCollins whom I haven't met but who I know played a role to bring *Blight* into the world: thank you, thank you, thank you!

Finally, thank you to my friends and family, who always cheer me on and support my work, and especially to my husband, Jeremy Duncan, who reads my drafts, brews the coffee, and never stops making me laugh. Without you, I would be much further along in my journey to becoming an incurable cat lady.